The yellowbacks... classics of popular fiction

The yellowjackets or yellowbacks were a great series of bestselling adventure and crime thrillers that had its origins in the mid to late 19th century following on from the 'penny dreadfuls'. They virtually began the mass market revolution of the early 20th century with a clear standard format and imprint/series livery (what would today be called branding). Hodder & Stoughton published the yellowjackets in two main series with series run dates of: 1923-1939 and later 1949-1957.

As the tagline ('where thrillers really began') on the back cover implies, the imprint and series focused on thrillers that were the bestsellers of their time. This current reissue or retro revival if you will, brings back many of these masterpieces, now classics in their own way and extends it further by including key titles from that period that were either great crime or thriller or even general commercial fiction (including sub-genres of noir, horror, gothic, romance, westerns, etc.) influences of their time. There are some perennial favourites and many rarities either lost or not easily available being revived in the current series. Writers and characters ranged from adventure heroes like Bulldog Drummond, Allan Quatermain, Richard Hannay or the Saint through thriller grandmasters Edgar Wallace and E. Phillips Oppenheim, crime and mystery maestros like Patricia Wentworth, GK Chesterton, Agatha Christie and the Detection club, to western and swashbucklers like Zane Grey, Max Brand, Captain Blood and even romance or general fiction classics like Hermina Black, Denise Robins, Marie Corelli or Stella Morton. These were books that had storytelling at their heart and always entertained.

The yellowbacks had both hardback (with varying design elements) and paperback (which built the series look) versions with the latter still carrying the imprint 'yellowjacket'. The current reissues pay tribute to both and use an amalgam of elements from both editions while retaining the complete yellow (or 'mustard-plaster') livery with the author's name in blue beveled type with a 'simulated emboss' effect and a white outer 'outline', and the book title in black. These reissues retain the distinctive size of the original mass market paperback and follow the three main category variations— the thrillers (crime, westerns, mystery, adventure) had blue lettering for the author's name, while Romance and softer general fiction had red; and other categories like humour had green.

For more detail and a full list of titles visit https://www.hachetteindia.com/home/yellowbacks

SKIN O' MY TOOTH

SKIN O' MY TOOTH

Baroness Orczy (full name: Emma Magdalena Rozália Mária Jozefa Borbála Orczy de Orci ; 1865 –1947), usually known as Baroness Orczy (the name under which she was published) or to her family and friends as Emmuska Orczy, was a Hungarian-born British novelist and playwright. She is best known for her series of novels featuring the Scarlet Pimpernel, the alter ego of Sir Percy Blakeney, a wealthy English fop who turns into a quick-thinking escape artist in order to save French aristocrats from "Madame Guillotine" during the French Revolution, establishing the "hero with a secret identity" in popular culture.

Orczy was born in Tarnaörs, Hungary, the daughter of the composer Baron Félix Orczy de Orci (and Countess Emma Wass de Szentegyed et Cege. Emma's parents left their estate for Budapest in 1868, fearful of the threat of a peasant revolution. They lived in Budapest, Brussels, and Paris, where Emma studied music unsuccessfully. Finally, in 1880, the 14-year-old Emma and her family moved to London, England where they lodged at 162 Great Portland Street. Orczy attended West London School of Art and then the Heatherley School of Fine Art. Although not destined to be a painter, it was at art school that she met a young illustrator named Henry George Montagu MacLean Barstow, the son of an English clergyman; they were married at St Marylebone parish church on 7 November 1894.

They had very little money and Orczy started to work with her husband as a translator and an illustrator to supplement his meagre earnings. John Montague Orczy-Barstow, their only child, was born on 25 February 1899. She started writing soon after his birth, but her first novel, The Emperor's Candlesticks (1899), was a failure. In 1903, she and her husband wrote The Scarlet Pimpernel, first as a play. She had conceived the character while standing on a platform on the London Underground. She submitted her novelization of the story under the same title to 12 publishers and was accepted by Greening before later signing on for the full series with Hodder & Stoughton.

Orczy's work (she wrote many sequels and it became a bestselling series) was so successful that she was able to buy a house in Monte Carlo: "Villa Bijou" at 19 Avenue de la Costa (since demolished), which is where she spent World War II. She was not able to return to London until after the war. Montagu Barstow died in Monte Carlo in 1942. Finding herself alone and unable to travel, she wrote her memoir Links in the Chain of Life (published 1947). She died in Henley-on-Thames, Oxfordshire on 12 November 1947.

SKIN O' MY TOOTH

Baroness Orczy

hachette

Skin O' My Tooth
First appeared in The Windsor Magazine in 1903 and then
first published in book form in 1928 by Hodder & Stoughton..

This Hodder Yellowback edition © Hachette India 2023
(Registered Name: Hachette Book Publishing India Pvt. Ltd.)
An Hachette UK Company www.hachetteindia.com

1

All rights reserved. No part of the publication may be reproduced, stored in a retrieval system (including but not limited to computers, disks, external drives, electronic or digital devices, e-readers, websites), or transmitted in any form or by any means (including but not limited to cyclostyling, photocopying, docutech or other reprographic reproductions, mechanical, recording, electronic, digital versions) without the prior written permission of the publisher, nor be otherwise circulated in any form of binding or cover other than that in which it is published and without a similar condition being imposed on the subsequent purchaser.

The texts in these editions in most cases have been reprinted as is, with minimal editorial changes and by and large no bowdlerizing for political correctness; though in some editions, a few words and phrases considered archaic, or those considered offensive now, along with archaic punctuation may have been modified in places to make the text more accessible to today's readers. The narratives, language, beliefs, social mores and/or cultural depictions, in these volumes are a reflection of their times and must be viewed as such. They may also contain certain cultural, racial and gender prejudices and stereotypes that may be outdated or clearly wrong then and wrong today; but their removal would be tantamount to claiming these prejudices never existed. The Publisher does not endorse or support those depictions or stereotypes; and these books have been made available for a discerning audience that will read it for entertainment value and a chronicle/record of popular fiction of past times.

Cover design by Priya Singh adapted from the original classic yellowjacket by
Hodder & Stoughton.

Cover illustration by Ishan Trivedi.

Series note: Some of the books in the series (unless otherwise credited) may have cover or inside illustrations from the original yellowbacks or early editions, and while full restoration has been attempted, some images may be grainy or faded due to the condition of the original material. The end notes or bonus material or blurb details may have been sourced from the public domain or free use publications such as Wikipedia and attribution is hereby made also allowing similar free use reproduction from here. Sources requiring further specific attribution may write in and further detailing and/or corrections shall be made in subsequent printings/editions.

Reprint specifications may be subject to change including but not limited to
finishes, paper, colour sections.

ISBN: 978-93-5731-073-4

Hachette Book Publishing India Pvt. Ltd.
4th & 5th Floors, Corporate Centre,
Plot No. 94, Sector 44, Gurugram - 122 003, India

Typeset in Electra LT STD 10/12.5 pt by Manipal Technologies Limited, Manipal

Printed and bound in India by Manipal Technologies Limited, Manipal

CONTENTS

1.	The Murder in Saltashe Woods	1
2.	The Case of the Sicilian Prince	21
3.	The Duffield Peerage Case	40
4.	The Kazan Pearls	61
5.	The Case of Major Gibson	91
6.	The Inverted Five	109
7.	The Turquoise Stud	139
8.	Overwhelming Evidence	165
9.	The Case of Mrs. Norris	196
10.	The Murton-Braby Murder	214
11.	A Shot in the Night	233
12.	The Hungarian Landowner	260

1

THE MURDER IN SALTASHE WOODS

We all called him "Skin o' my Tooth": his friends, who were few; his clients, who were many, and I, his confidential clerk, solus—and very proud I am to hold that position. I believe, as a matter of fact, that his enemies—and their name is legion—call him Patrick Mulligan; but to us all who know him as he is, "Skin o' my Tooth" he always was, from the day that he got a verdict of "Not guilty" out of the jury who tried James Tovey, "the Dartmouth murderer." Tovey hadn't many teeth, but it was by the skin of those few molars of his that he escaped the gallows; not thanks to the pleading of his counsel, but all thanks to the evidence collected by Patrick Mulligan, his lawyer.

Of course, Skin o' my Tooth is not popular among his colleagues; there is much prejudice and petty spite in all professions, and the Law is not exempt from this general rule.

Everyone knows that Skin o' my Tooth is totally unacquainted with the use of kid gloves. He works for the best of his client; let the other side look to themselves, I say.

Funny-looking man, too, old Skin o' my Tooth—fat and rosy and comfortable as an Irish pig, with a face as stodgy as a boiled currant dumpling. His hair, I believe, would be red if he gave it a chance at all, but he wears it cropped so close to his bulky head that he looks bald in some lights. Then, we all know that gentle smile of his, and that trick of casting down his eyes which gives him a look that is best described by the word "coy;" that trick is always a danger-signal to the other side.

Now, in the case of Edward Kelly, everyone will admit that that young man came nearer being hanged for murder than any of us would care for.

But this is how it all happened.

On Tuesday, September 3rd, Mary Mills and John Craddock—who were walking through the Saltashe Woods— came across the body of a man lying near the pond, in a pool of blood. Mary, of course, screamed, and would have fled; but John, manfully conquering the feeling of sickness which threatened to overcome him too, went up to the body to get a closer view of the face. To his horror he recognised Mr Jeremiah Whadcoat, a well-known, respectable resident of Pashet. The unfortunate man seemed to John Craddock to be quite dead; still, he thought it best to despatch Mary at once for Doctor Howden, and also to the policestation; whilst he, with really commendable courage, elected to remain beside the body alone.

It appears that about half an hour after Mary had left him, John thought that he detected a slight movement in the rigid body, which he had propped up against his knee, and that the wounded man uttered a scarcely audible sigh and then murmured a few words. The young man bent forward eagerly, striving with all his might to catch what these words might be. According to his subsequent evidence before the coroner's jury, Mr Whadcoat then opened his eyes, and murmured quite distinctly—

"The letter... Kelly... Edward... the other." After that all seemed over, for the face became more rigid and more ashen in colour than before.

It was past six o'clock before the doctor and the inspector, with two constables and a stretcher from Pashet policestation, appeared upon the scene and relieved John Craddock of his lonely watch. Mr Whadcoat had not spoken again, and the doctor pronounced life to be extinct. The body was quietly removed to Mr Whadcoat's house in Pashet, Mary Mills having already volunteered for the painful task of breaking the news to Miss Amelia, Mr Whadcoat's sister, who lived with him.

The unfortunate man was cashier to Messrs. Kelly and Co., the great wine merchants; so Mr Kelly, of Saltashe Park, also Mr Edward Kelly, of Wood Cottage, were apprised of the sad event.

At this stage the tragic affair seemed wrapped up in the most profound mystery. Mr Jeremiah Whadcoat was not known to possess a single enemy, and he certainly was not sufficiently endowed with worldly wealth to tempt the highway robber. So far the police had found nothing on the scene of the crime which could lead to a clue—footsteps of every shape and size leading in every direction, a few empty cartridges here and there; all of which meant nothing, since Saltashe Woods are full of game, and both Mr Kelly and Mr Edward Kelly had had shooting parties within the last few days.

The public understood that permission had been obtained from Mr Kelly to drag the pond, and, not knowing what to think or fear, it awaited the day of the inquest with eager excitement.

I believe that that inquest was one of the most memorable in the annals of a coroner's court. There was a large crowd, of course, for the little town of Pashet was a mass of seething curiosity.

The expert evidence of Dr Howden, assisted by the divisional surgeon, was certainly very curious. Both learned gentlemen gave it as their opinion that the deceased met his death through the discharge of small shot fired from a rifle at a distance of not more than a couple of yards. All the shot had lodged close together in the heart, and the flesh round the wound was slightly charred.

The police, on the other hand, had quite a tit-bit of sensation ready for the eager public. They had dragged the pond and had found the carcass of a dog. The beast had evidently been shot with the same rifle which had ended poor Mr Whadcoat's days, the divisional surgeon, who had examined the carcass, having pronounced the wound—which was in the side—to be exactly similar in character. A final blow dealt on the animal's head with the butt-end of the rifle, however, had been the ultimate cause of its death. As the medical officer gave this sensational bit of evidence, a sudden and dead silence fell over all in that crowded court, for it had leaked out earlier in the day that the dead dog found in the pond was "Rags," Mr Edward Kelly's well-known black retriever.

In the midst of that silence, Miss Amelia Whadcoat—the sister of the deceased gentleman—stepped forward, dressed in deep black, and holding a letter, which she handed to the coroner.

"It came under cover, addressed to me," she explained, "on the Tuesday evening."

The coroner, half in hesitation, turned the square envelope between his fingers. At last he read aloud—

"To the Coroner and Jury at the inquest, should a fatal accident occur to me this (Tuesday) afternoon, in Saltashe Wood."

Then he tore open the envelope. Immediately everyone noticed the look of boundless astonishment which spread over his face. There was a moment of breathless silent expectation among the crowd, while Miss Amelia stood quietly with her hands demurely folded over her gingham umbrella and her swollen eyes fixed anxiously upon that letter.

At last the coroner, turning to the jury, said—

"Gentlemen, this letter is addressed to you as well as to myself. I am, therefore, bound to acquaint you of its contents; but I must, of course, warn you not to allow your minds to be unduly influenced, however strange these few words may seem to you. The letter is dated from Ivy Lodge, Pashet, Tuesday, September 3rd, and signed 'Jeremiah Whadcoat.' It says:

> 'Mr Coroner and Gentlemen of the Jury,—I beg to inform you that on this day, at 2.30 p.m., I am starting to walk to Saltashe, there to see Mr Kerhoet and Mr Kelly on important business. Mr Edward Kelly has desired me to meet him by the pond in Saltashe Woods, on my way. He knows of the business which takes me to Saltashe. He and I had a violent quarrel at the office on the subject last night, and he has every reason for wishing that I should never speak of it to Mr Kelly and to Mr Kerhoet. Last night he threatened to knock me down. If any serious accident happen to me, let Mr Edward Kelly account for his actions'."

A deadly silence followed, and then a muttered curse from somewhere among the crowd.

"This is damnable!"

And Mr Edward Kelly, young, good-looking, but, at this moment, as pale as death, pushed his way forward among the spectators.

He wanted to speak, but the coroner waved him aside in his most official manner, while Miss Amelia Whadcoat demurely concluded her evidence. Personally, she knew nothing of her brother's quarrel with Mr Edward Kelly. She did not even know that he was going to Saltashe Woods on that fatal afternoon. Then she retired, and Mr Edward Kelly was called.

Questioned by the coroner, he admitted the quarrel spoken of by the deceased, admitted meeting him by the pond in Saltashe Woods, but emphatically denied having the slightest ill-feeling against "Old Whadcoat," as he called him, and, above all, having the faintest desire for wishing to silence him for ever.

"The whole thing is a ghastly mistake or a weird joke," he declared firmly.

"But the quarrel?" persisted the coroner.

"I don't deny it," retorted the young man. "It was the result of a preposterous accusation old Whadcoat saw fit to level against me."

"But why should you meet him clandestinely in the Woods?"

"It was not a clandestine meeting. I knew that he intended walking to Saltashe from Pashet through the Woods; a road from my house cuts the direction which he would be bound to follow, exactly at right angles. I wished to speak to him, and it saved me a journey all the way to Pashet, or him one down to my house. I met him at half-past three. We had about fifteen minutes talk; then I left him and went back home."

"What was he doing when you left him?" asked the coroner, with distinct sarcasm.

"He had sat down on a tree stump and was smoking his pipe."

"You had your gun with you, of course, on this expedition through the Woods?"

"I seldom go out without my gun this time of year."

"Quite so," assented the coroner grimly. "But what about your dog, who was found with its head battered in, close to the very spot where lay the body of the deceased?"

"Poor old Rags strayed away that morning. I did not see him at all that day. He certainly was not with me when I went to meet old Whadcoat."

The rapidly spoken questions and answers had been listened to by the public and the jury with breathless interest. No one uttered a sound, but all were watching that the handsome young man, who seemed, with every word he uttered, to incriminate himself more and more. The quarrel, the assignation, the gun he was carrying; he denied nothing but he did protest his innocence with all his might.

One or two people had heard the report of a gun whilst walking on one or other of the roads that skirt Saltashe Woods, but their evidence as to the precise hour was unfortunately rather vague. Reports of guns in Saltashe Woods were very frequent, and no one had taken particular notice. On the other hand, the only witness who had seen Mr Edward Kelly entering the wood was not ready to swear whether he had his dog with him or not.

Though it had been fully expected ever since Jeremiah Whadcoat's posthumous epistle had been read, the verdict of "Wilful murder against Edward St. John Kelly" found the whole population of Pashet positively aghast. Brother of Mr Kelly, of Saltashe Park, the accused was one of the most popular figures in this part of Hertfordshire. When his subsequent arrest became generally known in London, as well as in his own county, horror, amazement, and incredulity were quite universal.

2

The day after that memorable inquest and sensational arrest—namely, on the Saturday, I arrived at our dingy old office in Finsbury Square at about twelve o'clock, after I had seen to some business at Somerset House for my esteemed employer.

I found Skin o' my Tooth curled up in his armchair before a small fire—as the day was wet and cold—just like a great fat and frowsy dog. He waited until I had given him a full report of what I had been doing, then he said to me—

"I have just had a visit from Mr Kelly, of Saltashe Park."

I was not astonished. That case of murder in the Saltashe Woods was just one of those which inevitably drifted into the hands of Skin o' my Tooth. Though the whole aspect of it was remarkably clear, instinctively one scented a mystery somewhere.

"I suppose, sir, that it was on Mr Edward Kelly's behalf?"

"Your penetration, Muggins, my boy, surpasses human understanding."

(My name is Alexander Stanislaus Mullins, but Skin o' my Tooth will have his little joke).

"You are going to undertake the case, sir?"

"I am going to get Edward Kelly out of the hole his own stupidity has placed him in."

"It will be by the skin of his teeth if you do, sir, the evidence against him is positively crushing," I muttered.

"A miss is as good as a mile, where the hangman's rope is concerned, Muggins. But you had better call a hansom; we can go down to Pashet this afternoon. Edward Kelly is out on bail, and Mr Kelly tells me that I shall find him at Wood Cottage. I must get out of him the history of his quarrel with the murdered man."

"Mr Kelly did not know it?"

"Well, anyway, he seemed to think it best that the accused should tell me his own version of it. In any case, both Mr Kelly and his wife are devoured with anxiety about this brother, who seems to have been a bit of a scapegrace all his life."

There was no time to say more then, as we found that, by hurrying, we could catch the 1.05 p.m. train to Pashet. We found Mr Edward Kelly at Wood Cottage, a pretty little house on the outskirts of Saltashe Woods. He had been told of our likely visit by his brother. He certainly looked terribly ill and like a man overweighted by fate and circumstances.

But he did protest his innocence, loudly and emphatically.

"I am the victim of the most damnable circumstances, Mr Mulligan," he said; "but I swear to you that I am incapable of such a horrible deed."

"I always take it for granted, Mr Kelly," said Skin o' my Tooth blandly, "that my client is innocent. If the reverse is the case, I prefer not to know it. But you have to appear before the magistrate on Monday. I must get a certain amount of evidence on your behalf, in order to obtain the remand I want. So will you try and tell me, as concisely and as clearly as possible, what passed between you and Mr Whadcoat the day before the murder? I understand that there was a quarrel."

"Old Whadcoat saw fit to accuse me of certain defalcations in the firm's banking account, of which I was totally innocent," began Mr Edward Kelly quietly. "As you know, my brother and I are agents in England for M. de Kerhoet's champagne. Whadcoat was our cashier and book-keeper. Twice a year we pay over into M. de Kerhoet's bank in Paris the money derived from the sale of his wines, after deducting our commission. In the meanwhile, we have jointly the full control of the money—that is to say, all cheques paid to the firm have to be endorsed by us both, and all cheques drawn on the firm must bear both our signatures.

"It was just a month before the half-yearly settlement of accounts. Whadcoat, it appears, went down to the bank, got the cancelled cheques, and discovered that some £10,000, the whole of the credit balance due next month to M. de Kerhoet, had been drawn out of the bank, the amounts not having been debited in the books.

"To my intense amazement, he showed me these cheques, and then and there accused me of having forged my brother's name and appropriated the firm's money to my own use. You see, he knew of certain unavowed extravagances of mine which had often landed me in financial difficulties more or less serious, and which are the real cause of my being forced to live in Wood Cottage whilst my brother can keep up a fine establishment at Saltashe Park. But the accusation was preposterous, and I was furious with him. I looked at the cheques. My signature certainly was perfectly imitated, that of my brother perhaps a little less so. They were 'bearer' cheques, made out in a replica of old Whadcoat's handwriting to 'M. de Kerhoet,' and endorsed at the back in a small, pointed, foreign hand.

"Old Whadcoat persisted in his accusations, and very high words ensued between us. I believe I did threaten to knock him down if he did not shut up. Anyway, he told me that he would go over the next afternoon to Saltashe Park to expose me before my brother and M. de Kerhoet, who was staying there on a visit to England for the shooting.

"I left him then, meaning to go myself that same evening to Saltashe Park and see my brother about it; but on my journey home, certain curious suspicions with regard to old Whadcoat himself crept up in my mind, and then and there I determined to try and see him again and to talk the matter over more dispassionately with him, in what I thought would be his own interests. My intention was to make, of course, my brother acquainted with the whole matter at once, but to leave M. de Kerhoet out of the question for the present; so I wired to Whadcoat in the morning to make the assignation which has proved such a terrible mistake."

Edward Kelly added that he left Jeremiah Whadcoat, after his interview with him by the pond, in as excited a frame of mind as before. Fearing that his own handwriting on the cheques might entail serious consequences to himself, nothing would do but M. de Kerhoet as well as Mr Kelly must, be told of the whole thing immediately.

"When I left him," concluded the young man, "he was sitting on a tree stump by the pond, smoking his pipe and I walked away towards Wood Cottage."

"Do you know what became of the cheques?" asked Skin o' my Tooth.

"Old Whadcoat had them in his pocket when I left him. I conclude, as there has been no mention of them by the police, that they have not been found."

There was so much simplicity and straight forwardness in Edward Kelly's narrative that I, for one, was ready to believe every word of it. But Skin o' my Tooth's face was inscrutable. He sat in a low chair with his hands folded before him, his eyes shut and a general air of polite imbecility about his whole unwieldy person. I could see that our client was viewing him with a certain amount of irritability.

"Well, Mr Mulligan?" he said at last, with nervous impatience.

"Well, sir," replied Skin o' my Tooth, "it strikes me that what with your quarrel with the deceased, the assignation in the Woods, his posthumous denunciation of you as his assassin, and his dying words, we have about as complete a case as we could wish."

"Sir—"

"In all cases of this sort, my dear sir," continued Skin o' my Tooth quietly, "the great thing is to keep absolutely cool. If you are innocent—remember, I do not doubt it for a moment—then I will bring that crime home to its perpetrator. Justice never miscarries—at least, when I have guidance of it in my hands."

It would be impossible to render the tone of supreme conceit with which Skin o' my Tooth made this last assertion; but it had the desired effect, for Edward Kelly brightened up visibly as he said—

"I have implicit faith in you, Mr Mulligan. When shall I see you again?"

"On Monday, before the magistrate. I can get that remand for you, I think, and then we shall have a free hand. Now we had better get along; I want to have a quiet think over this affair."

3

On the Monday, Edward Kelly was formally charged before the beak; and I must say that when I then heard the formidable array of circumstantial evidence which the police had collected against our client, I sadly began to fear that not even by the skin of his teeth would Edward Kelly escape from the awful hole in which he was literally wallowing. However, Skin o' my Tooth hammered away at the police evidence with regard to the dog. The prosecution made a great point of the fact that Mr Whadcoat and Rags had been killed by the same rifle and at the same time and place, and the one point in Edward Kelly's favour was that neither his servants at Wood Cottage, nor the witness who saw him enter the wood, could swear that the dog was with him on that day. On the strength of that, and for the purpose of collecting further evidence with regard to the dog, Skin o' my Tooth finally succeeded in obtaining a remand until the following Friday.

Personally, I thought that there was quite sufficient evidence for hanging any man, without the testimony of the dead dog, but I am quite aware that my opinion counts for very little.

"Now, Muggins," said Skin o' my Tooth to me later in the day, "the fun is about to begin. You go down to Coutts's this afternoon and find out all about those cheques which caused the quarrel, and by whom they were presented. Don't mix the police up in our affairs, whatever you do. If there is anything you can't manage, get Fairburn to help you; he is discretion itself and hates the regular force. Beyond that, try and work alone."

I had done more difficult jobs than that before now, and Skin o' my Tooth knows he can rely on me. I left him curled up in an armchair with a French novel in his hand and started on my quest. I got to Coutts's just before closing time, saw the chief cashier and explained my errand and its importance to him, asking for his kind help in the matter. He was courteous in the extreme, and within a few moments I had ascertained from him that cheques on Kelly and Co.'s account, perfectly en règle, and made out to "E. de Kerhoet, or Bearer," had been cashed on certain dates which he gave me. They were in each instance presented by a commissionaire in uniform, who brought a card—"M. Edouard de Kerhoet," with "Please give bearer amount in £5 notes," scribbled in pencil in the same handwriting as the endorsement on the cheques.

"The amounts varied between £1,200 and £3,000," continued the cashier, still referring to his book. "Being 'bearer' cheques, and signed in the usual manner, we had no occasion to doubt them, and of course we cashed them. The first cheque was drawn on July 3rd, and the last on August 29th."

The cashier added one more detail which fairly staggered me—namely, that the commissionaire wore a cap with "Kelly and Co." embroidered upon it. If necessary, there were plenty of cashiers and clerks at the bank who could identify him. He was a tall man of marked foreign appearance, with heavy black hair, beard and moustache cut very trim. On one occasion when he left, he dropped a bit of paper which contained the name "Van Wort, Turf Commission Agent, Flushing, Holland."

I thanked the cashier and took my leave.

When I got back to the office, I found Skin o' my Tooth placidly sleeping in his big armchair. I had had a hard day and was dead tired, and for the moment when I saw him there, looking so fat, so pink, and so comfortable, well—I have a great respect for him, but I really felt quite angry.

However, I told him what I had done.

"Capital! Capital, Muggins!" he ejaculated languidly. "But, by Jove! That's a clever rascal. That touch about the name on the cap is peculiarly happy and daring. It completely allayed the suspicions of the cashiers at Coutts's. Now, listen, Muggins," he added, with that sudden, quick-changing mood of his which in a moment transformed him from the lazy, apathetic Irish lawyer to the weird human bloodhound who scents the track. "That foreign commissionaire is a disguise, of course; the cap hides the edge of the wig and shades the brow, the black beard and moustache conceal the mouth and chin, the foreign accent disguises the voice. We may take it, therefore, that the thief and his ambassador are one and the same person—a man, moreover, well known at Coutts's, since disguise was necessary. Do you follow me, Muggins? And remember, the motive is there. The man who defrauded Kelly and Co. is the same who murdered Whadcoat later on. Whadcoat was effectually silenced, the tell-tale cheques have evidently been destroyed. There would have been silence and mystery over the whole scandal, until the defalcations could be made good, but for Whadcoat's letter to the coroner and his dying words: 'The letter... Kelly... Edward... the other...'"

He paused suddenly and seemed lost in thought, then he muttered—

"It's that confounded dog I can't quite make out!... Did Edward Kelly, after all..."

It was that great "after all" which had puzzled me all along. "Was Edward Kelly guilty, after all?" I had asked myself that question a hundred times a day. Then, as I was silent—lost in conjectures over this extraordinary, seemingly impenetrable mystery—he suddenly jumped up and shouted—

"By Jove! I've got it, Muggins! 'The other.' What a fool I have been! Go to bed, boy; I want a rest too. Tomorrow will be time enough to think about 'the other.'"

4

From that moment Skin o' my Tooth was a transformed being. He always is when he has got a case "well in hand," as he calls it. He certainly possesses a weird faculty for following up the trail of blood. Once he holds what he believes to be a clue, his whole appearance changes; his great, fat body seems, as it were, to crouch together ready for a spring and there is a wild quiver about his nostrils which palpably suggests the bloodhound, only his eyes remain inscrutably hidden beneath their thick fleshy lids.

It was twelve o'clock the next day when our train steamed into Pashet station. We had a fly from there and drove down to Saltashe Park, the lordly country seat of Mr Kelly.

At the door, Skin o' my Tooth asked for the master of the house; but hearing that he was out, he requested that his card might be taken in to Mrs Kelly. The next moment we were ushered into a luxuriously furnished library, full of books and flowers, and with deep mullioned windows opening out upon a Queen Anne terrace.

The mistress of the house, an exceedingly beautiful woman, received us with every mark of eagerness and cordiality.

She welcomed us—or, rather, my esteemed employer—most effusively; and when we were all seated, she asked many questions about Mr Edward Kelly, to which Skin o' my Tooth replied as often as she allowed him to get a word in.

"Oh, Mr Mulligan," she said finally, "I am so glad that you asked to see me. I have been positively ill and devoured with anxiety about my brother-in-law. My husband thinks that I upset myself and only get hopelessly wretched if I read about it all in the papers, so he won't allow me to see one now; but, I assure you, the uncertainty is killing me, as I feel sure that Mr Kelly is trying to comfort me and to make Edward's case appear more hopeful than it is."

Skin o' my Tooth gravely shook his head. "It could not very well be more hopeless," he said.

"You can't mean that?" she said, while tears gathered in her eyes. "He is innocent, Mr Mulligan. I swear he is innocent. You don't know him. He never would do anything so vile."

"I quite believe that, my dear lady; but unfortunately circumstances are terribly against him. Even his dead dog, Rags, speaks in dumb eloquence in his master's condemnation."

"Rags!" she exclaimed in astonishment, "what can the poor doggie have to do with this awful tragedy? Poor old thing! it lost its way the very morning that the terrible catastrophe occurred. M. de Kerhoet was staying here that day, and I had taken him for a drive to Hitching before luncheon. On the way home I saw Rags in the road, looking very sorry for himself. I took him in the carriage with me and brought him home."

Skin o' my Tooth looked politely interested, but I hardly liked to breathe; it seemed to me that a fellow creature's life was even now hanging in the balance.

"Rags knew us all here just as well as it did its own master," continued Mrs Kelly, "and when my husband went out with his gun in the afternoon, Rags followed him, whilst M. de Kerhoet and I went on to a garden-party."

"And what happened to Rags after that?" asked Skin o' my Tooth.

"To tell you the truth, the awful tragedy I heard of that afternoon drove poor Rags out of my mind; then the next day, I am thankful to say, M. de Kerhoet left us and went back to Paris. I did hear something about the poor dog being drowned in the pond; he was a shocking rover, and really more trouble than pleasure to his master."

Mrs Kelly was sitting with her back to the great mullioned windows; she could not, therefore, see her husband, who seemed to have just walked across the terrace and to have paused a moment, with his hand on the open window, before entering the room. Whether he had heard what his wife was saying, I did not know, certain it is that his face looked very white and set.

"I remember now," continued Mrs Kelly innocently, "seeing my husband put away Rags' collar the other day in his bureau.

I dare say Edward will be glad to have it later on, when all this horrid business is over. You must tell him that we have got it quite safe."

I all but uttered an exclamation then. It seemed too horrible to hear this young wife so hopelessly and innocently denouncing her own husband with every word she uttered. I looked up at the motionless figure still standing in the window. Skin o' my Tooth, who sat immediately facing it, seemed to make an almost imperceptible sign of warning. Mr Kelly then retired as silently as he had come.

Two minutes later he entered the room by the door. He seemed absolutely calm and collected, and held out his hand to Skin o' my Tooth, who took it without the slightest hesitation; then Mr Kelly turned to his wife and said quietly—

"You will forgive me, won't you, dear, if I take Mr Mulligan into my study? There are one or two points I want to discuss with him over a cigar."

"Oh! I'll run away," she said gaily. "I must dress for luncheon. You'll stay, won't you, Mr Mulligan? No? I am so sorry! Well, goodbye; and mind you bring better news next time."

She was gone, and we three men were left alone. I offered to leave the room, but Mr Kelly motioned me to stay.

"The servants would wonder," he said icily, "and it really does not matter."

Then he turned to Skin o' my Tooth and said quietly—

"I suppose that you came here today for the express purpose of setting a trap for my wife; and she fell into it, poor soul! Not knowing that she was damning her own husband. Of course, you did your duty by your client. Now, what is your next move?"

"To place Mrs Kelly in the witness-box on my client's behalf, and make her repeat the story she told us today," replied Skin o' my Tooth with equal calm.

"And after that?"

"After that, you must look to yourself, Mr Kelly. I am not a detective, and you know best whether you have anything to fear when once the attention of the police is directed upon yourself. I shall obtain Mr Edward Kelly's discharge tomorrow, of course. Backed by Mrs Kelly's testimony, and, if need be, that of Mr Kerhoet, in Paris, I can now prove that the dog could not have been shot by my client, since it was following you on the afternoon that the murder was committed. Since the chief point in the theory of the prosecution lies in the fact that Mr Whadcoat and the dog were shot on the same day and with the same rifle, and seeing that the animal's collar was known to be in your possession the day following the crime, my client is absolutely sure to obtain a full discharge and to be allowed to leave the court without a stain upon his character."

Mr Kelly had listened to Skin o' my Tooth's quiet explanation without betraying the slightest emotion; then he said—

"Thank you, Mr Mulligan. I think I quite understand the situation. Personally, I feel that it is entirely for the best; life under certain conditions become abominable torture, and I have no strength left with which to combat fate. I did kill old Whadcoat in a moment of unreasoning fear, just as I killed Rags because he made too much noise; but, by Heaven! I had no intention to kill the old man, and I certainly would never have allowed my brother to suffer seriously under an unjust accusation. I firmly believed that justice could not miscarry; and while I thought that you were sharp enough to save him, I also reckoned that I had been clever enough to shield myself from every side."

He paused a moment and then continued; just like a man who for a long time has been burdened with a secret and is suddenly made almost happy by confiding it to a stranger.

"I had had many losses on the turf," he said, "and had made my loses good by defrauding our firm. It was a long and laborious plan, very carefully laid; but I was always clever with my pen, and my brother's signature and Whadcoat's writing were easy enough to imitate. Then, one day, I found an old uniform in the cellar at the office—my father used to keep a commissionaire when he had the business. It was about my size and gave me the idea for the disguise. It all worked right, and I knew that I could make my defalcations good at the bank very soon. It was a positive thunderbolt when, on the Tuesday morning, I received a letter from old Whadcoat, telling me that he was coming over to Saltashe that afternoon to see M. de Kerhoet and myself about a terrible discovery which he had just made. I knew he would walk through the Woods, and I found him sitting near the pond, smoking, alone. I only meant to persuade him to hold his tongue and say nothing to M. de Kerhoet for the present. But he was obstinate; he guessed that I was guilty; he threatened me with disclosure, like the fool he was, and I had to kill him... in self-defence."

Somehow, although he undoubtedly was a great criminal, I could not help sympathising with this man. The beautiful house we were in, all the luxury and comfort with which he was outwardly surrounded, seemed such terrible mockery beside the moral tortures he must have endured. I was quite glad when he had finished speaking, and Skin o' my Tooth was able presently to take his leave.

Only a few hours later, the evening papers were full of the sensational suicide of Mr Kelly in his Library at Saltashe Park. Almost at the same time that this astonishing news was published in the Press, the authorities at Scotland Yard had received a written confession, signed by Mr Kelly, in which he confessed to having caused the death of Mr Jeremiah Whadcoat in Saltashe Woods, by the accidental discharge of his gun.

A little frightened at first of any complications that might arise, he had said nothing about the accident at the time; then, when his own brother became implicated in the tragedy, and he felt how terrible his own position would be if he now made a tardy confession, the matter began to prey upon his mind until it became so unhinged that he sought, in death, solace from his mental agony.

"That man was a genius," was Skin o' my Tooth's comment upon this confession. "Strange that he should have lost his nerve at the last, for I feel sure that the crime would never have been brought absolutely home to him; at any rate, I could have got him off. What do you think, Muggins?"

And I quite agreed with Skin o' my Tooth.

2

THE CASE OF THE SICILIAN PRINCE

I doubt whether full credit was given to Skin o' my Tooth for the solution of that mysterious incident in the Saltashe Woods, which he—and no one else—brought about. Personally, I firmly believe that Kelly, of Saltashe Park, would have allowed his brother to hang, sooner than confess, if Skin o' my Tooth had not succeeded in absolutely cornering him. Now, in the case of the Sicilian Prince, no one could deny—but perhaps I had better say how it all happened.

The Swanborough tragedy was filling all London and provincial papers with its gruesome mysteries. Early on Tuesday morning, March 18th, the body of a man, shockingly mutilated, was found on the level crossing, just below the Swanborough station of the London and North-Western Railway. It is always difficult to dwell on the grim details which are the usual accompaniment to this type of drama; suffice it to say, in this instance, that the body was found lying straight along the metals, so that the passing express had gone clean over the trunk and face. What mutilation the train had left unaccomplished had been completed by the sparks from the engine. The face was unrecognizable, the hair had been singed, the flesh on hands and neck had been charred. The peculiar position of the body, so carefully laid down, with the feet pointing towards Swanborough station, and the head towards Bletchley, disposed of any theory of accident that may at first have suggested itself. Moreover, some articles of clothing—a coat and waistcoat—were subsequently found lying in a field close by. It was clearly either a case of murder—the unfortunate man having, presumably, been rendered unconscious and then placed on the metals—or one of deliberate suicide.

The grim tragedy immediately assumed the appearance of complete mystery. Though Swanborough is but a tiny, straggling village, and this part of Buckinghamshire but scantily populated, no one seemed to have missed a relative or friend, or to recognize the clothes that were found lying in the field nor those that were upon the mutilated body. The police had published a description of these clothes and articles, and of the body, as far as this could be done. The unfortunate man seemed to be about thirty-five years of age, five feet nine inches in height, and of slight build. He was evidently in the habit of wearing a green silk shade over one eye, for one was found lying on the ground quite close to the head; the right forearm showed a very recent wound caused by the burning of some acid—probably vitriol.

The people of Swanborough, however, in spite of the horrible gruesomeness of the tragedy, seemed to take very little interest in the elucidation of its mysteries; perhaps, too, they had the average English yokel's horror of having anything to do with the police. Be that as it may, it was not until the following day that a more enlightened or more enterprising villager bethought himself of walking to the police station and informing the inspector there that "maybe the murdered man was Mrs Stockton's lodger."

It appears that Mrs Stockton, who rented a small cottage not far from the railway, had had a lodger on and off for the past six months. No one in the village had ever seen him; if he ever went outside the cottage, he must have done so at nights;

but young Stockton had sometimes talked to the neighbours about his mother's lodger. He was a foreigner, he said, "and no end of a swell," with a name no decent body could pronounce, as it was about half a yard long. He was certainly very odd in his ways, for he used to go away quite suddenly and not come home for a week or so on end. Mrs Stockton never knew where he went to; and then he would turn up again, mostly in the very early mornings.

Life in rural districts is wonderfully self-centred; still, the police thought it odd that this tardy information did not come from Mrs Stockton herself or from her son, if, indeed, her lodger were missing just now. The detective-inspector immediately went down to the cottage. Finding the door locked, and getting no answer to his repeated knocks, he forced his way in, followed by two constables.

Parlour and kitchen were empty, but up on the floor above, in one of the three little bedrooms, the men found the unfortunate woman lying in bed with her throat cut. There was no sign or trace anywhere of young Stockton.

The mystery, of course, had deepened more and more. Nothing in the cottage seemed to have been touched; there were even a couple of sovereigns and some silver lying in a money-box. So far it appeared that two purposeless and shocking murders had been committed probably within a few moments of each other, as Mrs Stockton had evidently been dead a good many hours. The detective-inspector instituted immediate inquiries in the neighbourhood on the subject of young Stockton, who certainly had unaccountably disappeared. It seems that he was a platelayer by trade, lately in the employ of the North-Western Railway, but recently dismissed owing to ill-conduct.

A description of the missing man was telegraphed to every police and railway station in the kingdom, but so far not a trace of him had been found. The theory of the police was that he had boarded the very train which had mangled the body of his victim, and then dropped off it again a good deal farther down the line. Whether he had murdered the "foreign swell" for purposes of robbery, and killed his mother in order to get rid of an inconvenient witness, was, of course, a mere matter of conjecture; certain it is that he had vanished, almost as if the earth had swallowed him up.

2

From the first, Skin o' my Tooth was greatly interested in the Swanborough tragedy. The enigmatic personality of one of the victims, the veil of complete mystery which the murderer had succeeded in throwing over his crime, the "foreign swell" who lived in the English cottage, all appealed to my chief's love for what was dramatic and mysterious.

It was on the afternoon of the 20th, just after I had come in with the evening papers, that there was a timid rap at the outer office door. I went to open it, and, to my amazement, saw before me the daintiest vision that had ever graced our fusty old office in Finsbury Square. I had never seen such a lovely young girl. She could not have been more than seventeen or eighteen, and she was exquisitely dressed in something soft and black, and wore the daintiest pair of shoes I had ever set eyes on. She asked me if she could speak to Mr Mulligan immediately. It was such an unusual thing for us to receive visits from charming young ladies that for the moment I quite forgot to ask her name.

However, Skin o' my Tooth was quite ready to receive her, whoever she was, and the next moment I had shown the lady into the private office. She walked up to my esteemed employer and held out a daintily gloved hand to him.

"My name is quite unknown to you, Mr Mulligan," she began. "I am Miss Marion Calvert, and I would not have ventured to come like this to your office without any introduction, and all alone, but I want the best possible legal advice, and—"

THE CASE OF THE SICILIAN PRINCE 25

"Yes?"

"My friend, Miss Morton, who is engaged to Mr Edward Kelly, of Saltashe Park, told me all about you once, a long time ago, and how much you had done for Mr Kelly. I remember then making up my mind that if ever I were in trouble and wanted a lawyer, I would come to you; and now—"

She had undone her furs and seated herself beside the desk. Skin o' my Tooth gave me a wink. I knew what that meant. I was to sit in my usual corner behind the wooden partition—a position which my chief poetically called "behind the arras"—and take shorthand notes of everything the lady said.

"Mr Mulligan," she resumed very abruptly, "I was engaged to Prince Sieronna, who was murdered the other day on the railway near Swanborough."

"Then, indeed, you are in trouble," said Skin o' my Tooth very gently, "and that is why you have come to consult me. Tell me, what can I do for you?"

"I am afraid that my story will seem a very foolish one to you. I was only a schoolgirl then. It was six months ago," she explained with touching naivete. "I had just left school, and was going down to Buckinghamshire with one of the governesses to stay with my uncle, Mr Percival Lake, and his wife, when I first met Prince Sieronna. It was in the train between Euston and Swanborough, and he was so kind and attentive, and oh! so interesting. He told me that he was a Sicilian, and he talked about Italy and about Fascismo, and the Sicilians who had suffered in the war. He himself was an exile from the country he loved so well, because he had taken part in an anti-Fascist rising. He had large estates, but they were temporarily confiscated by Signer Mussolini; so he had to come to England, which he loved, and he lived in a small cottage amidst roses and lilies, and dreamt there of Italy and her liberty.

"You may imagine how delighted I was when he told me that this ideal cottage was in Swanborough, close to where my uncle lived, for I had hopes then that I should see him again. Well, Mr Mulligan, I won't bore you with all the details of what was the happiest time of my life. Mrs Lake was kindness itself, but she kept rather a strict eye over my movements. However, very soon I discovered that I could always slip out in the evenings, while she went to sleep over her game of patience, and then I used to meet Amadeo—Prince Sieronna—in the fields at the bottom of the garden. Very soon we had both realized that we loved one another passionately."

"But surely your uncle—?" suggested Skin o' my Tooth.

"My uncle was away during the first fortnight of my stay in Swanborough. When he came, things were very much altered. Someone—one of the servants, perhaps—had evidently spied upon me and had told him of my meetings with Prince Sieronna, for he read me a long lecture on the subject of foreign adventurers and English girls with money, and forbade me ever to see this Sicilian Prince again. Of course, I was obliged to obey him then, as he kept a pretty sharp lookout over my movements, and I saw nothing of Amadeo for a week; but the moment Mr Lake went back to town we were able to resume our happy evening meetings in the fields.

"This went on for some time, during which my love for my future husband grew with every obstacle my uncle placed in my way. But Mr Lake was often obliged to be absent from home on business, and you may be sure that Amadeo and I made the most of these happy intervals. We had agreed that we should be married as soon as I was of age and free to do as I pleased.

"During all this time, Mr Mulligan, I was in absolute ignorance of my future financial position, and Amadeo, with a delicacy that was positively sublime, and which put to shame Mr Lake's cynical insinuations, had never asked me any questions on the subject. I knew vaguely that my father had left me some money, under the trusteeship of Mr Lake, and

I concluded that I should have the use of my small fortune when I came of age.

"To my astonishment, however, on my eighteenth birthday, which was the ninth of this month, my uncle informed me that by the terms of my father's will I was now to become sole mistress of about £20,000 which he had left me. The next day Mr Lake took me up to his office in London and rendered me an account of his guardianship; he then placed into my hands a large packet, which contained my £20,000 worth of securities, chiefly railway and mining shares, he said, and told me that I was free now to do with them what I pleased. It had been ostensibly arranged that I should stay in London a few days with some school friends of mine, but, secretly, Amadeo and I had planned to spend long, happy days together. I took a room in Victoria Street, and he used to come up from Swanborough in the mornings sometimes, and we would go out to see the sights of London. We meant to get married almost immediately and go and live abroad. What with my money and the revenues from Amadeo's estates which Signor Mussolini was about to restore to him, we would be able to live, not only in comfort, but even in luxury."

She paused. It seemed as if she could not continue her narrative; so far it had been one of simple, delicate love romance, in which only the mysterious personality of the foreign adventurer appeared as a dim presage of coming evil; now, for the first time since the terrible tragedy occurred, the young girl—little more than a child—found herself forced to speak of it to a stranger, and her very nerves must have quivered at the ordeal. But Skin o' my Tooth did not speak. He sat in the shadow, watching the play of every emotion upon the delicately chiselled face before him.

"Last Monday, Mr Mulligan," she resumed at last, with an effort at self-control, "Amadeo went down to Swanborough in the afternoon, after having spent the day in town with me.

He meant to settle what small accounts he had in the village and stay in London until our marriage. I was sitting quietly at tea at a shop yesterday when I heard someone close to me read aloud from a newspaper the account of the mysterious tragedy at Swanborough. A man had been found killed on the level crossing, his body and head shockingly mutilated. A description of his clothes followed—one or two articles found near the body. Oh, it was terrible, Mr Mulligan! From those descriptions I knew that the murdered man must be my fiance, Prince Sieronna."

There was a long silence in the fusty old office. Skin o' my Tooth was giving the young girl time to recover herself, when he said quietly: "It must indeed have been hard to bear in your peculiarly isolated position. But you have not yet told me how I can be of service to you."

"Oh! It's about the money, Mr Mulligan—my whole fortune. Prince Sieronna had charge of it all, of course, and now I am penniless."

"You need have no fear; we can easily trace those securities for you; the thief won't be able to negotiate them."

"Oh, the securities!" she said naively; "they were all sold."

"Indeed?" was Skin o' my Tooth's very dry comment.

"Yes. At Amadeo's suggestion I instructed the brokers, Messrs. Furnival and Co., to sell my shares for me. They sent me a cheque for £20,000, which I endorsed, and Prince Sieronna cashed the cheque. He had all the money in notes, and he told me to write my name at the back of each. On the Monday we went round together to several foreign banks, where we changed our English notes into foreign money. You see, we intended to live in Paris, and meant to start for France almost immediately."

I wished then that I could have caught a glimpse of Skin o' my Tooth's face; as it is, I thought I heard the peculiar low whistle he usually gives when a point in a case particularly strikes his fancy.

"I see," he said at last. "And that money? Did the Prince carry it about with him?"

"He gave me fifty pounds, as I meant to go shopping after he left me; the remainder he kept in his pocket-book."

"H'm! Life's strange ironies!"

But, fortunately for her many illusions, the young girl did not catch the drift of this last remark, for she said with great vehemence: "You see now, Mr Mulligan, that there could be no question of accident or suicide. Prince Sieronna was murdered and robbed, and I have come to you so that you may help me to track his murderer."

"I will do my best," said Skin o' my Tooth, with a smile; "and at the same time we must hope to track your lost fortune for you. But I think that is all I need trouble you about this afternoon. Where are you staying?"

"I am still at 182, Victoria Street."

"Then I can easily communicate with you. I will see the detective-inspector in charge of the case, and, of course, let him know about the money, which should be found in the murderer's possession. Was the money French or Italian?"

She shook her head.

"I really couldn't tell you. You see, Amadeo saw to everything."

Skin o' my Tooth sighed. So much naiveté and blind confidence would be ridiculous were it not sublime.

Five minutes later I had shown the lady downstairs, and when I returned I found Skin o' my Tooth lounging in his big armchair.

"It was a case of biter bit with a vengeance, wasn't it, sir?" I said, with a laugh, whilst I carefully collected my notes. "This so-called Prince seems to have been as complete a scoundrel as the man who murdered him."

"Muggins, you're an ass!" was the only comment my esteemed employer made during the whole of the rest of that afternoon.

3

In the meanwhile the evening papers had brought no further news of the Swanborough mystery. No trace of the missing platelayer had been found, and it was pretty clear that at the inquest, which was fixed for tomorrow (Friday), the police would have no important evidence to add to the scanty scraps already collected and published.

"The local authorities will resent my interference in this case," said Skin o' my Tooth to me; "but I must chance that. If I leave them to blunder on as they have done over this murder, I shall never get Miss Calvert's money for her, for the scoundrel will succeed in slipping through our fingers."

He sent me down to Scotland Yard the next morning to make the necessary declaration with regard to Prince Sieronna's antecedents as related to us by Miss Calvert, and also to the missing quantity of foreign money. The detective-inspector who was watching the case was greatly excited to hear my news.

"This gives us the motive for the crime," he said, "and the foreign money in the possession of an uneducated Buckinghamshire yokel like Stockton is sure to lead to his discovery and speedy arrest. At any rate, the local people have asked for one of our men, so now that we have so much fresh data I will send Mason, who is very capable, down to Swanborough. I will give him instructions to place himself at Mr Mulligan's disposal should he require any local information."

When I went back to the office I found the car at the door and Skin o' my Tooth waiting for me with his hat on.

"Come down to Swanborough with me, Muggins," he said. "I have worked out this case in my own mind, and I want to ascertain, by studying the geography of the place, whether I am right or wrong."

We went down to Swanborough, and during the whole of the run Skin o' my Tooth never spoke a word. He sat leaning back in the car with that funny little smile of his playing round the corners of his fat mouth, and the thick lids drooping as if in semi-somnolence. But every now and then I caught a flash, a steely, almost cruel look, in his lazy blue eyes, and then his nostrils would quiver like those of a hound who has just found a scent. I knew those symptoms well. I had seen them in him whenever the sharp and astute lawyer was for the time being merged in the tracker of crime. Skin o' my Tooth had all the instincts of a bloodhound. Placed face to face with a murder, he would follow the trail of the assassin with almost superhuman cunning. He did not deduce, he seldom reasoned; he felt the criminal. I believe firmly that he scented him.

When we drew up outside the small country station a little after 2 p.m., we found that Mason, the detective, who was personally known to Skin o' my Tooth, had already come down by train. He was standing talking to the booking clerk when my chief went up to speak to him.

I think that he was none too pleased to see a lawyer mixed up in a case which he no doubt considered strictly the business of the police; but Skin o' my Tooth seemed to have armed himself for the afternoon with a limitless fund of Irish urbanity.

"I won't detain you long, Mason," he said, with a bland smile. "I should presently like to have a look at the body with you; and in the meanwhile, I dare say, while we walk through the village you will put me *au fait* of the latest news in connection with this interesting case."

"There is very little news," said Mason, with marked impatience. "The case is a very troublesome one, and if it is meddled with I don't believe we shall ever get at the rights of it."

"I see that you were having a chat with the young booking clerk here," said Skin o' my Tooth, quietly ignoring the detective's rudeness. "I wonder what his impression was of the Sicilian Prince. So few people seem to have seen him; but he always travelled up and down by train, so, of course, at the railway station they must have known him by sight."

"The porters and the booking clerk only saw him once, and that was on the Monday, when he came down by an afternoon train, and one man saw him soon after eleven the same evening. It was just after the last slow train had gone through, and they were closing the booking office; he was then walking along the line with young Stockton towards the level crossing."

"What sort of a looking man was he?"

"Oh, a regular foreigner, it appears, with thick black hair falling back over his forehead, and a heavy black moustache. He had a huge scar right across the left side of his face—from a wound, I suppose. They say it looked like a sabre cut, and it seems to have injured his eye as well, for he wore a guard over the left one. Anyway, he is quite unrecognizable now," he added grimly.

Mason had led the way along the platform while he was talking, and we had followed him. He was now walking along the railway line, about two paces in front of us. On our left a tall and neat hedge fenced off a field, and some two hundred yards ahead was the level crossing, where a road cut the line at right angles.

About twenty yards from the level crossing there was a wide gap in the hedge. Mason pointed this out to us.

"It is supposed that Stockton enticed his victim into the field under some pretext or other and rendered him unconscious there; then he dragged him on to the metals; at any rate, that is where the murdered man's coat and waistcoat were found; whether he took them off himself or whether Stockton took them off after he killed him, and why, remain a puzzle."

"A puzzle indeed," Skin o' my Tooth assented blandly.

"This gap," Mason went on, "Mr Lake tells me, used to be quite a small one. It has obviously been broken and widened quite recently."

THE CASE OF THE SICILIAN PRINCE 33

"Mr Lake?" queried Skin o' my Tooth.

"Mr Percival Lake. This field is his property; his house and grounds are at the opposite end of it."

"Oh! Ah, yes! I am glad to hear that, as I should like to call on Mr Lake before I leave Swanborough today."

We had come to a standstill on the very spot where the awful and gruesome murder of the mysterious foreign prince had been perpetrated. Skin o' my Tooth was looking at the surroundings and at the ground before him, and every now and then I could hear him snorting, and caught sight of that weird and quick flash in his eyes which gave his jovial, fat face such a cruel look. Then, without word or warning, he suddenly darted through the gap in the hedge into the field beyond. With an impatient shrug of shoulders Mason followed him, and I brought up the rear.

It was mid-December, and the ground was as hard as nails; a few patches of dead grass only showed here and there. We were in a field of about thirty acres, triangular in shape, with the same tall hedge surrounding it, and the house and grounds forming its apex. A road ran on either side of it, converging on the other side of the house.

The afternoon had rapidly drawn in. It was past three o'clock, and a thick mist had descended. Mason followed, with evident and unconcealed ill-humour, Skin o' my Tooth's peregrinations through that field. At first he had offered certain hints and volunteered some information, but at last he seemed to have resigned himself to the part of a bad-tempered man in charge of a lunatic.

We walked straight across the field to where the house and its thick shrubbery formed its extreme boundary. There, too, a small gate led to a cottage and tiny garden, which occupied a piece of ground that seemed to have been sliced out of Mr Lake's property.

"It is Mrs Stockton's cottage," explained Mason, in answer to Skin o' my Tooth's inquiry. Quite close to the gate there was a tool-shed, which seemed to interest Skin o' my Tooth immensely, for he lighted match after match in order to examine it inside and out. However, he expressed no desire to view the interior of the cottage, and at last, when I was quite numb with fatigue and cold, he turned to Mason and said quietly: "I am quite ready to go to the station now and have a look at the body."

For a moment I thought that Mason meant to go on strike, but evidently he had had his orders, or perhaps he, too, began to feel, as I had done so often, that curious magnetic influence of Skin o' my Tooth's personality, which commands obedience at strange moments and in strange places. Be that as it may, he refrained from making any remark, but, passing through the gate and cottage garden, he went out into the road. About five minutes' brisk and silent walk brought us to the village and then on to the little police station. Still without a word, Mason led the way into an inner room. There upon a deal table, and covered over with a sheet, lay the body of the murdered man.

4

It is not often—thank Heaven for that!—that I have to go through such unpleasant moments in my faithful adherence to my duty towards my employer. I shall never forget the terrible feeling of sickly horror which overcame me when Skin o' my Tooth so quietly lifted the sheet which covered the dead man. The whole scene is even now vividly impressed upon my mind—the small, low-raftered room, the electric light from the ceiling throwing its glitter upon the gruesome thing on which I dared not look, and upon the strange, bulky figure, so marvellously impressive at this moment, of my chief. Mason stood close by in the shadow. I could see that even he did not care to cast too long a look at the hopelessly mutilated face of the murdered man. Skin o' my Tooth, however, was quite unmoved. He had dropped the sheet, and calmly, one by one,

THE CASE OF THE SICILIAN PRINCE 35

he took up each garment from the pile of clothes which lay neatly folded beside the body.

"These were found upon the deceased, I understand?" he asked. The detective nodded.

"All," he replied, "except the coat and waistcoat in the field and the gloves, which were in the grip of the hand."

"And which this man could never have worn," commented Skin o' my Tooth dryly, "though they are quite old; they are two sizes too small for the hand."

There was a silence again for a few moments; then Skin o' my Tooth, having carefully examined each individual garment, put the last one down; then, placing his hand upon the pile, he said: "I hope for your sake, Mason—and for mine, too, for that matter, since it would save argument—that you have arrived at the only possible and complete solution of the so-called mystery."

"The only mystery in this matter," retorted Mason gruffly, "is the real personality of the deceased. We know who murdered him all right enough, though we don't know where the murderer may be at the present moment."

"The personality of the deceased is no mystery to me. He was a young man named Stockton, a platelayer by trade, and an inhabitant of this village," said Skin o' my Tooth, making this extraordinary announcement as if he were stating the most obvious and commonplace fact.

Mason shrugged his shoulders and looked almost appealingly at me, as if he wanted me to take charge of this raving lunatic.

"The only thing that puzzles me," continued Skin o' my Tooth imperturbably, "is that it never struck any of you gentlemen in charge of this case how very badly some of these clothes must have fitted this man."

"People don't always have their clothes cut by a London tailor," muttered Mason sarcastically.

"Undoubtedly. But in this case the fit is so erratic; while the trousers would be at least three inches too short, the coat sleeves would be much too long. This man could not have had these gloves on at all; and every time he wore these boots, which are not new, he must have endured positive torture, yet he has no corns on his feet."

"The clothes might have been a scratch lot, bought at a second-hand clothes shop," suggested Mason.

"A man does not buy second-hand boots that are much too small for him."

"What is your idea, then?"

"That they are another man's clothes," said Skin o' my Tooth quietly.

"But—"

"Note one thing more. The suit of clothes are good, such as a gentleman might wear; boots, gloves, hat—all are of an expensive kind; but the underclothes are of the commonest and coarsest make."

"That often happens," muttered Mason obstinately.

"It certainly in itself would mean but little were it not for the fact that with almost superhuman cunning everything has been devised in order to completely destroy the identity of the victim. From the clothes every tag and some buttons have been removed which might bear the tailor's name; on the forearm vitriol was used, in order, obviously, to obliterate some mark—tattoo, perhaps—which might have made the body recognizable, whilst the same corrosive substance destroyed the finger and toe nails, which might have told a tale."

"The accepted theory is that the deceased was engaged in some work which necessitated the use of sulphuric acid."

"That might account for the corroded finger-nails, if the man was particularly careless, but not for the wound on the forearm nor for the condition of the toe-nails. Think of it all carefully, Mason, and then bear in mind the fact that the only person who might by chance have identified the body, in spite of its mutilation, was also murdered."

"You mean Mrs Stockton?"

"The mother, undoubtedly," replied Skin o' my Tooth quietly. "Surely you see for yourself now that the body we have here before us is that of Stockton, the platelayer, whereas it is this so-called Prince Sieronna, this arch-scoundrel, thief, liar, and assassin, who so far has escaped the vigilance of the police."

"You may be right," murmured Mason, convinced, as I could see, in spite of himself, with the firm logic of Skin o' my Tooth's arguments; "but, as far as I can see, you have not by any means solved our difficulty. It was quite one thing to hunt for a Buckinghamshire yokel who would be trying to pass a quantity of foreign money and could not speak any language but his own, and quite another to search through the continent of Europe now for a foreigner, of whose real appearance I presume even your client, his sweetheart, is ignorant."

"You won't have to search through the continent of Europe, my man," said Skin o' my Tooth, with a jovial laugh. "You just apply—as quickly as you can, too, for the gentleman may slip through your fingers yet—for a search warrant and warrant for arrest of Mr Percival Lake, of Swanborough. You will find most of the £20,000 there in foreign money, Italian or French. That money belongs to my client, Miss Marion Calvert, who will file affidavits to this effect tomorrow."

"You are mad!" retorted Mason.

"Mad, am I?" laughed Skin o' my Tooth jovially. "Why, man, you know as well as I do by now that I am right. Why, I guessed the trick the moment Miss Calvert told me her pathetic little history; then I came down here, and I saw how admirably the geography of the place was adapted to that arch-villain's infamous plot for robbing his young ward. Why, you have only to remember three points to realize how absolutely right I am. Point number one: whenever Mr Percival Lake was at home

Miss Calvert could never see her sweetheart. The moment he was supposed to go back to town she found him at the trysting-place in the field; but always at night, remember, when the disguise, the scar, the black hair, would more easily deceive the young girl. It was only when he had got her money absolutely in his possession that he became more audacious and saw her in London in broad daylight."

"I have always thought that that scar and the thick, black hair meant a disguise," muttered Mason. "Some people are so clever at making-up, and Mr Lake is a little bald and clean-shaved."

"The change of costume was so easy of execution with that convenient little tool-shed in his own shrubbery, secluded from all eyes and, until recently, fitted with a good lock and key, which have since, very obviously, been removed. Why, nothing in the world could be more easy than for an arch-scoundrel like that man Lake ostensibly to leave for town in the evening, carrying his bag, and, walking through his field, to spend the night in the tool-shed, and emerge therefrom in the very early morning as Prince Sieronna; then to reverse this performance whenever the foreign adventurer had to resume his original part of Mr Percival Lake, Miss Calvert's stern guardian. Add to this point number two—that the man who played the trick on Miss Calvert must have known all about her financial position and the full terms of her father's will, by which she came of age at eighteen."

"That certainly brings it nearer home to Lake than ever. And your third point, Mr Mulligan?"

"That this so-called foreigner was supposed to have gone up to London from Swanborough very frequently during the week, when he met Miss Calvert in town nearly every day, and helped her to transfer her English securities into foreign money, and yet no one at the Swanborough railway station had ever seen him before the night of the murder. Then, he wished to show himself, openly, in the company of the platelayer, so that, when he had murdered Stockton and dressed up his body in his own cast-off disguise, everyone should fancy that they recognised in the mangled remains the personality of the Sicilian Prince. He did the murder at dead of night, of course, and in the privacy of his own fields; he used vitriol where the marks of identification might reveal the platelayer; then he murdered Mrs Stockton and slipped home quietly to bed. I dare say his wife was an accomplice. Some women are very loyal or very obedient to their husbands. But come along Muggins," he said, suddenly altering the tone of his voice and turning to me, "we must be up in town by 6.30 and it can't be far off that now; besides which, Mason will want to think all this over."

"No, I shan't, sir," said Mason firmly. "I am going up to Swanborough police station at once."

"What for?"

"To deliver my report and to get a warrant for the arrest of Percival Lake."

Everyone remembers the arrest of Mr Percival Lake on a double charge of murder. In his safe at his house in Swanborough were found French and Italian notes amounting in value to about £20,000. Tracked to earth, the scoundrel made but a poor defence. Fortunately for his relations, since he was well connected, he died of sudden heart failure during the subsequent magisterial inquiry, and was never committed for trial.

This all happened three years ago. Miss Calvert is married now, and has evidently forgotten her former passionate love for the mysterious Sicilian patriot.

3

THE DUFFIELD PEERAGE CASE

It was through the merest coincidence that Skin o' my Tooth got mixed up with this remarkable case, which brought him suddenly into such great prominence before the public, and was really the foundation-stone of his subsequent more fortunate career. In those days—it seems very long ago now—money was often very tight at the Finsbury Square office; it was spent as soon as earned, for Skin o' my Tooth never learnt its value, principally, I think, because he never exerted himself to earn it. The gentle art of self-advertisement was totally unknown to him, even in its most elementary stages, and had I not made friends with the sub-editor of the Surrey Post, and got him to insert that excellent puff, beginning: "Mr Patrick Mulligan, the most eminent and learned lawyer on criminal cases, is now in our midst," etc., etc., no doubt the Duffield Peerage Case would have drifted into other far less competent hands, and Heaven only knows what the upshot of it all would have been.

We had gone down to Guildford in connection with the Wingfield Will Case, and finding the sweet little Surrey town peculiarly attractive, Skin o' my Tooth had decided to stay on for a few days, and, under the pretence that he would feel lonely, he insisted on my remaining with him. We had spent a week of delightful idleness, and my chief had devoured a large supply of his favourite French novels, when the murder of Mr Sibbald Thursby, a noted solicitor of Guildford, threw the whole town into a veritable state of uproar. From the very first the wildest rumours were circulated on the subject of this appalling tragedy, and it became really difficult to sift the real facts from the innumerable surmises and embellishments indulged in by the imaginative reporter of the Surrey Post. The truth however, as far as I ultimately succeeded in gathering it for the benefit of my chief, who seemed interested in the case, was briefly this:—

Mr Sibbald Thursby had an office where he transacted his business in Guildford High Street, but he lived in a tiny house just outside the town, on the Dorking Road; his household consisting of himself and a man and his wife named Upjohn, who shared the duties of cook, gardener, maid and man of all works between them. On Friday last the Upjohns went upstairs to bed as usual at 9.30 o'clock, leaving their master at work in his study on the ground floor. This room had windows opening out on to the small garden at the back, and a little conservatory leading to it. Mr Thursby always bolted the windows and locked the conservatory the last thing before going to bed. The Upjohns heard someone knocking at the front door some ten minutes after they went upstairs, but both having already got into bed, they seem to have been too lazy to get up. Whether Mr Thursby himself let his belated visitor in or not, they could not say, for they heard nothing, and very soon were both sleeping the sleep of the just.

But next morning, when Mrs Upjohn went into the study, she was horrified to find her master lying on his side across the threshold of the conservatory door; his clothes—the clothes he was wearing the night before—were covered with blood, his face was obviously that of the dead. Upjohn, summoned by his wife's screams, quickly ran into Guildford for the doctor and the police: the former pronounced life to be extinct,

Mr Thursby's throat having been cut from ear to ear, obviously with the short, curve-bladed knife found in the conservatory. There had been no time even for a short struggle for his life on the part of the unfortunate solicitor. According to the theory immediately formed by the police, he had been attacked with extraordinary suddenness and fury; practically at the very moment when he was opening the conservatory door in order to let the assassin in. The latter must at once have gripped his victim by the throat, smothering his screams, and only used the knife when the poor man was already senseless. In failing backwards, Thursby had seized the portière curtain and dragged it down with him in his fall, otherwise nothing was disturbed in the room. The windows were found carefully bolted; the lamp even had been extinguished. The few little articles of silver and bits of valuable china in the cabinets were left untouched; the unfortunate man's watch and chain, the loose cash in his pocket, were found intact; and to the police the crime seemed as purposeless as it was mysterious.

At the inquest, which was held on the following Tuesday, a verdict of "Wilful murder against some person or persons unknown" was returned, and the public had perforce to rest satisfied that everything was being done to throw light upon this tragic and awful affair. But gradually a rumour, more persistent and positive, and less vague than others, began to find general credence. The Surrey Post had brought the news that a lady—a stranger to Guildford—had gone to the police to request the return of certain papers which had been in the charge of Mr Sibbald Thursby, and for which she held a receipt signed by him. Rumour went on to assert that a search was made for these papers, and that they had not been found, but that one of the constables, when he was carefully surveying the room where Mr Thursby was murdered, had discovered a handful of ashes of burned papers in the grate. Twenty-four hours later, the news had spread throughout England like wildfire that the lady whose papers had so unaccountably disappeared claimed to be the lawful wife of the Earl of Duffield, and that those papers were of paramount importance to the legal aspect of her claim and that of her son.

Skin o' my Tooth had stayed on at Guildford all these days, chiefly because the case interested him from the very first; with his unerring instinct in criminal matters, he had scented a mysterious complication, long before the many rumours anent the lady claimant had taken definite shape.

"I imagine Lord Duffield won't enjoy this washing of all his family linen in public, which seems to me quite inevitable," he said to me one morning, when he had read his Surrey Post.

We had just finished the excellent breakfast provided by the Crown Hotel, and Skin o' my Tooth had suggested the advisability of my running up to town to get him a batch of French novels, when one of the waiters came up to our table, with a great air of importance and mystery, and holding a card upon a salver.

"His Lordship is in his carriage," he murmured with the respect befitting so important an event, "and desires to have a few minutes' interview with Mr Mulligan."

I glanced at the card, which bore the name "The Earl of Duffield," while Skin o' my Tooth quietly intimated to the waiter that he would see his Lordship in the sitting-room.

Lord Duffield was a stout, florid, jovial-looking man of about fifty, decidedly military and precise in his dress and general bearing, but at the present moment obviously labouring under a strong emotion which he was making vigorous efforts to conceal.

"Mr Mulligan, I believe," he said.

"That is my name," replied Skin o' my Tooth. "To what can I ascribe the honour of this visit?"

"I read your name in the local papers, Mr Mulligan, but of course I had heard of you before, in connection—er—

with criminal cases. The present instance—but," he added, looking somewhat dubiously at my humble personality, "this gentleman—?"

"My confidential clerk, Lord Duffield. You need have no fear of speaking before him."

Satisfied on that point, Lord Duffield sat down, then he said abruptly—

"It is about this murder of Sibbald Thursby. The turn this affair has taken forces me to place the matter, as far as I am concerned, into the hands of a lawyer. Our own family solicitor is too old and has never had any experience of this sort; whereas you—"

"I am entirely at your disposal."

"To make the matter clear to you, I shall have to take you back some thirty years, when I, a young subaltern in a line regiment quartered in Simla, had no prospects of ever inheriting this title and property. When I was barely twenty, I fell in love, like the young fool I was, with a noted beauty of Simla, a Miss Patricia O'Rourke, whose reputation already at that time was none too enviable. After a brief courtship, I married her, in the very teeth of strenuous opposition on the part of all my friends; and less than six months after my marriage I had undoubted proofs that Miss O'Rourke was of more evil character than even Simla had suspected, for at the time she married me she had a husband still living—a man named Henry Mitchell, as great a blackguard, I believe, as ever trod the earth.

"Half crazy with grief and the humiliation of it all, I at last succeeded in obtaining sick leave, and soon sailed for England determined, if possible, to turn my back for ever on the woman who had blighted my life, and on the scene of my folly and my shame.

"Well, Mr Mulligan, I dare say that experience has taught you that grief at twenty is soon forgotten. Within a year of that saddest period of my life, my uncle, the late Earl of Duffield, lost his only son, and I became his heir. He obtained for me an exchange into the Coldstream Guards, and soon after that I married Miss Angela Hutton, the daughter of America's great copper king. The following year my uncle died, I inherited the title and property, and then my son Oswald was born, and I became a widower.

"In the meanwhile, Miss O'Rourke, or Mrs Mitchell, had disappeared from Simla. No one knew where she had gone to; some of my friends thought that she was dead.

"I was obliged to tell you all this, Mr Mulligan," resumed Lord Duffield after a slight pause, "so that you may better understand my position at the present moment. Remember that I have been during all these years under the firm impression that my marriage with Patricia O'Rourke was an illegal one, and that our son born of that union was not legitimate. I had what I considered ample proofs that Henry Mitchell was alive at the time that she married me. When I taxed her with the crime of bigamy, she not only did not deny it, but calmly told me to go my way if I liked. Now, after thirty years she has once more appeared upon the arena of my life. Not only that, but she has come forward with a claim — a strong claim for herself and her son. She has obtained affidavits, sworn to by people of unimpeachable position testifying to the death of Henry Mitchell in Teheran — where he had settled down in business — three clear days before her marriage to me.

"After thirty years?" commented Skin o' my Tooth in astonishment.

"She went to see Sibbald Thursby, who, as you know, perhaps, was the most noted lawyer in Guildford. He was a very old and very intimate friend of mine. She put all the facts before him and showed him all her papers. He came and told me himself that the affidavits were perfectly en règle, duly signed and witnessed by the British Consul in Teheran; one had been sworn by Dr Smollett, a leading English medical man, who attended on Henry Mitchell in his last illness."

"But why thirty years?"

"Well, it appears that she had all along been morally convinced that Henry Mitchell had died before our marriage; but she had lost trace of him for some months, and had been unable to obtain the necessary proofs to convince me of his death. However, when I left her, she resolutely set to work to obtain these proofs; but by the time she had succeeded, some years had elapsed, and she also had lost sight of me. She did not know that Lieutenant Adrian Payton had become the Earl of Duffield, you see. A mere accident revealed this fact to her, and, immediately realising her duty to her son, she then set sail for England."

"Mr Thursby, I understand, as a lawyer, thought well of the lady's claim?"

"He thought that there could be no two opinions on the subject."

"There usually are, though, in law," said Skin o' my Tooth, with a smile.

"Yes! And you may be sure that I did not mean to allow my son Oswald to lose his rights and become nameless without a struggle. But Sibbald Thursby had shown me the affidavits which my wife—I suppose I must call her that—had given in his charge, and I am bound to confess that her case seemed remarkably clear. Still, I meant to fight to the bitter end—then—"

"Then? And now?"

"Now? Have you forgotten what has happened? Sibbald Thursby has been murdered, and those same papers have been stolen or destroyed."

"According to you, by whom?" asked Skin o' my Tooth quietly.

"Ah! Heaven only knows! Look at me, Mr Mulligan. Am I capable of such a crime? And yet public opinion has already built a veritable scaffolding of base insinuations against me and my son Oswald. My wife has gathered round her a veritable army of partisans; the London papers utter scarcely veiled accusations, and the people of this county cut me in the street."

"But what about your son, Viscount Dottridge, I mean?"

"What about him, Mr Mulligan? I tell you there is an infamous conspiracy against him. He went out on the afternoon preceding Sibbald Thursby's death to pay a visit to some friends about twenty miles the other side of Guildford. He was on his bicycle, and rode home late in the evening. Just outside Guildford his tyre punctured badly; he was still five miles from Duffield, so he elected to have that puncture mended in the town sooner than walk his machine home. He left his bicycle at Rashleigh's, in the High Street, then thought he would kill time by having a chat with Sibbald Thursby. He went round to 'The Cottage.' It was then a little before ten. He knocked at the front door, but receiving no answer, he went away again and went for a stroll in the lanes until his machine was mended. He called for it at Rashleigh's at a quarter past ten; it was then ready, and he rode home."

"Yes. And—?"

"And while he stood for a moment irresolute upon Sibbald Thursby's doorstep, a couple of workmen saw him, and have informed the police of this fact. If you have read the local paper this morning, Mr Mulligan, you will have noticed that they announce 'Sensational Developments in the Guildford Mystery.' That sensation will be, I take it, that my son Oswald will be accused of having murdered Sibbald Thursby, in order to destroy the papers which would have robbed him of his inheritance."

"Of which crime you assert that he is innocent. Pray do not misunderstand me. Mine is at present an open mind; I have only followed the case very superficially. Since you have honoured me with your confidence, I will, of course, go very fully into the matter. Your position from a legal point of view is secure for the moment. Failing the proofs that Henry Mitchell was dead at the time of your marriage with Miss Patricia O'Rourke, your proofs that he only died after the marriage hold good and make your position unassailable. In that way, the murderer of Mr Sibbald Thursby has certainly done you—or, rather, your son—a good turn, for the lady may perhaps never succeed in getting her proofs together again. Teheran is such a long way off, and the creditable English witnesses are probably dead or dispersed by now. But, of course, there is public opinion, and no doubt you yourself cannot estimate at the present moment how far it will force your hand."

Lord Duffield groaned. "At present," he said, "I only seem to care about the danger to my son Oswald."

"Quite so; and if you will allow me, I will now at once see the detective-inspector in charge of the case, and you may rest assured that everything that can be done, will be done to throw daylight upon these unfortunate events."

Lord Duffield seemed as if he would like to prolong the interview. He looked to me as if he had something on his mind which he could not bring himself to tell, even to his lawyer. Skin o' my Tooth, with his keen insight, also noted the struggle, I am sure, for he waited silently for a moment or two. However, after a brief pause, Lord Duffield rose, shook hands with my chief, nodded to me, and with a few parting instructions he finally left the room.

2

I don't suppose that even Lord Duffield realised how very strong public opinion was already against him in this matter. The lady—small blame to her—had made it her business to let the whole town know the full history of her case, and I must say that, as it now stood, it did not redound to the credit of the noble lord and his son. The detective-inspector, on whom Skin o' my Tooth called that same afternoon, was quite convinced that Lord Duffield and his son had planned and executed the destruction of the documents. The murder, he admitted, might not have been intended, but merely committed as an act of self-defence, when the noble thieves had found their friend awake and alert, instead of in bed, as they had supposed. There was no doubt that Viscount Dottridge was seen to loiter round "The Cottage" at about ten o'clock at night. The Upjohns were firm in their statement that they had heard a noise at the front door at about that time. The theory of the police was that the young man had then gone round to the garden and tried the conservatory door; Mr Thursby, hearing a noise, had gone to see what the noise was, and was probably gripped by the throat before he could utter a scream.

"Personally, Mr Mulligan, I have very little doubt that his Lordship was in this game, somehow," concluded the detective-inspector at the end of our interview with him; "but I think you will agree with me that the position is remarkably difficult. What in the world am I to do? Duty is duty, and there must not be one law for the rich and another for the poor. The matter can't be hushed up now. Lady Duffield—I suppose she is that, really—won't allow the matter to rest. As long as she remains in the country, she will keep public opinion well stirred up. I wish she could be persuaded to leave the matter alone now. Even if we succeed in proving a charge of murder against Viscount Dottridge, it won't give her son any better chance to make good his claim, will it, sir?"

"Certainly not," replied Skin o' my Tooth; "and you have put the matter in a nutshell. As you say, it would be far better if the lady vacated the place and left you a free hand to hush up the scandal or not, according to the discretion of your chiefs."

It was clear from this interview that the detective-inspector did not know how to act. Torn between his respect for the title and position of the Earl of Duffield, and his own sense of duty in view of the many proofs in favour of Viscount Dottridge's guilt, he was certainly inclined to wait, at any rate until public opinion literally forced the hand of his chiefs.

But in the meanwhile, Skin o' my Tooth had announced to me his intention of seeing the lady who seemed to be the real centre of the many tragic events of the past few days.

We walked round to the "Duffield Arms," where we understood that she was staying, and two minutes later we were shown into the private sitting-room which she occupied at the hotel.

I must say that I looked with some interest at the woman round whom such exciting events seemed to have gathered. Though she must have been nearly fifty years of age certainly, there was even now a wonderful amount of fascination about her entire personality, and a power of magic in her blue eyes. Her son, whom she introduced to us as Viscount Dottridge, was with her when we came into the room, and it was quite impossible not to be struck immediately with the distinct resemblance which he bore to his father. Legally or not, this young man was undoubtedly the son of the Earl of Duffield. Nature had taken special care to prove that fact, at any rate; and my sympathies immediately went out to him and to his beautiful mother, for there was no doubt that Luck had treated them very roughly.

She received my chief very graciously, and, bidding him be seated, she listened with a smile to what I may term the presentation of his credentials.

"I am Lord Duffield's legal adviser in this matter," he said; "but I think I may safely say that I am the friend of both parties. Whilst I serve my client to the best of my ability, I have every desire—believe me—to be of service to you and to your son."

She shrugged her shoulders.

"I have been a fool, Mr Mulligan," she said. "I ought never to have parted with those papers. Now I fear that no one can help me."

"Surely you are wrong. There is no reason why the lost papers should not be replaced. It certainly may take some years and—"

"Money," she interrupted impatiently, "which I have not got. Those who murdered Mr Thursby and stole the papers knew what they were about. They have left me absolutely helpless; and even if the perpetrator of the dastardly outrage were punished with the full rigour of the law, I should still see my son ousted from his rights."

"Would you mind telling me the exact contents of the papers you considered most valuable to the furtherance of your cause?"

I thought she looked at him a little suspiciously then; but evidently reassured by his genial smile, she said—

"There were two sworn statements made—one by a Dr Smollett, who was a well-known English doctor in Teheran, the other by an English nurse named Dawson; both these persons were with Henry Mitchell at the time of his death, and remembered all the circumstances connected with it. Dr Smollett is dead now. As for the nurse, I have lost sight of her for ten years; it is very doubtful if I could ever trace her."

"But surely these statements were made before the resident British Consul at Teheran?"

"Oh, yes! of course they were. Sir William Courteen was Consul at the time. He subsequently became Governor of the Gold Coast, and died, if you remember, some three years ago."

"Fate has indeed dealt harshly with you," murmured Skin o' my Tooth with genuine sympathy.

"To tell you the truth, it never struck me at first that Lord Duffield would contest my just rights. When I understood that

Mr Thursby was a personal friend of my husband's, I left my papers in his hands, thinking that no doubt he would show them to Lord Duffield, who, feeling the unimpeachable justice of my claim, would resign himself to the inevitable and give willingly to my son, and his, what, after all, is his due."

"That being a very unlikely contingency now, Lady Duffield, might I ask you what you intend to do?"

"Failing my rights, Mr Mulligan, which I suppose from what you say will now never be granted to me, I can always fall back on that barren enjoyment—revenge. Yes, revenge!" she added with sudden vehemence. "He would deprive me of my position and leave my son nameless? I tell you, Mr Mulligan, that with Heaven's help I will so rouse public feeling against him that, when his son has been hanged for the murder of Sibbald Thursby, he in his turn will have to flee this country as a pariah and an outcast, for no honest man henceforth will shake him by the hand."

She had spoken with so much vindictive fury that I felt a cold shiver creeping down my back. Skin o' my Tooth, smiling blandly, was obviously smitten by the fire of her magnificent blue eyes.

"I think," he said, "you will reconsider your very severe mandate."

"Never."

"Surely, if my client realised that you had certain undoubted claim upon him—I only speak without prejudice; but you have a son, and revenge, though sweet, might not prove very useful in his career."

"I never looked upon it in that light," she said coldly, and rising from her chair, as if she wished to end the interview.

"You would not care to name a figure?" suggested Skin o' my Tooth insinuatingly—"without prejudice—"

For the first time during the interview she turned to her son and seemed to consult him with a look, but he shook his head very energetically.

"Not now," she said to Skin o' my Tooth, and then, with a charming smile, she intimated that she wished the interview to cease.

"You will, in any case, always find me at your service," concluded my chief blandly, as we finally took our leave.

3

As the days wore on, the mystery the Guildford tragedy seemed to deepen more and more. We had another interview with Lord Duffield, at which his son—the only son he would acknowledge—was present, and I must say that seeing those two men, typical of the English, country-bred, but high-born gentlemen, it was almost impossible to conceive that they could lend their hand to the dastardly murder of an old friend. Skin o' my Tooth had received overtures on the part of the claimants, who seemed to have finally realised that revenge was but sorry pleasure, and expressed themselves ready to accept a monetary compromise in return for their permanent residence out of England.

To my intense astonishment Lord Duffield fell in readily with this arrangement, which, after all, was nothing but a bribe, and first gave me the idea that perhaps he and his son had something on their conscience. It is quite certain that a constrained feeling seemed to exist between father and son. Undoubtedly I often caught Viscount Dottridge casting furtive glances at his father, and once or twice Lord Duffield looked long and searchingly at his son, then sighed and turned his head away.

I don't pretend to any deep insight into human nature, but it certainly struck me that these two men had begun almost to suspect one another. And no wonder! Who else but they had any interest in destroying the papers which would have made good the cause of the claimants? And I had seen the detective-inspector that morning, and knew that the police, forced into it by public opinion, egged on by the claimants, and convinced that they held sufficient proofs, had at last decided to apply for a warrant for the arrest of Viscount Dottridge.

That same afternoon Skin o' my Tooth at last obtained leave to go over "The Cottage." The police—who always resent outside interference in such matters—had so far on some pretext or other, always refused permission. But my chief was on his mettle. Lord Duffield had promised him £10,000 if he succeeded in elucidating the mystery and in averting the disgrace which threatened him and his son. Today, at last, Skin o' my Tooth was able, not only to make a vigorous effort towards obtaining that substantial reward, but also to indulge his passion for ferreting out the mysteries which lurk around a crime. I don't think I ever remember seeing his weird faculties more fully in evidence than over the elucidation of the Guildford tragedy—that faculty which literally made him feel the criminal before he held any clue to his guilt.

The late Mr Sibbald Thursby had been buried the day after the inquest, but in his house everything had been left just as it was the night of the appalling tragedy. The Upjohns had gone, refusing to sleep another night in a place where so terrible a murder had been committed, and as we let ourselves in by the front door our footsteps echoed weirdly within the deserted house. We were accompanied by two constables who, however, took but little interest in Skin o' my Tooth's wild ramblings through the tiny garden, the conservatory, and the study. It seemed as if he expected the ground to give him the final key to the mystery, of which he already had studied the lock; he was walking along with his eyes glued to the floor, his hands buried in the capacious pockets of his ill-fitting coat, and every now and then I could hear him muttering to himself—

"There must be a bit, only a bit—there always is."

Then at last he seemed to have found what he wanted, for he darted forward towards a fine large palm, all dead and dry now for want of water, which stood in an ornamental pot close to the grate. Inside the pot, and covered with dust and mud, there glimmered a piece of paper. Skin o' my Tooth seized it as if it had been a most precious piece of jewellery; then furtively he thrust it in his pocket, and signed to me to hold my tongue, as the constables had just come into the room.

After this short episode, Skin o' my Tooth expressed himself satisfied with all he had seen, and together we returned to the hotel.

Once alone in the privacy of our sitting-room, he took the dirty piece of treasure from his pocket, carefully knocked the dust out of it, and then spread it out smoothly before him on the table.

"You mayn't think it, Muggins," he said, "but this piece of dirty paper is worth an earldom and a good many other things besides, including the life of a man, who without this wee scrap would very probably have ended on the gallows. It is also worth £10,000 to me."

Eagerly I looked over his shoulder. The scrap of paper was about the size of my hand, and had obviously been torn off another larger sheet. The words I could decipher were:

"... ry Mitchell... anuary 22nd, 1871... my presence," and lower down, what was evidently a signature written in a different hand,

"... nor Dawson."

"And what is it, sir?" I asked.

"What an ass you are, Muggins!" he said impatiently. "Can't you see that this is all that is left of one of the affidavits which proved that Henry Mitchell died on the 22nd of January, 1871, or three days before Adrian Payton married Patricia O'Rourke? The signature is that of the nurse Dawson, who swore this particular affidavit."

"But it's no use in this state, is it, sir?"

"Oh, yes, Muggins. An affidavit is always useful, even in this condition. You look up a train for me. Early tomorrow morning I am going up to town with this scrap of paper."

He would not tell me anything more then, and the next morning he went up to town and stayed away all day. I saw the detective-inspector in the afternoon, who told me that the warrant for the arrest of Lord Dottridge was actually out, but that he had had a wire in the morning from Scotland Yard "to await further instructions."

"I fancy," he added with a grin, "that Mr Mulligan has not deserved his nickname this time. He can't get Lord Dottridge out of this hole, not even by the skin of his teeth."

In the evening, however, Skin o' my Tooth came home, dead tired and triumphant. I met him at the station, and together we immediately proceeded to the police-station.

"I have been waiting to see you, Mr Mulligan," said the inspector. "We cannot delay any longer, and tonight we must execute the warrant against Lord Dottridge."

"You can throw that warrant into the fire, inspector," replied Skin o' my Tooth quietly, "and tomorrow you can apply for another. You'll have to be pretty quick, too, as I fancy your game smells a rat already and may yet slip through your fingers."

"What do you mean?"

"Only this. When you kindly allowed me to view the scene of the interesting murder case you have had on hand, it was my good fortune to come across this interesting document."

And Skin o' my Tooth once more carefully unfolded that dirty scrap of paper on which he had set such store.

"What in the world is this?" asked the inspector.

"That is the very question put to me under the same circumstances by my clerk, Mr Alexander Stanislaus Mullins. The paper, inspector, is all that is left of one of the affidavits which were to prove the legality of certain claims made by a charming lady and her son. You will notice the signature,

'...nor Dawson.' I may tell you that the lady in question had lost sight since ten years of nurse Dawson, who attended upon her husband in his last illness. This illness occurred thirty years ago. We have no official knowledge as to when this affidavit was filed, beyond the fact that it was more than years ago; but if you will examine very carefully the paper on which it was written, you will notice a remarkably interesting fact."

And Skin o' my Tooth held up that dirty scrap of paper against the lamp, allowing the light to show through it. In the extreme corner, the water-mark, "C. & Sons," became clearly visible.

"Looking through the list of English paper-makers," continued my chief, quietly pointing at this with his thick finger, "I came across the name of Clitheroe and Sons, of 29, Tooley Street, London. This afternoon I interviewed the manager of that firm, who informed me that the lettering of the water-mark in this particular bit of paper indicated that it was manufactured by Clitheroe and Sons in 1899."

"I don't understand," gasped the inspector, staring with all his might first at the dirty bit of paper and then at the unwieldy, bulky figure of Skin o' my Tooth, as he quietly revealed the key to the mystery which had so long puzzled the astute detective.

"Yet it is very simple," he said, with one of his bland smiles. "Personally, I had suspected it all along, from the moment that I first saw Lord Duffield and his son, and realised that they had—if I may so express it—not the brains to carry out so daring, a crime successfully. Had that very amiable, but not otherwise brilliant, young man committed that murder, believe me, he would have left plenty of evidence of his guilt. The fact that you yourself, in spite of your acumen, had been unable to really bring the crime home to him, showed me that a cleverer head than his, and a subtler mind, had been at work: but until you favoured me with a permission to view "The Cottage," I had not a single indication on which to work. When I first saw the lady, I realised that hers might have been the head;

my instinct told me that her son's was the hand; but there seemed such a total lack of motive, the whole theory seemed so topsy-turvy, that I hesitated even to follow it up. Then you courteously allowed me to view the scene on which the crime itself was committed. At once the fact struck me very forcibly that whoever had come on that fateful night to steal the affidavits knew where to lay his hand on them. Nothing in the room or in the desk had been disturbed, and yet obviously the murderer would turn down the lamp as low as possible immediately his nefarious deed was done, lest the light from windows should reveal his presence. Then, again, you know, no doubt as well as I do, how seldom it is that a murderer does not leave a single trace or clue behind him. That is most fortunate in the cause of justice, otherwise many crimes would remain unpunished. I reckoned in this instance that a man after committing what I presupposed would be his first crime, would necessarily have his nerves very much on the jar. His hand, presumably, would shake, and in tearing up the papers by the very much subdued light of the lamp, and in the presence, of his victim lying dead on the door it is impossible, I say, that some scrap should not have escaped his trembling hands—you know how paper flutters—and lodged itself momentarily out of sight, ready to reappear as a damning witness against him."

The inspector was silent. I could see that he was hanging breathless upon Skin o' my Tooth's lips. And I, too, saw it all now before me, even before my chief gave us the final explanation of his unanswerable logic.

"In ascertaining the fact that this paper was manufactured two years ago, whilst purporting to have been written on and signed more than ten years previously, it became clear to me that the affidavits setting forth Miss Patricia O'Rourke's, alias Mrs Henry Mitchell's, claim were a pack of forgeries. From this conclusion to the understanding of her clever plan was but a quick mental problem. After all, it was simple enough. Having forged the documents, she entrusted them to Sibbald Thursby. Then her son chose his opportunity, the best he could find, to steal and destroy them. After that she hoped so to rouse public indignation against Lord Duffield by openly accusing him of the theft that he would either throw up the sponge altogether and recognise her rights, or at worst pay her a handsome compensation to clear out of the country and leave him alone. Remember, she all but succeeded. You yourself suggested this alternative as the simplest solution of the difficulty, and Lord Duffield was quite ready to fall in with these views."

"But as it is," suggested the inspector at last, "do you think we shall be able to bring the crime home to these people? They seem to have been very clever."

"You could bring the accusation of forgery and fraud undoubtedly home to her. You might succeed in proving the murder against her son, but I don't think that you will get a chance of doing either."

"Why not?"

"I think you will find your birds flown already."

"That would be tantamount to an acknowledgment of guilt, and then we could overtake them wherever they may have fled."

"It certainly is an acknowledgment of guilt, as you say," concluded Skin o' my Tooth, rising from his chair and stretching his great, loose limbs; "but personally, I do not think that you will overtake them if they have succeeded in making good their escape."

Skin o' my Tooth's prophecy proved to be correct. The detective-inspector, I think, has remained convinced to this day that my esteemed employer was not altogether innocent in the matter of the escape of Mrs Henry Mitchell and her son from the clutches of the law. They had left for London that very evening, and thence had gone to Dover, where all trace of them had ostensibly vanished. I believe that their lucky escape from justice cost Lord Duffield a pretty penny, but, of course, he felt that enough family dirty linen had been washed in public, and he was willing to pay a good sum to save even an illegitimate son from the gallows.

4

THE KAZAN PEARLS

You are quite right there: Skin o' my Tooth did have everything to do with the unravelling of that complicated knot which the sensational press at the time called the Great Pearl Mystery, and my opinion—which is shared by many in authority—is that but for the activities and courage of my chief, a grave miscarriage of justice would have been perpetrated.

What happened was this: the Countess Zakreoski, an American lady married to a Russian of great wealth, late of the household of the murdered Tsar, had dined one evening with her husband at the Majestic, their host being the Honble. Morley-Everitt, son of the Countess' first husband, who was Lord Everitt of Eode, and brother of the present peer. Mr Morley-Everitt was a very popular and smart young man about town, and a devoted attendant upon his stepmother, whom he helped in her entertainments and to whom he acted as a kind of secretary and factotum in her magnificent house in Belgrave Square. She, in return, kept him lavishly supplied with money, and the two were more like actual mother and son to each other than is usually the case with children of a former marriage.

The dinner party in question consisted, in addition to the Count and Countess Zakreoski and the host, of the Marquis and Marquise de San Felice of the Italian Embassy, Lady

Dewin, who was a connection of the Everitts, Madame Hypnos, a Greek lady, friend of Countess Zakreoski, and of a certain Major Gilroy Straker, lately come over from Australia, on some business or other connected with Empire products; he had brought letters of introduction from well-known people in Australia, to other equally well-known people in London. The party stayed on till rather late, and then went home in two motors, the one a large Rolls-Royce belonging to Count and Countess Zakreoski, and the other, a small Essex, belonging to Mr Morley-Everitt. The latter took Lady Dewin and Madame Hypnos with him, the others all went in the Rolls-Royce.

On that occasion the Countess Zakreoski wore—as she often did—the famous Kazan pearls, an heirloom of great value and historical interest, around which many a Russian romance has been woven: the pearls have been the envy and admiration of every jewel expert in Europe and America ever since they were first brought out of the family strong-room by Count Zakreoski and presented to his bride, the present Countess.

They consisted of three ropes, magnificent in size and lustre and perfectly matched; their value was said to be incalculable. They were insured for £60,000.

The Countess only discovered the loss of her pearls when she got home, and her maid helped to divest her of her cloak. I won't, of course, recapitulate all the details of the search which was immediately instituted, inside and outside the house, in the garage and the motor; there were telephone calls to the Majestic, to the police, to the chauffeur, and half the night was spent in setting the machinery going towards the recovery of the priceless gems. Subsequently as much as £10,000 reward was offered, and amateur as well as professional detectives were employed by the score, not only in England, of course, but all over Europe and America.

But all these efforts were of no avail. Day followed day and no news of the missing pearls. The police was hopeful still, but the public shrugged their shoulders and marvelled what the thief could hope for except the reward, as surely such remarkable gems would not easily be marketable.

The loss, or rather theft, of the Kazan pearls was however, only the first phase of an extraordinary tragedy, wherein accident and coincidence played their several sinister parts. It was about a fortnight later, and the sensation about the Kazan pearls had vanished in favour of a world-famed prize fight, when Madame Hypnos, who had many friends in London society, was found murdered in the flat which she occupied in Curzon Street, Mayfair.

The flat consists of three rooms and bathroom opening on a narrow passage; two of the rooms, bedroom and sitting-room, communicate with one another, the third is just a small kitchenette. The unfortunate woman's body was found lying on the floor of the sitting-room. She had been stabbed in the back with a large curved knife of Eastern design, which lay close beside her. The discovery was made by a Mr and Mrs Mortimer who had a flat on the same floor. They had been at the theatre, and on returning home had heard a fearful row going on in Madame Hypnos' flat. They paused for a moment or two on the landing in order to listen, and they heard Madame's voice shouting repeatedly:

"You shan't! You shan't!"

However, they felt that it was no business of theirs, and after a while they went unconcernedly into their own flat. About five minutes later they heard an awful shriek. Mrs Mortimer was in the kitchenette at the moment, heating up some cocoa, while her husband was in the bedroom changing his shoes. For a moment she felt paralyzed with horror. Suddenly she heard the front door of the flat across the landing open and close, and footsteps clambering downstairs. Then only did she put down the saucepan which she had been handling and ran to her husband. He, too, had heard the shriek and was debating in his mind what he should do when his wife ran in to him. Together they went out on the landing. The well of the stairs was in total darkness, which was odd, because one light was always kept up on each landing all through the night. These lights were controlled by a single switch in the main entrance hall, and someone must have turned that off after the Mortimers had gone into their flat. The man's first instinct was to run downstairs as fast as darkness would allow and turn the lights up again. When he came back to his own landing he found his wife almost swooning with terror. She was speechless and with trembling hand was pointing in the direction of Madame Hypnos' flat, from whence could be heard at intervals heartrending groans.

This time without pausing to think, Mr Mortimer ran into his own flat, got a poker, smashed the stained-glass panel of the door of Madame Hypnos' flat, put his hand through the hole, and turned the handle of the door. The wretched woman, who was lying in a pool of blood, was even then drawing her last breath.

Mr Mortimer sent his wife back to her own rooms and ran down to rouse the hall-porter and sent him for the police.

On the face of it, robbery appeared to have been the primary motive of the crime, because every article of furniture in the place had been ransacked: drawers had been pulled open and locks smashed; the mattress and pillows on the bed, as well as upholstery, had been ripped up, and with the same knife, probably, that had finally done the deed.

Inspector Richards, one of the most able men of the C.I.D., was at once put in charge of the case. A few facts immediately jumped to the eyes, others appeared there and then to obscure the main issue. One thing was certain, the murderer had been on familiar terms with his victim: the flat had not been broken into. Whoever it was who had come to visit Madame Hypnos that evening had been let in by her in the ordinary way. She kept no servant of her own; as a matter of fact, no one kept a servant in these little flats, which were what are known now as "service flats". The visitor had been made welcome by Madame: there was a half-bottle of whisky and siphon on one of the tables; two tumblers which had contained whisky stood on the mantelpiece, together with an empty cigarette box, and there were a couple of ash-trays filled with dead matches and cigarette ends.

But the great disappointment that confronted Richards was the total absence of finger-prints other than those of the murdered woman herself. These, strangely enough, appeared on both the tumblers that stood upon the mantelpiece, and also—though here they were very much blurred—upon the handle of the knife with which the crime had been committed. But beyond that, nowhere, although Richards, who is as keen after a clue of that sort as a bloodhound after a trail, put every single article in that flat to the finger-print test.

What he soon discovered, however, was the actual motive of the crime. To begin with, there was, lying close beside the fender, a torn and crumpled copy of *The Times*. It looked as if the reader had thrown the paper down in a fit of rage and stamped upon it. Richards smoothed out the creases and looked at the date; it was a week old. The page that lay uppermost was the front one, and there in flaring letters in the personal column was the advertisement of the assessors, offering £10,000 reward for the recovery of the Kazan pearls.

This gave Richards the clue of what the thief or thieves had been after. With more deliberation than he or they had displayed, he set to work to search the flat, and it was after three hours' minute search, when he had almost given up hope, that he chanced to turn over a gallipot that contained washing soda, and there, hidden underneath the soda, was a handful of pearls, some clinging to their string, others loose—one of the three ropes of the Kazan pearls.

Richards now was hot on the scent; inquiries from the hall-porter of the flats and also the other occupants of the block brought to light the fact that Madame Hypnos received many visitors—mostly in the evenings, and mostly men; the hall-porter thought that Madame was usually on the lookout for them; anyway, he never saw them halt on the landing. It seemed as if her front door would always be left ajar, so that the visitors could just push it open and walk in. Asked to describe some of these visitors, the man hesitated. He never, he said, saw any of them very clearly. One gentleman, he thought, had a black beard and curly black hair; he wore a slouch hat and an overcoat with the collar turned up to his ears. Another wore a heavy white cavalry moustache. He was lame and very stout. Madame had not been in the flats very long, and the hall-porter had not had time, as yet, apparently, to take stock of her visitors. But there was one young gentleman who had recently come once or twice to the flat. Mr and Mrs Mortimer had seen him too; he was young and tall, they said, with fair, curly hair and blue eyes and small toothbrush moustache. The first time this young man called was about three weeks ago, and he came quite openly and asked the hall-porter if Madame Hypnos lived there. After which Mr and Mrs Mortimer volunteered the information that on the evening of the tragedy that same young man had called at the flat; they were just off to the theatre when he got out of a taxi outside their front door. They took that same taxi on to the theatre. It was then a quarter past eight.

The taxi, advertised for by the police, was easily enough traced. The chauffeur said that he had originally been taken up by a gentleman outside the Dominions Club in Hanover Square and had driven him to a block of flats in Curzon Street, Mayfair, where a lady and gentleman had taken him to the Duke of York's Theatre. Inquiries at the Dominions Club elicited the fact that one of the members, a certain Major Gilroy Straker, had been one of the party at the Majestic when the Countess Zakreoski lost her pearls. He always kept a room, it seems, at the Dominions Club, having been one of its founders and therefore privileged. He was summoned to give evidence at the inquest, identified by the taxi-driver, the hall-porter of the flats, and Mr and Mrs Mortimer, and even before he had begun to give evidence the police obtained a search warrant against him, and amongst his effects in his room at the Dominions Club they found the Kazan ropes of pearls, with the one row broken and about fifty or sixty pearls missing.

2

At the close of his evidence Major Gilroy Straker was arrested, and the verdict of the coroner's jury was one of wilful murder against him. His arrest created a great sensation in London, more particularly in the little coterie that had taken him up. It was a very smart coterie, by the way, one chiefly made up of wealthy foreigners who had either made their home in England or were passing through. Countess Zakreoski and her husband were among its leaders; they had relations and friends all over Europe and America; no foreigner of distinction ever came to London without an introduction to the popular couple. They would sponsor the ladies and married couples, and Mr Morley-Everitt would introduce the bachelors to the smart clubs in London. In this instance both the Zakreoskis and Mr Morley-Everitt felt that they owed an apology to their friends for the introduction of Major Straker to this charmed circle. He had come to London with introductions to the Countess from friends of hers in Sydney, and she had, as it were, passed him on to Mr Morley-Everitt, her stepson. The latter had been more than kind in seeing to it that the young colonial, who, by the way, had served with distinction with the A.E.F., had a good time in London. This was an easy task, as the Major was good looking and an excellent dancer, and he had been made very welcome. With regard to Madame Hypnos, matters were not quite so simple. It seems that Countess Zakreoski had only been kind to her at the request of Major Straker: she had only had her once to tea at her own house, and Mr Morley-Everitt had—again at Major Straker's request—very kindly asked her to be of the party that night at the Majestic. On inquiry it turned out that neither Mr Morley-Everitt nor Count and Countess Zakreoski, nor any of the party that night, knew anything about Madame Hypnos beyond the fact that she was a friend of Major Straker.

Skin o' my Tooth, I must tell you, was from the first very much interested in this case: he always had a wonderful flair for intricacies and problems long before they cropped up in evidence. He and I went daily to Bow Street to hear the Australian Major give an account of how he came to be in possession of two ropes of pearls belonging to the Countess Zakreoski, whilst the third rope, or a part of it, was found in the flat of a lady whom he had visited the very evening on which she came by a violent death.

Of course, to most people his history appeared so curious as to be unbelievable. No wonder that the police turned his statements inside out and that the magistrate had no option but to commit him for trial. What Major Straker had told the police, the coroner, and the magistrate was this:

He had arrived in England, he said, about three months ago from Australia, where he had been managing director of a firm of wool merchants in Sydney. He had gone out to Australia when quite a lad, but had—until quite recently—a mother and sister living in Worcestershire, which was his original home. He had been to see them after he landed at Southampton, and then came up to London to have a good time. He was taking a long holiday, and had brought letters of introduction to Countess Zakreoski and one or two other people in town from some smart friends in Sydney. During the war he had helped to found the Dominions Club for colonial officers, and a room was from the first reserved for him there, whenever he should happen to come to London again.

Count and Countess Zakreoski and Mr Morley-Everitt were very kind to him; he soon made friends and went about a good deal. He had met Madame Hypnos at one of the smart charity balls at the Albert Hall. She was in the crowd at the buffet and appeared to be distressed at being jostled; he offered his services to get her something to eat and drink. She accepted gratefully; said she had been cut off from her friends in the crowd and was afraid that they had left her in the lurch. Major Straker had no cause for complaint: she was pretty and charming; he asked her to dance, and she was an exquisite dancer; then he asked her to supper, and she accepted. She suggested Eugene's, and thither they went. Mr Morley-Everitt happened to be there having supper with a friend; mutual introductions ensued; they all spent the rest of the evening very happily together, and finally the Major saw Madame Hypnos home to her flat in Curzon Street. She asked him to call again, which he did the very next day, and once or twice after that he took her to a theatre or to a restaurant. She did not seem to have many friends in London, and she did not tell him anything about herself; he never heard her mention the people who had left her in the lurch at the Albert Hall ball, and he asked no questions: he just took her as he found her, as any young man would take the friendship of a pretty woman who made herself agreeable to him. In the meanwhile it appeared that Mr Morley-Everitt had also been greatly taken by the pretty Greek widow—she did say that she was the widow of a Greek officer killed in the war—he had also called upon her and taken her out to theatre and restaurant; he had even gone to the length of presenting her to his stepmother, and finally asked her to the dinner-party he gave at the Majestic on the night when the Kazan pearls were stolen.

"That night," Major Straker went on with his statement, "I was driven home from the Majestic by Count and Countess

Zakreoski, and took leave of them outside their house in Grosvenor Square and started to walk home to the Dominions Club. It was long past midnight then, and I had just turned into Maddox Street when out of the narrow passage immediately behind St. George's Church two men fell upon me with the suddenness of lightning: one had me by the throat, whilst the other got hold of my legs and very nearly brought me to the ground. However, I had been what might be called a noted athlete in Sydney, and I was taught ju-jitsu by a famous Japanese exponent. Anyway, we had a brief but desperate struggle, my assailants and I, and they were already getting the worst of it when fortunately a policeman's whistle sounded somewhere quite close, and they took to their heels. So quickly did they run that by the time a couple of bobbies appeared at one end of the street they had disappeared down the other. Well, I didn't want to be bothered with any police, and I had suffered no damage from my adventure, so, before the bobbies finally arrived, I, too, had vacated the scene of action and turned into the Club."

All this, of course, you will say, appeared reasonable enough; it was the remainder of the Major's story which the coroner and the coroner's jury, as well as the police magistrate, absolutely refused to believe. Major Straker said, namely, that when he undressed that evening he found the pearls in the outside pocket of his smoking suit. He had not the remotest idea how they got there. Just for a moment the thought darted through his brain that the assault upon him was in some way connected with those pearls. But it seemed too preposterous a conjecture to be dwelt on for long. He looked out of the window to see if the policeman on the beat was anywhere about. If he had been, he would have run down and spoken to him about his find. But the street by now was quite deserted; not a soul in sight, and, as he felt just a little shaken by his recent fight with two determined stalwarts, he thought the best place for him now was bed.

"I had," the Major went on to say, "the fullest intention to take the beastly things to the Lost Property Office at Scotland Yard the very next day, but the first thing in the morning, before I had time to glance at any paper, a telegram was brought up to me. It was from my sister in Worcestershire. My mother had had a seizure. Her life was only a question of hours; could I come immediately? So, without thought of anything else, I threw a few things into a suitcase and was off to Paddington and down to Worcestershire by the first available train. I suppose that I did buy a paper at the station and that I glanced at it on the way, but I have no recollection of what I read. I was away a week or ten days, long enough to see my dear mother buried and to make arrangements about the letting of the house. My sister had a pal in London to whom she was very much attached, and she expressed a wish to go and stay with her for a few weeks, until she and I had time to think about the future.

"I suppose that when I left London I just stuffed those stupid pearls into a box; probably if they had been left lying loose in a drawer I should have seen them and taken them to the Lost Property Office as I had originally intended. But there it is! I thought no more about them, and, as you know, by that time the sensation about them had given place to something more recent. At any rate, I saw nothing about it in the papers. Amongst the letters which were waiting for me at the Club on my return were two or three from Madame Hypnos, asking very kindly what had become of me, and desiring me to come and see her. It seems that she had also telephoned more than once to ask after me, and when she was told that I was away she wanted to know my address, which I had quite forgotten to leave with the hall-porter. After that she again telephoned repeatedly to know if I had returned. Frankly, I was not in a mood to see anybody just then, but during the course of the day the lady telephoned again. This time the hall-porter, unfortunately, told her I was in and put me through without telling me who it was calling. She recognized my voice at once, and then entered into a voluble explanation about the loss of some beads, the last time we had dined together at Eugene's. She described the beads to me. 'Three long rows,' she said, 'of imitation pearls. They are of no value really, but I miss them rather, as they were good of their kind.'

"Still on the telephone she recalled the incident of her loss: 'Don't you remember?' she asked me, 'I told you that I had broken the clasp, so I took the heads off and stuffed them into the pocket of your coat. I forgot to ask you for them when we met again at Mr Everitt's dinner-party, and I suppose you forgot about them, too. You must remember!' Well! I didn't remember the incident at all, and told her so. I had found some pearls in the pocket of my coat, and she described these so accurately, clasp and all, that I had no doubt whatever that the pearls were hers, and that in the sorrow and worry consequent on my mother's death, I had just forgotten all about the incident which Madame Hypnos had described.

"You may think it all very strange," Major Straker went on with a shrug, "but I tell you, I know nothing about pearls. I had never handled any in my life, and I had not seen anything about any theft of pearls or reward for their recovery in any newspaper. When I arrived in Worcestershire my mother was dying; two days later she died; two days after that was the funeral: I had plenty to do without bothering about London papers. Anyway, I had no suspicion whatever as to the truth of Madame Hypnos' story, and I promised that next time I came to see her I would bring the beads along with me.

"She begged me to come at once. Well! I could not do so that day or the next, but on the Friday at about eight o'clock Madame telephoned again, and as I was sick of the whole thing, I got into a taxi and drove round to her flat with the pearls in my pocket. Madame, however, appeared quite indifferent when I gave them to her, which rather surprised me, considering all the fuss she had been making, and she left them lying on the mantelpiece. At one moment she got up to get something or other out of the next room, and while I was waiting for her, I picked up *The Times* which was lying on a table close by. The first thing that caught my eye was the advertisement for lost pearls in the 'Personal' column. I must say that I had to read it through three times before its full significance entered into my brain. £10,000 reward! And three ropes of pearls lost at the Majestic on such and such a night— but, even so, I was only vaguely conscious of the connection between this advertisement and my adventures with Madame Hypnos and those pearls. I remember picking them up from the mantelpiece and weighing them in my hands, when Madame suddenly re-entered the room. She stood for one moment in the doorway looking at me, her eyes blazing with fury. The expression on her face confirmed my vague suspicions. I taxed her with trying to cheat me out of the reward which I should get for the recovery of the pearls, and I deliberately stuffed them back into my pocket. But she was upon me like a vixen, tearing and scratching and biting, with teeth and nails. There was a curiously shaped knife on the table, and at one moment she seized that and would have gone for me, only that I managed to wrench it out of her fist. What she did succeed in doing, however, was to get hold of a part of the pearl rope that was protruding out of my pocket. We fought for that, and my! She was strong and artful. During the fight the rope broke, some of the pearls were scattered, and for an instant she slackened her hold on me in order to watch them rolling on the carpet. That was my opportunity: I had had enough of this fighting vixen, and I made a bolt for it. I was out of the flat before you could say knife.

"My intention was to restore the pearls to their rightful owner the very next morning, and claim the £10,000 reward. I did not see why I should not, although I had come by them in a mysterious way; I felt perfectly guiltless in the matter. The trouble was that when I had glanced at the copy of *The Times* in Madame's flat, I had not the time to make a mental note of the name and address of the assessors who were advertising for the pearls: and when I bought a copy of *The Times* that morning, the advertisement did not appear in the 'Personal' column. What I did see in the paper, however, was the murder of Madame Hypnos. Of course, I was horribly shocked, and very much intrigued to know what in the world had happened in that flat after my departure. Needless to say that I, at once, connected the tragedy with those wretched pearls. To be quite frank, I got a touch of cold feet after that, not in connection with the murder of Madame Hypnos, but because I realized that my story of how I came to be in possession of those pearls might sound unbelievable. I was going to see my lawyer next day; he is an old family friend, and I made up my mind to tell him the whole story and get his advice. Anyway, I could do nothing till I had got an old copy of *The Times* that had the name and address of the assessors in it.

"I don't think I was alarmed or even very much astonished when the following morning I received a summons to attend the inquest on Madame Hypnos. You know the rest: while I was in attendance at the coroner's court, the police had obtained a search-warrant and the pearls were found among my things. And"—the Major concluded with a quaint little sigh—"that's all there is to it."

3

The arrest of Major Gilroy Straker on a charge of murder was one of the sensations of that memorable London season, I forget who it was that advised him in the first instance and through the preliminary inquiry at Bow Street: I suppose it was the old family solicitor of whom we had already heard. Anyway, the evidence against the unfortunate man appeared overwhelming, and his own defence a story quite unbelievable: even the sensational press did not refer to the case as "mysterious." It seems that his youth had been rather wild, and that he had originally gone out to Australia in consequence of some trouble, which probably was no more than youthful folly, but which the police had raked up and were using in order to bolster up their case against the unfortunate young man. In the end the magistrate committed Gilroy Henry Straker for trial on the capital charge. He pleaded "Not Guilty" and reserved his defence.

A moving figure throughout the magistrate's inquiry, and also at the inquest, had been the sister of the accused, a pale-faced youngish woman whose eyes rested with the most tender solicitude and unvarying trust upon her unfortunate brother. It was the day after the magistrate had committed Straker for trial that she called upon Skin o' my Tooth. I saw her when she entered the office, dressed very quietly in black, her poor eyes bearing the traces of countless tears. She sent in her name, Mary Straker, and when I told her that Mr Mulligan would see her immediately, a pathetic look of joy lit up her sad face. As usual, I took my place "behind the arras," notebook in hand. Unseen, I watched the play of the poor girl's features throughout her interview with my chief.

She began by explaining to him that the solicitor, a very old friend of the family, who was looking after her brother's interests had himself advised her to call. "He is the biggest-hearted man in the world, Mr Mulligan," she said, "and the most modest. His firm has been established in Worcester for over a century, but he is old now, and he felt that he might not be able to do for my brother what a younger and more astute man could."

It seems that the fame of Skin o' my Tooth had reached that remote corner of England through his sensational defence of

Gaston Ricketts in the celebrated cattle-maiming case. Ricketts was a Worcestershire man and his acquittal had made a great stir in the county.

"My brother and I have got a little bit of money, Mr Mulligan," Mary Straker went on with a wan, little smile. "You only need to name your fee—"

But this part of the interview was soon got over. Skin o' my Tooth said very little—he never does say much—he just let her go on talking about her brother, his early youth, his misdemeanours, his life, which had been rather wild, then his departure for Australia, his determination to make good, his love for his mother.

"She died in his arms, Mr Mulligan," the girl concluded, with a catch in her throat; "and he swore to her then that he would continue to make good and always lead a straight life for her sake. To imagine for a moment after that, that he would go and quarrel with that bad woman over some wretched pearls, that he would murder her and then swear lies to the police, is impossible. He did not do it, Mr Mulligan. God knows he did not do it; but human justice does err at times, and—well, it's no use saying anything more—is it?"

I knew from the first that Skin o' my Tooth would take the case up. It was just the sort of intricate problem that would appeal to him.

He asked her a great many questions which at the time must have appealed as irrelevant to her as they did to me, such as whether her brother always wore a smoking suit when he went out to dinner, and whether he habitually wore gloves. But what he did say to her at the close of the interview was characteristic of him and of his methods.

"Can you," he asked the girl with that earnestness of conviction which had brought hope to so many despairing hearts, "can you cast aside all sorrow and fear outwardly for a time? Have you sufficient confidence to act a part under my guidance and sufficient pluck to see it through?"

She looked him straight between the eyes and replied briefly: "Any amount."

"Then listen to me," he concluded solemnly. "If your brother is innocent he shall not hang, for I will bring the murderer of Adele Hypnos to justice."

Matters being satisfactorily settled thus far, Skin o' my Tooth started on what he called his preliminary tour of inspection. He had a long interview with Major Straker, which apparently put him in rare good humour, after which I was allowed to accompany him and his friend Mr Alverson of the C.I.D. to Madame Hypnos' flat, where we were met by Inspector Richards, who was inclined to be both truculent and argumentative. He and Skin o' my Tooth had never been friends.

Many days had, of course, elapsed since the tragedy, and even a super Sherlock Holmes would have been hard put to it to find those traces of cigar-ash and burnt matches, or fragments of dust so dear to the amateur detectives of fiction. Richards had in his precise self-satisfied way reconstituted the crime for us, pointing to each and every object just as he had found it, when first he arrived on the scene.

Nothing had been moved except the body of the murdered woman: there were the glasses with the dregs of whisky in them, upon the mantelpiece, the curved knife lying on the floor, the gallipot with the washing soda, the open drawers, the torn furniture. Skin o' my Tooth, silent, with eyes downcast and a gentle smile upon his nice pink face, made no attempt to interrupt. When Richards had finished he went all over the flat with him and examined every object as it was pointed out to him.

"How do you account for the absence of fingerprints?" he asked Richards when the tour of inspection was ended.

The inspector shrugged his wide shoulders.

"Just my contention, Mr Mulligan," he said; "Straker is an experienced criminal. He very nearly escaped gaol, as you know, when he was only nineteen. He took the precaution in this instance to wear gloves. We found a glove button in this room, with a bit of the glove clinging to it, where it had been torn during the struggle with his victim."

"But you didn't find the torn glove among my client's effects, I understand."

"No, we did not," Richards replied. "He was clever enough to get rid of it before we came on the scene."

"Though not clever enough to dispose of the pearls before he went to Worcestershire. But there's no accounting for criminal psychology, is there?" Skin o' my Tooth concluded with his imperturbable smile. "May I see the glove-button, when next I call at the Yard?"

"Of course," the inspector replied laconically. "You can have a good look at it whenever you like."

4

"An innocent man's only hope of safety hanging on a glove button, with a scrap of yellow washing kid still attached to it!" Skin o' my Tooth remarked to me when we were back at the office. "Give me the evening paper, Muggins, and let's think of something else."

And not only did he think casually of something else, but he appeared deeply absorbed in the account of the loss of a flexible diamond and emerald bracelet belonging to a certain Mrs Dunfie. She had dined three or four nights ago at the Diplomatic Club, and on her return home had missed her bracelet. Advertisements and offers of reward had so far been of no avail. Skin o' my Tooth became quite excited over a short paragraph in the Evening News relating to this matter, and ordered me to bring him twenty or thirty of the latest back numbers of *The Times*. These we always keep at the office for a whole year, after which the files are accessible to the public at the British Museum. After Skin o' my Tooth had turned over fourteen or fifteen of the most recent numbers, he gave a sigh of satisfaction.

"You'll be interested to hear. Muggins, that Lady Orliffe lost a valuable diamond brooch the night she dined at Eugene's just three weeks ago."

After that he let the matter drop.

My chief wasn't at the office the whole of the next day, but I went round in the evening to see him at his rooms. He was sitting in dressing-gown and slippers reading a French novel: his face was pink, his eyes downcast, and I was quite sure that the smile which curled round his lips was not due to the humour of M. Dekobra.

"I've done a good day's work, Muggins," he said to me.

"I'm sure you have, sir," I replied. Then as he remained silent and still smiling I ventured to add: "Any further clues?"

"Only the glove button. Muggins," he rejoined with a sigh. "Only the glove button and an Italian waiter."

"Yes, sir?"

"We dine at the Majestic on Wednesday next, Muggins," he went on with a chuckle. "Swallow tails, you know, and all that."

"By ourselves, sir?"

"No, Muggins, no. I am the guest of the Count and Countess Zakreoski, and you will dine with Mr Alverson and Richards at the next table. You'll have some fun, Muggins, I promise you."

"I'm sure of that, sir," I retorted.

The following evening I was ordered by my chief to come round to his rooms at about ten o'clock. I found him in hat and coat, waiting for me: "Come along, Muggins," he said, "we're going out."

My chief's rooms are in the Adelphi. We took a taxi as far as the corner of Tottenham Court Road; then we walked up in the direction of Soho. Presently we turned into a smart-looking little restaurant in Percy Street. The name of the licensee over the door was Italian—Pincetti, I think it was—and the restaurant, I saw at a glance, was run on foreign lines—that is to say, the tables had been cleared of cloths, and so on, and the marble tops gave the appearance of a cafe rather than a restaurant. Some people—not many—sat about, some drinking coffee, others liqueurs, and so on. It all looked very clean and respectable. We sat down at a table in a corner of the room and ordered coffee; my chief asked for the evening papers; nothing happened for a time. Skin o' my Tooth appeared entirely absorbed in the Evening Standard, but I, over the edge of the Westminster Gazette, took stock of the company.

It was getting late. Signer Pincetti's customers went out in groups of twos and threes until only two tables, besides our own, remained occupied. At one of these sat a man who looked like a prosperous wine merchant or the manager of a successful catering establishment; he wore a top-hat on the back of his head, and had on a frock-coat, striped trousers, white spats, and a white waistcoat strained over a very portly stomach. His eyes were small and his face red and clean-shaven; a few strands of lank and greasy hair were carefully brushed across his bald cranium. He was in the company of two young women, who were smeared with paint up to their eyes and very showily dressed, and all the time that he talked with them, with great volubility, he was chawing the end of a fat cigar; though at times he raised his voice to make a facetious remark or utter a loud guffaw, he would quickly lower it again, and for the most part talked in a kind of hoarse whisper, quite impossible to follow. The women said very little; they smoked cigarettes all the time and giggled in response to the man's jokes.

At another table sat a quiet-looking man who might have had something to do with the Russian Ballet or been a member of the Queen's Hall Orchestra. He looked like a Scandinavian, but might have been a German. He had quantities of untidy, very fair hair, one unruly curl of which fell right down over his left eye, and a fair beard and moustache. His dress was very slouchy, and he wore his shirt in that horrible foreign fashion, open very low down at the neck, with a wide, soft kind of Eton collar and a huge butterfly bow of a tie. He was with a very quiet-looking middle-aged woman, and the two did not appear to hold much conversation together.

Behind the desk sat a fat, foreign-looking woman of the usual type, and a pale-faced boy in a white coat and black trousers was in attendance behind the bar.

I had just finished taking stock of this mixed company when a belated customer came in—obviously an Italian, who might have been a waiter. He was quite young and very neatly dressed. He threw his hat down on a chair and then sat down and ordered a vermouth. For the next quarter of an hour he appeared to be absorbed in an Italian newspaper which he had taken out of his pocket, but it struck me that he cast more than one glance in our direction. Presently he got up and went to the bar, presumably to pay for his drink, but I couldn't see exactly what he was doing, because his back was towards us. Then he went out of the restaurant. It was getting near closing time; the man in the frock-coat and the top-hat called to the waiter and paid for his drinks; the Scandinavian, on the other hand, did the same as the Italian and paid at the bar. We were the last to leave.

We walked for a bit and then took a taxi. As soon as we were inside, Skin o' my Tooth rubbed his hands together as if in complete satisfaction, and said:

"Now our little party will be quite complete."

Then he told me what he had done. He had prevailed on Count Zakreoski to organize a dinner-party at the Majestic which would comprise all those who had been present on the night when the Kazan pearls were stolen.

"I wanted not only the same guests to be there, but the dinner served by the same staff of waiters. At first I approached the Countess herself. She is a very handsome woman. Muggins, and knows her own mind; though I believe that her father was a window-cleaner in Seattle, she treated me from the height of her aristocratic position as if I were dirt. Her decision was final; she would have nothing to do with any scheme that might defeat the ends of justice. In her view, Major Straker had murdered his confederate, that odious Madame Hypnos, and the best thing that could happen would be that he should be hanged.

"I couldn't move her," Skin o' my Tooth went on with a chuckle, "until her husband unexpectedly appeared upon the scene. He was very stiff and pompous too, but appeared sympathetic, and, what's more, his magnificent wife seemed to stand somewhat in awe of him. Anyway, in spite of the lady's antagonism, I told him about my scheme, and in his pompous and condescending way he fell in with it, and simply ignored his wife's opposition. She was furious with me, of course, and if looks could kill I shouldn't be here now. The dinner-party was then fixed for Wednesday next, and Count Zakreoski promised me that he would invite all the same guests who had been present at the previous gathering. The next question was that of the staff of waiters. I went to the Majestic and interviewed the head waiter. A substantial tip got me what I wanted—namely, the man's promise that all the waiters who had served dinner on the previous occasion would do so again this time. Then he hesitated a moment and said: 'I was forgetting; Bocco is no longer here.' Bocco was one of the waiters, it seems, and he had left some time ago to go to Eugene's. I flew to Eugene, only to be told that Bocco was now at the Diplomatic. Here I ran my elusive gentleman to earth. I got Richards to set one of his men watching his movements, and heard this morning that Bocco went most nights to have a drink at the Restaurant Continental in Percy Street, also that he was apparently out of work, having lost his job at the Diplomatic a few days ago. Back I went to the Majestic, and once more by dint of a tip prevailed on the head waiter to offer Bocco a temporary job, and as Count Zakreoski has also fallen in with a pleasant little scheme of mine, I feel sure that our little party on Wednesday will be very successful."

I was rather intrigued to know why Skin o' my Tooth had been so keen on running that one waiter to earth. At the time of the loss of the Kazan pearls all the waiters had been closely interrogated, searched, and watched. I didn't quite see what the chief hoped to attain by this reunion of all the minor actors in the previous drama.

"It didn't strike you, Muggins," he said with a smile, "that Lady Orliffe lost her diamond brooch at Eugene's a fortnight after the Kazan pearls episode, and that Mrs Dunfie lost her bracelet at the Diplomatic a fortnight after that. Compare that with Bocco's odyssey, and you will understand why I am so keen on his being a member of our pleasant little party on Wednesday."

The evening came. Mr Alverson and Richards met me at my rooms, and we went on to the Majestic, well supplied with money for our dinner, given to us by Skin o' my Tooth. Soon after we arrived, Count Zakreoski's party filed into the restaurant. I had understood from my chief that he would be with them, but he certainly was not there. To my astonishment, however, a little later on I saw Mary Straker come in. She looked excessively pretty, and not only was she beautifully dressed, but she wore a beautiful row of pearls round her neck; indeed, I didn't recognize her at first, so different did she seem to the pale-faced, tearful girl I had seen at our office. She was accompanied by a stout, florid man of obviously foreign nationality, with thick black hair and heavy dark moustache. They sat at a table not far from Count Zakreoski's party.

It was towards the end of the dinner that Count Zakreoski, turning casually in the direction of Mary Straker and her foreign companion, seemed to recognize the latter and, rising from his seat, went to greet him most cordially. They talked as if they were old friends, and Mary Straker was then introduced to the Count. The result of this little episode was that Count Zakreoski persuaded Mary Straker and her companion to join his friends for coffee and liqueur in the lounge. Mr Alverson, Richards, and I also adjourned to the lounge, and the first thing I noticed was that it was the waiter Bocco who was serving coffee to Count Zakreoski's party. The next moment I had recognized my chief in Mary Straker's foreign companion. Never had I seen such marvellous disguise, and it said much for Count Zakreoski's powers of self-control that, though he was, of course, aware of the comedy, never for one instant did he betray nervousness or surprise.

The Countess was gay and chatty. She certainly was a very handsome woman. Mary Straker had evidently been given the task of flirting with Mr Morley-Everitt, and this she was doing to perfection. The party broke up just before closing time. My chief had appointed to meet me directly after that at the Continental Restaurant in Percy Street, whilst Mr Alverson and Richards lingered a little while longer in order to give final instructions to the staff of detectives outside, who were being told off each individually to shadow every single member of the party as well as every one of the waiters.

I was the first to arrive at the Continental. The place was not very full. Sitting at a corner table I noticed the florid man whom on our previous visit we had put down as a prosperous caterer. He was alone this time. Soon Skin o' my Tooth turned up. He was still in his marvellous disguise as the black-haired foreign plutocrat. I noticed that, as he entered, the florid man gave him a quick, searching look and then glanced across to the pale-faced boy at the bar, who gave an almost imperceptible shrug. Presently the young, shock-haired Scandinavian came in. He, too, was alone this time. The florid man gave him a sign, and he then went across and sat down at the other's table. They both glanced once or twice in our direction.

It was now close on eleven o'clock; all the other customers had left. There were only the four of us in the place: Skin o' my Tooth and I at one end of the room, the fair-haired Scandinavian and his florid friend at the other. Presently Skin o' my Tooth rose and went across to the other table.

"You will forgive my saying this to you, my friends," he said with a marked foreign accent, "that that ass Bocco will ruin us all if he goes on in that way."

Quick as lightning the whole aspect of the room had changed the moment Skin o' my Tooth began to speak. The boy at the bar ceased polishing his glasses, and came out, as it were, into the open; the fat woman at the desk had put down her pen, and, resting her elbows on the top of her books, appeared like a veritable statue of tense attention. Instinctively I had jumped to my feet, because I had seen that the shock-haired Scandinavian had suddenly thrust his right hand inside his coat. But Skin o' my Tooth remained perfectly bland: he put up his podgy hand with a gesture intended to calm the agitation of all these persons so keenly on the alert, and, without waiting for an invitation, he sat down beside the young Scandinavian.

"It would be a mistake to try and shoot me, my young friend," he said urbanely. "Shooting makes so much noise, what?... and the police, you know?... eh?... Would I know about Bocco if I was not your friend?"

Then, as the other two made no reply, but sat there sullen but attentive, the Scandinavian still with his right hand inside his coat, Skin o' my Tooth continued:

"Bocco made a mistake the night when he pinched the Kazan pearls... not? He had instructions to put them into the pocket of the young gentleman who sat at the left hand of our late lamented sister, Madame... what was her name?... Hypnos?... Like a fool he slipped those bee-oo-tiful pearls into the pocket of the young gentleman who sat on her right. And see what a lot of trouble we have had since... and our poor sister, Madame—er—Hypnos—what? She had to be put out of the way because she would not part with the few bee-oo-tiful pearls our young friend the Australian Major had unwillingly left in her lily-white hands... Pity, not. And now again this mistake... Tut-tut!..."

"What do you mean, and who the devil are you?" the florid man blurted out in a rage, while the Scandinavian half drew his hand from under his coat, and from where I stood I caught sight of a small Colt which he was clutching.

"Who the devil are you?" he echoed, muttering between his teeth.

"Luckily," Skin o' my Tooth replied with a smile, "I am the man in whose pocket that fool Bocco slipped the pearls which he pinched at Claridge's tonight, or we should have had more trouble... not?"

And, still smiling amiably, he drew out of his pocket the row of pearls which Mary Straker had been wearing at dinner. He passed them once or twice through his podgy hands, and then slipped them back quietly into his pocket. The others made a menacing gesture, and the pale-faced boy came a step or two nearer.

"Easy, easy, my friends," Skin o' my Tooth rejoined. "I am not going to quarrel with you over this business. I can't get on without you, and you can't get on without me, eh? In my nice little shop in Amsterdam I sell the trinkets which you find for me in England—not? I like you, my friends. I did not even quarrel with you when I did not get the Kazan pearls, which I should have had. So why quarrel now?"

Then he beamed at everyone around, including myself, and, pointing to me, he said:

THE KAZAN PEARLS 87

"That is a young English friend of mine. He had a little misfortune a few years ago in connection with that forgery affair on the Colonial Bank, and so he is very devoted to me—very devoted to me. Now, shall not our other young friend here put up the shutters, and we will all have a bottle, or even two, of the best champagne this elegant restaurant can supply. What?"

Again he beamed on us all. At another sign from him the pale-faced boy went to put up the shutters and closed the door of the restaurant. Skin o' my Tooth was rubbing his podgy hands contentedly together, the woman at the desk smiled benignly, and the florid man appeared quite cheerful. Only the Scandinavian still looked somewhat sullen. When the boy had closed the shutters he fetched a couple of bottles of champagne from the back of the bar and placed them in their ice-buckets upon the table; he also brought four glasses.

"No! No!" Skin o' my Tooth rejoined cheerily. "Are we not all friends? Are we not seven of us here to rejoice that that fool Bocco's mistake did not bring more trouble on us all? Madame, too, eh?" he concluded, making a polite gesture of invitation in the direction of the woman at the desk, who came forward obviously very pleased. We now sat round the marble-topped table, I on one side of Skin o' my Tooth, who had the Scandinavian on his left. He was still beaming on the company in general while he poured out the champagne. The florid man and the Scandinavian had exchanged a quick glance. I could see that suspicion still lurked in their minds. Then the Scandinavian shrugged his shoulders, and both the men dived into their pockets and brought out a pair of gloves, which they proceeded to put on, while Skin o' my Tooth continued to chatter pleasantly:

"Ah!" he said, turning to the Scandinavian, "a very wise precaution—very wise indeed. One never knows, eh? Finger-prints are tiresome things—not?—on glasses or bottles of champagne, eh? You are wise, my friend, very wise, to make it a hard-and-fast rule never to—"

The next moment he had grabbed the Scandinavian's right hand, and at the same time shouted to me: "Shoot, Muggins!"

Acting on his instructions, I was armed with a Colt that night. While Skin o' my Tooth gave the word of command, "Hands up!" which was instantly obeyed, he kept his eyes fixed on the Scandinavian, and his hand gripped the man's wrist. No one knows better than yours truly how steel-like my chief's grip can be, and I could see the Scandinavian's cheeks blanch with the pain. I had already fired off my Colt. It was a signal for Richards and his men, who had made their way into the house through the back entrance. They came into the restaurant with a rush. I was covering the florid man, who I thought was probably armed and might offer desperate resistance; the other two were obviously terrified and gave no trouble whatever.

"Take off that elegant fair wig from my friend here," Skin o' my Tooth said to Richards, "and the beard, of course. A charming disguise, my dear Mr Everitt," he continued blandly. "I myself was deceived the first time I saw you here."

Indeed, no one was more surprised than I was when, after Richards had removed the shock-haired wig and the beard, Mr Morley-Everitt appeared before us all, all the starch gone out of him, his face beneath its make-up wan and drawn from the terrible vice-like grip still upon his wrist.

"And now the glove, Richards," Skin o' my Tooth went on calmly.

Just for an instant Everitt made a desperate effort, not so much to free himself as to destroy the proof of his guilt in the murder of Madame Hypnos. Lowering his head, he dragged at the glove on his right hand with his teeth. But, of course, the effort proved futile. Already he was in the grasp of Richards and his men, who held his arms pinioned while Skin o' my Tooth quietly removed the glove. There was the tell-tale tear;

the button with the piece of kid still hanging to it fitted the place exactly.

Once the police held the principal members of this gang of malefactors, they quickly enough followed up the clue till they brought the whole lot to justice. All Skin o' my Tooth's deductions proved to be correct. The florid man—whose name was Pincetti, and who was the proprietor of the Continental Restaurant—was the head of the organization; Bocco the waiter and Morley-Everitt were his principal lieutenants, but there were about a dozen others, all of them young men about town, smart, impecunious, who had chosen this means of earning a livelihood. Bocco was a marvellous sleight-of-hand trickster; it was his business to detach the piece of jewellery from a woman's arm or neck, and he had orders to drop "the swag" into the pocket of any member of the gang who happened to be present. At the time of the theft of the Kazan pearls he had never seen Morley-Everitt without disguise. As Skin o' my Tooth so cleverly guessed, he had been ordered to slip the pearls into the pocket of the young man who sat on the left of Madame Hypnos, and by some unexplainable error he thrust them into Major Straker's pocket, who sat on her right.

Viewed from that angle, and with Sir Arthur Inglewood as his counsel, the case against the Australian soon collapsed. But the jury at the trial of Morley-Everitt did not, I suppose, consider the evidence of the glove button sufficient on which to find him guilty of murder. It went to prove that Everitt had visited the flat that night, but not that he had murdered the woman. Anyway, the whole gang got several years' hard labour, and are still doing "time." The Countess Zakreoski fought hard to get Morley-Everitt's share in the whole thing hushed up, but the husband refused to be a party to an attempt at trying to defeat the ends of justice. He had fallen in with wonderful sympathy with Skin o' my Tooth's scheme on behalf of Major Straker, and had played his own role in the comedy admirably.

I suppose, on the other hand, that he considered it luck that the Countess' name was not dragged into the case, for everyone was convinced that she herself was a party to the theft of her pearls; she probably knew nothing about the gang and thought that her stepson would be the one to restore the lost pearls to her and to receive the £10,000 reward offered by Count Zakreoski, her husband.

5

THE CASE OF MAJOR GIBSON

I have always wondered why Skin o' my Tooth was so unpopular in his own profession. He had very few friends among his colleagues, but those he had were certainly very staunch. I have heard it said that his ways were "unprofessional;" certain it is that he avoided actual litigation for his clients whenever that was possible. I suppose that would be called unprofessional.

Personally I never met a man of such varying moods. Over that Swanborough murder case he was alert, uncanny, and irritatingly active; over Major Gibson's case he always looked as if he were going to sleep and as if any trashy French novel were more interesting than the honour of his client.

Now, I remember when Major Gibson first called upon him and told him his story, I thought to myself:

"Here's the prettiest kettle of fish that ever Skin o' my Tooth had placed before him." He was a good-looking man, this Major Gibson; but the day he called at the office he looked as white as a ghost. He began by saying that unless Mr Mulligan would help him, he had made all arrangements for committing suicide.

I could see that he did not quite know how to begin; Skin o' my Tooth did not evidently come up to the imaginary portrait the gallant Major's imagination had drawn for himself. I must say that my esteemed chief looked particularly fat, pink, and inane that morning.

"I always like to hear the story from the beginning," he said as he quietly—without asking his client's leave—lighted a huge German long-stemmed pipe. For a moment I thought that the Major was going to make an ass of himself and leave the room and go and commit suicide, sooner than tell his tale to an ill-mannered Irish lawyer; but he was in a tight hole, and he kept his temper.

"About a month ago," he began at last very abruptly, "I was staying at Belcher Hall, Mr Everard's place in Rutlandshire. There was a good deal of gambling going on there in the evenings. I am not a rich man; I disapprove—on principle—of playing games of hazard; nevertheless, I played and lost one night—"

"Dates, please, wherever possible," interrupted Skin o' my Tooth quietly.

"October 18th," said Major Gibson, whilst I, knowing what would be expected of me presently, made as rapid shorthand notes as my imperfect training would allow. "At about 11 p.m. I at last left the baccarat-table at Belcher Hall, with my last possible cheque on my current account drawn to bearer, and promissory notes amounting to close on £8,000 in the hands of various gentlemen, my fellow-guests in the hospitable mansion of Belcher Hall. I must say that Everard was exceedingly nice to me later on in the billiard-room, when we had a smoke and a drink together. I was a fool, and mistook his kind words for genuine sympathy; I admitted to him that I had lost a great deal more than I could possibly afford, and that there was nothing for it but I must exchange into some Indian regiment and put off my proposed marriage until I had in some measure retrieved my heavy losses, or, if the lady were unwilling to wait, to give her back her word and her liberty. I think Everard must have understood how hard this would be to me. Only a month ago

I had become engaged to his wife's niece, Miss Marion Sutcliffe, to whom I was passionately attached. I am not a young man, and I do not fall in and out of love as quickly as some of my contemporaries."

He broke off abruptly; evidently the subject of Miss Marion was still a sore one.

"How long did the interview last—with Mr Everard, I mean?" asked Skin o' my Tooth quietly.

"At twelve o'clock precisely I left him, intending to go to bed; but as I knew I should find it very difficult to get to sleep, I strolled into the library, a beautiful room on the ground floor, with deep-mullioned windows. I meant to get a book and then retire to my bedroom. I remember that the room was quite dark when I went in, as the heavy curtains had been drawn closely across the deep window recesses. As I did not know where and how to switch on the electric light, I went up to one of the windows, meaning to draw the curtains aside and to let a flood of moonlight into the room. But the garden looked so fine and poetic, and I felt so moody and wretched that, quite contrary to my usual habits, I sat down in one of the deep window-seats and stared out, mooning, thinking of nothing in particular, into the garden before me. How long I remained there I cannot tell you. Certain it is that suddenly I became aware that someone was in the library besides myself. I had not heard the door open or shut, and I did not know who the someone was. I only inferred that it was a lady, for I could hear the tap-tap of high-heeled shoes upon the parquet floor as she, in her turn, went up to one of the windows."

Major Gibson paused a moment here, giving me time for the space of thirty seconds at least to stretch out my cramped muscles. Skin o' my Tooth had not said a word; he was looking down at the meerschaum bowl of his long-stemmed pipe, whilst a coy and gentle smile played round the fat corners of his mouth. Major Gibson passed his hand across his forehead once or twice; I know that he was cursing himself for the fool he had been at 1 a.m. on the memorable night of October 18th last.

"I can assure you," he said at last, "that nothing in particular crossed my mind when I heard the tap-tap of those high-heeled shoes; certainly the next moment I should have made my presence known to the midnight wanderer; but just then I happened to have my head turned towards the garden, and to have caught sight of the figure of a man cautiously making his way towards the library windows, whilst keeping as much as possible within the shadow of the trees. A second later I had heard a gentle whistle, the window farthest from the one in which I was sitting was opened, then shut, and I realized that the most discreet and prudent thing I could now do was to keep as quiet as I possibly could for the present, and, if I were detected later on, to feign a deep and uninterrupted sleep."

"Discreet and prudent," commented Skin o' my Tooth with a smile. "It is strange how we all differ in the meaning of those two words."

"I am wise, today now, after the event," retorted Major Gibson a little impatiently. "At the time I did not think I was doing the slightest harm, either to myself or to the two who were having this clandestine meeting at this extraordinary hour. Remember, the room was quite dark; the man, whoever he was, had evidently slipped in through the window, and no one had drawn the curtains. I heard some hurried whispers, then the man spoke impatiently. 'Have you brought them, anyway?' What the lady replied I could not hear, but it was evidently satisfactory, for he said quite loudly: 'That's all right—let's have a look.' I remember it struck me at the time that the midnight interview did not seem particularly tender. It came very soon to an end, too. Curiosity is supposed to be a feminine vice, but I can assure you that at that moment I was positively devoured with curiosity as to who the lady was who could thus risk the whole edifice of her social position for the sake of some individual who was evidently unscrupulous, and obviously was none too tender. I again heard the click of the shoes: the lady was returning to her own room, leaving the man to find his way out alone. I put one finger on the curtain, hoping to catch a glimpse of her, but I only saw the shimmer of a green satin frock as a ray of moonbeam caught it when she glided out of the room.

"I remembered all the ladies who were staying in the house; I had seen them in the drawing-room before that miserable baccarat party. I remember, too, that Mrs Everard, our beautiful hostess, who was very fair, wore a magnificent green satin gown. I also remembered that Marion—my Marion—Mrs Everard's niece, had looked bewitching in a clinging green frock all shimmering with beads. Of course, Marion was out of the question—you will understand that, won't you?—the very thought was preposterous; but Mrs Everard, my friend's wife, young, pretty—I assure you my head was in a whirl. I had not moved. I had forgotten the man until a flood of brilliant light startled me from my dream. I had pushed aside the curtains. Immediately beneath one of the electric light brackets, which he had evidently just switched on, a man was standing with his back to me; he was examining intently something which he held in his hand. My instinct was to knock him down then and there, like the foul thief he was; but I suppose I must have made a noise when I crossed the room, for he turned before I could reach him. I then saw what he held in his hand. It was the long rope of pearls which I had before now seen round Mrs Everard's neck.

"I really don't think," continued Major Gibson, after another little pause, "that I can tell you exactly what happened after that. All I can remember is that I had him on the floor, and that I would have killed him if he had not at last reluctantly given me back that rope of pearls."

"It did not strike you that it might be best to ring for some of the servants and to give him in charge like the thief he was?" asked Skin o' my Tooth after a while, during which he was contemplating the unfortunate Major through his half-closed lids.

"I thought of it for a moment—but—"

"But you did not do it?"

"No."

"Why?"

"Because he swore to make a scandal if I denounced him. I had not seen the woman, and I was not sure; but there, on the floor, close to the door, was a bunch of pink roses which I had given to Marion a few hours ago."

"I see," said Skin o' my Tooth, with a smile. There was silence in the room for a time, whilst I had a chance of cracking my knuckles, which were horribly stiff and cramped.

"I think I can guess what happened after that," said Skin o' my Tooth, at last taking the pipe out of his mouth. The Major did not reply, and he went on:

"You sent the thief about his business, and you yourself were discovered five minutes later with that rope of pearls in your hand, unable or unwilling to give an account as to how you had come by it."

Major Gibson nodded moodily.

"I met Everard just outside the library. He caught sight of the pearls in my hand, even before he had recovered from his surprise at finding me there at that hour. He asked me for an explanation. I could give him none—that is to say, I gave him one as near to the truth as I dared, which he, of course, disbelieved. I gave him back the pearls, and he told me at what hour I could get a train back to Town. He was supposed to be a friend of mine, but he thought me guilty. You see, he knew how heavily I had lost at cards. I had myself told him that I was sore pressed for money, and might have to break off my engagement, and even to leave for India—"

THE CASE OF MAJOR GIBSON

"Will you tell me what lie—I mean what explanation—you did give Mr Everard?" interrupted Skin o' my Tooth quietly.

"I told him that, on going into the library late at night to fetch a book, I had found a man there with Mrs Everard's pearls in his hands, that I had succeeded in getting the pearls from him, but that he, in his turn, succeeded in getting away through the window."

"He naturally asked you why you did not raise an alarm?"

"He did."

"And also whether you would recognize the supposed thief if you saw him again? Quite so. Your replies not being very lucid, he drew his own conclusions. But forgive my interrupting you. You have not quite finished, I think?"

"I haven't much more to tell you. It appears that the ladies went up to their rooms soon after twelve, the men staying down in the billiard-room to smoke. But at last everyone retired, and Everard himself was about to do the same when his wife—fully dressed still—met him on the stairs with the news that one of her most valuable strings of pearls had been stolen. She was putting away the jewels which she had just been wearing when she noticed that one of the cases was empty. Everard persuaded her to go back to her room, and he himself started on a tour of inspection round the House."

"And met you?"

"And met me, as you say."

"Then is that all you have to tell me?"

"That is all. Everard was up in time to see me before I left in the morning—he and Lord Combermury, the colonel of my regiment. Both tried to persuade me to confess, and promised, as an inducement, that if I made a clean breast of it to them, and agreed to exchange into some native regiment and to break off my engagement with Miss Sutcliffe, the whole matter should be hushed up."

"And you promised—?"

"I promised nothing."

"The result being—?"

"That the scandal has gone the round of the town. I have been requested to hand in my papers, and in my clubs it has been strongly hinted to me that I should be turned out unless I succeeded in clearing my character."

"And so far you have not attempted to mention the lady's name?"

"Would I not be branded as a worse blackguard than before for slandering a woman in order to try and save my own skin? And I was not sure, remember. I did not know who the lady was."

"Have you any conviction now?"

The Major hesitated a moment, then he said quietly, "No."

2

There was silence in the room for a long time after that. The Major was staring moodily into the fire, and Skin o' my Tooth was puffing away at his old German pipe, smiling gently to himself. Presently he began to hum a tune, and looked so coy, and fat and comfortable, no wonder he jarred upon the unfortunate Major's nerves.

"Well, sir?" said the latter at last very irritably.

Skin o' my Tooth smothered a yawn.

"I was waiting," he said.

"What for?"

"To hear what you are going to do."

Here the Major swore vigorously.

"Do you think I should be here now," he said, "if I knew? The few friends I have got left advise a slander action, and I have come to consult you, as someone has told me that you were the ablest man in London in cases of this sort."

"That 'someone,' no doubt, said to you that you had a jolly bad case and required an unscrupulous devil like

Patrick Mulligan to pull you through," remarked Skin o' my Tooth dryly.

I could see from the deep red on the Major's bronzed cheek that my esteemed employer had guessed right.

Skin o' my Tooth settled himself within the depths of his large, shabby leather armchair. He smothered another yawn with an attempt at politeness. He looked, in fact, as if he were getting very tired of the whole thing, and longed to get back to his favourite French novel, the yellow paper cover of which was even now protruding from one of the pockets of his ill-fitting coat.

"A slander action in this case would be a very ticklish matter," he said at last. "Mr Everard, against whom, I suppose, you would enter it, would plead justification, and you must own that the circumstances of the case are decidedly in his favour. He finds you in a very ambiguous position, and the explanations you give are terribly lame. You might get 'damages one farthing,' which would do you more harm than good, and effectually kill the last shreds of reputation you have got left. But there is one thing, of course, which can put you right, and that is a confession from the lady."

"Impossible!"

"Why?"

"Is it likely?"

"I think so. You have come to me for advice. It is the only one I can give. Some of my more eminent colleagues would, no doubt, suggest an action. But these same eminent gentlemen will tell you that Patrick Mulligan has no reputation to mar. His ways are tortuous, his means unscrupulous. Perhaps they are right. Are you willing to adopt these ways and means and follow my advice unreservedly? You will scrape through this hole by the skin of your teeth, I tell you, but I will pledge the evil reputation I have got that we'll obtain a confession from the unknown lady."

"It would have to be a public one now, I am afraid, to do me any good."

"It will be sufficient. I give you my—No! I won't give you my word; it wouldn't be much good to you; but ask the most disreputable character in the London slums when Skin o' my Tooth has said, 'I'll do it,' whether he is the man to break his word."

No wonder the Major looked a new man. I have seen many a poor chap look like that when once they have had a square talk with Skin o' my Tooth. By gosh! But he knows how to carry conviction with him; when he talks to a client or to the jury, it's all the same—they run after him like a pack of sheep.

"And now, my dear Major," he concluded, "which day will it be convenient for you to meet Mr Everard?"

"Meet Everard?" gasped the Major. "I wouldn't care to... "

"Sir," said Skin o' my Tooth, with his gentle smile, "just now I used the word 'unreservedly.' I will not move in this matter unless I possess your entire confidence."

The Major hesitated no longer. Skin o' my Tooth was his last straw. "You do what you think best," he said doggedly; "but Everard will refuse."

"Wednesday next, shall we say, at 3 p.m.? That will suit you? Muggins, make a note of that."

"Everard will refuse," repeated the Major.

"I think not," said Skin o' my Tooth, with a smile. "Have I your permission to proceed?"

"As you will."

"And you place yourself unreservedly in my hands?" For one brief second the Major hesitated, while his sharp, clear, honest eyes scanned quickly the fat, unwieldy figure huddled up in the armchair, the sleepy eyes with their drooping lids, the ill-fitting, shiny black coat, with that yellow-backed French novel protruding from its pocket. Skin o' my Tooth sat there, with that coy smile of his playing round the corners of his mouth.

Then the Major, with a sudden, frank gesture, put out his hand and said firmly: "Without reserve."

"Muggins, show the Major out," said my chief, with sudden, obvious alacrity. When I came back—having shown Major Gibson downstairs—I found Skin o' my Tooth absorbed in his French novel. I waited for a while; then, as he did not speak, I asked at last: "What am I to do now, sir?"

"Nothing, my boy, nothing," he said airily. "Confine yourself to not being an ass for the rest of the afternoon; that will always be something accomplished. In the meanwhile, you can hand me down 'Burke's Landed Gentry' from that shelf."

I gave him the book he wanted.

Then he added: "By the way, Muggins, copy out your notes on a sheet of parchment and engross them neatly. We may require them in that form later on."

3

Mr Everard, strange to say, was willing enough to meet Major Gibson and his solicitor, and talk the matter over amicably if possible. I fancy he is a decent enough sort of a man, and was only too ready to see the end of this unfortunate business; moreover, I don't suppose that he, either, cared to take his chances of defending a slander action. If by any chance Major Gibson did succeed in making his case good, he would get such thundering damages as even Mr Everard—rich as he was—would not care to pay. It was finally arranged that Major Gibson, accompanied by Mr Patrick Mulligan and myself, should be at Mr Everard's house in Park Lane on Wednesday at 3.30 p.m. Of course, Mr Everard's solicitor would be present; also Lord Combermury, and—by the special request of Major Gibson, as represented by Mr Mulligan—Mrs Everard and Miss Marion Sutcliffe.

I had not the least idea, of course, what Skin o' my Tooth was up to, but the whole of that morning, while he was reading his French novel, I saw him smile to himself with that funny, coy, and gentle smile which always meant mischief to his adversaries.

I remember feeling at that interview very like a character in a French play. Everyone wore a black morning-coat—except myself. Skin o' my Tooth's was very shabby, and fitted him badly, and from the tail-pocket a yellow-backed book protruded very conspicuously.

We were shown into a fine dining-room, oak-panelled, magnificently furnished. There was a large fire in the big open grate, and the two ladies, when we came in (I did not know which was Mrs Everard and which Miss Sutcliffe), were sitting close beside it.

Skin o' my Tooth put down his hat and drew from his pocket the notes of Major Gibson's case which I had made and carefully copied out and engrossed. This he placed on a little side-table which stood close to the mantelpiece. Then all the gentlemen sat down round the large dining-table, and the fun began.

Skin o' my Tooth started talking very quietly, I wondering all the time what he was driving at, and how he hoped to benefit the unfortunate Major by this extraordinary comedy; but he went on talking, and I must confess that never in my life had I heard such a fine string of lies so magnificently uttered.

"I must thank you, ladies and gentlemen," he said, "for so kindly acceding to my client's request. He felt, as I do—as you will, I am sure—that nothing could be more deplorable than the dragging of this unfortunate affair before the public. Major Gibson has been—quite involuntarily, I feel confident, but still grossly—maligned. I will ask you, gentlemen, not to interrupt me just now; you can have your fling at us later on; for the present you must allow me to state positively that Major Gibson is not only absolutely innocent of the ugly charge of theft proffered against him, but is even now the victim of a code of honour as chivalrous as it is misdirected."

Skin o' my Tooth then, with perfect suavity, started a highly-coloured account of the incidents in the library at Belcher Hall, as related to him by Major Gibson. The moonlit garden, the dark room, the tap-tap of the high-heeled shoes, the clandestine meeting. The half-dozen people there present, all except myself, did their best to try and stop him, to sneer at him; ejaculations, muttered in a whisper, broke out from every side. The ladies looked indescribably shocked and witheringly contemptuous. Mr Everard looked ready to knock Skin o' my Tooth down, and his legal adviser talked of "extraordinary allegations," of "slander," and "thumping damages." But Skin o' my Tooth sailed serenely on. When the interruptions became too loud, he shouted louder, and that was all.

"Now, gentlemen," he said, "when you have quite done calling me a liar, I can get on all right. I don't blame you. I don't even mind telling you that I called Major Gibson a liar myself when I first heard his tale. You see, he kept telling me that he had no proof, no witnesses to corroborate what he had said. Now, I am not one for believing that there is ever a truth without any proof; and when my client left me I said to myself there must be some proof, some witness somewhere. Major Gibson did not recognize the lady. Good! But in that large house and grounds of Belcher Hall, full to overflowing with visitors and servants, someone—I cared not who—must have seen that unknown woman in the green gown, or that man; some trace somewhere would be left of her passage or his, some sign, some indication, whether traced by man or by Fate."

Gradually, as he spoke, I noticed that the attitude of his hearers had become considerably modified. There were no interruptions now, no whispered comments. Mr Everard and the legal gentleman hung upon my chief's words. The Major himself looked as if suddenly a bright vista of hope had been opened before him. As for the ladies, one looked pale and breathless, while the other, leaning back in her chair, kept up that air of dignified hauteur which some English ladies know how to wear when certain matters which they deem objectionable are discussed in their presence. In fact, when Skin o' my Tooth paused for a moment and began fumbling in his pockets as if in search of something, this same haughty lady said quietly: "Do you think, Archibald, that in view of the matters which — er — Mr. — er — Mulligan seems fit to discuss here, I and my niece had better go?"

"I beg a thousand pardons," said Skin o' my Tooth urbanely. "I have finished, I assure you. Please do not go. The matter will interest you both. Have I your permission to proceed? Many thanks. It is not necessary, I think, for me to dwell here upon the ways and means I employed on behalf of my client. You may imagine that I left no stone unturned."

I was literally gasping, I can tell you. I am a pretty good liar myself on occasions. I would not enjoy Skin o' my Tooth's confidence if I were not. But I had to confess humbly to myself that in the face of Skin o' my Tooth's last assertion with regard to those stones, which to my certain knowledge were made of paper and were all yellow-backed, I was only a bungling botcher. But what I could not make out was what all his fumbling in his coat-pockets meant. I thought that he was looking for the notes, which I had written out so neatly, and which he had placed on the little side-table close to the mantelpiece. Not a bit of it. When I made a movement to get them for him, he looked at me, and I understood that I had better sit still and wait.

"I am quite sure," continued Skin o' my Tooth, after a dramatic pause, during which I noticed that his whole bulky figure seemed as it were to crouch ready for a spring, "that you will understand what a glorious day it was for me and for my client, Major Gibson, when at last my strenuous efforts were crowned with success. No, ladies and gentlemen! I was not mistaken. In that densely populated, magnificent mansion I had unearthed a man who, on that memorable night, was present near enough to the library of Belcher Hall to see the mysterious lady in the green gown give Mrs Everard's pearls to an unknown thief. This man saw the whole scene from beginning to end. Reasons which I will explain to you presently, but which seemed paramount to him, forced him to silence, until I compelled him to speak. He saw, and would know again, the man who, like a thief in the night, bullied, then robbed, the woman who was fool enough to ruin her reputation for his sake; he heard the whispered conversation, saw the necklace pass from her hand to his; he recognized the mysterious lady in the green gown, and picked up, after she left, something which had belonged to her, which he holds still..."

Skin o' my Tooth was surpassing himself. All of us there felt as if electricity filled the air. I am sure I was shaking with excitement from head to foot; both Major Gibson and Mr Everard were as pale as death, and I thought one of the ladies was about to faint. The other, whom I now knew was Mrs Everard, had risen from her chair; she was now standing close to the little side-table, almost immediately behind Skin o' my Tooth, who, suddenly dropping his voice and lolling placidly in his chair, said with gentle smile, in perfect matter-of-fact tones:

"Unfortunately, misfortune has dogged my steps, or rather those of my poor client. The witness I had so carefully unearthed died a couple of days ago most unexpectedly."

I wondered if I were mistaken, but I certainly thought that I heard a very obvious sigh of relief from somewhere. Certain it is that the spell of excitement under which we all had lain was broken, and one or two ironical comments came from that end of the table where Mr Everard sat with his legal adviser.

But I knew that Skin o' my Tooth had something up his sleeve; I knew that smile of his.

"However, before the man died, I had succeeded in persuading him to swear an affidavit stating all that he had seen. This affidavit I have brought with me today, and..."

Then I knew what he had been driving at all along. He was on the alert, and so was I. In the midst of his neatly-told lie he stopped and pointed to my notes, which were lying on the side-table quite close to the chimney.

"Give me that affidavit, Muggins, my boy," he said.

But before I could reach them, before even anyone else had realized what she was doing, Mrs Everard, as quick as lightning, had seized the notes and thrown them into the fire, while she turned on Skin o' my Tooth and said defiantly:

"At any rate, that unfortunate woman's name will now remain a secret for ever."

Then I understood. I cared nothing about burning my fingers, but I did want to rescue the remaining fragments of my notes, as I knew they would be wanted.

Mrs Everard was glaring at old Skin o' my Tooth as if she were a hungry tigress. If looks could kill, my esteemed employer would have been a dead man then. As it was, he smiled placidly, and taking the fragments of half-burned paper from me, he quietly smoothed them out and placed them on the table before Mr Everard; then he once more turned towards the angry lady.

"My dear lady," he said very gently, "I feel that I have behaved towards you absolutely like the cad my eminent colleague here present no doubt will call me. Just at this moment I know that you hate me for the odious comedy I had devised in order to extort an unwilling confession from you. Yes, my dear lady, a comedy and a confession. I don't think that I am the only man present who knows that the Hon. Thornby Oakhurst, your brother, is the grave thorn in a distinguished family's flesh. That with somewhat impulsive thoughtlessness you tried to be of material assistance to him at a time that he was actually flying from the police and unbeknown to your husband, is only natural. That in trying to shield him and your own family honour, you allowed an innocent man to suffer so severely is only what, under the same circumstances, most of your sex would have done. Let me in my turn confess to you, and to Mr Everard, to whom I must also offer my humblest apologies, that the only witness present on that fateful night was Major Gibson himself, and that the affidavit which you hoped to destroy consisted of my clerk's notes of the facts taken under my unfortunate client's dictation. There is no woman's name mentioned throughout its few pages, but I think you will admit yourself that in trying to burn that document you yourself with your dainty hand have plainly written your own."

It is wonderful with what dignity Skin o' my Tooth can speak when he likes. Mr Everard looked as if he had some difficulty in standing straight. He did not look at his wife, and she did not attempt to speak. What would be the outcome of this extraordinary scene I could not conjecture. Evidently Skin o' my Tooth was satisfied, for without another word he bowed to everyone, and, with Major Gibson, left the room, followed by my humble self. As I passed out of the door, I gave a final look round at the actors whom we had left on the stage. Mr Everard had gone up to his wife, who had fallen sobbing into a chair. Miss Sutcliffe was kneeling beside her, trying to comfort her, and Lord Combermury and the solicitor looked as if they wished themselves safely out of the way.

I must say Mr Everard behaved very well in the matter; both he and Lord Combermury made it their business to see that no shadow of a stain remained on Major Gibson's reputation, though Mrs Everard's name has, of course, never been mentioned.

Major Gibson was married to Miss Sutcliffe about a month ago, and Mr and Mrs Everard gave a magnificent reception in their fine house in Park Lane in honour of the bride and bridegroom. I suppose there was supper served in the room in which we had sat on that day.

Skin o' my Tooth was not asked to the wedding or to the reception. He would not have gone, anyhow.

6

THE INVERTED FIVE

I think that I have made it clear by now why it is that Skin o' my Tooth is not popular among his colleagues. We all know that there is prejudice and petty spite in all professions, and the Law is no exception to this general rule.

Moreover, Skin o' my Tooth is totally unacquainted with the use of kid gloves. He works for the best of his client; let the other side look to themselves, I say.

Now take the case of young Newton Dampier. If ever I saw a man with the fatal noose already round his neck, there he was: good looking, not particularly intelligent, not particularly straight-laced where women were concerned, but a gentleman for all that, he had got himself into one of the worst messes a man had ever floundered in, and had, it not been for Skin o' my Tooth... but I am anticipating.

How well I remember that morning when Sir Leopold Messinger first called at the office. I took in his card myself, and as I went through I glanced at it. The card told me nothing, save his name and that of his club—the National Conservative. I had vaguely heard the name before in connection with racing, yachting, and other plutocratic habits, including the fitting up during the war of his sumptuous yacht as a hospital ship for naval officers and the presentation of it to the Admiralty, which act of generosity got him his title and half a column of fulsome flattery in the evening papers. Glancing through the window of our outer office, I had already caught sight of a gorgeous Hispano-Suiza, which was in thorough keeping with our visitor's reputation for wealth, as well as with his appearance, which, despite his title and all that he had done for England during the war, was not altogether English.

A minute or two later, while one of the boys showed Sir Leopold into the chief's office, I took up my seat in the alcove, which, as I said before, Mr Mulligan so poetically calls "Behind the Arras." From this spot, sitting at my desk, notebook and pencil in hand, I could, without being seen, see and hear everything that went on during my chief's interview with his clients, and record in shorthand every word of the conversation that passed between them. I believe that this practice of using a confidential clerk as a faithful and secret recorder of interviews and conversations is peculiar to Skin o' my Tooth, and I am told that had it been universally known at the time that he was still in practice, he would never have seen another client across his doors. But it is neither my purpose nor my business to justify so great a man as Patrick Mulligan in any one of his actions. All I need say is that my shorthand notes have done much in their time to save a man's life from the gallows or secure the acquittal of one wrongfully accused.

But to return to Sir Leopold Messinger. As I said before, he was distinctly un-English in appearance; large, stout, florid, with black hair carefully brushed across his cranium to hide the first signs of oncoming baldness. He wore a perfectly cut suit of dark tweed and held between his thick fingers a large cigar. His eyes, on the other hand, were extraordinarily kind and benevolent, his voice was gentle and persuasive, and his manner toward my chief particularly courteous and even deferential. He came very quickly to the point.

The governess of his children, a French girl of good family, who had been with him about six months, had mysteriously disappeared. She lived alone in a small flat in Maida Vale and came daily to Grosvenor Square at nine o'clock, gave lessons to the children, stayed to lunch, went out for a walk with them, and after tea went back to her flat. On Saturdays she usually went home directly after lunch.

Last Monday (this was Friday morning) she did not turn up, nor had she sent a note of excuse, which was curious, but at the time aroused no definite suspicion. But day followed day and still no news of Mlle. de Mery.

"I began to feel anxious," Sir Leopold went on "and yesterday I drove round to her flat in Maida Vale. There a neighbour of hers, a respectable-looking woman whom I happened to meet on the stairs, told me that nothing had been seen or heard of the girl since the previous Sunday, when she started off, presumably for a walk, sometime in the afternoon. Now what had not occurred to my informant but struck me at once, was that last Sunday was a very foggy day. I tackled the woman about this, expressing my astonishment that she had done nothing in the way of informing the police when for days on end she had seen nothing of her neighbour. But you know what people are in that class of life—clerks, shop-assistants, and so on; they have so many worries of their own they don't trouble—as they call it—about other people."

Sir Leopold's large, kind eyes—in expression something like an amiable Pekingese—fixed themselves inquiringly on the chief. But Skin o' my Tooth's face was utterly expressionless. I don't know if you have ever seen him: vulgar minds have compared him to a Yorkshire pig. His skin was certainly roseate in colour, and he was what might be called corpulent. I think I mentioned before that he was as bald as an egg, and that his eyes were very small but penetrating, like gimlets. Usually they were expressionless, encased in their fleshy lids, but at times he would have a way of looking down and pursing his mouth, for all the world like a coy Mid-Victorian maiden. I could detect now a certain hesitation in Sir Leopold's manner, as if he were sorry he had come for advice to this fat fool of an Irishman. They all went through that phase, and Skin o' my Tooth, as keen an observer as anybody, never made the slightest attempt to gain their confidence. He just would let them flounder along. Invariably they came round, and after the first interview trusted him implicitly.

Sir Leopold appeared to be pulling himself together as if he were making a desperate effort to chase away a nightmare, then he resumed: "It took me some time to persuade Mrs Tomkins, or Hawkins—I think that was the name—firstly to make an attempt at effecting an entrance into Mlle. de Mery's flat, and when this was proved to be impossible, her front door being locked, to inform the police at once. I felt, you see, that it was more her business than mine, but it was only after we had argued the point for nearly half an hour and other neighbours had assembled, adding their shrill voices to those of Mrs Hawkins, that, in a fit of exasperation, I declared that I would go to the police myself at once, but that the Hawkins' were not to be astonished if the police blamed them severely for failing to notify them of this mysterious disappearance. This frightened the woman effectually, and she promised me that directly her husband came home—he was a clerk in an accountant's office—she would see to it that he went to the police immediately."

Sir Leopold paused, and I must frankly admit that at this point I was completely off the scent. The way I had figured it out in my own mind was that Sir Leopold feared to be involved in some way in the disappearance of his children's daily governess—that perhaps he had made love to her, even got her into trouble perhaps, and either he feared that the poor girl had thrown herself into the river, or he knew something about her fate, something that might land him in a criminal's dock. But, as I say, I was following the wrong scent. Sir Leopold Messinger had by now lost all traces of hesitation; his good-natured, doggie eyes were fixed with a pathetic, appealing glance on the chief, who sat behind his desk, immovable and coy, giving him no help in the unfolding of his narrative.

"I dare say you wonder, Mr Mulligan," he went on more glibly, "why I have come to you with this tale. I won't talk platitudes and speak of your reputation. When I tell you that a man for whom I have the greatest respect, not to say affection, may be involved in this mysterious affair, you will easily understand my coming for advice to the one man who can throw light upon it. I am speaking of my confidential secretary, Mr Newton Dampier. He has been with me for over two years. A finer, straighter character it would be impossible to conceive."

Sir Leopold paused once more; his cigar had gone out, he groped in his pocket for matches, struck one or two unsuccessfully, put down the cigar, pulled a handkerchief out of his pocket, and mopped his streaming forehead. But Skin o' my Tooth's fat, pink face expressed nothing at all. He glanced down in that coy, Early-Victorian manner of his on his highly polished finger-nails, then he said with apparent indifference:

"And what about this Mr Newton Dampier, Sir Leopold?"

"He was passionately in love with Mlle. de Mery," Sir Leopold replied slowly. Then he dropped his voice almost to a whisper and added: "On the Sunday afternoon in question he had arranged to call for her at her flat. They were going out for a walk together. This arrangement was rather vexing to me, because my family and I were spending the week-end with some friends at Brighton, and, as I had a great many arrears of correspondence to attend to, I wanted Dampier to come down with us. However, he put the matter of his engagement with Mlle. de Mery so urgently before me that I did not like to stand in the way of young lovers. My wife, the children, and myself motored down to Brighton on Saturday afternoon and returned on Monday morning. As I told you, we saw nothing of Mlle. de Mery either that day or the next. I questioned Dampier. He declared that he knew nothing about her—had, in fact, not seen her that Sunday afternoon; when he arrived at her flat, he rang and knocked in vain. She was obviously not at home, and had apparently forgotten her appointment with him. Dampier's manner was very strange." Sir Leopold continued with a grave shake of the head: "Even my wife, who is not at all observant, remarked upon his gloominess and obvious abstraction. During the next two or three days, whenever I tried to question him, he answered me evasively, sometimes almost rudely. Of course, I made allowances for all that—"

Sir Leopold gave a deep sigh; when he spoke again there was a quiver in his gentle, even voice, but he looked Skin o' my Tooth very straight in the face.

"One thing," he said slowly, "that Mrs Tomkins, or Hawkins, told me was that on the Sunday afternoon she saw a young gentleman, whom she had often seen before in the company of Mlle. de Mery, on the stairs, as if coming away from the girl's flat. Mrs Hawkins described him to me as looking very agitated and flushed, and as he went downstairs he was muttering incoherent words to himself."

"Disappointment," Skin o' my Tooth murmured gently, "at finding the lady gone."

"So it would appear, Mr Mulligan," Sir Leopold admitted with a sigh, "at first sight. But I must tell you that all along I was very uneasy about Dampier; his manner was so very strange. But what brought my anxiety to a head, and actually caused me yesterday to drive over to Mlle. de Mery's flat, was that in the morning, after I had dictated a couple of letters to Dampier, he told me that he had a terrible headache and asked me if I would mind his going home to rest for an hour or two. He hoped to be better by the afternoon, and would then return. Naturally, I urged him by all means to go and rest. After he had gone I had occasion to go to the room in my house where he has his desk and typewriter and does his work for me. There was a fire in the grate and some charred papers among the ashes. One of these, only partially burned, was lying in the fender. What prompted me to pick it up I could not for the life of me tell you. But I did pick that paper up, and I glanced at it. Here it is, Mr Mulligan," Sir Leopold concluded, and his trembling fingers fumbled in the pocket of his overcoat, drew out a pocket-book, and, extracting a creased, half-charred scrap of paper from it, held it out to my chief.

That letter—it was a mere fragment—was subsequently photographed, and here is a reproduction of it:

> *... no longer love*
> *... think it would be*
> *... at we do not meet*
> *... Sincerely your*
> *... Florine*

My chief looked at the fragment carefully, turned it over and over between his fat fingers, then asked briefly:

"The handwriting?"

"Unmistakably that of Mlle. de Mery," Sir Leopold replied. "I know it well."

"Anyone else know it?"

"Oh yes! My wife—the children—"

"And the signature?"

"Likewise. Her name was Florine. There must be a specimen of it in the children's exercise books." There was silence for a moment or two after that, Skin o' my Tooth sitting with his podgy hands clasped before him. I could hear the ticking of the old clock on the mantelpiece. Somehow I did not feel great interest in this commonplace tale of lovers' quarrel culminating in crime. One hears so many tales of that sort these days. I thought, too, that Mr Mulligan looked bored, and was marvelling whether he would refuse to take up the case on some pretext or other. Presently he asked his client: "And what is it, Sir Leopold, that you wish me to do in the matter? For the moment I don't quite see—"

"Of course you don't," Sir Leopold broke in eagerly. "I should have told you at once, but I am so upset, you understand? Newton Dampier is like a son to me, and, Mr Mulligan, I am as convinced as that I am alive that the boy is innocent, that I foresee trouble for him, and I want you to see that he gets out of it. Spare no expense, Mr Mulligan; I am footing this bill."

Once more there was silence in the fusty old room. I imagined that the chief was weighing the importance of the affair in his mind. Personally I didn't think that Sir Leopold's request stood much chance. Skin o' my Tooth at the moment had several Crown cases on hand notably one relating to some mysterious cases of cocaine smuggling; this in addition to his other work was taking up so much of his time that I had often recently heard him declare that he would not undertake any more work, unless it were of a specially interesting character. My astonishment was great, therefore, when, after a moment or two, he broke the silence which appeared to be weighing down Sir Leopold's spirits.

"Do you happen to know, Sir Leopold," he said, and with one podgy finger tapped the scrap of paper which he still held in his hand, "what caused Mlle. de Mery—is that the name?— to write this letter to your friend?"

Sir Leopold appeared to hesitate before he replied: "I don't know, Mr Mulligan—that is—"

"Had she another lover?"

"Yes!" Sir Leopold replied more resolutely. "She had, I am certain. Otherwise she never would—"

"Could he, for instance," Skin o' my Tooth went on as his client paused, obviously irresolute, as if unwilling to put his thoughts into words, "could he have been the man whom Mrs Hawkins saw on the stairs that Sunday afternoon?"

"I'm afraid not," Sir Leopold replied. "She described the man to me: tall, fair, curly hair, hazel eyes, slight toothbrush moustache. The description was unmistakable. Whereas the other man whom Mlle. de Mery had favoured of late was very dark and foreign looking—"

"Do you know him? Personally, I mean?"

"Yes! Horatio Dreyfus. He is a distant relation of my wife's. He came to lunch one day at my house, and there met Mlle. de Mery."

"And he lives?"

"Abroad mostly. But just now he is staying at the Majestic."

Without any further comment, Skin o' my Tooth touched the bell-push on his desk. This was the signal for me to slip out of my cubby-hole through a door behind me, and then ostentatiously to knock and enter by the main door of the office.

"Ring up Mr Alverson at Scotland Yard," the chief said to me, as soon as I appeared, "and ask him what has been done in connection with the disappearance of the French girl which was reported to the police last night."

I don't, of course, know what occurred between the chief and his new client in the interval while I was on the telephone, but when I returned I found Sir Leopold on the verge of tears of joy and gratitude.

"If you get the boy out of this mess, Mr Mulligan," he was saying, "there is no fee that you could ask me that I would find too high."

Skin o' my Tooth was twiddling a cigarette between his fingers, his eyes were downcast, and there was a gently coy smile playing round his lips. He listened apparently unmoved to Sir Leopold's expressions of exuberant gratitude then, and his calm appeared in strange contrast to the other man's excitement. He asked quietly:

"What did you know of this Mlle. de Mery, Sir Leopold, before you engaged her as governess for your children?"

"I didn't engage her," Sir Leopold replied; "my wife did. She had put an advertisement in *The Times*. Mlle. de Mery presented herself. She appeared pretty, refined, very well read: she had what the French call her Brevet Superieur, which showed her to have had a splendid education; she also had some warm letters of recommendation from the Mother Superior of a convent in Belgium who had known her intimately."

"And on the strength of these facts you engaged her?"

Sir Leopold shrugged his massive shoulders. "My wife took to her," he said, "and I must say that she never had cause to regret her choice. We were all of us very fond of Mlle. de Mery."

"And what about this convent in Belgium? Where is it?"

"Ah!" Sir Leopold replied with a quick sigh, "that's the trouble. My wife and I were trying to recollect the name and address. We questioned the children. But alas! Neither name nor address impressed itself upon our minds."

At this point Skin o' my Tooth looked up and caught my eye. I had, of course, to deliver the message which had come to me over the phone.

"What is it, Muggins?" he queried curtly. It was his pleasure, you understand, to call me Muggins, though my name is, as you know, Alexander Stanislaus Mullins. I gave him the message which I had received from Mr Alverson, a personal friend of my chief who is on the staff of the C.I.D. at Scotland Yard. He told me that, as a matter of fact, the body of an unknown young woman had been lying for two days at the Thames Police Court mortuary pending identification. The body was found under Wapping Bridge, and, according to the divisional surgeon's testimony, had then been in the water three days. The face had been so battered in by some heavy instrument that, in consequence of the terrible wounds so inflicted, decomposition had already set in very rapidly. Undoubtedly it would prove unrecognizable save to a very intimate friend or near relative. The body, on the other hand, had one distinguishing mark, a circular scar something like a large vaccination mark, on the right deltoid, which, in the opinion of the divisional surgeon, had been made comparatively recently by the application of corrosive acid.

There was no clothing of any kind on the body, but it was wrapped round from neck to foot in several yards of black material, like swaddling clothes, held in place by a large metal brooch of hammered metal, triangular in shape, with, in the centre, a large inverted FIVE. A stained linen handkerchief was knotted loosely round the throat—it had no initial on it, only a laundry mark—and underneath the handkerchief the neck showed the marks of a thin cord wound round with sufficient force to cause strangulation.

The police had already taken the usual steps to try and establish the identity of the victim of this terrible outrage when Mr and Mrs Hawkins, of Harberton Mansions, called with their story of the disappearance of a neighbour of theirs, a French girl living alone in the flat next to theirs. They were asked to view the body, but entirely failed to identify it. Mrs Hawkins had immediately fainted, and all Mr Hawkins could say was that the French girl certainly had hair the same colour and texture as that on the head of the deceased. Questioned as to the curious brooch found upon the body, they both said that they had never seen Mlle. de Mery wearing it.

While I delivered this message. Sir Leopold Messinger showed signs of the greatest distress; his agony of mind was pitiable to see, and when I had finished speaking he exclaimed in a voice broken with sobs:

"That brooch! I can identify it, Mr Mulligan, so can my wife and the children. The poor girl had it on one day, I remember.

I was very much interested in it because I had once seen one exactly like it somewhere abroad. I forget where. For some reason or other my wife got the idea that it was unlucky, and told Mlle. de Mery so, who laughingly promised that she would never wear it again."

"You didn't by any chance ask her at the time how she came by that brooch?" Skin o' my Tooth asked presently.

"Yes," Sir Leopold replied, "we did ask her. Naturally. But she answered rather curtly that it was a present."

"She did not say from whom?"

"No. But I remember that Horatio Dreyfus' name was mentioned in connection with the thing, and that both my wife and I remained under the impression that the brooch was given her by Horatio Dreyfus."

"Was Mr Dampier present when this episode occurred?"

"No. He was away at the time; he had gone up North for a couple of days for me on business."

After that there was a long pause. My chief was weighing the matter in his mind, and Sir Leopold's kind, doggie eyes were fixed more and more hopefully upon him. He had sufficient tact—I could see that—not to press his plea any further. Another word from him might have upset his chances altogether. As it was, after some two or three minutes of absolute silence, which must have seemed an eternity to the anxious man, Skin o' my Tooth said quietly:

"You may send Mr Newton Dampier to me tomorrow, Sir Leopold; I'll see him."

Once more Sir Leopold showed himself tactful and understanding. He did not indulge in profuse expressions of gratitude. Almost without another word, he rose to take his leave.

"At what hour shall I send him?" was all he asked.

"In the early part of the afternoon. Say at three o'clock."

Sir Leopold's whole expression had undergone a change. He appeared comforted now, almost cheerful. His last words to my chief before he left the office were spoken most solemnly: "The boy is innocent, Mr Mulligan," he said. "I would take my dying oath on that."

When I returned to the office after escorting him to the door, I found Skin o' my Tooth rubbing his podgy hands contentedly together.

"This is going to be an exciting case, Muggins," he said. "Just ring up Mr Alverson again, will you?"

What passed over the phone between my chief and his friend of the C.I.D. I didn't know at the time. When next I saw Skin o' my Tooth he was absorbed in the perusal of M. Victor Margueritte's latest French shocker.

2

At three o'clock precisely the following day Mr Newton Dampier came to see the chief. I, of course, was "behind the arras" during the interview and could study the young man's face and his manner. He appeared to me both dejected and "jumpy," but as far as I could judge he was not at present conscious of being in any kind of danger. No wonder that the poor young man was "jumpy." He had just been through the terrible ordeal of viewing the dead body of the girl to whom he had been so passionately attached. He had, however, been quite unable to swear positively as to her identity, although he, too, declared that the hair was certainly that of Mlle. de Mery.

Sir Leopold and Lady Messinger, who had also magnanimously come forward, could not do more either. But they did identify the brooch, and for the time being the police appeared satisfied that the deceased was indeed Florine de Mery who had disappeared from her flat in Harberton Mansions the previous Sunday.

Questioned by Skin o' my Tooth, Mr Newton Dampier managed to give a clear and straightforward account of his sentimental friendship with Mlle. de Mery. It had been an entirely happy one until that Sunday afternoon when he received a curt letter from her, telling him, in effect, that she no longer loved him and thought it would be best that they should cease to meet.

"How did you get that letter, Mr Dampier?" Skin o' my Tooth asked him. "There is no post in London on Sunday."

"I found it in my letter-box," he replied, "just as I was starting out to keep my appointment with Mlle. de Mery. How it got there I do not know."

"What have you done with it?"

"Carried it in my pocket the first few days," the young man replied with a sigh, "then threw it in the fire in an access of rage."

Skin o' my Tooth drew the fragment of charred paper out of his letter-case and placed it before Mr Dampier. "Is this a portion of it?" he asked.

"It is," the other replied. "But how did you come by it? I thought I had destroyed it completely."

"It was found—fortunately, by a friend who brought it to me."

"You mean Sir Leopold?"

"Yes! If it had come into the hands of the police—"

"The police?" young Dampier broke in excitedly. "Surely you don't mean—?"

"Well!" Skin o' my Tooth put in with his bland smile. "I put it to you—lovers' quarrels have led to murder before now."

Mr Dampier's eyes, filled now with horror, were staring at Skin o' my Tooth, while he passed a trembling hand once or twice across his forehead.

"My God!" he murmured hoarsely. "Murder? I? I confess," he went on more calmly, "that after I had read the letter I flew round to Mlle. de Mery's flat in a frenzy of grief. But I only meant to argue and to plead. I would no more have injured one hair of her head than I would deny my own existence."

And suddenly, without any transition. Skin o' my Tooth came out with what seemed an irrelevant question.

"Did you know a Mr Horatio Dreyfus?"

Dampier blinked his eyes once or twice like a man waking from a dream.

"Well, yes," he replied. "Slightly. Why do you ask?"

"Were you aware of his attentions to Mlle. de Mery?"

The young man appeared to hesitate a moment before he replied: "Yes, in a way I was, but I did not think that Florine— Mlle. de Mery, I mean—would ever respond to them."

"And do you know anything about the curious brooch with the inverted FIVE which was found upon her body?"

"No, Mr Mulligan, I don't. As a matter of fact, that brooch puzzles me. I never saw Florine wear it."

Skin o' my Tooth was silent for a minute or two after that. I was watching young Dampier, speculating how he would take the blow which was about to fall upon him. Guilty or innocent, it would stun him, but how would he behave afterwards? I had received the message from Mr Alverson not half an hour ago, so I knew what was coming, and I felt the tenseness of those few minutes; my nerves were taut as if stretched on a rack.

"Mr Dampier," Skin o' my Tooth now resumed very quietly, "you read in the paper, did you not? or Sir Leopold must have told you, that a handkerchief bearing a certain laundry mark was found knotted loosely round the throat of the deceased?"

"Yes, I knew that, Mr Mulligan," Dampier replied equally calmly.

"But you didn't know, did you? that the police had succeeded in tracing that laundry mark to a laundry which not only works for you, but which actually identified the handkerchief as one belonging to yourself."

I must say that he took the blow like a man. That he understood its full significance was undoubted, because his face became the colour of lead, and his eyes, which still stared at Skin o' my Tooth, became suddenly glassy.

"My Lord!" was all he said.

With this dramatic climax, and as far as important matters were concerned, the interview was practically ended, although Mr Dampier remained another half-hour in my chief's office, asseverating his innocence and answering various questions put to him by Skin o' my Tooth in a dazed though for the most part straightforward manner.

That he was in a tight hole he quickly realized. Skin o' my Tooth warned him that a warrant for his arrest on the capital charge would certainly be out before evening. But my chief was in one of his best moods. There was no resisting his optimism, or his confidence.

"If you are innocent, Mr Dampier," he said emphatically, "I will get you out of this hole. You may stake your life on that."

"My life is at stake," the young man rejoined. "But if you do not believe that I am guiltless of this foul deed—"

"I neither believe nor disbelieve," Skin o' my Tooth broke in with some impatience. "I haven't had time to think over that laundry mark yet," he added grimly.

When Mr Dampier had gone my chief sent for me. "Ring up Sir Leopold Messinger," he said, "and ask him kindly to arrange a meeting between Mr Horatio Dreyfus and myself. Tell him I would suggest his asking us both to lunch at his club tomorrow, as I don't want the meeting to appear pre-arranged."

3

That meeting, however, never took place, although Skin o' my Tooth actually went to lunch at Sir Leopold Messinger's house in Grosvenor Square. But the other guest was absent. The night before the body of a well-dressed youngish man of somewhat foreign appearance was found on a seat in Hyde Park with a silken cord tied tightly round the throat. Death was due to strangulation. The news reached Sir Leopold by telephone, just as he and Skin o' my Tooth were sitting down to lunch. No attempt had been made to conceal the identity of the victim of this terrible outrage. Visiting cards in his letter-case, which was untouched, revealed his name as Horatio Dreyfus, whilst "Majestic Hotel" was scribbled by hand in the corners. Inquiries at the Majestic elicited the fact that Mr Dreyfus had certainly been staying there, having arrived from Paris about a month ago. He went out a great deal, received some letters and telegrams. Beyond that nothing was known about him; and when the police searched among his effects, the one thing that was not found was his passport. But he had entered his name at the hotel as a British subject born in London. The hall-porter at such a large hotel as the Majestic was necessarily a very busy man, and apparently an incurious or unobservant one: he certainly did not remember, when questioned, the name of any person who at any time had called on Mr Dreyfus.

The chief reception clerk, on the other hand, was able to give the name and address of the bank on which the deceased had drawn the cheques for payment of his weekly hotel bills. Inquiries at that bank elicited the information that Mr Dreyfus had only been a customer for about a month, that he had been originally introduced by Sir Leopold Messinger, and that he still had a balance of about £200 to his credit. The police then got into touch with Sir Leopold, who had very little to say, except that the deceased was a distant relation of his wife's who had always been considered by the family as something of a rolling stone and a bad egg. Sir Leopold had only seen him very occasionally, either in Paris or some other Continental resort. About a month ago he turned up in London, apparently full of good resolutions—he was going to settle down in life, and he begged Sir Leopold to help him get something to do in the City or anywhere. He had about £500 loose in his pocket, which he professed to have won at Monte Carlo, and as a matter of goodwill Sir Leopold gave him an introduction to the manager of one of the banks with which he had business relations.

And beyond that, nothing. Neither Sir Leopold nor Lady Messinger seemed to know anything more about Mr Horatio Dreyfus. Advertisements and notices were sent out in all directions by the police, solicitors kept an advertisement going for three days in the personal column of *The Times*, but no one came forward able or willing to throw any light on the recent habits or doings of Mr Horatio Dreyfus. His personality remained as mysterious as the circumstances connected with his death. According to Lady Messinger's evidence at the inquest, he was an only child of parents long since dead, who at one time had considerable property in Germany. This they sold and settled down in London, where the boy was born. Lady Messinger knew them all, when they had a house in Lancaster Gate, but she had seen nothing of Horatio since his parents went back to Germany, which was over twenty years ago, when he was a boy of about fifteen.

The inquest in this case, as in that of the unfortunate Mlle. de Mery, was adjourned for a month to enable the police to collect further evidence. It was through his friend, Mr Alverson of the C.I.D., that Skin o' my Tooth got two remarkable pieces of information, which, so far as the Press was concerned, were still kept a secret: the one was that in this case, like in the other, the same shaped round scar caused by the application of some corrosive acid was found upon the body, on the right deltoid. The other strange fact was that the silk cord—a black one—with which the unfortunate man had been strangled was weighted with a metal pendant of exactly the same design as the brooch found on the body of Mlle. de Mery—namely, a triangle with, in the centre, an inverted FIVE.

And in the meanwhile my chief's latest client, Mr Newton Dampier, had been arrested on a charge of murdering Florine de Mery on a certain Sunday in November; he had been brought up before the magistrate and remanded; but there was no doubt that within the next day or two he would be committed for trial. Was I not right when I said that here was a man literally with the hangman's rope around his neck?

4

I must say that during the next few days Skin o' my Tooth appeared more interested in M. Dekobra's latest thriller than in the affairs of his client. Never once did he go and see him. He always sent me, and I would go and try and instil some measure of hope into the poor young man's dejected spirits. It was all very well for Skin o' my Tooth to say that he expected his clients to believe implicitly in him. But away from him such belief was liable to wear threadbare, and the first thoughts of despair would inevitably creep into the brain.

I alone knew that, as a rule, the more uninterested in a case Skin o' my Tooth appeared to be, the more passionate really was his enthusiasm for it; and the more trashy French novels he devoured — he never read the fine ones — the deeper were his thoughts in a wholly opposite direction.

During the third week in November, Newton Dampier, having, on Skin o' my Tooth's advice, pleaded "Not Guilty" and reserved his defence, was committed for trial on the capital charge. In the meanwhile the coroner's inquest on Mr Horatio Dreyfus was concluded with a verdict of wilful murder against some person or persons unknown, and that on the unknown woman, presumed to be Florine de Mery, with a verdict of wilful murder against George Newton Dampier.

A day or two later, when I was coming away from an interview with our client, I happened to take a stroll along the Embankment when I was accosted by a disreputable-looking character begging for alms. I tried not to listen to his tale, which was supposed to be that of a broken-down gentleman on his beam-ends—an ex-officer and so on—the usual tale. I hurried on after I had bestowed half a crown upon the creature, when an ironical laugh unexpectedly struck my ear. The broken-down gentleman on his beam-ends was none other than Skin o' my Tooth, so admirably made up that even I had failed to recognize him.

I was far too well trained to ask questions then; he took me by the arm and, whispering an address in my ear, he ordered me to meet him there in half an hour. I knew the place well, of course—a slum in Hoxton, where my chief rented a couple of rooms in an evil-looking lodging-house; here he kept every sort and kind of disguise, mostly filthy rags, also ragged uniforms and togs of all sorts. It was the sort of place where questions are never asked and where the police seldom penetrate.

When I arrived I found my chief already waiting for me. Without wasting time, he pointed to a bundle of rags and told me to put them on. Ten minutes later we emerged into the street once more, looking as seedy a pair of blackguards as anyone would wish to see.

Silently I followed Skin o' my Tooth as he threaded his way through the network of streets that lie around the river bank.

No one knew his London better than Skin o' my Tooth, and within an incredibly short time that peculiar smell made up of hemp, tar, oil, and coal-dust revealed the fact that we were nearing one of the docks. Presently we came to a halt, at a distance of about twenty yards from a gaily lighted restaurant, from whence came the strains of a lively jazz band. Here we took up our stand, a pair of silent, motionless figures, with our backs to a greasy, dank wall. Skin o' my Tooth had drawn a bundle of bootlaces from his pocket, and these, together with boxes of Swan vestas, he was apparently offering for sale. Many people passed us by; sailors or soldiers with their girls, foreigners of every description, Orientals from every clime; some dropped a few coppers into my cramped hand, some went by with an ugly word for two able-bodied oafs. Skin o' my Tooth never said a word, and here we stood for nearly two hours, after which we went back to Hoxton, changed back into our own clothes, and returned home, hardly having exchanged a word.

The next evening we went through the same performance, and again the evening after that. On the third evening, however, there was a change in our adventure. A man, short and slender in build, dressed in perfectly tailored clothes, was about to pass us by when Skin o' my Tooth's voice was suddenly raised in pitiful appeal: "For the love of God, sir," he cried, "you are a gentleman. Have pity on a broken-down wretch of your own class."

The man paused—instinctively, I think, rather than from any sense of compassion. He peered quizzically into Skin o' my Tooth's face.

"A broken-down gentleman, are you?" he asked with a sneer. "Lots of 'em about these days, especially in Limehouse, eh?"

His speech betrayed what I had already guessed from his face, which was sallow and flat-featured, with almond-shaped, up-slanting eyes. Underneath the soft grey hat which he wore his hair appeared black as coal. In spite of his Western dress, it was easy to guess that here was a man born in China.

But Skin o' my Tooth was continuing his piteous appeal. He had served as a temporary officer in the war, had been twice wounded, and mentioned in despatches. His son—and he pointed to me—had been gassed twice and had lost hearing and speech through shell-shock. He was entirely on his beam-ends and would do anything in the world—anything—to earn a decent living.

"An honest one?" the Oriental queried with his habitual sneer.

"Not necessarily," Skin o' my Tooth retorted boldly.

By way of an answer the other nodded in the direction of the restaurant, then he said curtly: "Wait here till five minutes before closing time, then go in there and we'll talk."

With that he strode away, and presently disappeared within the restaurant.

At five minutes before eleven my chief and I duly entered the gaily lighted place. No one took any notice of us. Indeed, there were others quite as disreputable to look on as we were. We sat down at a vacant table. The band had just ceased playing and were packing up their instruments. There was the usual hubbub and bustle attendant on closing time in these sort of places, and presently we found ourselves alone in the now dimly lighted hall. Everyone had gone. A Chinese boy was busy putting up the shutters.

After a while he came back into the hall, gave us nod and a wink, which we took to mean that we were to come along with him. We followed on his heels and he led us along a dark passage to what appeared to be a room built over the backyard of the house. Our guide knocked at the door. It was at once opened, and I caught a transitory gleam of a well-furnished room with a large desk in the centre and leather-covered club chairs, also of our friend—the Chinaman in Western clothes— and of another man dressed in an elaborate Chinese garment and wearing a black mask over his face. The next moment our guide pushed Skin o' my Tooth into the room and I was about to follow when the door was incontinently slammed in my face, and I found myself alone and in semi-darkness. Knowin that I had the part of a deaf and dumb man to play, did not call out, only tried to grab the Chinese boy who had brought us here, by the sleeve. He wriggled away, however, like an eel, and soon his shuffling footstep died away down the long passage.

I glued eye and ear to the keyhole, but could neither see nor hear anything. But after a moment or two I heard my chief's voice raised for an instant and then immediately subdued. It was not raised in any way in distress, but you may well imagine that I stood on guard at that door ready to hurl myself against it, if I got the least idea that Skin o' my Tooth was in any danger. Frankly, I had no fears for him. There was nothing about his person to suggest that he was anything but what he professed to be: a down-at-heel gentleman ready to undertake any shady job that would put a few pounds in his pocket.

I had been on the watch a quarter of an hour or so, when, feeling restless, I started pacing up and down the dark passage. There was a stairway at the end of it leading to the basement, and as I went by I heard the sound of crockery and banging of pots and pans, and above the din a man's voice speaking pigeon-English and raised in threatening accents. A second or two later there was a bang, a sound as of the smashing of crockery, followed by a woman's cry. Then a scuffle. I was on the point of running down the stairs to see what was happening down there, when a woman came rushing up, with touzled hair, eyes wild, and hands outstretched, who almost threw herself into my arms.

"Allee lightee!" came in sarcastic tones from down below. "Play the fool. Mr Wang Sen, he here directly."

I don't pretend to be either an athlete or a preux chevalier, but by the feeble light of a solitary gas-jet on the stairs I saw that I was holding in my arms a woman in distress. That she happened to be young and pretty did not in any way add to my desire to help her.

"What is it?" I whispered hurriedly. "Can I do anything?"

But she only moaned: "Oh! why don't they kill me? Why don't they kill me?"

"Come, we'll get the police!" I urged, and tried to drag her away with me. There was no one else about, and the bully down below showed no signs of coming up in pursuit. But the girl resisted me with all her feeble might.

"I can't, I can't," she whispered hoarsely, "I must go back."

Finding persuasion useless, I tried force. Here was clearly a case for the police to interfere for the protection of this woman who was obviously in the hands of bullies. So without more ado I picked her up in my arms—she looked half starved, poor thing, and was as light as a feather—and hastened along in the direction of the restaurant and the front of the house. It was pitch-dark, but by groping with one hand along the jamb of the door, my hand encountered the electric switch, and I turned on the light. The girl had by now partly lost consciousness. I deposited her on a chair and went round inspecting the place. The iron shutters were up all along the front, and the door through them was padlocked and immovable. I felt like a rat in a trap, and looked round despairingly at the unfortunate girl, marvelling what in the circumstances I could do for her. She half lay, half sat in a chair, her head down, her eyes closed: her dress, I forget of what it consisted, had slid off her right shoulder. And suddenly I felt myself giving a gasp, for there on the right deltoid was a round scar, in shape like a large vaccination mark.

I felt dazed and stupid for the moment, face to face, as I knew now, with some ugly bypaths of mysterious crime. If only my chief were here! And suddenly the comforting thought came to me that he would be here—soon—if only I had time to warn him, and he had time to think and to act.

I picked up the girl as if she were a bundle of goods and deposited her behind a screen which masked an iron stove in one corner of the room. I then groped in my pockets for a pencil and a scrap of paper, and scribbled the few words that would enlighten my chief—these had to be as few as possible, of course. After which I switched off the light, registering a silent prayer that the girl might not recover consciousness before we had an opportunity to get her away from this den of brigands.

A few seconds later I was back at my post against the door at the end of the passage. I squatted in the corner feigning to sleep, my nerves on the rack. How long my ordeal lasted I know not. Presently I heard some kind of hubbub and then a shuffling. The door was opened. Our original friend stood silhouetted under the lintel against the light. He clapped his hands three times. My chief was immediately behind him, and sitting straight upright at the desk was the man with the mask and the elaborate Chinese costume.

In answer to the clapping the Chinese boy presently appeared, shuffling along the passage, and the man I call our original friend said something in a language I did not understand—presumably Chinese. He then gave me a vigorous kick, whereupon I struggled to my feet. My chief helped me to get up, and I was thus able to pass the note which I had scribbled into his hand. All I had written was:

"Girl in distress, behind screen in restaurant. Immediate case for police."

5

The door of the back room had closed behind us. Our guide led the way along the passage once more through to the front restaurant. As we passed the top of the back stairs I thought I saw a grinning face peering upwards at us. Our guide switched on the light in the restaurant and then made for the iron door in the shutter. While he busied himself with the padlock, Skin o' my Tooth quickly glanced at my message, then, without any warning, threw one arm round the neck of the Chinese boy, smothering his screams. The scuffle was of the briefest, for my chief is both athletic and heavy. While he brought the boy to the ground, I made my way round to the back of the screen. The girl was slowly struggling back to consciousness. At sight of me a look of terror crept over her face, and before I could stop her she gave a piercing shriek.

Skin o' my Tooth had just silenced the Chinese boy by banging his head against the floor, but in a moment the house appeared alive with footsteps—shuffling footsteps hurrying, scurrying up and down stairs. We were indeed caught like beasts in a cage, our only apparent means of egress barred by iron shutters. But my chief is a man whose inductions are as swift as his actions. He picked up the girl who now was struggling like a wild cat, and shouted to me to follow him. He had reckoned, you see, that those devils over in the end room had secured for themselves a means of escape that way, in case the police ever came in by the front.

Scared, no doubt, by the woman's shriek, the two men in there had just opened the door when my chief, still carrying the woman, hurled himself against them and pushed them back into the room.

"Close the door. Muggins," he shouted to me as I slipped in in his wake, and he allowed the woman to slide out of his arms.

I had just time to close and bar the door. And there followed a scuffle such as I had never experienced in all my life. The man in the Western clothes very nearly did for me, I must say, while there was a veritable tornado going on at the further end of the room where the masked man and Skin o' my Tooth were at close grips. I do think that my last hour on this earth would effectually have sounded at one moment, but for a double hoarse cry which suddenly stayed the hand of my antagonist.

"Sir Leopold Messinger! By all that's wonderful!"

"Patrick Mulligan! By all that's damnable!" The tornado had momentarily subsided, but all I could see for a moment were two hands held aloft, one brandishing a black mask and a Chinese mandarin's hat, and the other clutching the wig and false beard which had so effectively transformed my beloved chief into a seedy, out-at-elbows gentleman.

At this point, fortunately for both of us, the girl seemed suddenly to realize that we were her friends. I only knew later why she had struggled so violently against our attempts to save her; for the moment I had only thought that she was either demented or just a fool. But now, when above the tattered Chinese mandarin's garments she saw the hot, steaming face and round Pekingese eyes of Sir Leopold Messinger, she seemed suddenly to recover her senses, and while the struggle between us four men still continued, she ran round and round the room, until she discovered a doorway, which she promptly threw open.

"This way," she cried, and in an instant she had switched off the light and plunged us all into darkness. But the outside air guided us. After a final desperate effort, I succeeded in breaking loose from my opponent. Skin o' my Tooth, by far the finest fighter of the lot of us, had rendered the over-fed, over-indulged plutocrat quite helpless already. The next few minutes saw us speeding out in the open toward the Commercial Road, the girl bravely keeping up with us.

6

It was a curious story which Skin o' my Tooth unfolded before the coroner at the resumed inquest on the body of the unknown woman presumed to be Florine de Mery. She was not Florine de Mery at all, and has remained unknown, poor wretch, to this day.

Sir Leopold Messinger was the head of a gang of cocaine smugglers. This gang consisted entirely of men and women who had been gentle people, who were on their beam-ends and were ready to do any dirty job for the sake of earning a competence. These Messinger would pick up mostly in the streets of London, Paris, or any other Continental city. Florine de Mery was one. Pursued, when quite a young governess in her first place, by the attentions of the son of the house, she had been put in the wrong by her employers and dismissed without character or reference. For a time she supported herself by teaching, but the relentless enmity of her employers, who were influential people, pursued her, and she fell on evil days. Messinger picked her up outside a squalid little cabaret in Paris where she had been working as kitchen-maid, and had just been turned out by the proprietress for refusing to accept the attentions of drunken customers.

So much for poor Florine de Mery. Horatio Dreyfus, rolling stone, gambler, out-at-elbows, was such another. He was no relative to Lady Messinger, who was as clever a liar as her husband. Wah Sen, who acted as butler in the Messinger household, was the instrument which Sir Leopold used for the punishment of any of the gang who dared to show signs of breaking away or of revolt. While he secured for himself an unimpeachable alibi, Wah Sen, silken cord in hand, would see to the effectual silencing of the recalcitrant.

During the interview which Skin o' my Tooth had with those scoundrels in the back room of the Limehouse restaurant, he learned some of the conditions which governed the enrolment of unfortunates into the gang of malefactors. They had to submit to being branded on the right deltoid with a distinguishing mark which would be recognized by every cocaine smuggler throughout Europe or the Far East. They were to play a lone hand, and never enter into any intimacy with their fellow-criminals. Obedience was, of course, to be implicit. At the slightest hint of an attempt at betrayal, death would follow, swift and sure. Wah Sen never failed. The inverted FIVE was the mark he left upon his victims to show to the others that his sinister hand had been at work. Thus by terror he held them. The poor governess, the out-at-elbows gentleman, the cashiered officer, were all equally held in bondage.

What caused Sir Leopold Messinger to engage Florine de Mery as governess to his children is difficult to say. She may have been peculiarly clever at the nefarious deed, and he may have wished to keep her under his own eyes and hand. She confessed later to Skin o' my Tooth that Sir Leopold had promised her some very special work, which would have brought her handsome remuneration, and ultimately gained her her freedom. But in the meanwhile he had discovered Dreyfus' growing admiration of the girl, and fearing that a secret intimacy would spring up between them, he decided on the death of both of them. It seems, however, that Wah Sen had also cast eyes of admiration on the pretty governess, and when the time came to execute the abominable orders of his chief, he chose some other unfortunate member of the gang for the foul deed, taking care to obliterate all traces of her identity. He kept Florine de Mery a prisoner, threatening her with the death of Newton Dampier unless she consented to link her fate permanently with his own. Whether she would ultimately have yielded to this threat, for she was very fond of Newton Dampier, I don't know. Skin o' my Tooth and I certainly arrived on the scene in the nick of time. The death of the young secretary had anyhow been decided on, as it was feared he may have learned something through his intimacy with Mlle. de Mery. But Messinger conceived the diabolical idea of first manufacturing such evidence against him as would prove him guilty of murder, and so put the police off any track which may have led to himself or to Wah Sen. I mean, of course, the handkerchief with the tell-tale laundry mark, and the fragment of the letter, which, it seems, was never written by Mlle. de Mery. He played the part of the distracted friend to perfection, and there is no doubt that had chance led him to any other lawyer or to an ordinary detective his last villainous schemes would have been completely successful.

Leopold Messinger was indicted at the Central Criminal Court for being in possession of I don't know how many ounces of cocaine. Other crimes, still more unavowable, were brought home to him, including that of being an accessory to the murder of one Horatio Dreyfus, and of an unknown woman. Wah Sen, committed at the same time on the capital charge, was duly hanged. Messinger got fourteen years. His wife and unfortunate children have disappeared.

But young Newton Dampier proved himself a true Briton, for he remained loyal, in spite of everything, to the girl he loved, and married her. He has gone out to Canada and is doing very well, I believe.

It was the black silk cord and the brooch of Oriental design which had first given Skin o' my Tooth an inkling of the truth. After that, the Chinese butler in the Messinger household set him thinking. He had Wah Sen shadowed, until he discovered that he was in the habit of frequenting a certain restaurant in Lime-house. Sir Leopold Messinger's identity as the leader of the gang was a revelation in the end. Skin o' my Tooth owned to me that he had not suspected this denouement.

7

THE TURQUOISE STUD

The mysterious drama began, as no doubt you remember, with the burglary in Lord Ap-Owen's house in Berkeley Square.

Let me remind you how it all happened.

At ten o'clock, or thereabouts, the servants had gone up to bed, with the exception of the butler, who had his evening out, and of a young footman named Cranston, who was still busy putting away a few things in the servants' hall. It was about half-past ten when there was a ring at the back door. Cranston, thinking that it was Mr Tabb, the butler, who perhaps had forgotten his key, went to answer it. No sooner had he opened the door when two men fell upon him; one struck him violently on the head, and before he could recover from the blow a scarf was wound tightly round his mouth, and his arms were pinioned and tied behind his back.

After that he must have lost consciousness, for he remembered nothing more until he heard, as in a dream, Mr Tabb's voice calling out lustily:

"Good heavens, Cranston, what the devil are you doing down there?"

Mr Tabb then untied his hands and took the muffler away from round his throat. He still felt very shaky, and his head ached furiously, but a hot drink and bed soon put him right, and by next morning he was none the worse for his adventure. Directly his Lordship returned he telephoned to the police, who sent an inspector round immediately. Cranston told him his story as circumstantially as he could. The passage, he said, leading to the back door was quite dark; as he thought it was Mr Tabb, he had not troubled to switch on the light; but there was a vague glimmer through the servants' hall door round the corner, and he had a short glimpse of his mysterious visitors, one of whom was tall and thin and had a small toothbrush moustache; he wore a light-coloured overcoat over his evening dress. The other was small and slender, more like a lad than a full-grown man; he, like his companion, wore a soft hat pulled down right over his eyes. Cranston was under the impression that he was the boss of the expedition, for he said something like "Now then, quick!" to the other man, just before the latter knocked him, Cranston, on the head.

But, as a matter of fact, the assault had been so sudden and so violent that the boy could not swear to anything; he was quite sure that he would not be able to identify positively either of the men, and he was not really certain whether there were two men or more.

Not much of a clue for the police to go on, you will admit. And while the wretched footman lay gagged and bound and unconscious down below, the burglars had found their way upstairs to Lady Ap-Owen's dressing-room; they had forced open a small safe and got away with jewellery and money to the value of £5,000.

The burglary in Lord Ap-Owen's house would have been a nine days' wonder and would soon have been forgotten except for the fact that it was followed, less than a week later, by another equally daring and equally mysterious.

On this occasion the victim was Sir Andrew Border-Peile, who owns that magnificent house in Prince's Gardens which has been talked about so much of late, and which is filled to repletion with art treasures and bric-a-brac of all kinds. The procedure of the miscreants was similar to that employed at the house of Lord Ap-Owen, which naturally led the public and police to conclude that the same gang had a hand in both. The only difference was that the ring was at the front door this time, but it was also at night when Sir Andrew and Lady Border-Peile were out to dinner and to a theatre afterwards. All the servants had gone to bed with the exception of the butler, an elderly man, who was sitting up awaiting the return of his master and mistress.

The second footman had just gone round to the garage, as the car had been ordered for eleven o'clock, and it was his turn to do duty beside the chauffeur. The butler then went to open the door, and no sooner had he done so than two men fell upon him, struck him a violent blow on the head, gagged and bound him as they had done in the case of Lord Ap-Owen's footman, and left him lying unconscious in the hall, where he was discovered an hour later by Sir Andrew Border-Peile, who had opened the front door with his latchkey, and was the first to enter the house. The burglars in the meanwhile had made their way to the reception-rooms upstairs and broken open some cases which contained a collection of Italian sixteenth-century jewellery of great value; they had also helped themselves to half a dozen or more eighteenth-century French and English miniatures and to some pieces of Elizabethan silver and gold ornaments. Altogether the loss was estimated at something like £30,000.

The butler, questioned by the police, was rather more circumstantial in his description of the men who had assaulted him than Lord Ap-Owen's footman had been. Though he only caught sight of them for a fraction of a minute, he saw them quite distinctly. There were two of them, he said. One was tall and thin with straight features, fair hair, and a small toothbrush moustache; the other was short and dark and very slender, more like a lad of about eighteen than a grown man. The butler was practically sure that he could identify the former if he saw him again, but he was a little more doubtful about the other. Both had their hats pulled down hard over their eyes, so that only the lower part of their faces was visible; but it was the tall, fair man who had knocked him, the butler, down; the young, dark lad had kept his hands buried in the pockets of his overcoat.

But unfortunately this was not by any means the last exploit of the daring gang, for less than a month afterwards they turned their attention to Sir Arthur Seligman's house in Carlton Gardens, and a week after that to the house of the American millionaire, Mr Josiah E. Habutt, in Park Lane, and always the same procedure: the ring at the front or back door, at about 10 or 10.30 on a night when the family happened to be out, the sudden assault, the obvious knowledge, not only of the house and its contents, but of the habits and routine of the household.

The footman at the house in Park Lane, as well as Sir Arthur Seligman's butler, both agreed that one of their assailants was tall and fair and had a small tooth-brush moustache, and the other short and dark and clean-shaven, but with that blue tint about the cheeks and chin peculiar to very dark people — especially foreigners — who have a strong growth of dark beard. This peculiarity, which had escaped Sir Arthur Border-Peile's butler, did away with the idea that one of the burglars was quite young — little more than a lad. In every instance, however, the miscreants, with their soft, broad-brimmed hats, had effectually succeeded in concealing the upper part of their faces.

Needless to say that by this time the public was getting restive. Everyone wanted to know what the police was about; householders in Belgrave and Mayfair no longer felt safe within their homes, and servants in those fashionable quarters of London could not be induced to sit up at night when the family was out. Presently, however, the newspapers had it that the police knew more than they chose to tell. As a matter of

THE TURQUOISE STUD 143

fact, they added, there were important developments pending, and the detective in charge of the case had already a clue as to the identity of the dark young man with the blue chin. He was supposed, on his last visit to a Mayfair mansion, to have left an important clue behind him. There were also hints of a conversation overheard in a Soho restaurant, and gradually the public was led to understand that the gang of burglars would turn out to be a set of swell mobsmen whose arrest was imminent and would cause unparalleled sensation in London.

Through Mr Alverson, who was Assistant-Commissioner in the Criminal Investigation Department and a great personal friend of Mr Mulligan, we knew that all these rumours were absolutely unfounded. The police held no clue whatever. But what the public never knew was that it was on Skin o' my Tooth's advice that the rumour that the C.I.D. did hold a clue was allowed to gain ground. My chief had discussed the case—in which, by the way, he took a keen interest—with Mr Alverson, and the discussion had, as you will understand presently, very remarkable results.

2

But in the meanwhile the mysterious burglars were undeterred by all these rumours. After one or two minor exploits, they created a further sensation by turning their attention to the house of Lady Mary Wern in Grosvenor Street. That charming and beautiful lady, whom all London knows through the numerous photographs of her published almost daily in the illustrated papers, had gone out to dinner that night with some friends. The women servants had, it appears, gone to bed, and the butler, a man named Lemon, was awaiting her Ladyship's return when there came a ring at the front door-bell. Lemon subsequently told the police that he went to answer it without the slightest fear or suspicion, but as soon as he had opened the door he was knocked down and left semi-conscious in the hall, whilst the miscreants made their way upstairs and once more got away with money and jewellery worth some hundreds of pounds.

Unfortunately, in this case the loss was not covered by insurance. Lady Mary Wern was a young war widow who had so far not thought of a second marriage. Her late husband, Colonel Wern, had seemingly left her very well off, for she kept up her house in Grosvenor Street in very nice style, entertained lavishly, went out a great deal, and was always dressed to perfection; but evidently she had no business head and had no one who looked after her affairs, or the matter of the insurance against burglary and theft would have been attended to before now.

It was at this stage of the mysterious drama that the name of Captain Alaric Stegand first came prominently before the newspaper-reading public. Captain Stegand was one of those young colonial officers who had found life in London very agreeable during the war when they were on leave. He was good looking, an excellent dancer, fine tennis-player, and so forth, and soon made many friends. Incidentally he fell desperately in love with Lady Mary Wern, a passion which she in no wise reciprocated. We must suppose that after a season or two he understood that his suit was a hopeless one. Lady Mary's friends declared that she told the young man this in no measured words; nevertheless, not only, it seems, did he refuse to take "No" for an answer, but his luckless love turned to insane jealousy. Even in public he was always ready with reproaches and unpleasant scenes, which very naturally irritated the lady beyond endurance, but what to her was still more unbearable, he took to dogging her footsteps, watching her wherever she went, questioning her servants, and generally playing rather the part of a jealous husband than of an unsuccessful lover.

Thus did the matter stand between these two when, on May 26th, the burglary occurred in Lady Mary Wern's house in

Grosvenor Street. Less than a week afterwards the affair took on a highly sensational turn, when the evening papers announced that a certain Captain Alaric Stegand, a well-known young man about town and member of one of the best clubs in London, had been arrested on a charge connected with what was called by the Press "the West End burglaries."

The police were, as usual, very reticent, but gradually certain facts leaked out, which led the public to draw a sigh of satisfaction at the thought that one at least of that gang of miscreants would speedily be brought to justice. The others would soon follow suit.

What had happened was simply this: Lady Mary Wern's butler had made a certain statement to the police. He told them that at the moment when he was struck violently on the head he had put out his hand to ward off the blow. As he did so his hand came in contact with the breast of his assailant; he grabbed at what turned out to be the miscreant's shirtfront; after that he turned giddy and sick and remembered nothing more until he came to, about an hour later. He struggled to his feet and turned on the light, which the burglars had taken the precaution to switch off. And there on the hall carpet, close to where he had measured his length on the ground, he found a shirt-stud consisting of a turquoise surrounded by tiny brilliants.

Of course, once the police got hold of that stud, they set the best brains in the C.I.D. to follow up the clue. But frankly, at first, little progress was made, for although the detectives soon discovered that the stud had been manufactured by the Jewellers' Alliance of Hatton Garden and Sloane Street, the firm was unable to furnish them with the identity of the customer who had happened to buy it. Many young gentlemen came in, the managers of both branches explained to the Assistant-Commissioner, and made purchases of jewellery over the counter; young ladies, too, would buy a present for their fiance or their brother. Names and addresses of such chance customers were not required and were not asked for.

In the end, as is so often the case in real life, when the hard-working detectives, weary of fruitless journeys and long, purposeless interrogatories, were beginning to lose heart, it was sheer coincidence that shed the first ray of daylight on this extraordinary and mysterious affair and led the police on the track of the owner of the turquoise stud. In this case the deus ex machina was a none other than a young footman named Thomas Hinks, who had been until quite recently in the service of Lady Mary Wern and was now valet to Captain Alaric Stegand, having been recommended to that gentleman by her Ladyship herself. Hinks had still been in her Ladyship's service the night that the burglary occurred, having only taken up his new duties a week or two later. He had, of course, been interrogated by the police, like the other servants of the Grosvenor Street household, and said that he knew about, and had seen, the turquoise stud.

It seems that on the very first evening that he waited on his new employer he noticed that Captain Stegand had a stud exactly like the one which Lemon the butler had found on the floor of the hall in Grosvenor Street after the burglary, and, what's more, it had obviously been one of a pair, for there was the case in which it was kept, with the place—obviously made for its fellow—empty. Thomas Hinks, who did not seem to be a particularly bright lad, had, nevertheless, so he told the police, thought it his duty to come and tell them of his discovery. Whereupon Chief Inspector Rogers, one of the ablest men at Scotland Yard, called personally upon Captain Stegand at the latter's rooms in Clarges Street. It was then close on eight o'clock in the evening. The Captain was out, but expected in any moment. He was going out to dinner, and Hinks was getting his things ready for dressing. He had his master's dress shirt ready with the one turquoise stud in it, and he was able to show Inspector Rogers the empty case, which, very obviously, was constructed to hold a pair.

When presently Captain Stegand arrived at his rooms and found himself being questioned by the police, he was highly indignant; denied, of course, having any connection with any gang of swell mobsmen, and when interrogated on the subject of the missing stud, he declared that he had no idea that the twin of the one which he always wore was missing from its case. As a matter of fact, he said he hardly ever wore two studs, and had certainly not done so for weeks, and therefore had never missed the second stud; whereupon Burke, who was with Inspector Rogers, and who is an uncommonly keen detective, had the brilliant idea of turning out the soiled-linen basket which stood in a corner of the Captain's dressing-room. And in the basket, sure enough, was a soiled shirt, with two stud-holes, recently worn.

"Has this shirt been in this basket for weeks?" Inspector Rogers asked coolly.

The Captain frowned, obviously completely taken aback by this mute contradiction of his positive assertion.

"I don't know," he said hotly, "I never wore that shirt, I swear it."

"Is your valet in the habit of wearing your shirts?" Rogers queried still quite coolly.

Thomas Hinks, obviously terrified out of his wits, looked ready to sink through the floor; the two police officers could not help smiling, when they compared his short, stubby figure with the tall, slim appearance of his master. The neckband of the Captain's shirt would not meet round Hinks' thick, bull-neck by an inch. Burke called the former's attention to this fact.

Captain Stegand shrugged his shoulders.

"I am just as much puzzled as you are," was all he said.

"Absent-minded," Rogers commented with a grin. "That's what you are sometimes, eh? Young gentlemen like you are often absent-minded."

Whereupon Captain Stegand lost his temper, which, of course, did not help matters. In the end he followed the men readily enough to the police station, where he was further questioned by the Assistant-Commissioner. Asked to state if he remembered how he had spent the evening of May 26th, the Captain answered promptly: "I remember perfectly; I was dining that night with a party of friends at the Savoy."

"And no doubt the party did not break up till close upon midnight—or later?" he was asked.

Just for a second or two the Captain hesitated, then he replied curtly:

"Earlier than that, I think."

"At what hour, then?"

"I could not say," he replied equally curtly.

But he gave, willingly enough, the names of his guests on that occasion.

The police did not detain him on that day, but you may be sure that he was closely watched, while investigations were rapidly pushed along and the Captain's story verified. He certainly had dined at the Savoy that night. The head-waiter had still the record of the tables which had been reserved by customers for dinner on that date: one stood in the name of Captain Alaric Stegand, with a party of eight. He was very well known at the restaurant, where he often entertained. But what was established beyond a doubt was that the party broke up soon after ten o'clock.

It seems that the whole party had assembled at 8.30 in the lounge, the whole party, that is, except one, Lady Mary Wern, who telephoned her regrets at the last moment saying that she had caught a slight cold and was unable to go out. Her absence appeared to cast a chill over the merry little party, but more especially over the host, so that the dinner fell rather flat, and by a quarter-past ten the last "good-nights" and "thank-you's" had been said. The host's silence and obvious chagrin was

THE TURQUOISE STUD 149

commented on by the ladies with some amusement, because everyone knew of Captain Stegand's hopeless passion for Lady Mary, of his insane jealousy of her, and his habit of dogging her footsteps, which had the effect of still further alienating the lady's regard for him.

The party having, as stated by all the guests, broken up at 10.15, Captain Stegand was asked how he spent the remainder of the evening, seeing that there was at least one witness ready to state that he had not come home until close upon midnight; a certain Mr Lucas Mander, who had rooms in Clarges Street, in the same house as the Captain, and who had seen and spoken to him on the doorstep coming in at about that time. But to this question Captain Stegand only gave a very evasive reply. He had walked about the streets, he said, aimlessly.

"In which direction?" the Assistant-Commissioner asked him.

"I walked up from the Savoy," the Captain replied, "and strolled for awhile in the Park."

"Nowhere near Grosvenor Street, I suppose?" he was asked.

"I may have been that way. I don't remember."

3

Thus, you see, the net was gradually being drawn closer round the suspected man. Captain Stegand's position was anything but an enviable one: firstly, there was the question of the turquoise stud, the exact fellow of one in his possession, and fitting into the empty space of a case, obviously made for it and its twin. The Captain swore that he did not even know that he had lost it; he did not, in fact, miss it as he so seldom wore a shirt with two stud-holes; and yet there was the tell-tale shirt recently worn and found in the soiled-linen basket.

Then came the question of the alibi—which was not one really, as the Captain found it quite impossible to account for over an hour of that memorable evening. He had walked the streets, he said, between 10.30 and close on midnight, and that was just the time during which the burglary had occurred in Lady Mary Wern's house and her butler, Lemon, was assaulted.

Thirdly, there was also the question of identification: there had been a hue and cry all along after a thin man with fair hair and a tooth-brush moustache, and Captain Stegand was tall, fair, thin, and wore a tiny moustache. And, what's more, Lord Ap-Owen's butler thought he could identify him as the man who had assaulted him, and Lemon, Lady Mary Wern's butler, positively swore that he was the man. But what brought matters to a head and decided the magistrate to grant a warrant for the arrest of Captain Stegand on a charge of assault and burglary was the testimony of two witnesses, an insurance clerk named Pomeroy and a girl, Alice Jenkins; these two came forward voluntarily in answer to an advertisement put in the daily paper by the police. They stated that at eleven o'clock on the evening of the 26th they were walking down Grosvenor Street when they noticed a gentleman in evening dress standing outside one of the houses, as if waiting for someone. They had failed to notice the number of the house, as they were on the opposite side of the road, but just at that moment a car drove up to that same house and a lady got out. She had on a dark cloak, and she was making straight for the steps which led up to the front door, when she caught sight of the gentleman in evening dress, and gave what sounded like a startled cry. Pomeroy and Miss Jenkins had passed on by this time, as the incident did not interest them particularly, but not before they had heard the lady say in a kind of rasping voice:

"What are you doing here?"

The gentleman appeared to mumble something, and then the lady, who by this time had rung the bell at her front door, said still more angrily:

"I call it an outrage—and you'll have cause to regret it one day."

THE TURQUOISE STUD

Questioned on the subject, Captain Stegand refused either to admit or deny the incident; but the two witnesses identified him quite positively as the gentleman in evening dress whom they had seen that evening in Grosvenor Street.

Nor did Lady Mary deny having seen and spoken to Captain Stegand outside her house on that occasion. She had not spoken of the incident before, because, as a matter of fact, she explained that, directly after the incident, and as soon as she entered her house, she heard of the burglary, which event put everything else out of her head.

Captain Stegand, then, was arrested on the 13th of June, rather more than a fortnight after the attack on Lady Mary Wern's house. After formal evidence of arrest was given before the magistrate, the accused was allowed bail—it was for a large sum, I remember—and that same afternoon he walked into our office and asked to see Mr Mulligan. I was not the least surprised to see him; his was just one of those cases which invariably gravitated in the direction of Skin o' my Tooth. Sitting as usual in my cubby-hole, I could see our new client clearly: the straight features, the fair hair, the tell-tale little moustache. He protested his innocence very vigorously, but admitted that his position was giving him and his friends a certain amount of anxiety.

"I seem to be floundering, Mr Mulligan," he said, during the course of the interview, "in a morass of adverse circumstances. That confounded shirt, for instance, I have no idea how it got into the soiled-linen basket, and I swear I never missed that second stud."

"We won't bother about the shirt and the stud just now," Skin o' my Tooth said with that quiet manner of his which always had the effect of calming fears and recreating hope. "We'll just concentrate, if you don't mind, on the actual evening of the 26th, and the hour when you left the Savoy and walked up to

Grosvenor Street. You did go straight to Grosvenor Street, did you not?"

"Yes," the Captain admitted, "I did."

"Why did you?"

Captain Stegand frowned. Obviously he did not like this kind of questioning, but Skin o' my Tooth, looking bland and fat and coy like a Victorian maiden in her teens, raised kind eyes to his.

"You must be frank with me, you know. Captain Stegand," he said quite pleasantly but with an unmistakable note of firmness in his voice, "or I shall be asking you not to waste your time and mine."

"You are quite right, Mr Mulligan," the Captain rejoined with engaging frankness, "and I should be a fool not to trust you implicitly. I left the Savoy that night intending to call at Grosvenor Street to see Lady Mary Wern if she was well enough to receive me. She had telephoned to me just before dinner that she much regretted not being able to join the party as she had promised to do, but she had a slight cold and was afraid to venture out. I was walking up Bond Street when I saw Lady Mary's car turn out of Grosvenor Street, and passing quite close to the kerb where I had come to a standstill, it went down Bond Street and then disappeared in the direction of Piccadilly. Lady Mary was sitting in the car. I did not think then that she had seen me, but I knew later on that she had. Well, Mr Mulligan," the young man went on with a sigh, "I don't see why I should conceal the fact from you that I am deeply attached to Lady Mary Wern, and that an almost insane sense of humiliation and jealousy caused me to forget what was due to her and to myself. Regardless of time or weather, I am ashamed to say that I took my stand outside her house determined to wait all night if necessary and to make what I suppose would be called a scene directly she came home."

"And when the lady did come home," Skin o' my Tooth put in with a smile, "she gave it you straight from the shoulder, eh? and you went home very much chastened, eh?"

"You have hit it," the young man admitted with a shamefaced sigh.

There was a slight, pause, during which I could see the Captain's anxious eyes fixed searchingly upon my chief.

"Well, Mr Mulligan?" he asked abruptly after a while.

"Well, Captain Stegand," Skin o' my Tooth replied slowly, "I don't think I need detain you further today. By the way," he went on, as if on an afterthought, "you know, of course, that while you were on the watch outside Lady Mary Wern's house the butler, so he states, was attacked by two burglars, who afterwards rifled the house and stole some valuable jewellery?"

"I know that now, Mr Mulligan," the Captain replied, "but I did not know it at the time."

"Didn't you see anything?"

"No."

"Not the two men who rang at the front door and knocked the butler down?"

"No. If I had I might have been of some use."

"Of course you might," Skin o' my Tooth assented blandly. "I hadn't thought of that."

"I suppose it all occurred just before I got there."

"I suppose so." Again there was a slight pause, a moment's silence, during which I had to be very careful—had to hold my breath almost—lest I betrayed my presence behind the arras. And presently Skin o' my Tooth rose, intimating that the interview must now come to an end. Captain Stegand still looked very anxious, and, obviously, there was something on his mind over which he was debating with himself whether he would speak of it or not. As usual, Skin o' my Tooth guessed what was troubling his client.

"In the words of the poet, Captain Stegand," he said quietly, "you must trust me not at all or all in all."

"I know, I know," the Captain retorted with a slight frown, "but it's always difficult—"

"Where a lady is concerned," Skin o' my Tooth said, completing the broken sentence. "But not in such a simple case as this, my good sir. What is it?"

"Well, all I wanted to say," the Captain rejoined, as if taking a sudden resolution, "is that you must keep Lady Mary Wern's name out of all this business. I can't bear to think that she should be worried. I would sooner—"

"Go to penal servitude for a crime you did not commit? Is that it?"

"Well! Not exactly, but—"

"Set your mind at rest, Captain Stegand," my chief concluded with a pleasant smile, "we needn't worry the lady about your affairs. And when all this has blown over, you can get married, and on your honeymoon forget all about it."

The Captain slowly shook his head, and for a moment or two his lips were tight set. Then he said with an attempt at light-heartedness.

"I am afraid she won't have me, Mr Mulligan. I offended her irretrievably that night, I am afraid."

"Well, you know." Skin o' my Tooth rejoined, "no lady likes to feel she is being watched by a jealous admirer. And," he added, "I suppose it wasn't the first time."

"I'm afraid not," the Captain admitted, "and I suppose I was a fool. She had already warned me once or twice, but—"

He sighed, and I felt really sorry for him: he seemed so depressed. But, nevertheless, he gave me the impression that in spite of his unfortunate love-affair, and his still more unfortunate position, he appeared to be comforted. Skin o' my Tooth had a wonderful way with him, especially when his clients thoroughly trusted him, and Captain Stegand very

THE TURQUOISE STUD

obviously did so. I was sorry for that young man, and firmly believed that he was the victim of circumstances. He certainly did not look to me the sort of man who could be the leader of a gang of daring miscreants; but then, of course, appearances are so often deceptive, and in any case they do not weigh in the opinion of the officials of the Criminal Investigation Department.

4

Two days later my chief desired me to call for him at his rooms in the Adelphi at eleven o'clock in the evening.

"Come just as you are, Muggins," he said to me, "and don't forget to slip your little Colt in your pocket as well as your police whistle."

He wouldn't tell me then where we were going, but as soon as I arrived at his rooms at the appointed hour, he said to me: "We are going to do a little bit of burglary on our own account. Muggins, and show them what we can do."

"Yes, sir," I said. "Where?"

"At the house of Lady Mary Wern, my friend. From private information received, I happen to know that her ladyship is going to the first night of Gabriel Cowlen's play, and won't be back before midnight. Now I have a particular reason for wishing to enter that house. We may get a rough reception, in which case I shall know that I have made the greatest mistake of my career; but," he added, with that inimitable chuckle of his, whilst he cast down his eyes and assumed that coy Early-Victorian expression which always meant mischief for an evildoer, "I make so few mistakes, that I am going to risk being put in charge of the police for housebreaking; and if any of the household look like attacking me personally, you can at once make play with your Colt. We are armed burglars for the time being, remember."

I have been trained never to make a remark when Skin o' my Tooth tells me of any of his plans, so without a word now I followed him. We took a taxi as far as Burlington House and then walked up to Grosvenor Street. I forget now the number of Lady Mary's house, but anyway, we got there after a few minutes' brisk walking and rang at the front door. It was quite mild, but there was a nasty drizzle, and I was glad that I had thought of putting on an overcoat. I confess to having felt strangely excited; this was just the sort of adventure that appealed to me, even though—or perhaps because—I hadn't the least idea what lay ahead of me. Skin o' my Tooth appeared to be highly elated. He was smoking a huge cigar, and while we waited on the doorstep he rubbed his hands together and chuckled audibly. We waited some time, and at one moment it seemed as if a shade of disappointment passed over my chief's fat, complacent features; the next, however, I once more heard that gleeful chuckle of his. Footsteps were crossing the hall, and a few seconds later the front door was opened by a middle-aged man, sleek and well groomed, in dress trousers and shirt under a morning coat—obviously the butler. Before I had time to realize what was happening, my chief's arm shot out and his clenched fist landed the butler full on the chest. The man staggered, at which I did not wonder, as I know the strength that lurks in Skin o' my Tooth's fat body, and would have measured his length on the hall carpet but for the fact that his hand came in contact with a heavy oak table, to which he clung, while making desperate efforts to recover his breath.

"Quick, man," Skin o' my Tooth now said aloud to me; "the dining-room silver first. Front room on this floor."

I remember that I was all at sea. But it was one of my chief's favourite jokes to spring all kinds of impossible adventures upon me, and then watch with amusement how quickly I succeeded in guessing his intentions. In this instance it was not very difficult. I knew that for some reason which I should understand later on we were supposedly swell mobsmen come to ransack Lady Mary Wern's house. I turned at once in the direction indicated to me by Skin o' my Tooth, but had not gone more than a step or two when the butler, suddenly regaining his breath, called out loudly:

"Thomas! Help! Quick!"

The door beyond the one leading to the dining-room flew open and a young man, short and of stoutish build, rushed out. At sight of us he paused, and for the space of a second or two he stared at us with eyes in which perplexity and fear were clearly indicated. The next moment I could see that he would have fallen on Skin o' my Tooth, but I had my Colt out already, and he threw up his hands.

"Ah, Mr Hinks," Skin o' my Tooth said with a pleasant smile. "I had no idea I should have the felicity of meeting you here. Well, my mate and I want you two gentlemen to go quietly back into the library while we have a little look round. Don't be anxious; we won't disturb the maids."

With his hands still up, the fellow Hinks backed into the library. The butler, to my astonishment, had made no attempt to defend either his friend or his mistress's house. To me he seemed more puzzled than frightened; presently he shook himself like a dog who has had a whipping, and straightened his clothes; then he took a step or two in the direction of the library door.

"The telephone is quite conveniently placed in there, I think," Skin o' my Tooth continued blandly. "You'll be able to call up the police, won't you?"

Hinks had already gone into the library. The butler appeared to hesitate for a moment or two, but without further parley Skin o' my Tooth gave him one of his vigorous punches, which sent him sprawling into the room in the wake of his friend. Skin o' my Tooth then closed the door and turned the key upon them.

"I suppose they will ring up the police now," I whispered.

"Not they," my chief replied with a chuckle; "but they may ring up the captain of their gang, or else make a bolt of it through the window; so while I see to one or two matters, both upstairs and down, you wait here with your ear glued to the keyhole. Should our friends in there attempt to use the telephone, give me our usual emergency call."

He switched off all the lights in the hall, and, guided only by his pocket electric torch, he made his way upstairs, while I remained in total darkness, with ears open for any sound that might come from the library; but none came. A few minutes later Skin o' my Tooth came down again. His fat face was beaming and he was rubbing his pink, podgy hand against his leg—a sure sign that he was pleased with the turn of events.

"No sound from there?" he asked in a whisper, nodding in the direction of the library door.

"None," I replied.

"They are still puzzled," he continued, "which is all to the good, as I didn't want to get the police in here too soon. There were one or two things I was not quite sure about. But now I know, so we'll just pretend that we have departed and then we can telephone to Alverson."

He said something at the top of his voice and then went to the front door, which he opened and reclosed with a bang; then, beckoning to me to follow, he tiptoed across the hall, and together we went down the back stairs, closing behind us the door, which cut the basement off from the hall.

"Now draw the bolts of the back door, Muggins," Skin o' my Tooth said to roe, "while I ring up Alverson. There's sure to be an extension to the telephone somewhere in the basement. I'll meet you here at the foot of the stairs in a moment or two."

I groped my way to the back door and undid the bolts. When I met my chief again I could feel that he was just chuckling with delight.

"Now we can quietly bide our time, Muggins," he said, "and I may safely promise you some fun."

We were in total darkness. I sat down at the foot of the stairs, and after a while Skin o' my Tooth sat down beside me. From time to time he drew a sigh of satisfaction or gave a quick chuckle of delight. He would not allow me to smoke, which was a terrible trial during that hour and a half while we sat there waiting.

"Just patience, Muggins! That's all we want now," he said to me.

Over our heads we could hear at first the two men rattling away at the library door; but it was stout and solid, and apparently they would not go to the length of breaking it open.

Whether after our supposed departure they had made up their minds to telephone for someone in authority over them, or whether one or both had got out by the window, we knew not. But Skin o' my Tooth had been right in his surmise: they did not wish the police to get mixed up in this affair until they had consulted with their chief, whoever he was.

Then all at once we heard the tooting of a motor-horn. A car drew up outside the house, and presently the front door was opened and we heard again the rattling of the library door, which was followed by confused and agitated talking and footsteps going to and fro. This went on for some time, the car still remaining outside the door. After a while we heard the door at the top of the back stairs being opened and a woman's voice saying:

"Shut up! I'd sooner see for myself."

A woman was effectively coming down the stairs; we could hear the rustle made by a heavily beaded gown and the clatter of high heels upon the oilcloth. The woman, whoever it was, guided herself by means of a small electric torch; a man in breeches and leather leggings followed close behind her.

And all at once Skin o' my Tooth switched on the electric light, which lit up the whole of the back stairs and left us both in shadow. The woman gave a scream.

"Who's there?" she called out.

"Only two poor burglars, lady," Skin o' my Tooth replied in a droning, nasal voice, "which can't get out 'cos the back door is locked, blarst it."

By the sudden glare of the electric light I had already recognized Lady Mary Wern. The man behind her might have been her chauffeur. He was tall and thin and fair and had a small toothbrush moustache. Lady Mary turned to him and said curtly:

"Call Lemon and Hinks down, Henry, and throw these men out."

"Ain't you goin' to telephone for the p'lice, lady?" Skin o' my Tooth said, almost whining. "My mate and I we haven't got a home, and we're really happiest sleeping in the p'lice cells or at Wormwood Scrubs. And our third mate, he's already off with a nice swag; so won't you telephone to the p'lice, lady?"

"Do as I tell you, Henry," was Lady Mary's reply to this strange request. "Where is Hinks?"

Hinks, in answer to a call from the chauffeur, had already appeared at the top of the steps, and Lemon was close behind him. The three men would already have been on us, only that Lady Mary was in their way on the narrow stairs. Now she stood aside, flat against the wall to enable them to pass.

"Let me telephone for you, lady," Skin o' my Tooth went on glibly. "I give you my word I'd rather."

He had turned in the direction where stood the telephone; quick as lightning, Henry, the chauffeur, took a flying leap over the banisters, down into the passage, with Hinks immediately behind him. In an instant they were right on Skin o' my Tooth, and a very unequal fight raged for a few seconds whilst I ran to the back door, tore it open, blew my police whistle, then turned back again, revolver in hand, covering the last man, Lemon, who threw up his hands.

I was not really afraid for my chief. He is a past-master in the art of self-defence and as powerful and heavy as a Hercules. He could tackle two men more easily than most people could tackle one, and he had the advantage of position with his back to the wall in a narrow passage. With one eye I could see a medley of arms and legs; with the other I watched every movement, not only of Lemon the butler, but also of Lady Mary. I had them both covered, but I knew very well that I would not dare shoot, whatever they did. I was not in danger of my life, and was not defending my own house and property, nor were my chief and I police officials discharging our duty.

But, of course, neither the lovely lady nor her three accomplices knew who we were. To them we probably were police officers on their track. I could see what was going on in Lady Mary's mind; she was making a superhuman effort to conquer her surprise and terror, and to make a bolt of it, either to conceal certain evidences which would tell against her, or to reach her car and drive away somewhere, anywhere, before the arrival of the police.

However, she had not the time for either of these means of escape, for the next moment we had Inspector Rogers here with Burke and a couple more men. The whole gang tried to brazen it out, of course; Lady Mary talked loudly of "outrage" and "miscreants" and "fools," whilst Henry the chauffeur and Hinks held the now unresisting Skin o' my Tooth pinioned against the wall, swearing that her Ladyship had been attacked by three armed burglars, one of whom had already got away. Rogers, however, allowed them to talk as much as they liked; he had his orders. These had been given to him by Mr Alverson, the Assistant-Commissioner, following the conversation which he had with Skin o' my Tooth on the telephone. He sent Burke and another man upstairs, and there in her Ladyship's wardrobe was the whole paraphernalia of a complete suit of man's clothes, together with the wig and the necessary make-up which she used when she accompanied one of her associates on a burglarious errand. It was she who was the dark, slender lad, who kept her hands in the pockets of her overcoat, as they, by their size and shape, might have betrayed her sex.

It transpired afterwards, chiefly through her own confession, that Captain Stegand had on more than one occasion spied upon her, as she called it. No doubt he was still far from guessing the truth, but she felt that at any moment something might betray her. Thwarted in her nefarious calling, terrified of being found out, that extraordinary woman, young, beautiful, adulated, devised the hellish scheme of throwing suspicion on the man who, quite unconsciously, was threatening her with exposure. Hinks, one of the gang who played the role of footman, took service with Captain Stegand, and the incident of the turquoise stud and the shirt in the soiled-linen basket was devised for the undoing of the wretched Captain and carried through by Hinks; a chance though very faint resemblance to Henry, who acted as chauffeur, did the rest. It was a cruel and wicked revenge to take on an innocent man, who, but for his timely visit to Skin o' my Tooth, might have drifted into the hands of a less skilful lawyer and fallen a victim to a miscarriage of justice.

As you know, Lady Mary Wern never stood her trial. While she was still out on bail she committed suicide by taking an overdose of veronal. Lemon, Hinks, and Henry, her three associates, each got five years. They were men, mind you, quite well born and well educated. What had brought them to this life of crime it is impossible to say. It may have been greed and extravagance, a desire to have a good time and plenty of money to spend without having to work for it; or it may just have been that mad desire for excitement and novel thrills which is such a common state in young people these days.

Of their guilt there was not the shadow of doubt. Certain finger-prints photographed after the attack on the houses of Lord Ap-Owen and of Sir Arthur Seligman, which it seemed at one time could never be traced to their owners, finally furnished the police with the last and most conclusive proof of the guilt of the three men. Strangely enough, no fingerprints could be traced to Lady Mary Wern; the evidence against her was entirely circumstantial — a question of time, false alibis, the make-up found by Skin o' my Tooth in her dressing-room, and so on; but her suicide, of course, set all doubts at rest as to her share in that huge and daring conspiracy. The attack on her house in Grosvenor Street was a blind, done in order to throw dust in the eyes of the police. The dust, however, did not settle in my chief's eyes.

"They were just a shade too clever," he said to me one day a propos of the case, "and there is no worse counsellor in the world than spite. That scheme about the turquoise stud very nearly proved the wretched Captain's undoing; but you remember the insurance clerk and his girl, who saw him standing outside Lady Mary Wern's house the night of the supposed burglary?"

"Yes, I do. I thought their testimony would do for the poor Captain."

"Not a bit of it. It should have proved his salvation from the very first, because if what Lemon the butler had said had been true, the Captain's shirt would have been crumpled, and with its missing stud have presented an untidy appearance which, to my thinking, would not have escaped the attention of the two witnesses. If you remember, they stated that at one moment the accused stood immediately under a street lamp and that they saw him quite distinctly."

"No! No!" he went on, with his coy and gentle smile, "those rascals wanted to be too clever, and the lady was in too great a hurry to vent her spite upon the wretched man. Perhaps if she had waited for a more favourable opportunity to enact the cruel comedy of the missing stud, she might have brought about a miscarriage of justice. Certainly that fellow Hinks was the cleverest rascal of the lot, because he was, of course, the chief performer in what we may call the farce of the missing stud; that touch of the soiled shirt in the basket was a stroke of genius, and I understand was his invention. As for me, Muggins, you know that I have a way of knowing if a man is lying to me or speaking the truth, and the moment I knew that Captain Stegand was not lying, I also knew that the mystery of the burglary in Lady Mary Wern's house and presumably all the other West End burglaries was to be sought inside that house in Grosvenor Street."

And I may as well tell you that when Skin o' my Tooth makes up his mind to a thing, he does not care what means he employs to achieve his end.

8

OVERWHELMING EVIDENCE

Skin o' My Tooth had several interesting cases of fraud to deal with recently, but none, I think, quite so sensational as what was known as the de Momerie succession case. Funny name, isn't it? It comes from Aombrai in Normandy, and the family is one of the oldest in the country, although its members have never figured conspicuously either in politics or in the social world. A title has never come their way, nor have they ever sought to obtain one; you may take it that they are probably too proud to figure in the honours' lists of today. But if you look through the rolls of the early Middle Ages you will come across some de Momeries in various important capacities, mostly in connection with county administration; there have also been several bishops in the family in the course of the centuries, and an Admiral de Momerie greatly distinguished himself in the seventeenth century during the wars against the Dutch.

However, the family history and family traditions of the Momeries have nothing to do with the succession case which created such a sensation a couple of years ago, and which cost the rightful heir half his fortune in legal expenses before he finally established his claim to the entailed estates of Mumbray in Glebeshire; indeed, it is to my chief, Mr Patrick Mulligan, that the present squire owes the fact that he, and not the astute adventurer who claimed those estates, has remained in possession. But it was literally by the skin of his teeth that he won the case, and never did my chief more fully deserve his nickname.

Now let me remind you how it all happened. The old Squire de Momerie, who was a Lieutenant-General in the army, and had served with distinction in the Ashanti and Zulu wars, as well as in New Zealand, was a man cursed with a violent temper. Some thirty years ago he quarrelled with his eldest son, for no apparent reason except that the young man had led rather a wild life at the 'Varsity' and run somewhat heavily into debt; not a very unusual thing for young men to do. But, anyway, the father appears to have taken a very high-handed attitude toward his son in this matter, with the result that young Arthur de Momerie decided to cut his stick, and left home determined to gain his independence by starting life anew somewhere in the colonies. He embarked on the Jenowe en route for South Africa. He arrived in Cape Town all right, and, according to all accounts, he and two or three young jackanapes with whom he had chummed up during the voyage, proceeded to paint the town red for about a month; they got themselves mixed up in various scuffles with the police; young de Momerie even spent some days in prison. Presently, however, there came one of those wild rumours of a fresh goldfield up country; there was a mad rush for claims, and in this rush, somehow or other, all trace of Arthur de Momerie appears to have been lost. Whether he ever reached the new fields and pegged out a claim as some said, whether he quarrelled with his associate, as others declared, and was found one day in his shack with a knife between his shoulder blades, whether he disappeared voluntarily or involuntarily, no one ever knew. From time to time rumours would reach his old home in Glebeshire that he had been seen in various parts of the world, in Africa, Argentina, or China; there was talk at some time that he had been found starving in a doss-house in New York, and at another that he was a noted cinema star, owning a magnificent property at Hollywood and earning £1,000 a day. But, needless to say, none of these rumours was authentic. One thing only was certain, and that was that Arthur de Momerie had cut his stick with a vengeance, and that if he was alive—which, of course, was more than doubtful—he had given up all desire to return to his old home.

His mother had died in the meanwhile; some said of a broken heart.

There was an only daughter, Gertrude, who became one of the most baffling and mysterious personalities in that remarkable case. She was the eldest of the family, and about a year before Arthur left home she had married her first cousin, Archibald de Momerie. This marriage from the family point of view was a most unfortunate one, Archibald being looked upon by all his kindred as a wastrel; in those days society young men and women had not yet taken to the stage as a profession; actors were still held, especially in county society, to be rogues and vagabonds—and Archibald de Momerie was not just an actor, who played in Shakespearian productions at the Lyceum, but he was actually on the music-hall stage—blacked his face and reddened the tip of his nose, wore false eyebrows and a diminutive hat, and sang comic songs—so said "the county" with hands uplifted and eyes turned up to heaven in holy horror.

Needless to say that the old Squire was furious about this marriage; Arthur, too, who was still at Oxford then, and had not yet quarrelled with his father, took a very high tone of disapproval which Gertrude seemed to have resented far more bitterly than she did her father's more arbitrary opposition. Indeed, the Squire actually forbade that actor-fellow, as he called him, the house, whereupon Gertrude, highly incensed, declared her intention never to set foot inside her ancestral home again. As for Arthur, when his turn came to quarrel with his father, he found neither sympathy nor affection in his sister, and it was universally understood that as a matter of fact it was Gertrude who had brought Arthur's extravagances to her father's notice and thus precipitated the quarrel.

Be that as it may, the old Squire was now certainly cut off from his two elder children. The second son, Henry, alone stuck loyally to his father. Just before the outbreak of the war, when all news concerning Arthur de Momerie, however wild and unauthenticated, had ceased to drift Mumbraywards, Henry, then a man approaching middle-age, and a Major in a smart cavalry regiment, was naturally looked upon as the future Squire. He had married the daughter of one of the neighbouring big-wigs, and had a young family of his own. They made their home in London, and only paid short visits twice a year to Mumbray. Then came the war. Major de Momerie quickly rose to the rank of Lieutenant-General, distinguished himself on several occasions, was mentioned in despatches, and retired from active service soon after the Armistice, with a G.C.B. The Squire, now an old man, had continued to live in his magnificent home, in a kind of splendid loneliness; his temper, so it was said, had not improved with time, but he was greatly respected, nevertheless, for the grand way in which he kept up the old county traditions of generosity towards his tenants, regular attendance in church, and lavish subscriptions to local sports and local charities.

He had seemingly in a measure forgiven his daughter, Gertrude. Mrs Archibald de Momerie had not kept to her word that she would never set foot inside Mumbray again. She did more than set foot inside it, she spent not only weeks and months, but some years under the paternal roof. Her husband, according to her, had not done so badly; he had had several good engagements in America and Australia, and it was while he was abroad fulfilling these engagements that Gertrude took more and more frequently to spending her time with her father. It was her brother Henry, always kind and affectionate, who had originally brought about the reconciliation. But Archibald de Momerie proved more resentful, and to the end refused to have anything to do with his father-in-law, who was also his uncle, by the way, and he certainly never did set foot inside Mumbray from the day of his marriage to that of his death—a matter of thirty years. He did now and again, it seems, visit England, but never came to Glebeshire. His wife on those occasions would join him in London. During the war, it seems, he remained in the States, where it appears that he had made quite a name for himself in the cinema world; at any rate, that was what his wife said, and this, of course, was another reason why the proud old Squire of Mumbray never would receive his son-in-law as a gentleman and an equal. All the same, he must have had a pretty good reputation as a cinema producer, because some time after the Armistice Gertrude de Momerie gave it out that her husband had received a splendid offer to manage a moving picture company which had just started production in Russia.

This was about a year before the death of the old Squire, which occurred early in 1923. Archibald de Momerie went out to Moscow in February of that year, and his wife, disdaining the advice of her friends, had actually decided to join him in that distressful city, when her father's health, which had been failing for some time, took on a sudden turn for the worse, and she elected to remain at Mumbray in order to look after him.

It was generally conceded that Gertrude de Momerie nursed her father most devotedly to the end. Great, therefore, was everybody's astonishment, and great must have been her chagrin and disappointment, when it transpired that all that the old man had left her in his will was a paltry £500 a year.

A couple more years went by. General Sir Henry de Momerie was now installed at Mumbray with his family. Having retired from active service, he now devoted the whole of his time to the management of his property and to keeping up the same old traditions which had obtained in his family for hundreds of years; incidentally, he had been very generous to his sister, and supplemented her annuity by settling another £500 a year upon her.

Gertrude de Momerie was now a widow. It was generally understood in the county that her husband had not been able to battle against the rigours of a Russian winter. She had a very sad tale to tell of how he contracted bronchial trouble almost as soon as he arrived in Moscow: hard work, overstrain, not to mention privations, to which he was not accustomed, did the rest. He never had been very strong, it appears, and of course the life of a cinema producer is not always a bed of roses. Gertrude received a telegram from him telling her how ill he was, and begging her to come out to him. She started very pluckily, so she declared, but after a terribly trying journey she arrived in Moscow just too late. Her dear Archibald had died in the hotel where he had made his quarters, and she had a truly terrible time out there, far from home and kindred, alone amongst none too friendly strangers, surrounded with red tape and formalities of all sorts. The funeral, without any religious ceremony, was, she declared, a nightmare, which she was vainly trying to forget.

After that she settled down in a flat in London. But she seldom came to Glebeshire since her widowhood, even though she remained on terms of close friendship with her brother Henry and his wife.

2

The first intimation of the sensational affair occurred when Sir Jeremiah Pomfrait, who was the de Momerie family solicitor, and had been one of the executors under the late Squire's will, received a communication from Messrs. Cussens and Cussens, solicitors, of Bedford Chambers, announcing the arrival in

England of Mr Arthur de Momerie, eldest son of the late Squire, who demanded an account from Sir Jeremiah of the administration of his father's estate, of which he was now ready to take possession.

A post or two later there came a letter for General Sir Henry de Momerie, beginning, "My dear Four-penny," and ending, "Yrs. affectionately, Barebones." The body of the letter contained a brief announcement of Arthur's arrival in England and his proposed visit to Mumbray; but the point of that letter consisted in the two nicknames, which had been used by the two brothers toward one another when they were schoolboys. Arthur in those days had been known as Barebones because he was very thin and large-boned, and Henry had been known as Fourpenny for no particular reason.

The whole thing partook of the nature of a thunderbolt. I cannot, of course, tell you what General de Momerie's feelings were on the spur of the moment; what he did do was, firstly, to hold his tongue about the matter to his wife, and then to wire to Sir Jeremiah Pomfrait, asking him to come over to Mumbray as soon as possible. He also, on further thought, wired to his sister Gertrude.

Thus there was a regular family gathering, at which, however, Lady de Momerie was not present. As it happens, I am in a position to relate exactly what turn the discussion took, as Skin o' my Tooth subsequently had all the details from Sir Jeremiah's notes. The latter, I must tell you, took the stand that the whole thing was an imposture. He spoke of the Tichborne case, and of Arthur Orton, the butcher; but the General could not, it seems, get over that letter he had received with those once so familiar nicknames.

"Fourpenny," he had said at the beginning of the interview with a sigh of puzzlement; "no one but Arthur ever called me 'Fourpenny,' and it is forty years since last I heard anyone call me that. And then 'Barebones'—that beats me, too—who could possibly know after all these years that I used to call old Arthur 'Barebones?'"

Gertrude de Momerie was silent, too, in her way; but hers was the way of uncompromising incredulity.

"Just another Arthur Orton," she agreed with Sir Jeremiah in her own determined manner. "You may take it from me, Sir Jeremiah, that if Arthur had been alive all these years he would not have left my father or my brother Henry alone; he would have been constantly at both of them, or at me, with demands for money. People said, I know, that he had made good, and that he was resentful, and therefore had made no attempt to return to Glebeshire. Well! I don't believe it. Arthur was not one to make good, and I am far more inclined to believe the story that he ended his days in a doss-house in New York."

"Don't say that, Gertrude," the General put in gently. "It is unkind to the memory of Arthur—if he is dead."

"Dead!" Mrs de Momerie retorted acidly, "of course he is dead. Wouldn't he have gone on sponging on father if he was not?"

"But," the General argued with a sign of puzzlement, "Arthur never sponged on father, as you put it, from the time he left home."

"Not during the first few years," Gertrude was willing to admit, "but afterwards he did."

"I never heard of his doing so," the General rejoined firmly. "I think father would have told me if he had heard from poor old Arthur."

"Apparently he did not, though. But I know for a fact that Arthur did write to father, and when father did not respond to his demands for money, he wrote to me and tried to sponge on me."

"How do you mean? Arthur tried to sponge on you? How? When?"

Gertrude de Momerie did not reply immediately; she sat with lips tightly set, and eyes fixed searchingly upon her brother. Sir Jeremiah Pomfrait put it down in his notes that she gave him the impression at the time as if she half-regretted what she had said, and was trying to make up her mind whether to speak more fully or to entrench herself behind a barrier of silence. At last she said:

"Arthur wrote to me on two or three occasions, the last time just before the war. The burden of his letters was always the same; that he was on his beam-ends, that he had asked father for help, but had received no reply to his letters. He begged me to do something for him."

"And," the General asked, "did you?"

"Yes," Gertrude replied, "I did."

"You never said anything to me about it."

"I thought you knew."

"How should I know?"

"I thought father must have told you."

Once more there was silence in the stately room where this strange family conclave was being held. Mrs de Momerie was no doubt beginning to feel that her attitude with regard to the supposedly dead brother had aroused, both in Sir Henry and in the family solicitor, a certain measure of mistrust, not to say antagonism, against her.

"Have you kept any of those letters you speak of, Mrs de Momerie?" Sir Jeremiah asked after a moment or two.

"I am not sure about all of them," Gertrude replied. "But I know I can lay my hands on the last one."

"When was that written?"

"Just after the outbreak of the war."

"As lately as that!" Sir Henry broke in, with a note almost of horror in his tone and in the look which he threw to his sister. "Great heavens! You should have told me, Gertrude," he added indignantly.

"I thought you knew," Gertrude reiterated obstinately.

"One moment, please," Sir Jeremiah now put in coolly. "Let us have all these facts correctly."

He turned and faced Mrs de Momerie squarely.

"You had a letter, you say," he asked her, "from your brother Arthur soon after the outbreak of the war?"

"Yes, I did," she replied coolly.

"Where from?"

"From Edmonton, Alberta. I was to send the reply care of the Canadian National Stores there. Arthur told me that he had been working on a farm in Alberta for the past two years, that he thought of joining the Canadian Expeditionary Force, but that he had been unable to save a sixpence and wanted a little money to get himself a few necessaries. He also told me in the letter that he had written to father, but had received no reply whatever, so he supposed that the old man was as obstinate and as irreconcilable as ever."

"That is false," the General broke in hotly. "I don't believe that father ever got the letters; they were kept back from him—"

He was glaring at his sister now in open hostility, and Sir Jeremiah had to intervene quickly before more fatal words had been spoken.

"One moment, Sir Henry," he begged, and then turned once more to Gertrude de Momerie.

"Now, Mrs de Momerie," he said, "you say that you still have the letter in question?"

"Yes," she replied, "I have."

"What about the handwriting? Without having that other letter before you, should you say that the one which Sir Henry received yesterday was written by your brother Arthur?"

And Sir Jeremiah placed the fateful letter beginning "Dear Fourpenny" before Mrs de Momerie. Frowning, her face pale, her lips once more tightly set, she examined it carefully.

"Nothing," she said dryly and, of course, irrelevantly, "will convince me that this letter was written by Arthur. He was killed at Loos. I have proofs—"

"My dear Gertrude," the General broke in with obvious impatience, "how like a woman! Sir Jeremiah did not ask you what were your convictions. He wanted to know if the handwriting in this letter is, in your opinion, that of our brother Arthur."

"I am quite sure that it is not," she replied stoutly.

"It does not resemble Arthur's handwriting, you mean?" the General insisted.

"I don't think it does."

"Well," Sir Jeremiah now resumed composedly, "if you are right, Mrs de Momerie, it will greatly strengthen our case. Now tell me: you say that in answer to the letter which you received in 1914 you sent your brother some money. In what form did you send it?"

"I sent him a couple of five-pound notes."

"Registered?"

"No."

"Did he acknowledge receipt?"

"He did not. But I concluded that, as my letter was not returned through the Dead Letter Office, he received it all right. On previous occasions when I sent him money he never condescended to acknowledge it."

"We shall have to trace the Canadian National Stores at Edmonton," Sir Jeremiah observed, turning for the moment to Sir Henry; "it should not be difficult."

Then he turned once more to Gertrude de Momerie. "I need not worry you much more, Mrs de Momerie," he said; "one or two little points, and I have finished. Tell me: weren't you surprised when you received that letter from Canada?"

"No," she replied. "During the previous five-and-twenty years I heard from him three or four times. His last letter had come from New York about 1908 or 1909. I remember he said something then about trying his luck in Canada."

"Have you still got that New York letter?"

"I am afraid not."

"Or any previous ones?"

"I don't think I kept any of them."

"But do you remember anything about them?"

"I remember which years I received them and where they came from."

"Ah! That is both good and important. And their contents?"

"Vaguely. But I may have kept one or two," Gertrude de Momerie went on hopefully. "I'll have a good search and let you know."

"You said something just now," the lawyer rejoined, "about having proofs that your brother Arthur was killed at Loos. What did you mean?"

"Just this," she replied. "In the Edmonton letter Arthur said that he meant to join the Canadian Expeditionary Force; he also said that when he took on work as a farm labourer he had dropped his name, and just called himself Arthur, and that he would enlist as John Arthur. Well, I followed the list of casualties in the Canadian forces pretty closely, I can tell you. John Arthur was reported missing, probably killed, after the Battle of Loos. That is nearly ten years ago," she went on coldly, "and I have not heard from him since."

"Until now," the General exclaimed almost involuntarily.

Gertrude de Momerie shrugged her shoulders.

"An imposter," she declared firmly.

"I wish I could think so," Sir Henry retorted with a sigh.

"I am inclined to agree with Mrs de Momerie," Sir Jeremiah put in. "In any case, our policy is one of splendid inactivity. We say nothing; we do nothing. Let the other side attack us; the burden of proving their case lies with them. In the meanwhile we shall collect all possible evidence that will upset their claim. I shall get in touch at once with the Canadian National Stores, also with the Canadian War Records Office, and Mrs de Momerie will kindly send me the Edmonton letter and any other letters she may find. Failing any other letter from your brother Arthur, Mrs de Momerie, I should like you to write me out a tabulated list of those which you remember having received from him, with their contents, as far as possible."

"I am afraid that my sister could hardly be relied upon for that," Sir Henry remarked with a sigh.

"And why not, pray?" Gertrude snapped out sharply.

"You have prejudged the case, my dear," her brother replied quite gently but firmly; "your dislike of Arthur has gone to the length of robbing him of any chance of seeing father before he died or obtaining his forgiveness."

"You mean," she retorted dryly, "that I kept father from seeing Arthur's letters—stole them, in fact. I must thank you for your generous estimate of me."

"My dear," Sir Henry rejoined mildly, "by your own showing—"

"By my own showing," she broke in tartly, "my poor husband and I were the only two members of the family who ever did anything for Arthur; although he behaved like a perfect cad to us at the time of our marriage. But it was Archibald who gave him food and shelter when he was literally starving in New York. How do I know," she went on vehemently apostrophizing her brother, "that he never wrote to you for help? You say he didn't, but how do I know? You place such a Christian construction on my actions that you must forgive me if I do the same by yours. And I tell you straight and as an absolute fact that at least on two occasions when I was staying at Mumbray there was a letter from Arthur, and all father did was to read the letter through once, and without a word throw it straight into the fire."

"I don't believe it," Sir Henry protested hotly. Gertrude shrugged her shoulders and said nothing more. Sir Jeremiah, perplexed and worried, did not know what to make of this heated wordy warfare. He put it down in his notes that Sir Henry gave him the impression of a man groping only for truth, and, above all, desirous of righting a wrong at any cost to himself, if a wrong had indeed been committed. Sir Jeremiah's estimate of Mrs de Momerie, on the other hand, was less complimentary. He certainly had the impression that she was not altogether guiltless of having kept open the breach between the late Squire and his eldest son; whether she had gone to the length of suppressing letters was another and graver mystery which only coming events would reveal.

3

The man who claimed to be Arthur de Momerie was at that time fifty-six years of age or thereabouts. His story was that after his quarrel with his father he had gone to South Africa, made a fortune in the gold-fields, and intended to return home when a murderous attack made upon him laid him on a bed of sickness for months, during which his partner robbed him systematically of everything he possessed.

When at last he recovered sufficiently to be about again, the partner had fled the country, and he, Arthur, found himself practically destitute and with shattered health. He felt too obstinate and too proud to return home until he had made good again. But all his efforts in that direction proved of no avail. He knocked about the world in three continents, but never succeeded in saving a penny. At one time he had sunk so low that he slept in a doss-house in New York. Putting his pride in his pocket, he had made one or two appeals to his father, but the old man had proved hard and irreconcilable. In New York, when he was absolutely on his beam-ends, he met his cousin Archibald, who was then playing a minor part at one of the theatres. Archibald took pity on him and got him a place as scene-shifter, and literally kept him from starvation for years until he, Arthur, finally went to Canada, hoping to get work there on a farm. For some time before this he had dropped his name, as he felt his was too high-sounding for the wretched vagrant that he had become. He was calling himself John Arthur, and it was under that name that he presently joined the Canadian Expeditionary Force. He fell into the hands of the Germans after the Battle of Loos and remained a prisoner until well into 1919, when the camp was broken up and he drifted eastwards to Poland and then north, first to Lithuania and then to Sweden, earning a precarious existence in various ways, chiefly as waiter or barman in the hotels of Warsaw or Stockholm.

More recently he had made his way into Holland; and it was at Amsterdam, in the bar of an hotel where he was serving, that he had heard a party of English visitors talking about Glebeshire and his old home. And thus, by what amounted to a miracle, he heard that his father was dead and that, his own death being presumed, his brother Henry had become the Squire of Mumbray. In a moment all the love for home and kindred revived in his heart; he collected what little money he had and took steamer for England; on the casual advice of a fellow-traveller, he sought out Messrs. Cussens and Cussens, put his case before them, wrote to his brother Henry, and now awaited the day patiently when justice would prevail and place him in possession of his rightful heritage.

Public sympathy, as soon as the whole story became known, was almost unanimous in favour of the claimant. The whole thing was romantic and appealed to the popular imagination.

On the other hand, General Sir Henry de Momerie also had his share of sympathy and, above all, of respect. He was behaving all through like a high-minded gentleman. Acting on his solicitor's advice, he remained in possession of the estates, but it was obvious that this was merely an official attitude; his private one was, equally obviously, a passionate desire to see justice done.

From the first he believed in the claimant, and but for Sir Jeremiah's stern advice would have welcomed him with open arms as his long-lost brother and given up Mumbray to him without any intervention from the law. He could not get over that letter with the two nicknames. Nobody who was alive now, he argued, except his sister Gertrude, could possibly know about those. True, he had not seen his brother Arthur for over thirty years; he himself was a schoolboy of sixteen at Wellington College when the quarrel between father and son occurred, but he had an old photo of Arthur when the latter was a boy at Eton, and there was a picture by Ouless, B.A., of their mother with her three children, then aged thirteen, eleven, and three respectively, and even those in the county who were most sceptical and who were for ever quoting the Tichborne case could not deny the resemblance which undoubtedly existed between the old pictures of Arthur de Momerie as a boy and the middle-aged claimant of today. Any more than any eye—but a prejudiced one—could fail to see that the handwriting of the letter beginning "My dear Fourpenny" was, to the last stroke and the last dot, exactly similar to the one written to Mrs Gertrude de Momerie from Edmonton, Alberta, just before the war.

Indeed, in the Chancery action brought by the claimant for the recovery of his lawful inheritance, Sir Jeremiah Pomfrait and the eminent counsel engaged on behalf of Sir Henry de Momerie had some very hard nuts to crack; so hard that they failed in the attempt. That case lasted fourteen days, two of which were taken up by the learned judge's summing up. There was a formidable array of witnesses, some of whom swore positively that the claimant was Arthur de Momerie, whilst others swore equally positively that he was not. The most important witness for the defence was Mrs Gertrude de

Momerie; her attitude was one of uncompromising hostility toward the claimant: she denied on oath that he was her brother, refused to see the slightest likeness between him and her brother Arthur, or the slightest resemblance between the handwriting in the Edmonton letter and that of the claimant today.

But there were certain points which even she could neither deny nor explain away. I must tell you that she had made an affidavit which, she declared, or rather hoped, would cause the whole fabric of the claimant's story to fall to the ground. Unable to produce any but the last letter, which she stated to have received from her brother Arthur before the war, she gave particulars of the missing letters—the approximate date, the place of origin, and the contents.

Now, the claimant, on his side, had lodged an affidavit stating that he had written to his father and to his sister at different times during the twenty-five years preceding the war, and he also gave the approximate dates of those letters, outlined their contents, and named the places where they were posted. Those which he said he had written to his father could not, of course, be substantiated, but as far as the others were concerned his statements coincided point by point with those made by Mrs Gertrude de Momerie.

He had a trying ordeal in the witness-box, which lasted from first to last nearly six hours. Sir Marbury Illcott, the eminent counsel for the defence, had him under cross-examination during the greater part of the time. With the help of a lavish expenditure of money, time, and ingenuity, the defence had built up a theory that the claimant was actually a man named John Arthur, who had knocked about the world, and become acquainted at one time with Arthur de Momerie, and learned from him the various details of past life and past events at Mumbray. To prove this theory, two witnesses had been brought over all the way from Canada, two men who had known and worked with a man named John Arthur on a farm at Alberta; they had lost sight of him at the outbreak of the war, but were told that he had joined the Expeditionary Force. They had known nothing about his circumstances over in England, but always understood that he was a gentleman and had wealthy connections.

Of course, that was all very well as far as it went. The military records of the Canadian Expeditionary Force also went to prove that this same John Arthur had, in spite of his age, succeeded in enlisting in the 2nd Division, and that he was reported missing after the Battle of Loos. But the whole of this theory fell to the ground during the examination and cross-examination of the claimant, whose memory of past events and incidents that had occurred not only at Mumbray, but during his school days at Eton and his university life at Oxford was positively prodigious. No third person could have had such intimate knowledge, unless one was prepared to suppose that Arthur de Momerie had years and years ago made up his mind that a certain John Arthur should impersonate him one day and claim his inheritance, and had deliberately primed him in all those details with a set purpose. That, of course, was an untenable theory. On the other hand, Sir Henry de Momerie, from a spirit of justice, and his sister, from a spirit of spite, had instructed their counsel with regard to all those numerous little details which they declared no one living except themselves or their brother Arthur could possibly know anything about. But never once was the claimant found to be wrong in any essential fact.

Indeed, it is safe to assert that it was the claimant himself who won his own case in the witness-box. Judgment was entered for him amidst cheers—quickly suppressed—from the public, and in the end, when Sir Henry de Momerie was seen walking up to his motor with his arm in that of his newly found brother, a hearty cheer greeted him from the crowd which was waiting outside the Law Courts, and some young people started to sing: "For he's a jolly good fellow!"

And when Gertrude de Momerie presently appeared, she was greeted with more than one decided "Boo!"

4

Now the last act of that curious drama began with the death of Sir Jeremiah Pomfrait. It occurred less than six months after the claimant had settled down in Mumbray, and been enthusiastically called upon by all the county.

Sir Henry de Momerie had stayed on with his supposed brother for a time, in order to help him with the management of the estate and make him acquainted with his tenants and employees. Lady de Momerie had once more settled down in London with her children; she had taken a house in Park Street and the General intended shortly to join her there. Quite apart from the entailed estates, his father, the old Squire, had left him personally quite a considerable sum of money for life in trust for his younger children: Lady de Momerie, too, had a small fortune of her own, and of course he had his pension, so the family was still quite well-off, but not sufficiently so to allow of Sir Henry continuing to give his sister Gertrude £500 a year. However, he was such a kind man that I am sure he did what he could in that direction. He was very much cut up at the death of Sir Jeremiah Pomfrait, who had been a friend of his family for so many years. Little did he guess, when he appeared as one of the chief mourners at the funeral, that this event would be the indirect means of restoring to him his filched heritage.

It was just about the time when that unfortunate Captain Stegand so narrowly escaped penal servitude for burglary, thanks to the courage and ingenuity exerted on his behalf by my chief, and Skin o' my Tooth's name was on every lip. Neither he nor I were, therefore, the least surprised when on a fine July morning a charming, exquisitely dressed lady came to our musty old office and sent in her card, "Lady de Momerie," to my chief.

She had come, she said to Skin o' my Tooth, as soon as she was closeted alone with him—I, "behind the arras" as usual—entirely on impulse. She had met Captain Stegand in society and liked him, and had admired the marvellous way in which his vindication and the punishment of the true evil-doers had been brought about.

Skin o' my Tooth, looking benign and coy, sat before her with eyes downcast and lips pursed, looking very unlike the daring man of action who could bring any miscreant to justice. From my point of vantage I could see a slight frown of puzzlement and of disappointment pass over the lady's brow as she contemplated in silence for a moment or two this; fat and benign Irishman, in whose hands she had decided to place the fate and fortune of her family.

And suddenly he raised his eyes and gave her just one encouraging look. I know that glance. How often had it not brought a poor afflicted creature out of the depths of despair to the first sight of hope! Lady de Momerie was a middle-aged woman, extraordinarily handsome and elegant, but even her beauty took on a more youthful appearance after she had encountered that hope-giving glance.

"Mr Mulligan," she resumed quietly, "let me tell you at once that in all probability you will call me a visionary and advise me to go back home and be content with the life which Providence has mapped out for me. Well, in a way I am content. I am extraordinarily happy with a husband who is one of the kindest and most generous of men; I have three children whom I idolize. But it is because I idolize my children and because my husband is so generous and kind that I cannot bear to see them and him defrauded by one of the most outrageous impostors that ever succeeded in throwing dust into the eyes of justice."

"Ah!" Skin o' my Tooth remarked with a sigh of satisfaction, "you have come to talk to me about the de Momerie claimant?"

She nodded acquiescence. I, too, felt elated at this turn of events, for I knew that my chief had just longed to have one of his fat fingers in that mysterious pie. And now he asked eagerly: "You have some new evidence?"

"No — not that — but —"

"A theory, a suspicion?"

"Neither."

"Then why — ?" Skin o' my Tooth queried with a frown of impatience.

"Why am I taking up your time, you mean?" she broke in with a little catch in her throat. "I can't tell you, Mr Mulligan. I know nothing beyond what transpired during the law case; but I just feel it in my heart that the man is an impostor, and that there is only one man in the world who can unmask him, and that is you."

"Did you ever have a talk with Sir Jeremiah Pomfrait about this?"

"Yes. Once. After the law case. He said that the evidence had been positively overwhelming, and that in any case nothing could be done, now that judgment had been pronounced. He admitted to me that he was just as convinced as I am, and as I suppose my sister-in-law Gertrude is, that the man is an impostor, but he really did not see how he could have combated the evidence successfully. Of course, he was already very ill when I had this conversation with him. Some of his friends believe that he broke his heart over that case."

"Very likely," Skin o' my Tooth rejoined dryly. "And I don't wonder at it."

"What do you mean?"

"That Sir Jeremiah Pomfrait was an old-fashioned lawyer, and went altogether wrong in that case..."

"Then you agree with me?" Lady de Momerie exclaimed eagerly.

Never had I seen my chief look less convincing or astute than he did at this moment, sitting opposite that eager and beautiful woman, with pink cheeks and eyes downcast, like the caricature of an Early Victorian maiden. His black, broadcloth, ill-fitting suit, his bald head, his loose collar and shabby tie, the French novel that protruded from his coat-pocket, all contributed towards the completion of the picture of supineness and inattention which he presented. I could see tears of disappointment gather in Lady de Momerie's eyes. But the next moment, psychologically, everything had changed. Lady de Momerie smiled, and a look of hope and trust illumined her handsome face. She held out her hand with an engaging gesture to my chief, who took it between his own podgy ones and patted it gently.

And this psychological transformation had been wrought solely through Skin o' my Tooth raising his eyes and giving his client just one look.

"Have you patience, Lady de Momerie?" he asked. "Can you wait?"

"How long?"

"It might be a year — or even more. I am waiting for a certain eventuality to occur. Directly after that I can go ahead."

"Will you tell me what it is?"

"Not on your life," he replied with a smile.

"But if it does not occur?"

"It will. I give you my word."

5

Nothing much did occur during the next six months, and my chief strenuously refused to see Lady de Momerie during that time. Poor woman! She must by this time have been on the verge of despair. In the meanwhile Sir Henry had joined her in their London house; the new Squire of Mumbray was now comfortably installed in the magnificent old house, and was leading there such a gay and giddy life as would have caused his sober ancestors to turn in their grave. He entertained lavishly, and spent his money freely. The Mumbray estates had of late increased immensely in value, as now practically the whole of the industrial town of Whittal was built upon land belonging to the new Squire.

You may imagine how the fact of his being a bachelor tended to increase his popularity with the ladies; but for the time being, at any rate, he appeared impervious to every effort that was made to draw him into the net of matrimony. At the same time, with all that entertaining, he did feel the want of a hostess at Mumbray; and presently the county was rather astonished to hear that a reconciliation had been effected between himself and his sister Gertrude. Everyone felt that the Squire showed a real Christian spirit by forgiving her spiteful opposition to his claim. Anyway, Mrs de Momerie arrived at Mumbray and soon installed herself there as the virtual hostess. Gossips declared that she would see to it that her brother never married, and that no new mistress of Mumbray should ever oust her from her enviable position.

It was soon after these events that my chief's interest in the de Momerie case appeared to revive. He did not say much to me, because that was not his way; but I knew at the time that he went down into Lancashire and stayed in a small village called St. Anselm's Cray. I also knew that he remained in constant communication with an old woman who lived there and whose name was Mrs Crowther. After that I was allowed to accompany him to Rugby, but was still kept in the dark as to what he was up to while he had an interview with an old lady who had, it seems, been the matron of one of the houses, thirty or more years ago, and with Dr Fernichan, now retired, who was in practice in Rugby until the war. I may as well tell you that whenever my chief returned from any of those interviews his nice, pink, fat face was beaming, and from time to time he gave that favourite little chuckle of his, which proclaimed that he was satisfied with the way a case was progressing.

Soon after our visit to Rugby—that is to say, in August, 1924—Skin o' my Tooth elected to spend his annual four weeks' holiday in Glebeshire. He rented a small house, quite close to Mumbray, and took me down there with him. Through the kindness of a neighbour, who was a client of my chief's, the latter was introduced to the Squire of Mumbray and to Mrs de Momerie. He was asked to dinner, and even I received invitations to the big garden and tennis parties that had become such a feature of the social life of Glebeshire.

It was at the second of those wonderful parties that Skin o' my Tooth, after having tipped me the wink to follow him, went and took a vacant seat beside Mrs de Momerie, who was watching the tennis. He entered into conversation with her, and presently said casually:

"I wonder, Mrs de Momerie, if you ever knew my friend Mr Archibald de Momerie, the actor and cinema producer?"

"Why, yes!" she replied. "He was my husband."

"No! Really?" Skin o' my Tooth exclaimed, with well-feigned astonishment, "though, of course, the name being such an uncommon one, I guessed that he must have been some relation. But your husband—? Why, he never told me he was married."

"No?" she rejoined coolly. Then added after a second or two, "Where did you meet my husband, Mr Mulligan?"

"In New York," he replied boldly. "He was playing in—let me see—in—oh! I shall forget my own name next—what was it poor old Archie made such a success in, in New York?"

"I really couldn't say," the lady replied coldly. "My husband played many successful parts in his day, both in New York and elsewhere."

"I have no doubt of that," Skin o' my Tooth assented blandly.

He held her glance, although she did give a quick look round, as if trying to find some other guest who would release her from the society of this inquisitive meddler. But for the moment everyone was engrossed in watching the tennis.

"Do just mention one or two of dear old Archie's successes, Mrs de Momerie," Skin o' my Tooth went on with perfect unconcern. "I was so fond of him, you know, and I am so vexed that my memory should be so poor. Tell me what he was playing in just before America came into the war. You must remember that?"

"I really don't, Mr Mulligan, and you must please excuse me. The Duchess has just arrived."

She rose and walked away, leaving Skin o' my Tooth sucking at his cigar, and with an enigmatic smile round his lips.

We were not asked to the next garden-party at Mumbray, but we met the Squire and Mrs de Momerie at the house of our kind neighbour. This time Skin o' my Tooth entered into conversation with the Squire.

"I was so interested in your law case, Mr de Momerie," he said, "because of my old friend Archie. You said he had been so kind to you in New York. That was just like him. What theatre was he playing in when you met him?"

"I really couldn't tell you," the Squire replied abruptly, and turned his back on my chief.

That same afternoon Skin o' my Tooth also got in a few words with Gertrude de Momerie.

"I am going to Russia shortly, Mrs de Momerie, on behalf of a client who is interested in a cinematograph company out there. Marvellous strides those Bolsheviks are making in the industry. I wonder if it is the same company dear old Archie worked for when he was in Moscow?"

"I really couldn't tell you," Gertrude de Momerie replied.

"I could easily find out, couldn't I?" Skin o' my Tooth rejoined blandly; "there have not been more than two or three cinematograph companies operating in Russia since the war. What was the name of the one dear old Archie was connected with?"

But Gertrude de Momerie had already turned away from him. I thought that she was ill, for, as she turned away, she swayed slightly and steadied herself by clinging to the back of a chair.

The next day Skin o' my Tooth wrote to the Squire of Mumbray asking for an interview. This was refused. He wrote again, and was again refused. He called, and was denied admittance. In the meanwhile he had placed certain facts in the hands of the police, also certain affidavits; and presently the claimant and Mrs de Momerie received a letter which they could not very well disregard. Accompanied by Assistant-Commissioner Alverson and myself, my chief made a formal call at Mumbray.

I could not help admiring the woman under the terrible ordeal which she had to undergo during this interview. Mr Alverson stood by incognito; he had three plain-clothes men waiting outside in the garden. I, of course, was too insignificant a personage to be taken notice of by those two clever scoundrels. For clever they were, and scoundrels too, of that there remained not a shadow of doubt, though Mrs de Momerie tried to brazen it all out, and the claimant continued to posture and to bluster like the true actor that he was.

Skin o' my Tooth, however, was the finer actor of the two. The way he began by lulling those two into a semblance of security by talking of dear old Archie was marvellous.

"Dear old chap," he said blandly; "one of the best, you know; but there were certain little irregularities over in New York which we shall have to explain. It will be quite easy, my dear Mrs de Momerie," he went on glibly, because the lady, thrown off her guard for the moment, looked more puzzled now than frightened, "and we will begin by establishing an alibi. Dear old Archie went out to Russia, I understand, in 1920 under contract with a cinematograph company. Now, if we have the name of that company we'll get a proper affidavit from them, sworn before the British Consul at Moscow, that in 1920 they had an English gentleman named Archibald de Momerie in their employ. And so, my dear Mrs de Momerie—"

He paused with pencil poised in one hand, notebooks in another, while Gertrude de Momerie passed her tongue once or twice over her dry lips. "How can I give you the name of a Russian company," she said boldly at last. "It was an outlandish name, and I don't know Russian."

"Ah, well! Never mind, then," Skin o' my Tooth went on suavely. "We must find other means of disproving the scandalous gossip which avers that poor old Archie never was a successful actor in New York, nor a cinema producer anywhere, that after knocking about in various big cities in the States he drifted to Canada, and under the name of John Arthur worked on a farm in Alberta, enlisted in the Expeditionary Force, fell into the hands of the Germans after the Battle of Loos, and after many vicissitudes drifted back to England. Would you believe it, dear Mrs de Momerie? those evil tongues actually say that dear old Archie never went to Russia, and therefore did not die there, but that he is very much alive at the present moment and sitting opposite to me now as the popular Squire of Mumbray."

He sat there so benign and so bland, with podgy hands folded before him, beady eyes watching the play of emotion on the face of those two scoundrels. They looked still brazen and still bold outwardly, but to me they appeared like two unfortunates who, finding themselves suddenly on the edge of a precipice, had looked down and turned giddy.

"Of course, that is all a pack of lies—" the claimant began in a loud, dictatorial voice.

"Of course it is, my dear sir," Skin o' my Tooth assented calmly. "Did I not say that we would disprove it all? Why, I am going to Moscow myself next week to defy the Bolsheviks and find out all I can about that cinematograph company which cost poor old Archie his life."

"It will cost you yours if you don't look out," Gertrude de Momerie said spitefully.

"Oh, I'll look after myself, dear lady," my chief went on, still smiling benignly. "Now, last week when I went over to Loamshire to see dear old Mrs Crowther—" He paused abruptly and then queried with well-feigned anxiety: "You are not feeling well, Mrs de Momerie? Can I ring for something for you?"

Even now she was marvellous, and though her face was the colour of ashes, she said quite firmly: "I am quite well, I thank you. As you were saying—?"

"I was saying that dear old Mrs Crowther was ever so kind to me and so chatty. You know she was your dear husband's nurse, and she told me about that awful burn on his left arm, which he got when he was a schoolboy at Rugby, playing with fireworks. It left a terrible scar from the wrist right up to the elbow—You are sure you are not ill, Mrs de Momerie? Do let me get you something... Well, as I was saying, Mrs Crowther told me that the scar was still there when she saw Archie just before he left for America in 1905. His mother had just died, and he had gone down to Loamshire to wind up her affairs. She left little, if anything, poor dear. Mrs Crowther had remained with her as a maid after Archie had grown up—"

"The old woman is a liar, I should say," Gertrude de Momerie retorted coolly. "Archie's mother was always too poor to keep a maid."

"Ah! Really? How interesting! Now, strangely enough, when I went on to Rugby I came in touch with the matron of the house in which Archie was during his schooltime. She well remembers the dear boy, and also the terrible accident which caused the scar, and the doctor who attended to him at the time—quite an old fellow now—was kind enough to show me his notes about the case. It was a very serious one, and Dr Fernichan assured me that even after fifty years the resultant scar would still be visible, as the flesh was literally scorched to the bone—A glass of water, Mrs de Momerie... or a drop of brandy... I am sure you are ill..."

"Now then... stop that!" This came suddenly from Mr Alverson, as the claimant, or rather Archie de Momerie, as he undoubtedly was, suddenly rose and tried to grip Skin o' my Tooth by the throat. Mr Alverson, who is quick and powerful, soon overpowered him, however, and then sounded his whistle, whereupon the plain-clothes men entered the room by the tall French windows, and Mr Alverson then drew from his pocket the warrant which he held for the arrest of Archibald and Gertrude de Momerie on a charge of conspiracy and fraud.

They went quietly enough both of them. I think they were absolutely dazed with this sudden collapse of the edifice of lies which they had so carefully built up. Their trial on the double charge did not last nearly so long as the original Chancery case had done. Some of the evidence which finally brought them both to justice was absolutely amazing. To my mind, the woman was the more remarkable of the two: the way she had not only planned the fraud for years, but finally put it into execution, was nothing short of staggering. Equally remarkable was the way in which she had played the various roles which she had assigned to herself, such as the sorrowing widow after the supposed death of her husband in Russia, and the circumstantial tale she told of her journeying out to Moscow to see him and finding him already dead in an hotel, of the funeral, and so on; also there was her role of a bitter opponent to the claimant, her reluctance to admit the slightest resemblance in his features or handwriting with her brother Arthur; all that was so admirably done that it was worthy of a better cause.

Directly after the trial at the Central Criminal Court, Sir Henry and Lady de Momerie had an interview with my chief in a private room. Naturally they were eager to know, now that there was no longer any doubt as to the guilt of de Momerie and his wife, what had led Skin o' my Tooth to suspect them at all.

"The case of that scoundrel in Chancery was so overwhelmingly in his favour," they argued.

"It was because it was so overwhelming," my chief replied, "that I turned my attention to the one member of the family who never was mentioned once throughout the case. He was dead, and there was an end of him. But as I was absolutely convinced that Arthur de Momerie was dead, and that the claimant was an impostor, I tried to piece together the few facts I knew about him with the tale he told in court, and I came to the conclusion that, as no one living save an actual member of the family could possibly have known all the minute details of home life which the claimant rattled off so glibly, and as no one but a member of the family could have borne such a striking likeness to the dead man as to deceive those who had known the latter intimately, he could be none other than Archibald de Momerie, cousin and brother-in-law of the rightful Squire; always remembering, of course, that over thirty years had elapsed since either Arthur de Momerie or Archibald had been seen in Glebeshire.

"So I set to work to trace Archibald's early life and family history. That sort of thing is, of course, child's play, once one has the end of the thread in hand. It was only because everyone, including Jeremiah Pomfrait, was so entirely convinced that Archibald de Momerie had died in Russia that no one thought of picking up his tracks.

"It has been an amusing case," he concluded. "Please don't thank me. It is I must thank you for allowing me to have a finger in the pie."

9

THE CASE OF MRS NORRIS

I have always known Skin o' my Tooth to hold the axiom that justice is invariably on the side of the cleverest lawyer. I might as well at this point record the fact that he held the learned gentlemen of the Bar in complete and withering contempt. "They are a necessary evil in the High Courts," he would say; but then, to my esteemed employer, everybody in a court of law, from the judge downwards, was "a necessary evil." He would have liked some arrangement by which he could have argued out a criminal case with another lawyer, that side to win who got the best of the argument.

I can recall one or two very narrow shaves, where a judge and jury's decision really seemed a matter of tossing a halfpenny; it might go either way, and my chief fully deserved the nickname which the public had now universally bestowed upon him. But of the many interesting cases with which Skin o' my Tooth was associated after the Duffield peerage case had brought his name so prominently before the public, none, I think, seemed at the first glance so intricate, and demonstrated his weird gifts more marvellously, than the case of Mrs Norris.

She was a pale, delicate-looking woman; I should not say more than twenty-five years of age, and no doubt among her own friends would be called pretty. Of course, when Skin o' my Tooth saw her in Holloway she was evidently worn out with sleepless nights and half crazy with the horror of the position in which she found herself. Her speech was very incoherent, and the curious mixture of self-accusations and vigorous protestations of innocence, together with the marked obstinacy of her general attitude, would have irritated any man less devoted to his calling than Skin o' my Tooth.

The facts, as far as they were known to the police and the public, and as far as Mrs Norris herself was willing to admit, were briefly these:

On Thursday, April 17th, the inhabitants of Shircroft Mansions, Maida Vale, were startled at eleven o'clock at night by loud screams proceeding from one of the flats. Very soon the door of No. 22 was thrown violently open, and Mrs Norris, who occupied the flat with her husband, came out on the landing, loudly calling for help.

To the neighbours, who immediately responded to her call, she seemed like one demented; her eyes were starting out of her head, her face was livid, and with trembling fingers she was pointing towards her own apartments, whilst, in answer to every query, her quivering mouth murmured repeatedly:

"In there—in the sitting-room!"

At last Mr Daniell, from No. 23, less nervous and excitable than the other neighbours, made up his mind to ascertain what it was that had so completely shattered Mrs Norris' nerves. One glance into the sitting-room, where the electric light was fully turned on, told him the whole gruesome tale. The body of Mr Norris was lying on the floor, with his throat cut. There was no doubt that he was dead—the body was rigid, the face livid, whilst the eyes stared up at the ceiling with a look of infinite terror; in his hand the unfortunate man held, tightly clutched, the razor with which evidently he had put an end to his life.

Following Mr Daniell's example, a few of the neighbours had crowded into the small flat; a young fellow from No. 20, who owned a bicycle, suddenly bethought himself that perhaps a doctor or the police would be needful at this juncture, so he went off, leaving a select few to gaze awestruck and helpless at the rigid body, and to offer well-meant but wholly ineffectual comfort to the half-crazed young widow.

It was, of course, very late in the night when at last the detective-inspector from the station, accompanied by two constables and the police divisional surgeon, came in response to the call from the cyclist. After that the crowd of eager and inquisitive neighbours had, perforce, to retire within the precincts of their respective flats.

From the very first the general public refused to believe in the suicide theory. The morning papers already on the following day threw out vague hints of possible sensational developments. The coroner's inquest held on Monday only confirmed what already everyone had suspected—namely, that Mr Norris had been murdered. The doctor declared that the wound in his throat had not been caused by the sharp razor found clutched in the dead man's hand; it had been inflicted by a much blunter instrument. Now, no knife of any kind was found upon the scene of the tragedy, but a few drops of blood were noticed by the detective-inspector upon the earthenware sink in the kitchen, showing that the murderer had washed his hands and his instrument there. Probably after that he found the razor in the dressing-room, and placed it in his victim's hand in order to raise the question of suicide.

But it was the examination of Mrs Norris which furnished the truly sensational element of the tragedy. She repeated before the coroner what she already had told the police—namely, that on the fateful night she had been out to dine with a friend in the neighbourhood of Swiss Cottage; she came home at eleven o'clock at night, and, going straight into the sitting-room and turning on the electric light, she saw her husband lying on the floor, dead. Horrified beyond measure, she had

THE CASE OF MRS NORRIS

screamed for help. She, too, had at first believed in the theory that Mr Norris had for some unaccountable reason committed suicide; certainly he had no enemy, to her knowledge, and she professed herself quite unable to throw any light upon the mysterious affair.

It appears, however, that her attitude, when originally questioned by the police, was so strange, her confusion and excitement so manifest, that Mason, the detective who had charge of the case, set to work to immediately verify her statements. He saw the friend with whom Mrs Norris had dined the evening of her husband's death, but he also ascertained that she left that friend's house at half-past nine o'clock.

Pressed by the coroner, now she seemed absolutely unable to give any account as to how she spent her time between 9.30 and 11 p.m. She had walked about the streets, she said; but as the night of the 17th had been pouring wet, this statement was, to say the least, peculiar. Unfortunately for her, no one in the Mansions had heard her come in; the outside doors not being closed until 11.30, anyone could easily come in or go out unperceived.

The owners of the other flats in the same building could not give the police much help in the matter. One statement in connection with the Norrises, however, was quite unanimous among all witnesses—namely, that the quarrels between husband and wife amounted to positive scandal. According to Mr Daniell, at No. 23, scarcely a day passed in the Norris menage without a domestic squabble. It was generally supposed that the young wife's extravagance and love of dress, and the husband's ungovernable temper, were the causes of this disunion. On the very night of Mr Norris's death, Mr and Mrs Wyatt, in the flat immediately below his, heard at half-past ten o'clock at night the sound of a scuffle overhead. So loud was it that Mrs Wyatt suggested that her husband should go upstairs and intervene, as she was quite sure Mr Norris was murdering his wife.

I don't think that anyone could blame the police for the course they adopted in this very mysterious affair; they arrested Mrs Norris on a charge of murdering her husband. Brought before the magistrate, she pleaded "Not guilty," and reserved her defence. All along she had repeated her story with wonderful obstinacy—she had dined with a friend, and from 9.30 to 11 had walked about the streets alone. Her whole manner on that subject was confused in the extreme. That there was something here which she wished to hide, was apparent to everyone. But the lie told against her, of course; and were it not for the fact that the magistrate was a peculiarly humane and kindly man, who took pity on her lonely position, and remanded her so that she might obtain legal advice immediately, there is no doubt that she would at once have been committed for trial.

2

It was at this point that Mrs Norris' relations approached Skin o' my Tooth, with the view that he should undertake her defence. The case had interested him from the first, and he was quite ready to give the unfortunate woman the benefit of his great skill.

We saw her in Holloway. She was obviously immensely relieved at having legal advice, and seemed inclined to be less reticent than she had been hitherto.

"I may have acted very thoughtlessly, Mr Mulligan," she said; "but I had no one to advise me; and, really, I have been half-crazy with this horrible accusation hanging over me."

"I think you were very foolish to make such a secret of how you spent your time between 9.30 and 11 on that fateful night; an alibi in a case like yours is imperative. I hope that you have quite made up your mind to be absolutely frank with me."

"I am afraid that when you hear how simple the explanation is, you will think me worse than foolish."

"It doesn't matter what I think at this point," remarked Skin o' my Tooth dryly.

"After I left my friend at 9.30," she began, speaking, I thought, with strange nervousness, "I went on to see another friend, in Hamilton Terrace, with whom I stayed until past eleven o'clock."

"As you say, it is extremely simple," said Skin o' my Tooth, who had noticed her curious and constrained manner, and was looking at her through his thick and fleshy lids. "The alibi is quite perfect. Of course, your friend will corroborate this statement."

She hesitated very palpably; then she added: "I took a taxi to go home—no doubt the driver can be found."

"No doubt; but it was a dark night, and the driver may not be able to identify you accurately. Still, it is additional evidence, your friend's being, of course, the most valuable. Will you give me her name and address, so that I may communicate with her immediately?"

Again Mrs Norris hesitated visibly for a moment before she replied:

"Lady Ralph Morshampton, 196, Hamilton Terrace."

Her attitude was a puzzle to me, and I could see that Skin o' my Tooth was both mystified and vexed. However, he dropped that point for the moment, and questioned Mrs Norris on the probable motive of the murder.

"The police tell me that the rooms had evidently been searched through and through, possibly for money or valuables. Do you know of anything that may have tempted a murderer?"

"Nothing," she replied most emphatically. "We were in very modest circumstances; we never kept money in the house, beyond a few pounds, and we had no valuables of any kind."

"And you cannot account for the wild search which was evidently made through the rooms for something? You know that the dressing-bag was turned inside out, the drawers emptied; even the books in the bookcase were disturbed."

"I don't understand it," she replied, with a return of that strange, nervous wilfulness which was so unaccountable, and which had already so much prejudiced her case; "I cannot account for it in any way."

With marked impatience Skin o' my Tooth rose to go. I could see that he was within an ace of throwing up the case, for it was clear, of course, that Mrs Norris was not absolutely frank, even with him. But the case had gripped him, and this additional puzzle only aroused his further interest in it; it seemed literally to bristle with mysteries. He controlled his rising temper for the moment and took leave of his client, promising to call again early the next morning.

"Why does that woman lie to me?" he said savagely, the moment we were outside. "She knows or guesses the motive of that murder, I'll swear. Is she guilty herself, after all, or is she shielding a friend? And what in Heaven's name has Lady Ralph Morshampton to do with it all?"

I, of course, could not answer these intricate questions, and we returned to Finsbury Square in silence.

We found that during our absence from the office the boy had introduced a visitor into Skin o' my Tooth's private room.

"A lady, sir," he explained. "She wouldn't give her name, and she wouldn't wait here, so I had to show her in."

I followed my chief into his private office, where the visitor was waiting. She was a lady very elegantly dressed, who rose with languid grace to greet Skin o' my Tooth as he entered. "Mr Mulligan?" she asked.

"That is my name," replied my chief, as he drew an easy-chair forward for her and seated himself at his desk, viewing his elegant visitor with more than professional interest.

She seemed a little troubled at what to say next, and looked across at me somewhat doubtfully.

"My confidential clerk," explained Skin o' my Tooth. "As trustworthy as myself. Still, if you wish it, he can go."

"Oh no! Not at all. Since he has your confidence, I have nothing more to say. I did not leave my name with your office boy, Mr Mulligan, as I would wish, as far as possible, that my interview with you should remain confidential. I am Lady Ralph Morshampton. No doubt you know my husband by name: and I came to see you about a matter connected with the murder of a Mr Norris, in Shircroft Mansions."

"Indeed!" commented Skin o' my Tooth.

"Yes," she continued, with more composure. "I know a good deal about this Mrs Norris, who is accused of murdering her husband. As a matter of fact, I think I can explain to you the reason why that cruel and dastardly crime was committed."

"Indeed!" repeated my employer, quite unmoved.

"As a matter of fact, Mrs Norris was in my house only an hour or so before she committed that awful crime. She was pursuing a policy of blackmail against me, Mr Mulligan; and finding that her poor husband would not be a party to that ignoble policy, she made him its victim."

"I don't quite understand."

"I must try to make it quite clear. Before my marriage, Mr Mulligan, I was on the stage; and as it happened just before I was engaged to Lord Ralph Morshampton, a villainous scandal circulated amongst my envious colleagues, coupling my name with that of Adam Norris, a young dramatic author of much promise. Fortunately, that scandal never reached the ears either of the Marquis of Camberiey, my father-in-law, or of the exalted society of which I was about to become a member. I was the daughter of a gentleman, and had always acted in Shakespearian drama only. Society, after my marriage, tolerated me from the first, but now, after strenuous efforts on my part, it has finally accepted me. I have a position within its circles which many envy. In the meanwhile, Adam Norris also married. Through some unaccountable carelessness on his part, which amounts practically to a sin, his wife got to know of that old and buried scandal anent himself and me. He had been fool enough to keep my letters. I believe they were distinctly compromising. I really had not remembered them at all, but Mrs Norris, having caught sight of them once by accident, bethought herself of doing a bit of illicit traffic with them. She was inordinately fond of finery and gaiety, passions which her husband's somewhat modest position would not allow her to indulge in. She wrote to me one day offering to sell me my old letters for a couple of thousand pounds and a few introductions in good society. Now, Mr Mulligan, I am the wife of a very rich man, with plenty of money at my command with which to gratify any passing whim. In this case it was my whim to pay money down and regain possession of those letters sooner than allow my husband and my friends to know of their contents. I wrote to Mrs Norris asking her to come and see me on Thursday evening, the 17th. She came at about ten o'clock, and we had a short interview, in which it was agreed between us that I should give her £4,000 and no introductions, in exchange for the letters. I must tell you that she informed me then that she had not got the letters. Her husband had them still; but she seemed to think that she would have no difficulty in obtaining possession of them. I could not tell you exactly at what hour she left me," concluded Lady Ralph Morshampton coldly, "but I imagine that she went straight home—well—and that she had some difficulty in persuading her husband to give up those letters. What do you think yourself, Mr Mulligan?"

"I was merely wondering, Lady Morshampton, whether you are really convinced in your own mind that Mrs Norris actually murdered her husband?"

"I really have not given that subject a thought. I merely came to you today because I thought that probably she would have given you her own version of her interview with me, and that you might take it into your head to cite me as a witness on her behalf. You will see for yourself, I am sure, that this would do your client no appreciable good; on the contrary, I would furnish the prosecution with a strong additional weapon against her—a motive."

"You forget. Lady Morshampton," retorted Skin my Tooth, taken aback in spite of himself at the extraordinary display of callousness and egoism, "you forget that citing you as a witness would also give an additional motive in my client's defence."

"I don't understand."

"The question of time."

"Oh! That is very vague." she retorted placidly. "I did not wish the servants to know of Mrs Norris's visit; that is why I had fixed the hour ten o'clock, when they were all at supper. I was on the watch for her, and opened the door to her myself. I let her out when our interview was over—I could not tell you at what time that was—and I am quite sure that none of the servants even knew that she had been in the house."

"But your husband?"

"Lord Ralph was in the smoking-room when Mrs Norris called. I heard him go out a quarter of an hour or so later, and he certainly did not come in until after she left."

"Therefore, if I cite you as a witness—"

"You do so at Mrs Norris' risk and peril," said Lady Ralph Morshampton, rising from her chair, and cooler than any cucumber. "I tell you that I could not swear positively at what hour she left me, and I know that she took a taxi lower down the road. I live in Hamilton Terrace, so it was only five minutes' drive at most. I think," she added finally, as she moved gracefully towards the door, "that I have succeeded in convincing you that it would be more prudent to leave my name out of this case altogether, have I not? Perhaps, after all, Mrs Norris was wise and did not mention her visit to me, in which case there is no harm done, as I know I can rely on your discretion. By the way, I have not got those letters yet; will you tell Mrs Norris that the bargain still holds good? Thank you so much. Good morning, Mr Mulligan. A very wet spring, is it not? Let us hope we shall have fine weather for the Easter holidays. Don't trouble to see me down. I haven't my car, of course, but I shall get a taxi outside."

When she had gone Skin o' my Tooth turned to me with a heavy grunt.

"For Heaven's sake, Muggins," he said, "let's have some air! Open those windows. Even the slushy London air is preferable to the moral atmosphere this elegant lady has left behind her."

3

We saw Mrs Norris in prison that same afternoon. The interview was somewhat stormy, as Skin o' my Tooth was furious with her. Nothing enrages him so much as a want of absolute confidence on the part of a client, and I am quite sure that in this instance he would have thrown up the whole case and let Mrs Norris literally go hang, but for the fact that the ever-increasing mysteries in connection with it had roused all his passion for what was interesting in the history of crime.

There was no doubt that Lady Ralph Morshampton's narrative had added fresh mystery to this already bewildering case. Mrs Norris, sternly questioned by Skin o' my Tooth, corroborated it in every detail. The reason why she had so obstinately held her tongue on the subject was because she felt convinced that her attempt at blackmailing, and her avowed interest in obtaining possession of certain letters belonging to her husband, would furnish the prosecution with an additional terrible weapon against her. Moreover, she felt instinctively—and there her instinct did not err—that Lady Ralph Morshampton would prove a bitter enemy whom it would be unwise to drag into the case more than was absolutely necessary.

"I did not dare tell anyone, Mr Mulligan," she pleaded pathetically. "Don't be hard upon me. I was quite convinced that something would turn up to prove that I did not commit that awful crime. I don't believe now that justice can err quite to such an extent."

"You certainly have done your level best to damage your own case," growled Skin o' my Tooth, somewhat mollified; "but now tell me, at what time did you leave Lady Ralph Morshampton?"

"It was just after eleven. I took a taxi and told the driver to put me down at the corner of Elgin Avenue. Shircroft Mansions are just a few yards further on."

"But what about the letters?"

"I haven't got them, Mr Mulligan. Just before the inquest, and before I was accused, I looked for them in their accustomed place, but they had gone."

"Where was their accustomed place?"

"Between some books in the bookcase. I don't think that my husband attached much importance to them. Anyway, I knew that I could easily get at them at any time."

"The police did not find those letters, I know," said Skin o' my Tooth to me later in the day. "It is clear, therefore, that the murderer succeeded in getting hold of them, and clearer still that the crime was committed in order to obtain possession of them. Now, if Mrs Norris speaks the truth, she was with Lady Morshampton until past eleven, when she went straight home."

"Perhaps, after all," I suggested, "Mr Norris committed suicide, and his wife, on coming home, merely hunted for the letters, and, not finding them in their accustomed place, turned the room topsy-turvy before giving the alarm."

To my astonishment, Skin o' my Tooth did not receive my suggestion with the scorn which I feel sure it deserved, and which he usually bestows upon my attempts in that direction. It was clearest of all to me that my esteemed employer was completely at sea for the moment.

"You shall find out for me, Muggins, whether Mrs Norris did speak the truth or not. I give you two days to do it in, and mind you don't mention the subject to me during that time. You know how to set to work, of course?"

"I think I do, sir. In any case, I will have an advertisement ready for all the daily papers tomorrow, and police notices all over the town, for the taxi-driver who drove a lady from Hamilton Terrace to the corner of Elgin Avenue on Thursday, April 17th, at about 11 p.m."

"That's all right, Muggins. You are not quite such an ass as you look. Fire away, then; and whatever you do, don't speak to me for two days."

The next morning my advertisement was in every paper and my notices all over the town. Twenty-four hours after that I knew the name, address, and number of the taxi-driver who drove a lady at the hour, on the day, and to the destination I had mentioned. Unfortunately, he had not seen the lady's face, and certainly would not know her again.

In the meanwhile, life at the office was anything but pleasant. Skin o' my Tooth was in one of those tempers of his during which it was not good to talk to him. That he had got some fixed idea in his mind about that murder I was then already quite sure. I knew the symptoms so well. For all the world like a great frowsy hound smelling blood, he sat for hours curled up in his armchair, smoking his long-stemmed German pipe, whilst even his beloved French novels were discarded. Every now and then I would see that weird and cruel spark flash in his lazy blue eyes. Then I knew that the tracker of blood was on the scent, that he held a clue, and that his mind had already solved the problem which would bring the murderer of Mr Norris inevitably to justice.

I told him the result of my investigations when the two days had elapsed. It was then ten o'clock in the morning, and we had both just arrived at the office.

"Sit down, Muggins," he said. "I expect a visitor."

I could see that he was very excited. He went himself to the door when presently a heavy step was heard in the passage. Skin o' my Tooth's visitor was a big, burly fellow, wrapped from head to foot in a huge overcoat. The word "taxi-driver" seemed to be written all over his rubicund countenance. He had a copy of the Daily Mail in his hand, to which he was pointing somewhat anxiously as he walked into the room.

"You're the gent, ain't you, sir," he asked presently, "who put this 'ere advertisement in the Mail?"

"Yes. I did put that advertisement in; and I got your letter this morning, so you see that I was expecting you."

"Ah!" remarked the man, with a grin of satisfaction. "It says 'ere that you'd give 'un a fiver reward. What you want to know is 'oo drove a gent from 'Amilton Terriss to somewhere near Helgin Havenue on the evening of April 17th?"

"That's it exactly."

"Now, I drove a swell from top of Carlton 'Ill to the corner of Helgin Havenue and Maida Vale at about a quarter past ten on that night. It was pourin' wet; and when I 'ad dropped 'im I went into the Lord Helgin for a drink. Now, about three-quarters of an hour later that same swell picked me up again just as I was turning into Maida Vale, and I took 'im back to 'Amilton Terris."

"You don't know to what number?"

"No, I don't; but I'd know that swell again if I saw him. I thought 'e looked as if 'e'd been drinking when 'e drove home—his clothes were all anyhow. 'E 'ad on a silk scarf round his neck, which 'e left in my cab."

"I suppose you won't mind throwing that scarf in with the most valuable information you have been good enough to give me," suggested Skin o' my Tooth, "and for which I shall have much pleasure in handing you the promised five-pound note?"

A broad grin illuminated the worthy chauffeur's countenance. He drew from his pocket a large coloured silk scarf, which he placed on the desk. Then he stretched out a very large and very grimy fist towards the crisp bank-note which Skin o' my Tooth was holding out towards him.

"I am mighty glad, sir, that my effort of memory is worth all that to ye," he said sententiously.

"Not to me, my man," said Skin o' my Tooth, with a smile, "but to an unfortunate woman whom your excellent memory has saved from the gallows."

"Lor'! It ain't a case of murder, is it? I don't like that."

"Remember that you told this young gentleman here and myself that you would know the swell again," said Skin o' my Tooth sternly.

"Yes. I would," replied the man, scratching his shaggy old head, "but I don't like to be mixed up with p'lice and things."

"Must do something for your five-pound note, eh?"

"Well, sir, p'r'aps you're right."

He was inclined to be loquacious, but Skin o' my Tooth, having got what he wanted, was eager to be rid of him. I showed the amiable driver out. I was longing to ask my chief a hundred questions. I found him sitting beside his desk, carefully examining the coloured silk scarf.

"There are stains on it, Muggins," he said quietly. "I am in luck today."

"But I don't understand, sir. What was the advertisement about, and who was 'the swell' who drove from Hamilton Terrace to Elgin Avenue and back?"

"Why, Muggins, you are even a bigger ass than I took you to be. The swell, my boy, was Lord Ralph Morshampton, the murderer of Adam Norris."

"But—"

THE CASE OF MRS NORRIS

"I suspected it the moment I saw that very elegant, very egoistical woman of the world, but I was afraid that it would be very difficult to prove. It was, no doubt, all settled between him and his wife, and Lady Ralph arranged that the interview between herself and Mrs Norris should take place at a moment when it would be most convenient for my lord to tackle the unfortunate dramatic author; this insured the wife being safely out of the way. I don't suppose for a moment that murder was premeditated. Lord Ralph Morshampton probably lost his temper, and, finding Adam Norris obdurate, knocked him down."

"But what made you think of it all, sir?"

"Only this, Muggins, that when people tell a lie I immediately look about me for the motive which made them tell that particular lie. Lady Ralph Morshampton, if you remember, told me that her husband is a very rich man, and that she had plenty of money at her command with which to gratify any passing whim. Now, that is not true. Lord Ralph Morshampton is a younger brother of the present Marquis of Camberley. His father, the late Marquis, left each of his sons an annuity of £3,000 a year, payable out of the estate.

"My inquiries into Lord Ralph Morshampton's financial position, as compared with the lie his wife had told me, gave me the first inkling—call it intuition if you will—of the possible state of the case, for clearly Lady Ralph could not indulge in the luxury of buying those letters for £4,000, however eager she might be to possess them; her appointment with Mrs Norris, therefore, was a feint, either in order to gain time or in order to devise some other means of gaining possession of those letters. After that, Muggins, taking it absolutely for granted that the murder was committed for the sake of those letters, it became easy enough to reduce the number of people interested in their possession to three; there was Mrs Norris, who wanted to sell them, and Lady Ralph Morshampton, who wished to destroy them. Putting aside the question that the murder was really far too gruesome and horrible for any woman of refinement to have committed, it soon became an established fact that the two ladies were actually together at 196, Hamilton Terrace at the time that the murder was being perpetrated. You remember that the people in the flat below the one occupied by Mr Norris heard the noise and scuffle at half-past ten. There then loomed before me the question of Lord Ralph, the husband. I made inquiries among the servants of Hamilton Terrace and among the neighbours, and learned that he was passionately fond of his wife, and ever eager to hide her past history before his relatives and friends; he, too, then, would have a motive—far stronger than any, since it concerned the woman he loved—to bury for ever a scandal which might injure her position in society. Having got the motive, I soon sought for proof. I remembered that Lady Ralph Morshampton herself had said that her husband left the house at a quarter past ten. I surmised that he would go to Shircroft Mansions to see Adam Norris, and that since he would not have much time at his command, he would go there in a taxi. I advertised in the terms you know already, and got this morning the very proof I sought for. You see, the whole matter became child's play once I had a clue."

"It was instinct, sir," I said, with genuine admiration, "marvellous intuition."

"Call it reflection, my boy, and you'll be about right. You see, the moment those letters were destroyed the Morshamptons' name slipped, as it were, right out of the case. My lady was right when she concluded that I could never have cited her on Mrs Norris' behalf. She was quite ready to see the unfortunate woman go to the gallows, and to swear anything that would achieve that end. That is why I am inclined to think that she planned the whole thing, while her husband was but half willing. Now, Muggins, run along and take this muffler to Scotland Yard. Mrs Norris comes up before the magistrate tomorrow. Poor woman! She has had a narrow shave; but what a fool she has been!"

Mrs Norris was discharged by the magistrate.

Everyone remembers, no doubt, the awful sensation caused by the suicide of Lord Ralph Morshampton in his house in Hamilton Terrace. As there is always a special law for those in his position, the whole matter of his guilt in the murder of Adam Norris was most effectually hushed up by the police, and the public never got to know the name of "the swell" who drove to Shircroft Mansions at a quarter past ten on that fatal night.

10

THE MURTON-BRABY MURDER

There is no occasion for me, I take it, to chronicle here the various cases which, following on that of Mrs Norris, have made Skin o' my Tooth's name a familiar one throughout England. The Dartmouth Murder, the Trentham Will Case, and many others, are too well known to bear repetition; but I am not quite sure whether the public—the newspaper reading public, I mean—ever fully realized all the difficulties which surrounded the case of young Mr Spender-Cole in connection with the Murton-Braby tragedy. To be quite candid, I was one of those who firmly believed in Mr Spender-Cole's guilt, and even now—but that is neither here nor there, for the facts, after all, cannot be denied, and they were as follows:

It appears that at eleven o'clock at night on Wednesday, August 14th, there was a sudden alarm of fire in the small farm belonging to Mr Earnslaw, which is immediately behind his house.

He was not yet in bed, and evidently intended at once to go and see what was amiss. Anyway, less than two minutes after the alarm of fire was raised, a loud cry of "Help!" and "Murder!" was heard from the direction of the house. Servants from the house and from the farm ran to the spot whence had proceeded the cry, and, to their horror, found Mr Earnslaw lying on the ground just outside the back door, and bleeding profusely from a wound in the chest.

The fire in the farmyard was quickly extinguished, and but little damage was done, but poor Mr Earnslaw's injuries proved to be mortal. He had been stabbed with terrific violence with some large clasp-knife or other weapon of that description, and only lived long enough to state that in the darkness, and also in the suddenness of the attack, he had not been able to recognize his assailant.

It became a terribly hard task to break the awful news to Miss Barbara, Mr Earnslaw's only daughter. She had been in her room, quietly getting into bed, while the awful tragedy which rendered her an orphan was being enacted downstairs; and as her room was in the front of the house, she had not heard her father's cry for help, and only vaguely the noise connected with the fire, to which she had paid no attention.

She proved herself to be, however, much more sensible, cool, and level-headed than anyone would have given so young a girl credit for. With wonderful clearness and presence of mind she gave the necessary orders for conveying her father to his room without causing him needless pain, and then despatched two of the farm servants to Bletchwick for a doctor and the police.

From the very first the whole of the newspaper-reading public took the keenest interest in the extraordinary circumstances which attended the Murton-Braby tragedy. Murder, pure and simple, without any attempt at robbery, has always a great element of excitement and sensation connected with it; it at once suggests some great, all-absorbing, evil passion as its mainspring—revenge, love, or both combined; bitter enmity or deadly hate. In the case of the murder of Mr Earnslaw, the difficulty with which the police had to contend did not so much consist in ascertaining whether he had a bitter enemy at all, as in trying to discover which of his many enemies hated him sufficiently to risk hanging for the sake of putting him out of the world.

Mr Earnslaw was supposed to hail from New Zealand, I believe; but beyond that—even in the dens of gossip which English country places usually are—no one knew anything about his antecedents. It was generally supposed that he had made his money—of which he seemed to have plenty—in illicit traffic of some sort. At a time when the whole Empire was teeming with enthusiasm and loyalty, he was that peculiar anomaly, a colonial pro-German. His views on that subject, which he aired with arrogant freedom, did not tend to make him popular in the county.

Why he had chosen to settle down in the guise of an English country gentleman, in a remote Somersetshire village, no one knew or cared; and as far as the county families were concerned, he was left severely alone. On the other hand, a certain amount of genuine sympathy was shown to Miss Barbara in her isolated position. The fact that she was peculiarly good looking may have had something to do with this sympathy—at any rate, on the part of the male members of those same county families. One or two rumours, even, had been lately current in the immediate neighbourhood of Murton-Braby, of an impending marriage between Miss Barbara Earnslaw, daughter of Mr Earnslaw, of Murton Farm, and one or the other of the eligible county bachelors, foremost among these supposed aspirants being the young Earl of Alderdale and Mr Spender-Cole.

Needless to say, the relatives of both these young men did their utmost to give these rumours the lie, an alliance with the daughter of the notorious pro-German meaning probable social ruin in loyal Somersetshire. Moreover, Mr Earnslaw himself strongly objected to the attentions paid to his daughter, and more than one servant at Murton Farm could testify to the quarrel which ensued when the master peremptorily forbade Mr Spender-Cole ever to set foot inside his house again.

This quarrel occurred precisely in the morning of August the 14th, and it was the evening of the same day that Mr Earnslaw was murdered.

2

The police were, of course, severely criticized for bringing forward a witness of the mental calibre of James Pecover. But how it happened was this: it seemed at first quite impossible to obtain the slightest clue with regard to the murderer of Mr Earnslaw. In the country, at eleven o'clock at night, most servants have already gone to bed; no one was about in Murton Farm until the alarm of fire sent everyone out of doors, and then everyone rushed towards the more distant haystack, whence the flames and smoke proceeded, and busied themselves with hose and pump, while the unfortunate master of the house was being murdered less than a hundred yards away. The murderer had thus been able to slip away from the grounds absolutely unperceived. In spite of the most strenuous efforts on the part of McMurdoch—one of the most able men on the detective staff—there did not come to light the faintest trace which might have led to the identification of the murderer. Completely at a loss where to turn for a clue, the police at the inquest—which was held in the dining-room at Murton Farm, on the 17th—had to admit that they had no evidence to place before the coroner. At this juncture Mrs Pecover, the wife of Mr Earnslaw's head gardener, timidly suggested that she was quite sure her son could throw some light upon the mystery. He had been, as was his invariable custom, mooning about the garden that evening, and she thought, from what he had told her, that he had seen something.

James Pecover was a vigorous but half-witted lad, who sometimes, when he was sane, helped his father in the garden, but otherwise was quite helpless and incapable; in his childhood his parents had believed him to be tongue-tied;

and even now that he was grown up he hardly ever spoke, and then only under the pressure of some strong excitement. The only person who had any influence over him, and who even, at times, succeeded in turning the half-witted lad almost into a rational being, was Miss Barbara Earnslaw. She had been wonderfully kind and patient with him, and the poor, half-witted creature had in consequence bestowed upon her what little affection he was capable of. His indignation at the murder of Miss Barbara's father expressed itself with peculiar intensity; and his mother said that it had been quite pathetic to watch the efforts of his feeble mind trying to explain a certain something which he had evidently seen.

Of course, it was a moot point whether such a person should have been allowed to make a statement at all; nor had the police, I know, the faintest intention of taking serious notice of James Pecover's evidence; but they did hope that his half-coherent statement might give them the first inkling of truth in the impenetrable mystery which surrounded the crime.

Examined at the inquest, James Pecover, however, refused to speak. He stared about him with an inane smile on his soulless face. After ten minutes' patient questioning, the coroner would have given up the task but for Miss Earnslaw, who came to the rescue with that same wonderful self-possession which had characterized her throughout this trying ordeal.

"My father has been cruelly murdered," she explained. "Whatever I can do to bring his murderer to justice, I will undertake, however painful the duty may be."

The coroner adjourned the inquest until the morrow; and when the public had retired. Miss Barbara, aided by him, attempted with almost superhuman patience to elicit information from the poor idiot.

At a word from her, James Pecover was ready to speak. He had, as usual, strolled about the garden the whole evening; whether he had heard the alarm of fire or not, he could not say;

anyway, he paid no attention to it, but remained in the garden close to the house. He saw someone standing among the shrubs close to the back door. Then Mr Earnslaw came out, and there was a sudden scuffle and a scream. Pecover had not quite realized what had happened; the next thing he remembered was seeing Mr Earnslaw fall forward and his assailant run away. Then he, too, fled, for he was frightened and sick.

"You did not see who it was that struck my father?" asked Miss Barbara.

The idiot nodded.

"Do you know who it was, then?"

Again James Pecover nodded excitedly.

"Then it was somebody you know?"

"Yes, Miss Barbara," he stammered.

"Who was it?"

The idiot's face expressed a hopeless blank.

Patiently the coroner, aided by Miss Barbara, named in turn every person employed about Mr Earnslaw's property, and also some of the tradespeople of Murton-Braby or Bletchwick, with whom the arrogant pro-German had been notedly unpopular. But to each of these names the idiot shook his head with emphatic energy.

At last, moved by a sudden thought, Miss Barbara got up and left the room. She returned two minutes later carrying a large packet of photographs.

"Now, James," she said very gently, taking the idiot's hand in hers and forcing him by the magnetism of her great sympathy to look straight into her eyes, "look through these pictures and see if among them you can find that of the man who killed my father and left me an orphan."

James Pecover evidently understood what was expected of him, for with extraordinary care and deliberation he looked at each photograph and put it on one side. Suddenly, with violent energy, he took up a picture of a young man, and, pointing at it with trembling fingers, he said with perfect coherence: "This is the man, Miss Barbara. I saw him as plainly as I see you. He wore brown knickerbockers, a Norfolk coat, and a straw hat. He killed Mr Earnslaw. I saw him. Give me the chance and I'll kill him, too!"

The coroner took the photograph from James Pecover's trembling hands. It was that of Mr Spender-Cole.

3

The coroner, I understand, refused to take any official cognizance of James Pecover's statements. At the adjourned inquest on the Monday following, he was not brought forward as a witness, and a verdict of "Wilful murder against some person or persons unknown" was returned. But Miss Barbara had no legal scruples of any kind. She determined to bring the murder of her father home to its perpetrator; and directly after the verdict she saw McMurdoch, told him of the clue she held, and begged him in any case to follow it up, if only to set her mind at rest and prove its falseness.

The results were such that even the detective was taken aback. Within forty-eight hours he had collected evidence to prove that Mr Spender-Cole was seen, by three witnesses who passed him on the road, to enter the grounds of Murton Farm at about a quarter-past ten on the evening of the 14th; he was then wearing the brown knickerbockers, the Norfolk coat, and straw hat described by James Pecover. His servants and family at Bletchwick Towers said that he was out the whole of that evening, only returning home at half-past eleven. Then, the whole question of Mr Earnslaw's quarrels with the young man was raised. Mr Spender-Cole had had several open disagreements with the Colonial pro-Boche, and on the very morning preceding the crime Mr Earnslaw had, in most insulting terms, forbidden him the door.

THE MURTON-BRABY MURDER

Miss Barbara's attitude throughout this time was one of passive coldness. Though many people in the county believed that she had been attached to Mr Spender-Cole, and would have married him but for her father's peremptory and strenuous opposition, her only wish in the matter was to bring her father's murderer to justice, whoever he might be. She heard with the same perfect impassiveness that the police had, after very arduous investigation and with due forethought, at last decided to apply for a warrant for the arrest of Mr Spender-Cole on the capital charge.

Throughout all these preliminaries Skin o' my Tooth had watched the case with unflagging interest. He had on more than one occasion declared to me that it was one of the most exciting ones he had ever come across, and expressed the hope and the belief that whoever was accused of the murder, that person should entrust his defence to him. It was only natural, when the evidence became so overwhelming against Mr Spender-Cole as to call for his arrest, that his relatives should place the unfortunate young man's case in the hands of the ablest lawyer in the British Isles. The Spender-Coles are very wealthy county people, Bletchwick Towers being one of the show places in Somersetshire. Skin o' my Tooth knew that money would be no object, and that his own interests as well as his professional enthusiasm would allow him to throw himself heart and soul into the mazes of the exciting case.

We journeyed down to Bletchwick on a fine August afternoon, and the next morning saw Mr Spender-Cole in gaol. He was a good-looking young fellow, I thought, somewhat of the gipsy type, with very dark skin and large, brown eyes. He appeared very delighted to see my chief, in whom he expressed his fullest confidence.

"You can get me out of this, Mr Mulligan, I know," he said quite cheerfully. "I have not done this thing, whatever I may have wished to do, and I am sure that no grave miscarriage of justice will occur in my case."

"I am equally convinced of that fact," replied Skin o' my Tooth pleasantly; "and, therefore, if you are wise, you will tell me the whole truth, good or bad, about this unfortunate business."

"Well, I am afraid some of it is pretty bad, Mr Mulligan," said the young man, blushing even underneath his swarthy skin. "You see, I unfortunately did go to Murton Farm on that night, less than half a hour before that murder was committed; and as I went to see a lady, my visit had necessarily to be kept secret."

"A lady?"

"I had better be quite frank with you, Mr Mulligan. My terrible position will account for my somewhat unchivalrous attitude. You must know that for some time I had been very deeply attached to Miss Barbara Earnslaw, and had every reason to believe that my love for her was reciprocated. She frequently wrote me in terms of the deepest love, and had pledged herself to me with all the passion her strong nature was capable of. I worshipped her, and she had made me supremely happy, and I was only too ready to make her my wife before all the world as soon as she would give her consent. But her father saw fit to disapprove of me as a future son-in-law, hence the many quarrels that arose between us. But I hoped to break down—some day soon—that barrier of filial deference which Barbara still placed between me and my wish to make her my wife. I thought I had at last succeeded, Mr Mulligan, when suddenly without any warning her feelings for me seemed to change. She treated me with marked coldness and refused even to come and see me at our usual trysting-place. I begged for an explanation. In reply I had a curt note from her, requesting my presence in the shrubbery at Murton Farm on the evening of the 14th, at about ten o'clock, and demanding that I should bring with me all the letters and tokens I had ever received from her. It was a terrible blow, Mr Mulligan, for of course I knew at once that something was amiss. I met Mr Earnslaw that morning, for, like a love-sick idiot, I haunted the precincts, of Murton Farm all day. He took that opportunity of forbidding me his house; and I had then to remember that he was Barbara's father, or I should have knocked him down. However, I obeyed my orders, and was in the shrubbery by a quarter past ten. It all occurred just as I had feared. I was given my congé, with but a few regrets for the past happy time. The Earl of Alderdale had asked Barbara to marry him, and she, with all a woman's love of title and position, then threw me over for these without a pang. I gave her back her letters, for she coolly explained to me that no shadow of scandal must ever touch now or in the future a Countess of Alderdale. Then I went away, for there was nothing more to be said. But I did not kill Mr Earnslaw. Why should I? Alive or dead, he could not balk me now. It was she who did not care; I could see she was not acting on compulsion — it is easy to see that, isn't it?"

He paused a moment in his narrative and stared absently before him. It was clear to me that the cheerfulness he had exhibited at the beginning of the interview was only outward show.

"You have not told me what happened after you had said goodbye to Miss Earnslaw and given up her letters," said Skin o' my Tooth after a while.

"Oh yes! She walked with me as far as the gate, for it was very dark, and I think she was afraid I might betray my presence by stumbling or losing my way."

"At what time was that?"

"It was five minutes to eleven when I left the gate. I remember looking at my watch."

"Why did you not tell all this to the detectives who were trying to get up the case against you?"

"Because at first I thought that Miss Earnslaw would tell all that was necessary, when she saw that I was in trouble, and, after that—"

"Yes? After that?"

"Well, somehow after that it seemed too late. As I had not spoken at first, and Miss Earnslaw had said nothing, I thought I should seem such an awful cad if—"

"If?" repeated Skin o' my Tooth, as the young man seemed to hesitate.

"Well, if she denied the whole thing, you see."

"Yes; I think I see," rejoined my chief quietly.

Of course, at the time such a thing appeared to me positively preposterous. If Mr Spender-Cole spoke the truth—and I had no reason to doubt it—surely no woman would allow a man to remain under a false accusation for the sake of her own social reputation, however highly she might prize it. I suppose that Skin o' my Tooth's estimate of human nature was not so optimistic as mine, for he did not discuss the point with the young man; he succeeded, however, as he always does, in instilling into his client a firm belief in the truth and justice of his cause, and when he left him, after another half-hour's pleasant talk, there was no doubt that Mr Spender-Cole's cheerfulness was no longer only on the surface.

Having left Bletchwick Gaol, Skin o' my Tooth sent me on to the Crown Hotel, where we were putting up, and told me to wait for him there while he drove on to Murton Farm.

"I expect nothing from the interview, Muggins," he said to me, "but I fancy I would rather like to cross swords with Miss Barbara Earnslaw."

He said this with one of his pleasant, jovial smiles and that funny casting down of the eyes which gave him quite a coy look. I watched the car disappearing down the dusty road, and then I strolled into the hotel bar and sat on one of the seats, with my hands buried in my trousers pockets, to think the whole matter out.

But think of it as I would, my solution to the mystery remained very preposterous—either that Mr Spender-Cole had told a lie, or that Miss Barbara had set fire to her father's hayricks and then murdered him, which, of course, on the part of a young girl but a little over twenty years old, was, to say the least of it, unlikely.

Less than an hour later I saw my esteemed employer's fat and slouchy figure strolling down the road. He came in and sat down next to me, and I could see that same pleasant, amused smile hovering round the corners of his fat mouth.

"Well, sir?" I ventured to say at last.

"Well, Muggins," he said, with a chuckle, "my interview with Miss Barbara Earnslaw was of the briefest. She professed herself entirely at a loss to understand why I had troubled her at all with Mr Spender-Cole's affairs. Her acquaintance with him, she said, was of the slightest. The suggestion that she had at any time had any intimacy with him she absolutely repudiated, qualifying it as unpardonable impertinence; and, of course, to the story that she had an interview with him just before the murder of her father, and herself saw him out of the gate, she gave most emphatic and haughty denial."

He chuckled again, smiling quietly to himself. Then he added, with a touch of genuine enthusiasm: "But, by Jove! Muggins, she is a handsome woman."

4

The next morning Mr Spender-Cole was charged before the local magistrates, and, formal evidence as to his arrest having been given, Skin o' my Tooth had no difficulty in obtaining a remand for him, pending the production of some important evidence.

During the past few hours, ever since his interview with Miss Earnslaw, Skin o' my Tooth had scarcely spoken a word. I could see that beneath that fleshy mask of his, thoughts were crowding in his mind thick and fast; and when I heard him ask for a remand for his client, pending important evidence, I knew that already in that shrewd brain the whole history of the mysterious crime had been reconstructed.

After we had had some luncheon we walked down to Murton-Braby, the pretty little village which nestles on the outskirts of the Doespring Woods, a couple of miles from Bletchwick. Skin o' my Tooth had asked McMurdoch to accompany us, and the detective, whose belief in Mr Spender-Cole's guilt was firmly rooted, treated us the whole way to all the arguments which tended to prove his case.

We made a halt by the gate of Murton Farm, and as we did so it was opened, and a lady and gentleman on horseback came out, attended by a groom. She certainly was one of the handsomest women I had ever seen, and she sat her horse with perfect ease and grace.

"Miss Earnslaw and the Earl of Alderdale," whispered McMurdoch to me. "They are to be married, I believe, as soon as her mourning is over."

They certainly made a very handsome couple, and mentally I endorsed my chief's enthusiastic praise of Miss Earnslaw's beauty. She frowned a little, I thought, when she recognized Skin o' my Tooth and the detective, both of whom had bowed respectfully to her as she passed, and for a moment it seemed to me that she meant to stop and speak to them; but the next instant she had cantered off with Lord Alderdale down the shady road.

I watched her until she was out of sight; and when I turned I saw that Skin o' my Tooth had gone up to the man who had opened the gate, and who still stood there leaning against it, also watching the two retreating figures down the road. I don't think that in the whole course of my life I had ever seen a face so full of hopeless despair and dormant passion as was that of this man.

"Hallo, Pecover!" ejaculated McMurdoch jovially.

Hearing the name, I looked at the young man with still keener interest. This, then, was the half-witted creature whose irresponsible statements had brought poor Mr Spender-Cole within measurable distance of the gallows. Skin o' my Tooth touched him lightly on the arm.

"She is very beautiful, isn't she, James?" he asked with that kindly sympathy which he knows so well how to impart to his voice.

James Pecover sighed and then looked inquiringly at my chief, as if wondering whence came all the sympathy.

"No wonder you love her so much," added Skin o' my Tooth.

The young man did not speak; his eyes expressed all that he would have said.

"Suppose you let me come into the lodge and give me and my friends some tea? We have come all the way from Bletchwick to see Miss Earnslaw; and now, you see, she has gone out riding, and we would like to wait until she comes home."

Quietly he pushed open the gate, and, taking James Pecover's arm, he led him towards the lodge. The gardener and his wife were both out. The young fellow, however, as if under the spell of Skin o' my Tooth's kindly sympathy, led the way to the pretty little parlour, where he soon began to spread the table for tea. My chief watched him with unceasing persistency as he moved to and fro in the room, getting tea and bread and butter ready with that mechanical precision which often characterizes the dull-witted. McMurdoch said nothing. He, too, felt at that moment, as I did, that wonderful magnetic influence which seemed to emanate from the uncouth Irish lawyer when he was in the pursuit of his favourite occupation, the investigation—

or, rather, the instinctive scenting—of crime. When everything was ready. Skin o' my Tooth sat down before the tea-party and said cheerfully: "This is excellent, James. Now I'll pour out tea for everyone. You sit here beside me."

I watched him as he poured out the tea, and suddenly he took a flask from his pocket and emptied half its contents into one of the cups, which he then filled with water. It was brandy, I could see, and he passed that cup to James Pecover, whose dull eyes had glistened as he took it from him.

"It does improve tea, doesn't it?" said Skin o' my Tooth, as he quietly watched the young man swallow down the contents of that cup at one gulp.

"Now we can talk," he added, noting the immediate change which had come over the dull, impenetrable face of James Pecover. His eyes brightened up, a warm glow spread over his cheeks; he smacked his lips once or twice and then handed his cup to Skin o' my Tooth, with the laconic word:

"More."

"Oh yes; presently. It is good, isn't it? But you have to tell me one or two things first; then you shall have some more."

"Yes! Yes! I'll tell! Give me more! I'll tell!" murmured the idiot excitedly.

"You shall tell me first of all," said Skin o' my Tooth, quietly fingering his flask and leaning across the table, "why you killed Mr Earnslaw."

A look of almost demoniacal hatred, which positively made me shudder, lighted up the half-witted creature's face.

"I hated him!" he hissed between his clenched teeth. "He horsewhipped me—struck me with his horsewhip—there—in the shrubbery! You can see the marks—across my back!"

And feverishly, with trembling hands, he loosened his coat and flannel shirt, and, bending his neck, showed his back, across which great purple marks still testified to the truth of what he said.

"I expect you deserved that horsewhipping, James," said Skin o' my Tooth coldly.

This added fuel to the raging fire of James Pecover's wrath. His excitement grew in intensity, and as it did so it loosened his tongue, already quickened by a taste of the brandy.

"Ay!" he said, "and he deserved the blow I struck him there, right in the chest! He struck me with his horsewhip, because—once—I don't know how it was—I found Miss Barbara alone in the shrubbery—I loved her, and I kissed her—I couldn't help it—she was so beautiful. She was angry and told Mr Earnslaw. He horsewhipped me, and I killed him. I put a light to the hayricks—I knew he would come out to see what was wrong; so when I had fired the ricks I went back to the house and waited for him. When he came out I stabbed him."

It would be impossible to render with any exactitude the curious, weird tones, so full of the most deadly hatred, with which that dull-witted creature had spoken. And now, when he had finished, he still repeated with the obstinacy so characteristic of the feeble-minded: "I stabbed him—I killed him! He horsewhipped me!"

"Why did you fasten your guilt on Mr Spender-Cole, then?" asked Skin o' my Tooth sternly.

"I was frightened—and I knew he was in the garden. I had seen him—with her—I hated him because she loved him."

"And you thought you could get rid of two enemies at once, eh? That was very ingenious. But where did you get the knife with which you stabbed Mr Earnslaw, and what did you do with it afterwards?"

"It was my own knife—I used to kill rabbits with it. I threw it into the rhodo bush when I had done with it; then the next night I buried it."

"Under the rhodo bush?"

The idiot nodded. The excitement was slowly but perceptibly dying out of his eyes. The effect of the brandy had been sudden, as is usually the case on feeble brains, but it was not lasting; the alcohol seemed to have pervaded his body, his limbs looked heavy, his head nodded, then drooped forward upon his chest. Once or twice he roused himself, the look of deadly hatred stole again into his bleary eyes, and he repeated slowly:

"He horsewhipped me, and I killed him!"

Skin o' my Tooth placed a finger to his mouth, and gently McMurdoch stole out of the room, while we remained watching beside the idiot.

Ten minutes later the detective came back. He was carrying a bundle, which he quickly placed upon the table and then unfolded. It was an old working coat, covered with stains and mud; the stains all down the front were obviously those of blood; wrapped in it was a large clasp-knife, covered with the same gruesome stains. We were all three examining these things, while James Pecover nodded in an inane fashion across the table, murmuring incoherent words to himself, when a frightful shriek caused us all to turn quickly towards the door.

Mrs Pecover, the gardener's wife, was standing there, her eyes staring horror-struck at her son's coat and knife lying upon the table. She had not spoken a word, but her awful shriek seemed to have roused her son from his idiotic apathy. With a cry half of mad rage and half of hopeless terror, he sprang up and with one bound fell upon Skin o' my Tooth, gripped him by the throat, and dragged him down with him upon the floor, where the madman's shrieks drowned Skin o' my Tooth's feeble call for help. McMurdoch and I had some difficulty in extricating my chief from the wild grip of the maniac. With a last effort at intelligence, James Pecover had, I suppose, realized that with his kindly sympathy Skin o' my Tooth had set a trap for him, into which he had fallen.

Had they been alone together at the time, the madman would have made short work of my chief, in spite of the latter's powerful physique. As it was, McMurdoch and I succeeded at last in dragging James Pecover away. Then, with Skin o' my Tooth's help, who had quickly recovered himself, we managed to hold him down. Mrs Pecover, terrified, had sunk sobbing into a chair.

"I had brought the sedative with me, as well as the stimulant," remarked my chief presently, as he drew a small phial from his pocket. "I thought that I should probably need both. Give me the cup, Muggins. I think I can get him to drink this."

When James Pecover had taken the draught, which he did without a murmur, he became quite quiet, and soon McMurdoch suggested one of us going to Bletchwick for assistance. Mrs Pecover had recovered herself sufficiently to realize the gravity of the situation. She went herself round to the garage and got the chauffeur to drive me down to Bletchwick.

"I shouldn't be sorry," she confided to me with that stolidity so peculiar to people of her class, "to get 'im put in the asylum. I tell you, sir, I 'ave lived a life of terror ever since the day Mr Earnslaw laid 'is whip across the lad's back. 'E 'as not been the same boy, and I tell you my life nor 'is father's 'ave not been safe since."

With the same stolidity she and her husband saw their idiot son conveyed to Bletchwick, escorted by two constables whom I had fetched. He was quite quiet, and gave no further trouble. He was taken to the county asylum the next day, by order of the magistrate as he was certified hopelessly insane.

The next day Skin o' my Tooth placed before the magistrate the proofs of James Pecover's guilt, and Mr Spender-Cole was, of course, exonerated from all blame in connection with the murder of Mr Earnslaw.

I once asked my esteemed employer what had originally made him think of the idiot as the probable culprit.

"Well, you see, Muggins," he said, "to me it seemed obvious that the murder was committed by someone who knew the ways of the house and its master very well. The hayricks were fired in order to attract Mr Earnslaw out of doors, and the person who fired them knew exactly where to lie in wait for his victim. The whole thing was so cunning that it suggested the work of a madman. James Pecover's accusation of Mr Spender-Cole being a false one, my thoughts naturally turned towards his accuser. You can always loosen an idiot's tongue with stimulant. I suppose many humanitarians would blame me for resorting to such means; but surely the life of an innocent man was worth the destruction of the last glimmer of reason in the brain of a homicidal maniac."

"At one time I actually thought that Miss Barbara Earnslaw murdered her father."

"Oh no! She was too dainty a lady for that; but she would have allowed Spender-Cole to hang sooner than clear him by admitting her clandestine meeting with him. I hear, by the way, that she is officially engaged to the Earl of Alderdale; so she has achieved her heart's desire, and Mr Spender-Cole has remained chivalrous to the last."

11

A SHOT IN THE NIGHT

I find it really difficult to disentangle from the mass of notes which I took at different times while I was in Mr Mulligan's employ those that relate to cases which gripped the attention of the public, and those which from their peculiar nature and intricacies specially appealed to me personally. But I don't think that I shall be far wrong if I put on record the circumstances which so nearly brought that unfortunate Mr Legge-Bright to the gallows—indeed, would have brought him there but for the extraordinary courage and intuition displayed on his behalf by Skin o' my Tooth.

The tragedy occurred about a couple of years ago. At that time Mitre Court, a pretty Queen Anne house not far from Oakminster, was occupied by a childless couple, Mr and Mrs Greeneadge. Mitre Court had been originally a farmhouse, built over two hundred years ago in the simple elegant style of the period. There were only six rooms altogether in the main square building; three on the ground floor and three above. The front door gave straight on the fine hall and really beautiful staircase; immediately on the left as you entered there was a small boudoir, and facing you was the door leading into the large morning-room, with a small dining-room leading out of it on the right. Upstairs were three bedrooms, one large and two small.

About twenty years ago an annexe was added to the main building; this now contained three or four servants' bedrooms, the kitchen, and the other offices. There were two doors of communication between the house and the annexe, one on the half-landing going up the main staircase, and the other on the right of the front door facing that of the small boudoir.

I am obliged to give these simple architectural details so as to make it clear how it was that though Mr and Mrs Greeneadge were fairly well to do and kept three or four servants, they were entirely isolated at night in their part of the house. The walls of Mitre Court were extraordinarily thick, and it was a long way from the best bedrooms upstairs, down the main staircase to the half-landing, then through the communicating door, which for appearance's sake was masked by a heavy curtain, then down a few steps to the butler's room, the first along a passage, on which gave the other servants' rooms.

Mrs Greeneadge had often remarked quite lightly that she and Mr Greeneadge might easily be murdered in their beds before the servants heard any sound proceeding from the house. She herself slept in the large bedroom over the morning-room, and Mr Greeneadge occupied the one above the front boudoir, whilst the one above the dining-room was a spare-room often occupied by a guest.

And now when I have told you that a door, always barred and bolted at night, gave straight from the morning-room into the very pretty garden at the back and that the garden was encircled on that side by a ha-ha beyond, which was a six-acre field surrounded by tall elm-trees and a containing wall, I shall have put before you the main features of the very pretty house where the tragedy occurred.

This part of England, although so near to London and other busy centres, always strikes one as extraordinarily lonely.

A SHOT IN THE NIGHT

Standing, say, on the flat roof of Mitre Court, one would see great stretches of meadow and corn land, with here and there, dotted about, clumps of walnut or elm trees, amid which nestle other dwelling-houses, mostly of the same type as the one where Mr and Mrs Greeneadge had their home. The absence of hedges and the flatness of the country accentuate in a measure the sense of vastness which the view over the country gives, vastness seldom if ever met with anywhere else in England. I have heard these parts compared to certain corn-growing districts in mid-Europe.

The Greeneadges led rather a lonely life. He was a man retired from business, whose principal income—amounting to £1,500 a year—consisted of an annuity paid to him by his nephew, Ralph Legge-Bright, to whom he had made over his business on that consideration. This he had done about two or three years before he met the present Mrs Greeneadge and married her. She was a youngish and attractive widow, noted for her athletic prowess on the tennis court and golf course, he a man then approaching fifty, and no doubt he often regretted the transaction whereby he had parted from his lucrative business for a mere annuity. It turned out subsequently that he and his wife did at different times discuss the question of her financial position after his death; he had not at the time thought of taking out a life insurance, as his was not what an insurance company would call a good proposition; the premium, in any case, would have been very high. Husband and wife decided therefore that they would settle down at Mitre Court, and live as simply as they could, merely setting aside every year as substantial a portion of the annuity as possible for the ultimate benefit of Mrs Greeneadge.

One point more in this affair is worthy of note, and that is, that just before Mr Greeneadge retired from business in favour of his nephew he had had a very serious illness, from which one or two expensive specialists decided that he would never recover; they only gave him two or three years at most in which he might still enjoy life. Mr Greeneadge took this verdict philosophically; he was a bachelor then, with no near relations to mourn his death when it occurred, but on the advice of those same expensive specialists he decided to retire from business and take the remainder of his life as easily as possible. His nephew, Ralph Legge-Bright, was clearly indicated as his most desirable successor in the management of the old family business, but as he had no capital available for a purchase outright, it was arranged that the retiring vendor should receive an annuity of £1,500 for life.

Two years later, not only had the so-called doomed man recovered from that fatal illness, but he was enjoying the best of health, and finally one fine day he announced his marriage to Ethel Mary, relict of the late Somebody or Other of Tooting. Great, I imagine, must have been Ralph Legge-Bright's chagrin. He had reckoned on purchasing the business from what was practically a dying man, and on having to pay the annuity for two or three years at most, instead of which he now saw himself faced with the likelihood of being saddled with a huge annual payment, which might go on for the next ten or fifteen years—or even longer.

Horrible thought! And the health of Mr Greeneadge went on improving, and every time Ralph Legge-Bright went to stay at Mitre Court he found his uncle looking gayer and considerably younger than before. Relations between the two men became more and more strained, and Mr Greeneadge— now a middle-aged man verging on sixty—made no secret of the fact that he made a shrewd guess as to the cause of his nephew's ill-humour. And the idea greatly tickled him.

"I am living too long for my nephew, that's what's the matter," he would say with a chuckle; "he is just longing to see me underground. But there's a lot more he'll have to pay me, before I gratify his wish."

Then came the war. Ralph Legge-Bright, who was running a business that employed a couple of hundred men, and was considered of national importance, was exempt from military service, but in the end strenuous work with a diminished staff brought on a nervous breakdown. He came down to Mitre Court for a rest cure. He came for a fortnight and stayed three months. The business after the Armistice was going through a period of deadly slump; the payment of the annuity to Mr Greeneadge must by this time have become an almost insupportable burden. Relations between uncle and nephew became more and more strained, and servants even were often witnesses to violent quarrels between them. These quarrels were invariably followed by fits of sullenness on the part of Mr Greeneadge, who, according to the butler's testimony, would often pace up and down the length of the morning-room muttering words that sounded like:

"The cad; the ungrateful skunk! But I'll teach him a lesson—" or words to that effect.

But although these quarrels became more and more frequent as the years went by, the visits of Ralph Legge-Bright to Mitre Court went on just the same. In fact, he came much more often than he used to, and would stay either for long week-ends, or at holiday-time for days and weeks on end. The only member of the party who kept her serenity throughout this trying time was Mrs Greeneadge; she came and went with perfect unconcern in this atmosphere of warring elements; always smiling, always cheerful, she would keep conversation going while her husband sat glowering at the head of the table, and Ralph Legge-Bright hardly had a civil word in his mouth. Not that there was any question of husband and wife not being on the best of terms, but from what the servants said subsequently it seemed as if Mrs Greeneadge kept a perfectly open mind and did not take sides in the quarrels between the two men. She spent most of her time in keeping up her splendid physique, became president of a noted feminine philathletic club, and collected trophies and silver cups which she won at various sports and athletic competitions.

2

And that is how matters stood at Mitre Court during the time immediately preceding the tragedy. It was mid-September, Mr Legge-Bright was staying at Mitre Court, and during his stay he had been asked once or twice to shoot at Gaunters, Lord Westerham's place close by. A neighbour whose house was not far from Mitre Court had on those occasions always called for him in his car and driven him over to Gaunters, but on this day the neighbour was either sick or away from home — I forget which — and Mr Legge-Bright very naturally asked his uncle to let him have the use of his car and chauffeur. A very simple request, surely, which however Mr Greeneadge categorically refused.

A violent quarrel ensued; Mercer, the butler, heard snatches of it, so did the housemaid, Emma Tozer.

"I don't keep a car for your entertainment, my friend," was one of the remarks which Mercer overheard. It came, of course, from Mr Greeneadge.

"If I didn't sweat blood in your damned business," Mr Legge-Bright retorted, "there would be no car for you, or Mitre Court for a matter of that. It would be the workhouse most likely."

"Or the grave — what?" Mr Greeneadge went on with a sneer. "You would like that best, wouldn't you?"

Whereupon Mr Legge-Bright said emphatically: "I would!" and he added a few strong expletives, which Emma Tozer, the housemaid — who we may take it had her ear glued to the key-hole — was too genteel to repeat.

At this moment Mrs Greeneadge came in, all smiles, ready dressed to drive out to Oakminster for shopping.

"Gaunters is not much out of my way," she said, as soon as Mr Legge-Bright in a few sulky words had told her the cause of this newest quarrel. "I will drop you there, and no doubt you will find somebody to drive you back this evening."

She tripped up to her husband, put her arms round him and murmured softly: "Dear old bear, aren't you?" and kissed him most affectionately. Then she added lightly: "Come along, Ralph. We'll pick the car up at the garage."

Mercer, the butler, who was in the hall by that time and opened the front door to let Mrs Greeneadge and Mr Legge-Bright out, overhead her say: "You must not take any notice of Edward, Ralph. His bark is worse than his bite. He is getting old, you know, and he has a lot to put up with."

"Not half so much as I have," Mr Legge-Bright retorted. "The old devil! I wish some of those murdering Irish would put a bullet into him by mistake."

This I must tell you was a reference to certain Irish roughs who were supposed to be haunting the neighbourhood with a view to shooting a highly unpopular ex-Irish Secretary, who had recently bought a property close by.

When Mercer went back to his master in the morning-room he found him in a state of great agitation. He was pacing up and down the room, muttering to himself; Emma Tozer, who had been busy dusting the dining-room, declared that just before Mercer came in Mr Greeneadge had burst into tears like a child, and cried out some such words as: "Intolerable! I can't—I can't—"

It seemed as if in recent years his whole nature had changed. He had become silent and morose in the extreme, and would fly into a rage at the slightest provocation, or else fall into fits of terrible depression.

However, on this occasion he appeared to be more calm as the day wore on. Mrs Greeneadge came home in time for lunch and chatted away quite pleasantly, in spite of the fact that her husband was rather taciturn and only answered her in monosyllables.

Of course, people may say what they like, and materialists may scoff: I am only an old-fashioned fellow and something of a fatalist. I think I have seen too many dramas and tragedies in human life not to ascribe to Fate—sheer, blind Fate—her just share in the ordaining of our destinies. Now take this Mitre Court case: wasn't it just a blind Fate that decreed that on this very day after the more than usually bitter quarrel between Mr Greeneadge and his nephew, Mercer, the butler, should slip on the stairs with a heavy tray and hurt his hip? If that accident hadn't happened, if Mercer had been about as usual, the terrible tragedy which cast its black pall over the pretty Queen Anne house and nearly brought an innocent man to the gallows would never have occurred, simply because Mercer would in the usual order of things have answered the front door bell. But, as it happened, Mercer did fall on the stairs and hurt his hip, and therefore could not answer the front door bell because he had to go to bed. In consequence of all this, Emma Tozer, the housemaid, had to bring in tea; she also had to put up the shutters and bolt and bar the back door.

She sounded the dinner-gong a quarter of an hour later than usual, and then only on being peremptorily ordered to do so by Mr Greeneadge. She meekly suggested to him that Mr Legge-Bright had not come in yet, and should cook keep something hot for him. But Mr Greeneadge replied quite roughly: "Certainly not. If Mr Legge-Bright chooses to be late for dinner, he can go without."

Mrs Greeneadge was just coming downstairs at the moment and, as usual, she poured oil on the troubled waters.

"It is all right, Emma," she said. "Mr Legge-Bright is sure to be in directly. Just serve dinner, will you?"

But Mr Legge-Bright was not in directly, and the dinner proceeded in silence on the part of Mr Greeneadge, and in an effort at conversation on that of his wife.

Emma Tozer cleared away the dinner things. When she finally took away the coffee tray, Mrs Greeneadge said to her:

"Don't trouble about the front door, Emma; I'll let Mr Legge-Bright in when he comes."

At ten o'clock the three servants went to bed. Mr Legge-Bright had not yet come in. Cook, it seems, was rung for by her mistress at about 9.30, and just as she was coming through the door from the annexe into the front hall, Mrs Greeneadge came out of the morning-room, and cook heard Mr Greeneadge's voice saying very loudly and determinedly:

"He can sleep out in the ha-ha for aught I care."

Well! You know what a pusillanimous lot female servants usually are, especially country servants. It did not, therefore, surprise even the police or the coroner when those three at Mitre Court—cook, housemaid, and kitchenmaid—made no attempt to move out of their rooms when shortly before eleven o'clock that night they heard a ring at the front door, and this preliminary ring followed by more ringing, banging, knocking, and repeated shouting. It was very obviously Mr Legge-Bright wanting to get in. Mr and Mrs Greeneadge had gone up to bed about half an hour before then, all lights were out, windows, shutters, and doors barred and bolted for the night. Incidentally it had started to rain about this time, and rather heavily.

The noise at the front door went on for about five or ten minutes, the dogs barking all the time, so that there was really a din, as the servants said, fit to wake the dead. Poor old Mercer was the only one who tried to get up, but he was so bruised and stiff that he could not manage for a long time to get his trousers on, and by the time he had succeeded in that necessary operation the noise had ceased, and he concluded that Mr Greeneadge had come down ultimately and let Mr Legge-Bright in. Mercer was glad enough then to crawl back to bed. I must tell you that the chauffeur did not sleep in the house; he lodged in a cottage at the top of the road, about half a mile away.

Up to this point, then, the inmates of Mitre Court agreed as to the sequence of events on that memorable night, as well as on the exact time when they occurred, but, after this, evidence became somewhat more vague and certainly conflicting. Emma Tozer, the housemaid, whose bedroom window gave on the back of the house, said that some little time after the noise at the front door had subsided, she heard a final bang louder than the rest, but from whence this came she couldn't say. She thought at the time that it came from a burst tyre in the road, and certainly not from the neighbourhood of the back door, which was not very far from her bedroom window. The girl admitted that she had been far too frightened all along to attempt to go and open the door to Mr Legge-Bright; she was quite sure that Mr and Mrs Greeneadge had heard the noise, and if neither of them got up to let their guest in, it was obviously not her (Emma's) place to do so, after the orders which she had received.

So finally, the noise having subsided, she turned over and went to sleep. Hardly had she dozed off, however, when she was awakened once more, this time by what she distinctly recognized as the sharp report of a gun, not far from her bedroom window. The report was followed by absolute silence save for the patter of the rain. The sound also aroused her room-mate, the young kitchenmaid, who, it seems, had gone fast asleep after the noise at the front door had subsided, and had heard nothing at all until the sound of the gun wakened her. Mercer had been in too much pain to notice anything at first beyond the intermittent banging and knocking. As a matter of fact, neither he nor Mrs Dickon, the cook, whose rooms were in the front of the house, heard any sound at all except the report of the gun.

After that all four servants seemed to have cowered in their beds like so many scared rabbits until Mrs Greeneadge came running into cook's room. She was in her dressing-gown and slippers and had a small electric torch in her hand.

"Dickon, Dickon," she called in a terrified voice, "do come. Mercer can't move, and I am sure something awful has happened."

Mrs Dickon jumped out of bed and quickly slipped on some clothes. Her mistress appeared terrified, as white as a sheet, panting, and her teeth chattering; she seemed hardly able to stand, and pressed her hand against her heart (her chest, Mrs Dickon called it), as if she couldn't get her breath.

"Oh! I am so frightened, Dickon," she kept on murmuring. "I am so frightened. Mr Greeneadge was so angry and... Oh! I am so frightened!"

Dickon caught hold of her by the elbow and led her through the hall and into the morning-room. On entering the morning-room she switched on the electric light, but Mrs Greeneadge at once switched it off again.

"We shouldn't be able to see," she said under her breath.

"What 'm?" Dickon asked stolidly.

Mrs Greeneadge did not reply, only pointed to the back door. It was wide open. Dickon took the electric torch and went to the door. It was still raining very heavily. To use her own words, her knees were shaking so that she could hardly move, and she felt sick and faint. Nevertheless, she went on and turned the light of the torch upon the step, where she had caught sight of a dark, huddled mass. Then she gave an awful cry and all but fell down in a faint, for there, lying half in the path and half over the step, with the rain streaming down upon it, was the body of Mr Greeneadge, face downwards, hatless, his arms outspread, his overcoat, soaked through with wet and mud, lying partly over him and partly over the path.

"Is he dead, 'm?" Dickon asked, terrified.

And Mrs Greeneadge nodded in silence. Dickon turned away, sick and faint, and all she could do was to hurry back to

Mrs Greeneadge's side, for the latter had evidently reached the end of her tether; she just gave one long sigh and fell in a dead faint on the floor.

Imagine those three female servants after that. It must be admitted that the situation was so awful that it would have scared hardier natures than theirs. In their own stupid parlance, they would sooner have died than lift that inert and huddled mass from the doorstep, and thus ascertain at least whether their unfortunate master was dead or not. You know what women are: either they surpass in coolness or heroism anything any man can do, or—if they happen to be cowards—then their cowardice is almost unbelievable. My experience is that in all emotions and all weaknesses, in all virtues and in all vices, women invariably outdo the men.

But this is beside the point.

In this case the cook, Mrs Dickon, had just sufficient sense to get the other two servants out of bed, and, after they had carried Mrs Greeneadge upstairs and laid her on her bed, to send the two girls together over to the cottage where the chauffeur lodged, with orders to come along immediately. This took some persuasion, too, I imagine. But anyway, Emma Tozer and the kitchenmaid went on, and Dickon sat down to watch over her mistress.

Nothing happened for the next quarter of an hour except that Mrs Greeneadge came to. Then the chauffeur, Frank Barker, turned up with the two girls, who already had given him a highly coloured account of what had occurred. The first thing he did was to telephone to the police, which, of course, should have been done before; then he had a look at his master's body, turned him over, and tried to lift him. He gave it as his opinion that Mr Greeneadge was indeed dead. He had a wound in the chest, in the region of the heart, his shirt-front, waistcoat, and underclothes were saturated with blood. The three women, huddled one against the other, did not dare to look. After that the party adjourned to Mercer's room, there to talk over the events of this night.

Barker's presence in the house seemed to have spread an atmosphere of comparative calm over the household. He had seen all sorts of terrible sights during the war, and whilst everyone waited anxiously for the arrival of the police he regaled them with stories, which, though terrifying in themselves, helped to pass away the time.

Upstairs, Mrs Greeneadge lay on her bed like a log, moving her head upon the pillow from side to side, and moaning piteously.

3

The Mitre Court tragedy was, of course, seized upon as a titbit by all the sensation brokers in the country; but at first little, if anything, leaked out beyond the bare facts; and to the public the story was one of a quarrel between two men for a motive that was variously put down as jealousy or else of a financial nature, a quarrel which culminated in a cold-blooded murder.

The police were naturally very reticent, as the personages involved were not of the class usually associated with a crime of that sort. The Greeneadges were well-known people, and Mr Legge-Bright, on whom suspicion immediately fastened, had, on the very day preceding the tragedy, been a guest at a shooting-party given by one of the chief magnates of the county. That suspicion had fastened on Mr Legge-Bright could not be denied. His enmity with his uncle was well-known throughout the neighbourhood, and many friends before now had been at pains to understand how he could have continued to accept the hospitality of a man for whose death he had so often and so openly longed. The ladies over their tea-tables, and the men at the County Club, soon came to the conclusion that Mrs Greeneadge had all along been the attraction which brought Legge-Bright so frequently to his uncle's house.

"See," they argued, "how she always threw herself in the breach and poured oil over troubled waters. She would not allow a deadly quarrel between the two men because she wanted Legge-Bright to continue his visits to the house."

Questioned by the police, she did her very best to shield the young man in every way she could; so much so, in fact, that at one time she was warned by the chief inspector in charge of the case, because of a statement which she had made and which was subsequently disproved.

In the meanwhile it had transpired that the business in which Mr Legge-Bright was engaged, and which he had acquired from his uncle under what had seemed very easy terms at the time, was far from prosperous. As a matter of fact, for the past two years it had been run at a loss, owing to the heavy annuity which he had to pay to Mr Greeneadge. The latter had on several occasions been asked to make a fresh arrangement with regard to the business, but had invariably and categorically refused. There was more than one business friend who was able to testify that the annuity had been openly discussed between uncle and nephew, and there was one friend in particular—a Mr Hurd-Smith—who had been asked to mediate with a view to obtaining a modification of the original agreement, but Mr Greeneadge's final word on the subject was invariably this: "If properly managed, the business should bring in a clear profit of £3,000 a year. I made it yield me that amount when I was at the head of it; but then, I neither drank, nor gambled, nor spent my nights at a night club. I worked. We all worked in those days. One thousand five hundred pounds a year was the sum we agreed on when I sold the business. To accept less would be horribly unfair on my wife. She would have to modify her style of life; we should have to give up Mitre Court. I have just taken out a life insurance policy and have a heavy premium to pay on that; but I had to do it because I can't tell from one day to the other whether that young wastrel won't ruin the business altogether, once I am underground and no longer there to pull it out of the slough if need be. No! Most emphatically no! I don't see why I should be called upon to make sacrifices in order to enable my nephew to cut a jaunty figure in society."

This conversation occurred less than a year before the tragedy. Mr Greeneadge was, of course, an old man by this time, who did not even attempt to understand post-war conditions in trade, and no doubt he held the firm belief that his nephew was perfectly able to pay him the annuity out of the business: and all Legge-Bright's protests to the contrary only had the effect of irritating him and bringing on further bitter quarrels between the two men.

This and other matters then became gradually known to the public. Newspaper men have a wonderful way of ferreting out such things. Two days before the inquest, for instance, it was known that Mr Greeneadge had been shot in the breast at close range, with a revolver which happened to be his own property. It was found lying in the road the other side of the boundary wall, which in itself was over forty yards from the back of the house where the body lay. The shot had pierced the heart through and through. Death must have been practically instantaneous. The unfortunate man was fully dressed, in the smoking suit and dress shoes which he had been wearing for dinner; his overcoat he had evidently just thrown across his shoulders when he went downstairs.

Thus the first day of the inquest revealed very little more than what the public and the newspaper men already knew. The police asked for an adjournment pending further investigations. Interest by now had, of course, centred round the revolver. Medical as well as other scientific opinion was unanimous in declaring that suicide was out of the question. It would have been impossible for the deceased, after being hit in the way he was, to have had sufficient strength to walk forty yards to the boundary wall, fling the revolver out into the road, then walk forty yards back again and fall down dead on the doorstep. The very idea of such a thing was preposterous. Everything, therefore, went to prove that the unfortunate man could not have committed suicide, and that he was shot by a person at present unknown, who, after firing off the revolver at close range, had made good his escape across the garden and over the boundary wall, and then thrown the revolver down in the road.

How, then, did the unfortunate man's own revolver come into the hands of the murderer? The servants at Mitre Court — both indoor and outdoor — had told the police that Mr Legge-Bright prided himself on being a first-class revolver shot. He had persuaded Adams, the gardener, to help him set up a miniature range at the bottom of the six-acre field, and not only would he spend a great deal of his time at revolver practice when he stayed at Mitre Court, but he persuaded Mrs Greeneadge to join him, and every now and then she would go down with him to the miniature range and try her hand at revolver shooting.

Now, on the day preceding the tragedy, right up to the very hour when it occurred, Mr Legge-Bright had not been inside Mitre Court. He had gone off in the car in the morning for a day's shooting at Gaunters. The question, then, was: Had he put his uncle's revolver in his pocket before starting? It was certainly not very likely. A man does not usually carry a revolver about with him when asked to a shooting-party.

Mrs Greeneadge, who had driven Mr Legge-Bright over to Gaunters in the car, declared emphatically that he had no revolver with him, only his gun. When she was asked how she could possibly know that, seeing that if Mr Legge-Bright did have a revolver with him, he would have had it in his pocket, she was forced to admit that she had no real means of knowing. This, in fact, was the occasion on which the chief inspector had to warn her to be more careful in what she said; and this was because the butler, Mercer, had made a remarkable statement, proving that Mrs Greeneadge had, at any rate, some doubt whether Mr Legge-Bright did take the revolver with him that morning or not. It was soon after luncheon and just before Mercer met with his accident; he was crossing the hall with a tray laden with silver and glass when Mrs Greeneadge called to him from upstairs.

"Mercer," she said, "have you seen your master's revolver anywhere?"

Mercer had not, and Mrs Greeneadge went on: "You don't know by any chance if Mr Legge-Bright took it with him this morning?"

"No, 'm, I do not," Mercer had replied. A moment or two after that he had slipped with the tray in his hands, and the incident which he now related had escaped his memory until he was questioned by the police. He said that the revolver in question was the one which Mr Legge-Bright habitually used for practice, and it was usually kept in the drawer of a bureau in the hall. Mercer understood from Mrs Greeneadge, though he could not quote her exact words, that she wanted to have her practice at the miniature range that afternoon, and he was under the impression that she could not find the revolver and did not therefore get her practice.

Mrs Greeneadge, now seriously warned, was bound to admit the truth of the incident as related by Mercer. She remembered now quite well that she did want to practice at the range that day, but had to give up the idea because she could not find the revolver.

There were one or two more incidents, some of them trifling in themselves, which also came to light during the course of the inquest. For one thing it was demonstrated that two shots had been fired from the revolver, although one only had caused the death of Mr Greeneadge. This, in view of the fact that the weapon was constantly in use for target practice, would have meant little, but for Emma Tozer's story of the loud bang which she had put down to a burst tyre, and which, according to her, occurred some little time before she heard the report of the gun at the back door. Also, there was some story of Mr Legge-Bright having promised to give a display of his prowess with the revolver on a very fine range which Lord Westerham had set up at Gaunters, on the very day that he, Legge-Bright, went there for the shooting, but for some reason this display did not come off. Two of his fellow-guests at the shooting party told this story to the coroner, and they were closely questioned as to whether the question of Mr Legge-Bright having his own revolver with him or not had cropped up, but both of them refused to swear one way or the other.

But you see, don't you, how a net was being gradually tightened round the unfortunate man. The police had, very naturally perhaps, quite made up their minds that he did slip his uncle's revolver into his pocket that morning before going to Gaunters, with the idea of giving a display of his prowess on the range there as he had promised to do. With that same revolver and on that same evening he killed his uncle in an access of rage, provoked, no doubt, by being refused admittance into the house, and also perhaps by rough and insulting words spoken by Mr Greeneadge when the latter finally went to speak to him at the back door.

Everything, the police argued, pointed to him as the murderer; never had circumstantial evidence led more conclusively to one man, and only one as the author of a crime. Mr Greeneadge had no other enemy in the world; his private life had been raked through and through, and no other human being was discovered who could possibly have wished him ill, or who could have benefited by his death. Though he certainly had become dreadfully morose and ill-tempered of late, he was on the best of terms with his wife; his servants did not mind his sullen ways, and the people of the neighbouring village had nothing much to do with him. The only person in the world who wished him ill, and that for obvious reasons, was his nephew, Ralph Legge-Bright. The business was being carried on at a loss entirely owing to the huge annuity which had to be paid to Mr Greeneadge, and the latter had obstinately and persistently refused to make any modification in the original agreement. The quarrels between the two men had often been of a violent character. Legge-Bright had not only declared quite openly that the old man had lived too long, and that he wished to see him in his grave, but he had more than once gone so far as to use threats, whilst on the night of the tragedy he certainly had been subjected to grave provocation. It seems that at about half-past eleven he had turned up at the Wheatsheaf, the local public-house up the road, and had roused the landlord, asking for lodging for the night. He was well known in the neighbourhood, and was, of course, admitted, but the landlord said afterwards to his wife that: "Mr Legge-Bright, he don't seem like hisself. Too much drink, that's what's the matter with him. I wouldn't give him no more. My licence, I says, won't allow me. But, Lor', he nearly went for me 'cos I said that." I don't think I need record any other detail in connection with the inquest, which dragged on its weary course for several days. But in the meanwhile the police had already applied for a warrant against Ralph Legge-Bright, and he was brought before the county magistrates charged with the murder of Edward Greeneadge by shooting him with a revolver.

Legge-Bright at once sent for Skin o' my Tooth, who had done some business for him before this; he, of course, advised the young man to plead "Not Guilty," and to reserve his defence. Legge-Bright was then committed for trial at the next assizes, and as Skin o' my Tooth immediately remarked with his accustomed flippancy, "The fun was then ready to begin."

4

I don't know whether I have sufficiently impressed upon you the fact of Skin o' my Tooth's extraordinary intuition and, of what was more remarkable still, his belief in his own unerring powers. The moment he had, as it were, his client's very soul stripped naked before him, and was convinced of his innocence, his mind fastened on the salient facts of the crime and within twenty-four hours he had the whole tragedy before his mental vision. He saw every phase of it, and concentrated on proving what he knew to be the truth.

Thus it was with this case. After half an hour with Legge-Bright, and a day spent in questioning Mrs Greeneadge and the servants at Mitre Court, he knew exactly what had happened on that tragic night. The actors in the drama moved before his mental gaze like puppets ordered by him to bear their parts. But the question was to prove it. I must tell you that as soon as the police were called in at Mitre Court they took possession of the place—that is to say, those portions of the house which the deceased must have traversed when he went to meet his death. His own room, with everything untouched and left just as it had been that night, was locked, as was also the morning-room. No one was allowed access to the back door, where, unfortunately, footprints had been eradicated by the rain, almost as soon as made. The servants were permanently relegated to the annexe and not allowed to come into the house. Mrs Greeneadge had left the morning following the tragedy and was staying with a sister in London.

Never shall I forget my first impression of that house, when I accompanied my chief there on his first turn of inspection. The Assistant-Commissioner, Mr Alverson, of Scotland Yard, who was Mr Mulligan's intimate friend, was with us, and the three of us wandered through the deserted rooms, which I declare had an odour about them as of the grave. Skin o' my

A SHOT IN THE NIGHT

Tooth had already propounded his theory to Mr Alverson, and what he did now was to point out to his friend and to me all the facts which tended to prove his assertions.

He led us first of all to the late Mr Greeneadge's bedroom. It was perfectly tidy; the bed had not been slept in; it was neatly turned down as any well-trained housemaid would leave it, with the pyjamas laid tidily upon it, and on one of the chairs the dressing-gown was carefully laid, and below it the bedroom slippers. On a chest of drawers in one corner of the room the police had laid out the clothes which the unfortunate man had been wearing on the fatal night; the dress suit, shirt, underclothes, overcoat, and so on, all terribly soiled, then the socks and shoes, as well as a pair of walking shoes, which Mr Alverson explained were lying in the room when the police were called in, and which were picked up by the chief inspector and submitted to close examination. The shoes were the property of the deceased; Mercer had testified to that. A considerable amount of mud clung to them, and this was analyzed by the great expert, Mr A. E. Marshall, and pronounced to be composed of the same elements as the soil in the garden of Mitre Court. Mercer had put forth the theory that probably Mr Greeneadge had gone out into the garden either before or after dinner; he did go out like that sometimes, it seems, "to have a look round," and, as it was raining, had slipped off his dress shoes and put on some thicker ones, and then changed back into his dress shoes again for dinner. As this really seemed the only possible explanation, it had, perforce, to be accepted.

"Why should we accept it, my friend?" Skin o' my Tooth queried blandly in response to Mr Alverson's explanation.

"Simply because there is no other," Mr Alverson retorted. "They are the late Mr Greeneadge's shoes. He must have had them on that evening, as they were thrown down under the foot of the bed, just as a man would throw his shoes down if he was in a hurry to change."

"And do you mean to tell me that the careful housemaid who laid out her master's pyjamas and dressing-gown with such meticulous care, would have left a pair of dirty shoes in the room?" Skin o' my Tooth rejoined with slow emphasis.

"They may not have been there when she tidied the room."

"She said in evidence that she tidied her master's room just before she went up to bed at ten o'clock. The shoes were not there then. The wretched man would hardly have gone out after that hour just to have a look round in the pouring rain."

"But, hang it all, man, the man did wear his shoes and did go out in them—"

"Who says that he wore his shoes and went out in them?"

"But—"

"Someone wore his shoes—someone went out in them," Skin o' my Tooth went on quietly, "which is quite another proposition."

"But who could—?"

"Why not his wife?"

Mr Alverson gave a gasp. For a moment or two his face expressed a kind of blank amazement; then gradually I could see his air of puzzlement yield to one of understanding, then of incredulity: "Are you accusing that young Mrs Greeneadge of having murdered her husband?" he exclaimed indignantly.

"Not I," Skin o' my Tooth replied blandly. "I merely accuse her of having worn her husband's shoes and walked about in them for a time in the rain."

"But with what object, in Heaven's name?"

"To realize the sum of £10,000 on her husband's life insurance policy, which I am afraid, however, the insurance company will, after my defence of Legge-Bright, refuse to pay her."

Mr Alverson looked more puzzled than ever.

"Then you think that—?"

"I don't think, my friend," Skin o' my Tooth broke in gently; "I know."

"What?"

"Simply that old Greeneadge shot himself in this very room; and that the bang which Emma Tozer put down to a burst tyre in the road was nothing but the shot which ended this poor old chap's life. Remember, my good man, that Greeneadge had nothing to live for. The business out of which he derived his annuity was going to the dogs, and his wife's affection had gradually been alienated from him. It's no wonder to me that on this night, when so many things had already occurred to upset him, he finally decided to put an end to everything."

"But," Mr Alverson argued, "how do you construct Mrs Greeneadge's role in all this?"

"Into the one overwhelming desire," my chief replied, "to make her husband's death appear as murder, instead of suicide."

"But why?"

"Because the old man had insured his life for £10,000 less than a year ago, and, as you know, the insurance company would in the event of a verdict of 'suicide' refuse to pay Mrs Greeneadge the money. And remember that that £10,000, except for a small sum which had in the course of years been put by for her benefit, was all the money she could look forward to in the world. The poor old buffer didn't, I suppose, think of that in his despair, or, if he did, perhaps he dismissed the thought. But she thought of it all right, and that is why she acted as she did. I don't know if Legge-Bright cared enough about her to think of marriage, but, anyway, with his business entirely ruined, he hadn't much to bless himself with. You don't suppose for a moment, do you, that she did not hear the shindy which Legge-Bright was kicking up at the front door? and haven't we been told by every witness that she was always ready to pour oil on the troubled waters and smooth down the tempers of both men? Don't you think that, hearing the noise, she would naturally get out of bed, ready to let the belated guest in, if her husband wouldn't do it?"

"Then why didn't she let him in?"

"Simply because Greeneadge proved to be more obstinate, more violent, stronger, too, this time, both morally and physically, to enforce his will than before. Legge-Bright should not be allowed inside the house. But who can tell exactly what passed between husband and wife, while Legge-Bright cursed and swore and hammered away at the doors? What quarrel, what argument, what taunt, brought about the final tragedy? But the tragedy had been premeditated by Greeneadge; the revolver which usually rested in a drawer of the bureau in the hall was in his own desk throughout the day, while he pondered, and thought, and brooded over the wreckage of his life. Then maddened no doubt by something she said, by thought of that man who had robbed him of his wife's affection as well as of his fortune, he suddenly took up the revolver and shot himself then and there in the region of the heart. Can you see the wretched woman now? Aghast! Terrified! Pausing for one minute only to ascertain if indeed her husband was dead? forgetting for the moment the very cause of all this trouble—Legge-Bright—who tired of banging on the doors had at last made up his mind to go off and spend the night at the Wheatsheaf.

"I can see her wondering—and thinking—then gradually, self-interest overcoming fear and horror, realizing that in consequence of this suicide she would lose the £10,000 which stood between her and penury. And her cool, calculating mind at once set to work to solve this puzzle; how to give the tragedy the appearance of murder. This meant first of all the clearing away of any trace of blood that might appear on carpet or furniture; fortunately for the woman's scheme the shot fired at such short range had caused a wound which had soiled the poor man's clothes, but no more. Then the body! And here we must remember that we have no ordinary woman to deal with, but an athlete, a person of great physical strength and fitness. For a woman like that to wrap the man's overcoat around his body so as to avoid any possible stain on her own clothes, and then to carry the body down a flight of steps and across a room was easy enough. I can see her in my mind, carrying her gruesome burden, afraid only of one thing, that one or other of the servants might venture out as far as the hall—and see her.

"Luck and the cowardice of the servants favoured her. She reached the back door unseen, and was able to lay the body face downwards on the step with the overcoat lying half across it. But there was still the revolver to negotiate. Let it be found as far removed from the body as was possible with the resources at her command; but for this her own footsteps must not betray her; the rain might obliterate them, but it was best to be on the safe side. So she ran upstairs once more, picked up the revolver, and then had the presence of mind to slip on a pair of her husband's shoes over her own slippers, before she ran down again ready for her task. Mind you," Skin o' my Tooth went on, "I will do the woman the justice to say that she had probably forgotten for the moment all about Legge-Bright, and the possibility of any suspicion fastening upon him. All that was in her mind was the idea of her husband's death appearing as an accident or a murder, instead of a suicide. The revolver, as you know, she flung over the wall into the road, and then she slipped back into her room to throw a last look around for any possible trace of the tragedy, and incidentally to wash her hands and face. When all and every trace had been obliterated she finally went and roused the servants—and you know the rest.

"That is the line of defence I am going to work on, on behalf of my client, who, of course, is innocent of the murder. I don't think that I am much mistaken in my belief that Mrs Greeneadge at this hour would give much to undo the mischief which she has done. Remember that she has done everything in her power to combat the suspicions which she feels may presently bring the wretched Legge-Bright to the gallows. Short of an actual confession, she has been prepared to swear to anything that would exonerate him. She is the chief witness for the Crown, but we have briefed Sir Philip Scott-Daimler for the defence, and I think you will find that Mrs Greeneadge will break down under cross-examination."

She did. Skin o' my Tooth was right, as usual. Sir Philip Scott-Daimler accepted his theory and worked upon it with all the skill which has rendered him famous at the Criminal Bar. His cross-examination of the poor woman was masterly. Frankly, I was sorry for her. Her full confession created an unparalleled sensation; and no wonder, for, misdirected though they were, the resourcefulness and courage which she had displayed on that fatal night in order to carry through her idea were nothing short of marvellous.

As Skin o' my Tooth had guessed, that idea did come to her almost as soon as she realized that her husband had indeed committed suicide, as he had more than once, it seems, threatened to do. She was herself reduced to penury through his death, and as in a flash the thought came to her to give it the semblance of accident, perhaps, or else murder. There had been talk, she remembered, of those Irish roughs who were known to haunt the neighbourhood. They might have come to the door—Why not?... Mr Greeneadge may have picked up his revolver before he went down to meet them... There might have been a scuffle, during which the weapon was wrenched out of his hand and turned against him by one of the gang... Again, why not?...

With this in mind, she lifted her husband's body and carried him downstairs and deposited him on the steps of the back door, just as Skin o' my Tooth had conjectured. With the same strength of purpose she flung the revolver over the wall into the road, having taken the precaution of slipping her husband's shoes over her own. We must think of her, of course, as a woman of iron will and stern determination, as well as of great physical strength, or she never could have gone on with the tragi-comedy. When you think that after she had disposed of the revolver and returned to the back door, and stepped over her husband's dead body in order to re-enter the house, she had the presence of mind to take off the tell-tale shoes before she entered the morning-room, then to run upstairs and place the shoes neatly under the bed, run down again, call Mrs Dickson, and play her role as she did, you will agree with me that there was an exceptional woman.

One thing only was decidedly in favour of her plan: she was practically sure that no one would see her. Mercer was helpless in bed; the female servants would certainly not get out of theirs, unless actually summoned, and, their rooms being in the annexe, very little noise, if any, would penetrate through the thick walls that separated them from the house.

She was, of course, right in her surmise. The cause of death appeared so obvious that it was practically never questioned, and she would have been quite safe on that score but for the fact that suspicion had fastened on Legge-Bright, and that the latter happened to have turned for legal advice to Skin o' my Tooth.

What the poor woman would have endured, or how she would have acted if an innocent man had actually been condemned to the gallows, it is impossible to say. She was certainly a remarkable woman in many ways, with a mind as athletic as her body.

And all that for so little! Ten thousand pounds insurance money! But there are any number of instances in the annals of crime when a criminal will risk the gallows or a life sentence for a five-pound note.

12

THE HUNGARIAN LANDOWNER

It all began with the visit to our office of a high personage closely connected with the Imperial Family of Austria, whose name I am not at liberty to mention, but to whom I will, with your permission, refer as the Archduke.

He had come to consult Skin o' my Tooth about a very delicate affair, which would require great tact and discretion, and had done this on the recommendation of Sir Henry de Momerie, who had at one time been British Military Attache at the Court of Vienna. Before embarking on the main portion of his story, our exalted client threw a quick glance about him; his eyes, I could see, rested for one second upon the heavy curtain behind which I was installed.

"We are alone, of course, Mr Mulligan?"

"Of course," my chief replied unblushingly. The conversation, I must tell you, was carried on in German, a language with which I am familiar, though I do not speak it fluently. My chief, I must tell you, speaks it like a native. Indeed, his linguistic powers are nothing short of marvellous. Not only does he speak French, German, and Italian as easily as he does English, but in the course of his world wanderings he has acquired a smattering of half a dozen more or less exotic languages. I know, for instance, that he has a fair knowledge of Japanese, that he speaks both Spanish and Russian, and I once heard him carry on an animated conversation with an Hungarian.

"I must begin by telling you, Mr Mulligan," the Archduke resumed after a while, "that before the war I had in my service a family of highly respected and devoted Hungarians named Varlay. There was an oldish man who was my chief gamekeeper, his nephew, whom he had adopted and who was my personal body servant, and his daughter, who was beautiful, modest, and charming in the extreme; so much so, in fact, that I as a young man fell desperately in love with her. Had I not been hedged in with family traditions which I could not override, I would gladly have married her. But this I could not do without the consent of my cousin, who was the head of our family, and a regular autocratic tartar; failing his consent, I should have been forced to renounce my titles and dignities and quite a large portion of my estates. Katinka—that was her name, sir—was, on the other hand, too proud to accept any other position in my house but that of my lawful wife. Well, sir, I could not very well quarrel with my family then—it was during the first stages of the war—and Katinka would not put her pride in her pocket. I suppose you would argue from this that there could not have been much love on either side, but that is as it may be. Anyway, I felt that I could no longer keep the Varlay family in my employ, nor would they have cared to remain; but I still entertained a great deal of esteem for them and deep affection for Katinka. With a view to compensating them collectively for the trouble brought upon them by our unfortunate love affair, and also with a view to providing for Katinka with a handsome dowry in the years that were to come, I presented old Varlay with a small property which I owned in Southern Hungary. To a Hungarian of any class, from the highest to the lowest, the ownership of land is the Ultima Thule of ambition. The

Varlays therefore left my service comparatively happy and thoroughly satisfied."

The Archduke paused one moment, and I was glad of a breather. Of course, I am only giving you the gist of what he said, my knowledge of German not being sufficient to enable me to take shorthand notes.

"'Two or three years went by,' the Imperial Highness went on, after he had satisfied himself that he still held Skin o' my Tooth's full attention. "There came the Armistice, the revolutions in the conquered countries; my family, as you know, fell on evil days. On the other hand, the Varlays had had nothing but luck. On the property which I had light-heartedly given them a rich oil-well had been discovered. Old man Varlay was in a fair way of becoming a millionaire. His nephew had distinguished himself in the war, been severely wounded, and invalided home just before the revolution. In the winter of 1922 the old man took his daughter for a holiday on the Lido. Here they fell in with a man named von Wildemeer, who was cutting a great figure just then in the various Continental resorts, where wealth and aristocracy, and, I may add, adventurers of all nations congregate. Though of German descent, the man had a British passport, and had therefore presumably established his British nationality. Well, sir, to my horror and astonishment, I learned presently through the medium of the newspapers that my still-beloved Katinka had married this man, whom I already suspected of being an adventurer or worse. Whether she was coerced into the marriage or merely was influenced by pique, I know not. I had during the past few years made many attempts to get in touch with her once more; but she always refused to see me. Again, I cannot tell you whether this was due to her own choice or to coercion from her father."

"And thus ended a perfect idyll," my chief remarked with a sigh and a benign look directed at his distinguished visitor.

"Not altogether," the Archduke rejoined. "My interest in Katinka will only cease with my life. And now," he continued, "I come to the main point of my story. About a month ago I happened to be in Budapesth, and there I met Anton Varlay, the old man's nephew, and therefore Katinka's near relative. He had been in town some time, he told me, settling his affairs, as his uncle had recently died. I, of course, asked him news of Katinka; at once he appeared troubled. He had had a letter a day or two ago from Wildemeer, begging him to come over to England immediately. Katinka, never very strong, had consulted a London specialist, who advised a serious operation. Von Wildemeer, distracted with grief, begged Anton to come at once so that Katinka should have someone of her own kindred near her, in case matters took on a fatal turn. Naturally," the Archduke went on, "I pressed Anton with questions. He told me that von Wildemeer and his young wife were now permanently settled in England, and that he, Anton, had just been down to the Sleeping Car Company and booked his berth on the Paris-Calais express for the following day. We then took leave of one another, but not before I had made Varlay give me his word of honour that he would send me news of Katinka directly he arrived in England."

"Well," Skin o' my Tooth asked, "and did he?"

"Not a word, sir," the Archduke replied, "and I have been nearly mad with anxiety."

"You wrote to him, I suppose, or telegraphed?"

"I didn't know where to find him; London is a big place. But I did go to the length of wiring to the principal hotels, but in each case had the reply: 'No one here of that name.'"

"But what about this man Wildemeer?"

"That's just it, Mr Mulligan," the Archduke exclaimed. "I want you to help me to find him."

"This Mr. — er — Varlay — is that the name? Didn't he give you the man's address?"

"No."

"Or where he himself would be staying?"

"No."

"Don't you think that perhaps 'no news may be good news'? He may have forgotten to write, or Mrs Wildemeer may have stopped his doing so."

"I nourished that hope for some time, Mr Mulligan, although I knew Anton Varlay to be a man of his word; but I made tentative inquiries in the Banat, where his property is situated, and found that neither his administrator, nor his lawyer, nor his bankers had heard a word from him from the moment he left Budapesth a month ago."

"Was it your idea, then, to come to England and look for your friend?"

"For him and for Katinka," the Archduke replied resolutely. "I am convinced that there is some villainy afoot on the part of that scoundrel Wildemeer."

"Does your Highness know much about him?" Skin o' my Tooth queried blandly.

"I know," the Archduke replied with a shrug, "that, far from being a man of wealth, he is just an adventurer, and was at one time, under various aliases, pretty well known to the police in Central Europe. I am certain that he only married my little Katinka because he thought that she was an heiress, and that her life must be a perfect hell now that he knows she is not."

Again there was a pause. Skin o' my Tooth, I could see, was pondering over what he had heard, and I, who knew every line of expression in that funny pink face of his, could also see that he was puzzled.

"Let me get this question of the property with the oil-well a little more clear," he said presently. "It was left, you say, to your friend, who has disappeared?"

"To Anton Varlay. Yes."

"By his uncle?"

"Yes."

"Absolutely?"

"Absolutely."

"Why didn't the old man leave it to his daughter? or at any rate leave her a reversion?"

"For the simple reason, sir, that his daughter had married a foreigner, and that a Hungarian of that class hates to see the land in the possession of any foreigner."

"Very good," Skin o' my Tooth assented with a nod, "in that case, as Mrs Wildemeer has no interest in her relative's estate, her husband would have none either, and therefore one great motive for foul play is at once eliminated."

"Yes, that is so," the Archduke admitted. "And I will confess to you, sir, that this is the chief cause of my trouble. There seems no motive for foul play, and yet—I am sure—"

You should have seen Skin o' my Tooth at that moment, huddled up in his huge armchair, his black clothes sitting all anyhow on his unwieldy person, his face and hands shiny and pink, his eyes downcast, for all the world like an Early-Victorian maiden listening to her first proposal. I could see a frown of impatience and disappointment gathering like a thundercloud on the Archduke's brow.

"You will understand, Mr Mulligan," he said at last, "that it is impossible for me to go to the English police myself about this matter for a dozen reasons. Firstly, I do not wish for my family's sake to have my name mixed up in an affair which will probably end in the criminal court; secondly—"

"Pardon me," Skin o' my Tooth broke in blandly, with an elegant gesture of his podgy hand, "but I find your first reason such an excellent one that I need not trouble you with eleven more."

Again the Archduke frowned. He didn't like this fat, frowzy Irishman's levity, and was, I am sure, half wishing he had not come. There was an awkward silence, and I could hear the tap-tap of an impatient foot on the worn linoleum. And then suddenly the whole atmosphere in the office appeared changed. The Archduke's frown had vanished, his foot no longer tapped impatiently. With an engaging gesture he held out his hand. "I can see that I may trust you, sir," he said.

"You may bet your boots that you can," Skin o' my Tooth replied as he shook the young man warmly by the hand.

And this change had come about just because Skin o' my Tooth had suddenly looked up and encountered his client's puzzled glance. It was wonderful how much that man could convey just by one look.

The Archduke, I may tell you, went away full of hope and trust.

2

Tentative inquiries by the police elicited nothing of any value. True, it was established that a man armed with a Hungarian passport, on which he was described as Anton Varlay, landed proprietor, a native of Temesvar in the Banat, and so on, had gone through the passport examination office at Dover on the 28th of last month, and that he was met there by a gentleman with whom he drove away, luggage and all, in a Wolseley four-seater, which belonged to a well-known garage at Croydon; but who was the hirer of that car on that particular day, or whither it was driven, remained a mystery. All that the owners of the garage could remember was that a gentleman whom they did not know called on that afternoon; he wanted to hire a car without a chauffeur; he gave a name and address which, of course, were fictitious, but he not only paid for the hire of the car in advance, but left a fairly substantial sum on deposit as a guarantee that the car would be returned the following day in perfect condition.

He brought the car back the following forenoon; the deposit was, of course, refunded to him, and there the transaction ended. As for the destination of the car and the use to which it was put, the garage proprietors could say nothing. It had been driven about 200 miles, or rather more than the distance from Croydon to Dover and back, and it had been seen on the road by an A.A. man as far north as Hendon. There were, this man said, three occupants in the car and a small quantity of luggage.

That was as far as information went. Skin o' my Tooth had put the police on the track, and they would, of course, pursue investigations, but in the meanwhile I could see that my chief was anxious. Close on four weeks had gone by since Anton Varlay landed at Dover, and since that day no one with whom he had any connection, either in this country or in Hungary, had heard a word from him. Skin o' my Tooth had had some correspondence with the police at Budapesth. They had confirmed the Archduke's account of the Varlay family in general, and had ascertained that Anton Varlay had obtained an English visa on his passport about a week before he left for England. After that, as far as the Hungarian authorities were concerned, the earth might have swallowed up that unfortunate young man. I must say that both the police in Hungary and the people whom Varlay employed in the administration of his property were extraordinarily supine. They seemed to think that the whole matter was the business of the English police; it was for Scotland Yard, they argued, to find this young man who had landed safely at Dover, and they washed their hands of the affair.

When I tell you that all possible inquiries had been set on foot to trace an Anglo-German named Wildemeer, who had a house presumably somewhere in the neighbourhood of London, and had a young Hungarian wife, and that all such inquiries had failed, you will understand how difficult had become Mr Mulligan's task. Wildemeer had disappeared just as effectually as young Anton Varlay. "We shall have to do something more venturesome," Skin o' my Tooth said to me one day, "or we shall be too late."

"You suspect murder, then," I asked.

"Murder for a motive which escapes me for the moment," he replied, "but murder nevertheless. But we shall see."

The next morning the following advertisement appeared in the "Personal" column of *The Times*.

> "A gentleman, middle-aged, with sound knowledge of several languages, would undertake work in any capacity. Russian, Hungarian, and Japanese a speciality. Legal or other documents accurately translated. Write Box XV 193, The Times, E.C.4."

This was the "something more venturesome" which Skin o' my Tooth had planned. All day and the next he waited anxiously for a reply to his advertisement. It was repeated on four consecutive days. On the fourth day he had an answer. It was a letter written on business paper which bore the heading: Thomas Peppitt, Commission Agent, 153, Tilney Street. It was signed Thomas Peppitt, and requested advertiser to call at the office on the following morning at 10 o'clock. There was a P.S. stating that the office was on the third floor, and that there was no brass plate on the door.

"I may be wrong," Skin o' my Tooth said with a chuckle, "but I think—" He paused a moment, then concluded dryly: "I think, Muggins, that we shall have some fun."

The following morning when I arrived at the office I found my chief so fantastically attired that when I first beheld him I genuinely failed to recognize him. Sparse black hair stood out in tufts all over his cranium: a beard and moustache that looked as if they had been gnawed intermittently clothed his chin and upper-lip. He wore a broad-brimmed black felt hat, a soft shirt and collar none too clean, steel-rimmed spectacles, and a bright green tie. He looked for all the world as if he had a bomb ready for explosion in either pocket of his brown velvet coat. He started off for Tilney Street very gaily telling me to wait for him at the office; he might be back in an hour, and he might be all day.

Now, as I told you just now, my role in this affair was absolutely nil; what there was of it consisted in waiting all that day and the next and the intervening night in an agony of anxiety. Most of the second day I spent in Mr Alverson's private bureau. Though it is a hard and fast rule in our office that I never speak of my chief's affairs to anyone without his sanction, I felt that the circumstances this time were so unusual and the eventualities so awful to contemplate, that that rule must be broken at all costs. Mr Alverson was as anxious and upset as I was. He promised me the utmost discretion, but at the same time he at once set secret machinery going to find out something about my chief's mysterious disappearance. He agreed with me that it was unlike Skin o' my Tooth not to have telephoned or otherwise communicated with me or with him. That he had not done so sounded ominous.

"He is either being held in duress," Mr Alverson remarked thoughtfully, "or of course he may have been taken to some remote village whence telephonic communication is impossible. I refuse to believe," he concluded, placing his kindly hand on my shoulder, for he saw that I was terribly anxious: "I refuse to believe that anything more serious has happened to him."

He went himself, and allowed me to accompany him, to 153, Tilney Street. Together we climbed up to the third floor, where we were confronted by three doors, two of which bore nameplates. The third one was locked. We inquired at the others, and in each instance were told that the third office on this floor had been unlet for about a mouth, but that a few days ago two persons came to look over it—two men, one of whom seemed the clerk, or perhaps servant, of the other. They had apparently obtained the key from the house agent. They returned again a day or two later—yesterday, namely—and spent about an hour on the premises, during which time they received the visit of a third party.

The clerk who gave us this information could not give us a very accurate description of the three individuals in question; he had not noticed them particularly. All he could tell us was that one was very tall and handsome, with reddish-fair moustache, and was dressed like a gentleman; the other had a stubby, red beard, and wore a broad-brimmed Homburg hat all the time. The man who came yesterday to visit those two was, in the clerk's opinion, obviously a foreigner; the description which the witness gave us of him tallied in every respect with my chief's disguise.

It seems that after the interview the three men went downstairs together and entered a traveller's brougham which had been waiting at the door. To trace an ordinary traveller's brougham through the maze of traffic round about Shaftesbury Avenue was for the moment an impossible task. Mr Alverson and I, having ascertained the name and address of the house agent in charge of the premises at Tilney Street, went on there, but our inquiries in that direction were fruitless. They never entrusted the key of those offices to anyone; a clerk always accompanied any intending tenant who wished to view the rooms; nor had they any recollection of a tall, handsome gentleman with a fair moustache making any inquiries about the premises. Obviously someone with a felonious intent had gone to the place, taken a wax imprint of the lock, and used the premises for some nefarious—at present unknown—purpose.

I confess that I went home that afternoon in a state bordering on frenzy. The whole of that day went by and the next and the intervening night with no news from my chief. Mr Alverson was kindness itself, and assured me that if another twelve hours went by without news, he would take it upon himself to set the entire machinery of Scotland Yard in search of my chief.

"I am convinced that he is all right," he said over and over again to me; "and that my life and yours won't be worth an hour's purchase when he knows that we have interfered in his affairs."

I could not share his optimism and what I endured within the next twelve hours beggars description.

It was not until the small hours of the following morning that—but I must not anticipate. Suffice it for the present to say that Skin o' my Tooth himself told me and Mr Alverson of the adventure which befell him after he left our office on that memorable morning to go to 153, Tilney Street.

3

I think I'd better give you Skin o' my Tooth's account of his adventure in his own words. He gave it to Mr Alverson and to me, and I made shorthand notes of the most salient portions of his narrative.

What he said to us was this:

"Precisely at ten o'clock on the morning you both know of, I walked up the half-dozen flights of steps to the third floor of 153, Tilney Street; when I reached the landing I paused a moment or two wondering which of the three doors facing me I ought to enter, when one of them was opened and out came a man, whose chief characteristics were a stubby red beard and somewhat darker, stiff, unruly hair. He professed to know at once who I was, and, anyway, appeared to have been on the lookout for me. He asked me to step into the office. It was entirely devoid of furniture, floor-covering, and even blinds, and the dust lay thick everywhere. On my left there was a door which bore the legend PRIVATE, and through this I was ushered into an inner office almost as void of furniture and certainly quite as thickly coated with grime as the other.

Moreover, it was very dark, as a tattered blind was drawn down over the window.

"There was a table in the middle of the room, also a chair on which sat with his back to the window a tall, broad-shouldered man dressed something like a family lawyer or a member of the Stock Exchange. He wore large, bone-rimmed spectacles with tinted glasses. But I need not describe him any further: you have both seen him by now.

"A great joy entered my soul," Skin o' my Tooth went on with a chuckle. "We have all seen that kind of mise-en-scene before, and the very first glance had told me that here was quarry for my friend Alverson, even if this well-dressed gentleman was not the actual person I was after. But I was pretty well sure by now that he was. Of course, he began with a long rigmarole about having borrowed this office from a friend for a few days, without having seen it previously; I stood by—since there were no chairs—twiddling my hat and sniffing as if I had a bad cold.

"Then followed a still wilder rigmarole about his being over in England for the purpose of negotiating various landed properties in Central and South-Eastern Europe; his trouble at the moment being that a wealthy client of his was desirous of completing the sale of a piece of land in Southern Hungary before he died. He was very ill, so my interlocutor explained, and wanted this transfer done and his signature affixed as soon as possible. It was a question of righting a great wrong, and if this sale did not go through, the land would pass to the government of Yugo-Slavia, who, as I surely knew, were the deadly enemies of Hungary and the Hungarians.

"Of course, I listened to all that trash with the utmost deference and interest, and when my friend paused in order to take breath, I asked him humbly in what way I could be of service to him. 'You will translate into Hungarian,' he replied to me, 'the deed of sale which my client's English lawyer has prepared for him; when that is done the document will only require my client's signature, and as you will be on the spot, you might as well sign as a witness. By the way,' he went on airily, 'what is your name and occupation, and where do you live?'

"I told him that my name was Wilhelm Mullenkamp, that I lived at 175, Mill Street, Upper Tooting, that I had been a lawyer's clerk, but that, unmerited misfortune, etc.—This seemed to delight him, for he asked me quite jovially if I had ever 'done time.' I assured him that I had not, and also that I was both willing and able to do the required work for him, as I was thoroughly conversant with the Hungarian language. 'What could be better?' my amiable friend retorted glibly; 'why shouldn't you come with me right away? We can get the business completed today, and there will be a £5 note for you for your trouble.'

"Of course, this time," Skin o' my Tooth resumed after a slight pause, "I knew that I was on the right track, and was blessing the inspiration which led me to put the advertisement in *The Times*. I followed my friend down the stairs, the other with the red stubby beard bringing up the rear. Down below one of those large, one-horse broughams, such as are used by commercial travellers, was waiting at the door. My friend graciously invited me to step in, which I did."

But at this point Skin o' my Tooth's narrative was broken into by an exclamation from Mr Alverson.

"And do you mean to tell me, Mulligan, that you got into that vehicle then and there, in the company of those two murderers—?"

"How else should I have known where they kept that wretched young man hidden?" Skin o' my Tooth retorted blandly.

"Couldn't you have—?"

"I could have done nothing that suited my purpose better than to go and investigate everything for myself. Anyway, I went, and, as I expected, found the inside of the brougham in total darkness, with shutters—not merely blinds—on all the windows. My friend made a casual remark about his eyes being worried by the light, which, of course, I ignored. I had been made to sit beside him, with the red-haired beauty opposite me. The drive lasted over an hour; I tried to keep some idea of my bearings, but after a while the want of air, and no doubt some subtle soporific also, made me more and more drowsy. Neither of my companions spoke, and presently something roused me with a jerk. Apparently I had dropped asleep.

"We had now come to a standstill. The two men got out and bade me follow them. As I stepped out on the pavement I took a quick glance about me; we were in a street of semi-detached houses with the usual small gardens front and rear, and a railway embankment at the back. A train rushed through just at the moment, and through the space between two blocks of houses I caught sight of a L. and N.E. engine. From this and the lay of the land I made out that we were somewhere in the neighbourhood of Finsbury Park or South Tottenham. But, needless to say, I was given no time for further investigation. The man with the red beard took me by the arm and I allowed myself to be bundled into the house, not without noticing that it bore the number 171, and that No. 173 attached to it was to let.

"You will laugh when I tell you that the very first thing that struck me when I entered that house was the smell of steak and onions; not an unpleasant smell in itself, but it simply pervaded everything.

"I was shown into the dining-room on the ground floor, and my new employer told me very jovially that I had better have lunch with him. I accepted with alacrity, but begged leave to telephone first to my mother, who would be expecting me home. 'Sorry, my friend,' he remarked dryly, 'but there's no telephone in the house, and the nearest public one is half a mile away, and luncheon is getting cold.' I could see that

THE HUNGARIAN LANDOWNER 275

the two hyenas, now they were in their lair, took less trouble to try and throw dust in my eyes. I naturally appeared as unsuspecting and innocent as they could wish. In the course of lunch my new friend told me that his name was de Florian, and that he was Italian; he also talked a lot more trash about his international affairs.

"We were waited on by the red-haired man, whom de Florian—I will call him that, if you don't mind—addressed as Smith.

"After lunch my employer took me to a room on the second floor at the back of the house; there was a table facing the window; the latter was of thick ground glass; there were also a couple of chairs, an armchair—very shabby—some bookshelves, and other bits of dilapidated furniture. De Florian took a book from one of the shelves, and placed it on the table before me. 'My work,' he said curtly, 'I want it translated into English. The client I spoke to you about is away for a couple of days. You can fill in the time by doing this important work. You will stay in the house for the present. I will pay you £2 a day in addition to the £5 I promised you, and I will lend you what you require for the night. Any letter you write you can give to Smith; he goes to the post every day at five.'

"There was a packet of manuscript paper on the table, a blotting pad, a fountain pen. De Florian gave me some cigarettes and a box of matches, then he went away.

"I glanced at the book. It was in Hungarian and entitled 'Memoirs of a Hungarian Aristocrat at the Court of Francis Joseph I.' Of course, the translation was a blind, and equally, of course, I was a prisoner in the house. I tried to open the window; it was securely fastened, and I couldn't move it. I began by getting through a certain amount of the translation; then when it got dark I sat down and thought things over. The situation interested me, and I thought of Muggins getting more and more anxious about me, and hoped he would not make an ass of himself. I was left alone the whole of that blessed afternoon, and I had got through at least five thousand words of the Hungarian aristocrat's memoirs when my friend Smith unceremoniously burst into the room and told me that dinner would be on the table in a quarter of an hour. I asked him to show me to my room so that I could get a wash, and this he did. The room was a horrible hole next to the one where I had been at work, and the window here, too, was of thick glass and absolutely immovable. 'Good!' I thought, and sailed serenely downstairs. The smell of steak and onions was more marked even than before. As we had had that delectable dish for luncheon, I wondered whether we were going to have it again.

"To my astonishment, when I entered the dining-room I found not only de Florian sitting at the table, but a young and charming lady, whom he introduced to me as his wife. She was very beautiful, and would have been ravishing but that she looked so ill, and that her eyes showed obvious traces of tears. She never said a word all through dinner, and I only once caught a quick, inquiring glance which she furtively directed at me. The rest of the time she sat with her eyes fixed on her plate, while de Florian talked and lied like a gas-meter.

"After dinner she left me to the sweet companionship of her precious husband, and presently we could hear the sweet strains of her voice coming from the next room. She was singing some of those lovely Hungarian folk-songs, so full of passion and melancholy, with which Hubay and Brahms have made us familiar. Even if I had had the slightest doubt of the identity of de Florian, I should have had it set at rest now. This was the Archduke's sweetheart, Katinka Varlay, a prisoner, like myself, of this scoundrel Wildemeer, alias de Florian and what—not besides, but, unlike myself, a prisoner who had long ago given up hope.

THE HUNGARIAN LANDOWNER

"At ten o'clock she murmured something that resembled 'Good-night.' Smith then brought in whisky-and-soda, which I declined, and presently I went up to my room. And so to bed. It was, of course, ages before I could get to sleep; but I must have dozed off at one time, for suddenly I woke with a start, certain that I had heard a human cry. Did I mention that there was no electric light in the house? and that in an airless room I had not fancied the idea of going to sleep with the gas half-turned on? Fortunately I am one of those methodical people who never go anywhere without a small electric torch in my pocket. I switched that on and sat up in bed listening. Over my head I heard a heavy tread and a murmur of voices, then nothing more.

"Nothing more occurred until about three o'clock the next day. I had had breakfast alone, worked at those silly memoirs until lunch-time, and had had lunch with de Florian and his silent, melancholy young wife. Needless to say that I had distinct proof now that I was indeed a prisoner. All doors, including the street door, were securely locked against me, and the windows were barred, shuttered, and padlocked at night. Not that I wanted to get away yet; I wanted to get to the bottom of the mystery of Anton Varlay before I did that; and those two scoundrels were quite clever enough and ready to make a bolt of it directly they discovered that I had given them the slip. I also strongly suspected that there were more than the two rascals in the house.

"At three o'clock, then, de Florian came into my room and gave me the draft of a document in English for translation into Hungarian. It was, as I expected, a deed of sale for the sum of £20,000 sterling of property including some oil-wells, executed by Anton Varlay in favour of his cousin, Katinka Varlay, wife of Simon D. Wildemeer, of London, England, and contained the ominous sentence: 'Receipt for which I hereby acknowledge.'

Thus was the main portion of the infernal plot revealed to me; soon I should, I hoped, be in possession of the rest. Over one thing I was reassured: Anton Varlay was still alive.

"Wildemeer, alias de Florian, sat in my room smoking cigarettes while I got the translation ready. When I had finished, he picked up the documents, both the English one and the translation, and curtly ordered me to come along with him. He led the way upstairs to a room just above mine, and I followed him in. Although it was still daylight out of doors, the curtains were drawn and the gas was alight. There were two people in the room—a revoltingly fat female and, sitting in an armchair by the mantelpiece, a man who at the very first glance appeared to be dying.

"When we entered he looked up at Wildemeer just like a dog that expected a beating. But Wildemeer beamed and smiled at him and said jovially: 'Hallo, Anton! Feeling better today—what?' The fat female then shrugged her shoulders and remarked dryly: 'Oh, he's all right now! He won't give us trouble.'

"I can assure you," Skin o' my Tooth went on emphatically, "had I been sure that there were not more than the two rascals and the fat female in the house, I would have taken my chance of knocking them down then and there, one after the other, and getting the wretched Anton Varlay and Katinka out of the house as best I could; but I had already heard Smith's footsteps on the stairs behind me, and another besides that. Heroics, I felt, would only have sealed poor Anton's doom as well as my own.

"Wildemeer now put the two documents on the table, and, taking a couple of rubber stamps and an ink-pad from his pocket, he proceeded to stamp the documents, and finally he affixed a couple of postage stamps of high value upon them. I had already noted that the rubber stamps bore the legend 'Hungarian Legation, London.' Wildemeer now held

THE HUNGARIAN LANDOWNER 279

a fountain pen out to Anton. 'Now then,' he said genially, 'sign here, will you?' But Anton did not take the pen. 'I won't sign,' he said huskily. 'Don't be a fool,' Wildemeer retorted quietly; 'you owe it to Katinka, if not to yourself.' Anton, however, was obstinate. Sign he would not, and I was admiring his pluck and obstinacy when Wildemeer did a very funny thing. He went up to a kind of large oak cupboard which stood in a corner of the room, and he threw open its doors. Immediately I became conscious of that awful smell of steak and onions which had worried me all along. I was looking at Anton at the moment, and in a flash the whole of the devilry was made clear to me. These fiends were starving the wretched boy into submission to their schemes, and putting on the screw by giving him food to smell when he was more than usually obstinate. Even now he turned green and fell back in what looked like a deathly swoon. God! but I had some difficulty, I can tell you, in keeping a serene, unsuspecting face. I tried hard to look a complete fool, and fortunately I succeeded, for Wildemeer murmured quite genially: 'That's the worst of this house, the smell of cooking pervades everything.' Then he added: 'Well, we won't worry the poor fellow any more today. I dare say he'll feel better tomorrow. The worst of it is that the young rascal has already had his cheque for £20,000, the proceeds of the sale, and so long as he does not sign these transfers, I, as the agent of the buyer, am responsible to her for the amount.' He then led the way out of the room, taking the documents away with him.

"When I was ready to go up to bed that night, he said to me: 'Tomorrow will see this business through, I am sure, and then I suppose you will wish to go back home.' Well, of course, I had realized by now that there was no time to be lost if that wretched young Varlay was to come out of this house alive. You must remember that, though I knew myself to be a prisoner, I had not before this desired to escape. But now matters were different, tonight, at all risks, I must get out of the house and in touch with the police.

"Love laughs at locksmiths, and so does yours truly, and at one a.m. I started on my adventure. I crept downstairs, feeling my way by the light of my small torch. My intention was to explore every mode of egress first, and if the worst came to the worst and I found every door locked against me, to return to my room and make a bolt of it by smashing the window, at risk, of course, of rousing the entire gang of murderers. It was for the sake of that wretched Anton that I was anxious and hopeful to make a noiseless exit out of this hospitable house.

"Presuming that Wildemeer and his wife occupied the floor just below me, I did not try the doors on that landing, but made my way soundlessly to the passage on the ground floor. The street door was securely fastened, and so were the doors of the dining and sitting-rooms, which gave on the passage. None of these could be made to yield without a considerable amount of noise. I next made my way down to the basement. Here I found a kitchen and other small offices, the doors of which were open, but the windows had wooden shutters in front of them, held in place by a flat iron bar, which was secured by a padlock. I put my friend Smith down as a good workman for that kind of job, as houses in South Tottenham or Finsbury Park are not usually provided with fittings of that sort.

"Anyway, there was no possible egress that way. For a moment the thought of a file went through my mind. If I could file one of those iron bars through... I opened the drawer of the kitchen table and dresser in the vague hope of finding such a thing, when suddenly, without the slightest warning, I felt a terrible blow on the top of my head. I saw stars, I can tell you, and the next moment I had measured my length on the stone floor. What happened next is, of course, pure surmise. I imagine that Smith slept somewhere down in the basement, that I had made more noise than I had supposed, and that during the time that

THE HUNGARIAN LANDOWNER 281

I was engaged in opening the kitchen table drawer the rascal had caught me in the act, crept up behind me, and knocked me down. After which he would naturally go up and tell Wildemeer what he had done, and the two rascals would then decide whether it would be worth while to murder me at once or wait for another opportunity. Right through my state of semi-consciousness I was dimly aware of the sound of movement somewhere in the house, and presently of the tinkling of a bell. You know how consciousness gradually returns. Well, in this case it was that persistent tinkle which brought my perceptions back with a jerk.

"The telephone! Heaven be praised! There was a telephone somewhere near, and if only those murderers up there gave me five minutes' grace... It was pitch dark, of course. But now for a bit of luck. When I had opened the kitchen drawer I had my little electric torch in my hand, half concealed in the pocket of my coat. If in falling I had not put it out of gear, I would be able to act more surely and more expeditiously. I groped in my pocket. The torch was there. It worked all right. Thank God for that. I struggled to my feet.

"You know I have the physique of a horse, and, though I felt giddy enough, I could stand and I could walk. The sound of the tinkling bell guided me. The telephone was just outside the kitchen door. Three more minutes and all would be well. I took off the receiver—just in time, I think, because in the dim distance above my head I had vaguely detected the sound of the opening and shutting of a door, and voices and movement more clear than before. I would have given much to have known who rang up this den of thieves at this hour of the night, but there was no time for that. I waited sixty interminable seconds, while from the upstairs landing came the sound of Smith's voice in voluble conversation, followed by some hard swearing from Wildemeer. My God! Those seconds! I can tell you I've never known time go by so slowly. Then at last I felt

I could safely call up the Exchange again, and I don't think that ever in my life did I hear a more welcome 'Hallo!' I replied: 'Put me through in double quick time to the police station nearest to the place I am speaking from, and give them this telephone number at the same time and tell them to ring up at once as they value their lives.' Fortunately the operator at the other end was both quick and intelligent, and so was the police-sergeant who got through to me within the next two minutes. Heavens above! Those two minutes! When I tell you that I could hear Smith and Wildemeer coming down the stairs, you may imagine how I felt. Luckily, like so many foreigners, they carried on a voluble conversation all the time, and paused on the half-landing, no doubt in order to settle the special way in which I was to be silenced for ever. Then at last I was through to the police station, told them to locate the house through its telephone number, to send half a dozen men here at once, and to force an entrance into the house. I gave them my name, which is pretty well known at every London police station, and finally hung up the receiver. Just in time, I assure you. Those murderers were already in the passage just above me. But I was all right now; I switched off the torch and crawled back to the kitchen, where I deposited myself so heavily on the stone floor that I gave my poor old skull another crack that made me see a constellation of stars once more. I did feel pretty sick and queer now, and, I suppose, must have looked it, for I was only vaguely conscious of the approach of those two beauties, and after a while of Wildemeer's voice saying pleasantly: 'Isn't he dead yet?' There were some murmurs which I did not quite catch, and then a woman's voice, which I took to be that of the fat female — it certainly wasn't Katinka's — said: 'Clear out, you two. I'll turn on the gas. It saves a mess.'

"Pleasant, wasn't it?" Skin o' my Tooth went on with his inimitable chuckle. "And she did it, too, the old devil. I could hear her stamping about the room; no doubt she was busy stopping cracks and crevices round doors and windows and stuffing paper up the chimney. Then off she went, and within the next minute I already became conscious of that sickening smell of gas. I groped for the torch in my pocket. It wouldn't work... Well, I won't bore you with an account of the next few minutes, which I spent in total darkness, sick and giddy with the cracks on my head, and trying to locate the spot whence came that awful smell of gas. I really thought that I was in for it this time, when suddenly, at the moment when resignation to Fate was my dominant sensation, I heard the loud clang of a bell, followed by banging and hammering at the front door.

"The police at last! The sound gave me a certain recrudescence of strength. I groped for the door now, found it luckily enough, just as my senses were going, and all I know is that presently I was found by Sergeant Murray, sprawling face downwards and arms outstretched, across the passage outside the kitchen door.

"I believe that the fat female fought like a demon when Murray and his men finally broke into the house. Smith tried to make a bolt of it through an upstairs window, but was caught in the attempt. As for Wildemeer, he just collapsed: nerve, and the pluck often associated with villainy, completely deserted him."

4

Nerve and pluck! Heavens above! Have you ever heard a more thrilling narrative of nerve and pluck told with such good humour and modesty? Skin o' my Tooth seemed to take his adventure as a matter of everyday business.

The whole gang, I must tell you—there were four of them, apparently, as Skin o' my Tooth had indeed suspected—was charged with attempted murder. Anton Varlay and my chief prosecuted. The ingenuity which Wildemeer had displayed throughout his hellish plot against Anton was nothing short of marvellous. And it must have taken some doing too. He got the wretched boy over from Hungary and into the house which turned out to be in Reporton Street, South Tottenham, which he had rented for the purpose. Here he welcomed him and then tried by every possible means to get him to make over his property to Katinka. At last he hit on the hellish idea of starving his man into submission. He had every kind of villainy at his fingers' ends, and knew exactly how a Hungarian legal document ought to look. He got the rubber stamp made to represent the Hungarian Legation; but his difficulty was that he did not know enough Hungarian to manufacture a document that would appear plausible in the courts over there. Katinka, I think—who was a brave little woman—would have allowed herself to be killed before she lent a hand to the villainy, and I imagine that Wildemeer was on the lookout for someone when Skin o' my Tooth's advertisement appeared in the nick of time. Who Smith was, and what share he was to have had in the transaction, was never really established. The third man had to be discharged, as nothing could be proved against him. But what did come out at the trial was that the fat female was the one and only Mrs Wildemeer, so that pleasant gentleman added bigamy to his pretty catalogue of delinquencies.

Anton Varlay and Katinka went back to Hungary after the trial. Poor little woman! I wonder if our friend the Archduke has made up to her for all she suffered in the past. I hope so! He seemed a decentish fellow, and there are no longer any family traditions to keep up these days!

A fan of Sherlock Holmes? Then meet Solar Pons

The original fan fiction from the great August Derleth—the Sherlock Holmes of Praed Street.

"the best substitutes for Sherlock Holmes known."
– Vincent Starrett

"an excellent series of adventures in detection in their own right." – *The Chicago Tribune*

For more details and a full list of titles:
visit https://www.hachetteindia.com/home/yellowbacks

Assembling the greatest detectives all together

Covering the full range and history of detective fiction.
From Zadig, *The Moonstone*, and Dupin through Sherlock Holmes, Loveday Brooke, Montague Egg, Lord Peter Wimsey, *The Thinking Machine*, Father Brown down to Solar Pons.

For more details and a full list of titles:
visit https://www.hachetteindia.com/home/yellowbacks

WELCOME BACK TO THE GOLDEN AGE